Champagne Days

Rob Russo

iUniverse, Inc.
New York   Bloomington

CHAMPAGNE DAYS

iUniverse books may be ordered through booksellers or by contacting:

iUniverse
1663 Liberty Drive
Bloomington, IN 47403
www.iuniverse.com
1-800-Authors (1-800-288-4677)

ISBN: 978-1-4401-3870-6 (pbk)
ISBN: 978-1-4401-3871-3 (ebk)

Printed in the United States of America

iUniverse rev. date: 5/8/2009

Dedicated to

Snoopie, Mom, Aunt Lily, Edith, Jean, and

All my Other Loved Ones and Friends

and

Eartha Kitt

Who made Turkey famous

Contents

CAST OF CHARACTERS
(Listed Alphabetically by **First** Name)

Ahmed Yalvac	A simple spy
Cizre	A young Kurd/friend of Midyat
Corey Brotano	Young American/in Air Force
Corum Zile	Minister of Communications/Government Ministry
Drew Johnson	American sergeant/operates Guest House
Friday Lebal	Wife of American army captain
Gobasi	Turkish taxi driver who befriends Corey
Hank Myrons	Colonel/American adjutant U.S. Army
Jean Burdur	Chief Inspector Turkish Secret Police
Kyle Muenster	American/ Corey's best friend
Midyat	A young Kurd/friend of Cizre
Nurtan Ordu	Kyle's Turkish girlfriend
Pegu Gediz	A Turkish girl in Samsun, Turkey
Penelope Myrons	Wife of Hank Myrons
Rob Rizzo	American Captain stationed in Izmir
Saadet Sivas	(Madam Sivas) older clairvoyant Turkish woman
Turan Karapinar	Rising inspector in Turkish Secret Police
Ty Manners	American airman from Maine
Urdanur Besni	Turkish woman who works in JAMMAT
Vance Leigh	A trouble maker
Winston Lebal	Captain/U.S. Army/husband of Friday
Yuksel Ispir	Turkish/friend of Nurtan

LOCALES

JAMMAT	American Headquarters
Guest House	Temporary housing for Americans
Yozgat Hotel	Located near Old City of Ankara
The Gece Klub	Turkish nightclub/Off-Limits to Americans
Intim's	Nightclub hang-out for some Americans
Motor Pool	Garage(s) where military vehicles are maintained
The Compound	

"May your days be long

In the land of the living,

And all your pain:

Be Champagne"

An Old Gaelic Proverb

The President of the United States is Dwight D. Eisenhower

PROLOGUE

*   *   *

Winston and Friday

San Antonio, Texas - August 1955

The next moment was frantic. With no particular purpose in mind, she looked toward the door and suddenly he was standing in the threshold–the red light of an exit sign shining down upon him. As he walked toward them, he pushed his way through the many revelers adorning the long bar. The closer he came, the more hatred and determination she could see in his eyes. Silently, she wished that this time it would be different. But the closer he came the more she knew that this was going to be the same. She was getting tired of this. And she also feared for the life of her young male companion.

Now he was in front of them and fire flew from his eyes.

The ambulance sped through the streets of the city while its siren shattered the night air. Like a shooting star piercing the darkness, it eventually screeched to a halt in front of the emergency entrance on the side of a hospital. No sooner had it stopped when a male Intern and a Nurse emerged from the building. The Intern flung open the doors of the vehicle and, assisted by the Nurse, lifted a Soldier out and onto a mobile stretcher. All this was accomplished as the Driver was disembarking.

"What have we here?" asked the Intern in a hurried tone.

"Not sure," answered the Driver. "I picked him up at a sleazy bar not too far from here. He was roughed up by another soldier."

"Roughed up?" echoed the Intern; "this guy looks pulverized."

The Driver was about to offer more views on the subject but the Intern and Nurse quickly disappeared into the building with their new patient.

1

Sighing nonchalantly, the Driver got back in the ambulance to await his next urgent call. He glanced at his watch: three a.m. He did not notice the man dressed in army fatigues who stood near the hospital entrance. The insignia on the man's shoulders indicated that he was a captain.

Intensely dragging on his cigarette, Captain Winston Lebal leaned against the building and thought back on the earlier part of the evening. How she had told him she was meeting her girlfriend. How he had suspected otherwise and had followed her. How he had found them together–kissing in a booth at the back of some dingy hang-out for soldiers. How he had beat up the enlisted man without a moment's hesitation and how he had used brass knuckles to do so.

As Winston put out his cigarette and field-stripped it, a taxi stopped in front of the hospital. The woman who hurriedly disembarked was plainly dressed in a silken white blouse and a narrow black skirt. Friday Lebal headed for the entrance doors but stopped when Winston blocked her path. They were completely alone in the early morning hour.

"Are you proud of yourself?" Friday asked coldly. Her voice was deep and seductively outstanding.

"satisfied." He paused. "for now."

"What is that supposed to mean?"

A smile crowned his uncomely countenance and remained there. It was a technique he prided himself on: not letting people see how really angry he was. Disarming someone by looking pleasant created an uneasiness. Perhaps even a sense of danger.

"tonight was your third affair." He paused again. "at least that i know of. the first two i couldn't actually prove, but tonight i caught you. your friend only got a beating. the next guy may get a fatal message."

"And risk your precious army career," she snapped.

Silence and an even broader smile were his only reactions.

"Why don't you divorce me?" she continued.

"because I love you."

"You love yourself. Then your fucking army."

"then why don't you divorce me?"

"For practical reasons. No money, no family other than you, no place to go and for the children's sakes. They need a father and you _are_ good to them, at least."

For several moments, they lapsed into respective thoughts. They glared at each other like two antagonistic youngsters contemplating a schoolyard brawl.

"let's go home," Winston finally said.

"I want to see how my friend is." She took a step forward; he blocked her by firmly grabbing her shoulders.

"you will listen to me!" he ordered.

"So will the army if I tell them about the stunt you pulled when we were previously stationed in San Antonio."

For the first time, the smile left his face. He released his grip and stepped backward. That incident had been a rare moment in his life. And she damn well knew it. His only solace was that she could not prove such an accusation. It was the only time he had ever sold government car and truck parts for his own profit.

Despite their marital problems, they were held together by a strange bond. Their almost uncanny, similar backgrounds comprised the mortar of their relationship. Both were products of the orphanage system. And neither of them ever wanted to feel so completely alone again. So they tolerated each other's idiosyncrasies.

Winston stepped aside. "go in, if you must."

The anger was now gone from her face. She had won this skirmish.

"Wait for me," Friday replied, while entering the hospital; **"I won't be long."**

Calm now for the first time in hours, Winston walked from the hospital entrance to the parking lot. Near his jeep, he noticed a sole rabbit emerge from behind a bush. It stopped to play with some object that the Captain could not discern.

On a sudden diabolical urge, Winston spotted a rock and threw it at the vulnerable little animal. A scream of pain spewed from the rabbit and echoed in the early morning air. The innocent creature crawled a few inches then fell dead.

Winston would give his wife one last chance, he decided. But it would definitely be the last one. If ever she had another affair, it might prove to be fatal to that lover.

Just like the rabbit!

*   *   *

August 1955 – My Last Night in

Staten Island, New York City

The colorful lights adorning the rides of our South Beach Amusement Park had long gone to sleep. Even the cleaning crews had done their jobs and left. We lay on the cool sand under the boardwalk. But it was a long thoroughfare and we were most decidedly not alone. Territorially scattered throughout the entire length of the promenade were couples just like us.

"I'm going to miss you, Corey," said Edith, after a long silence.

Why hadn't I said it first? Now when I do, she won't believe me.

"Me, too," I managed to utter.

"You're going to miss you too?" joked Edith. She had a quick and excellent sense of humor.

I laughed and kissed her on the forehead.

"They'll probably give me a leave after basic training so I'll see you in a couple of months."

Not too far away from us another couple had conveniently brought along a portable radio which was playing "You Belong to Me" by Jo Stafford.

"I guess you will be seeing many foreign places. Will you write to me and tell me about them? Better yet, take some pictures and send them to me."

"If that's what you'd like, I'll do exactly that."

There was a bit of an awkward silence–partly because it was our last night together and partly because we had been partying all day in our own special way. We had driven around the Island visiting my favorite spots which I would not be seeing for a long time. And I had had my last hamburger at Al Deppe's. We stopped to say goodbye to some relatives, went to dinner, walked along the fairway, rode almost all the rides in the amusement park and when it closed we found our spot under the boardwalk where we made love–both of us for the first time.

I was extremely nervous but Edith was calmer and very patient with me and everything seemed to turn out all right. But the strangest part of the whole experience was that I was not madly in love with Edith. I was extremely fond of her but I didn't perceive those sensations they talk about in poems and songs. Didn't feel the ground shake or hear heavenly music.

This troubled me because I had always been a hopeless romantic. I loved all the "boy meets girl" movies and even cried when the guy didn't get the gal or one of them died. But somehow I did not feel that strongly about Edith. *Maybe I really can't fall in love.*

"Does the Air Force allow you to decide where you want to be stationed?" asked Edith.

"They probably give you several choices and then send you where they want to."

"Is there anyplace special you want to go, Corey?"

"I've always wanted to see Paris, so they'll probably send me to some place on the other side of the world."

From that nearby radio we could hear the D.J. announce the hour at 3:30 A.M. It was a signal which meant it was time for us to go. We stood up and I kissed Edith for a very long time before we started walking to her car. I would not be seeing her when I caught the Air Force bus in downtown Manhattan at seven A.M.–a few hours from then.

I wanted no one to see me off–not even my parents–because I could not tolerate goodbyes. And I would not start this new adventure in my life by crying in front of a group of guys I was destined to spend my near future with.

When we kissed for the very last time at Edith's door, I could hardly tear myself away from her. Though I was not intensely in love, she did represent an era of my life in which I had always felt protected and safe. Now I was going out on my own, and it frightened me.

As I walked away from Edith, I wondered if I would ever see her again. "Keep safe, Corey," she whispered loudly; "keep safe."

*   *   *

Kyle

Manhattan, New York City – August 1955

Kyle Muenster–from Knightdale, North Carolina, stood in front of the New York Paramount Theatre in Times Square. The pictures and artwork that decorated the front of the theatre–under the marquee and surrounding the box office–bewildered Kyle. There was nothing as elaborate as that back home, he noted.

And they all gave you two shows for one, he marveled. On the screen was Barbara Stanwyck in something called "Double Identity" and, In person was The Andrews Sisters, some other guys and Harry James. For the price of fifty-five cents before noon, it sounded like a good deal.

Kyle looked at the ten bucks in his wallet. Having had hitchhiked into the city just that morning from Pittsburg he had to find a place to stay and a job to get. Ten dollars wasn't going to last that long.

He went into the Horn and Hardart Automat Restaurant a few blocks away and was fascinated by the rows of tiny glass windows behind which lay sandwiches and desserts. A customer could only open one of those windows by putting some nickels into the slot next to each one. *For shur they didn' have nothin' like this in Knightdale,* grinned Kyle. The food even tasted better comin' from them windows.

He left the restaurant and stepped into the hot sun. Having eaten a great deal, he was suddenly lazy and not ready to make big decisions. Since it was only 11:30 A.M. he could go see that show at the *Patromount*: multi-syllable words always confused Kyle and he usually mispronounced most of them. At least that movie house would be cool and he could rest awhile before deciding what to do.

After the show was over he was passing by one of the many smaller lobbies scattered throughout the spacious theatre when he spied an older woman sitting on a couch and smoking a cigarette. With his best foot forward he sat beside her and asked for a light.

"But you ain't got a cigarette in your mouth," she said, slightly bewildered.

"Then Ah guess Ah needs one of them, too," smiled Kyle, devilishly.

The woman fell under his spell and they talked for over a half hour. They seemed to be getting along very well and Kyle once more prided himself on being so great with the ladies. Then he made a mistake. He suggested they could sleep together provided she had some cash. She became highly insulted.

She raised her voice, indignantly protested that she was not a prostitute and loudly called for an usher. Kyle grabbed his sachel and hightailed it out of the theatre. He ran across the street—dodging the on-coming cars as if he were on a football field. When he reached the other side, he was halted by a wide guy in a blue uniform.

"Are you tryin' to get yourself killed, Blondie?"

"No. Some ole gal was chasin' me," lied Kyle.

When the wide guy laughed, Kyle calmed down and told the true story —including having just arrived in the Big Apple.

"Well, your problems are solved, my friend. This here shack behind me is a recruiting station. Join the Air Force and we'll pay you—as well as provide housing and three meals a day. And no woman can ever touch you 'cause you'll belong to Uncle Sam."

Kyle liked the wide guy's blue uniform so he promptly joined the United States Air Force.

———————

Ty

Portland, Maine – August 1955

Twenty year old Ty Manners stood next to his lawyer in a courtroom in Portland and listened reluctantly but attentively as the Judge read his sentence.

As no stranger to bucking heads with authority, Ty had heard many sentences passed down to him–all of which were subsequently suspended because his father was Congressman Charles T. Manners, a highly respected gentleman both on the Hill and in his own district.

The youngest of six sons, Ty was constantly in trouble, especially in high school where he chose to hang out with the wildest kids: those who drank, smoked pot and participated in various acts of vandalism. When their collective allowances ran out, they even resorted to mugging people. The unofficial gang continued its recalcitrant ways past the twelfth grade.

Today's sentence would be no different than the others, thought Ty. After all it wasn't anything earth shattering; it was only robbing a liquor store and giving the owner some bruises here and there. *This will be a breeze and within hours I'll be out on the street again doin' my thing.*

"Tyler William Crawford Manners," began the Judge; "it is the decision of this court that you be sentenced to five years hard labor in the state penitentiary!"

Ty showed no emotion as he patiently waited to hear the part about the suspended sentence and how this would be his "last chance" once again.

"This time there will be no suspended sentence, Mr. Manners!" The Judge emphasized the word "no".

As murmuring swept throughout the courtroom, the color of Ty's face turned from tan to death pale. It was the very last thing he had expected to hear. It hit him so hard that he began to sway and may have fallen if not aided by the lawyer.

After several painful moments, the Judge continued.

"However, in deference to your esteemed father who is one of our country's best politicians, and must bear the unfair burden of having you as an offspring, I will amend my sentence with the following proviso. I will give you a choice of two avenues." The Judge hesitated. "Do you understand me, Manners?"

"Yes, Judge," said Ty, softly. He would not give the asshole the respect of calling him "your honor".

"You many serve your five year sentence in prison or you may join a branch of the military service. I would suggest the French foreign legion but I do not want to jeopardize our relations with France. –You have five minutes to make your decision!"

While Ty lauded himself on being unruly and difficult he simultaneously considered himself to be a clever guy. There was only one answer he could give.

"I'll take the service, Judge."

"Fine. And I hope the military will straighten you out. Heaven knows you definitely need a personality renovation. –You will sign up today and leave tomorrow."

Then, for the benefit of the spectators in the courtroom, the Judge attempted levity by borrowing from the movies.

"I want you out of town before the sun goes down!"

––––––––

Colonel Myrons and Family

American Guest House, Ankara, Turkey – August 1955

In a two story residential building, a mature Turkish woman was greeting several new acquaintances.

"Merhaba, Colonel. That means 'hello' in my language, and may I welcome you to our fair city. My name is Urdanur; it is pronounced exactly as it looks: Ur-da-nur. In fact, the Turkish language is phonetic. All one has to do is simply sound out a word."

"T-That's very informative," smiled the Officer. "I am Colonel Hank M-Myrons, t-this is m-my wife M-Mrs. Penelope M-Myrons, and t-this is our daughter, S-Sandy. And if I understand correctly, you are a liaison between your people and m-mine, and t-that we will be working closely t-together."

"That is correct, Colonel," smiled Urdanur.

Then she continued her presentation.

"This building is called the American Guest House. You may stay here– free of charge–for a month until you can secure permanent lodgings. And that handsome young gentlemen over there;" she paused and pointed to a man standing behind a desk and involved with helping another couple; "is American Sergeant Drew Johnson. He will show you to your rooms very shortly."

The Colonel nodded his head as he thanked his new Colleague.

"For now, however, I will take you downstairs to the cafeteria and we can all enjoy a casual lunch and get to know each other. – Please follow me."

"I mus*t* insis*t* tha*t* we ge*t* our rooms, firs*t*!" harshly demanded the Colonel's wife.

Urdanur appeared surprised at the unexpected outburst and looked to the Colonel for confirmation; he simply nodded in the affirmative–albeit with a modicum of embarrassment.

"As you wish," replied Urdanur, with a feigned smile. "Then go to the desk and wait behind the couple that Sgt. Johnson is talking with."

As she abruptly headed toward the desk, Mrs. Myrons said, "I wait behind no one. I am a Colonel's wife!"

———————

The Airman

Sampson Air Force Base, New York – August 1955

Basic training was not nearly as difficult as the Airman had expected. It was almost the end of six weeks and he had found the regimen to be quite easy and almost fun. And he prided himself on being the top man in the squadron—except for Gonzales. That lowlife from Puerto Rico had been a thorn in his side since the first day.

Gonzales was the cockiest guy he had ever seen. Gonzales excelled in every aspect of training that they encountered. He was the first to finish any obstacle course, the fastest at preparing for inspection, an expert marksman and even the cheeriest guy on mess hall duty. Though most of the other guys in the squadron seemed to tolerate Gonzales, the Airman hated him more each day. He was not used to being number two and he would _not_ stay in that position for long.

In addition, Gonzales had done things to him which pissed him off. Gonzales always pushed ahead of him on line for food, repeatedly beat him in poker in the clandestine games held after lights out, taunted him because he was only the second best on the shooting range, and spread the word that the Airman masturbated every night.

The Airman also suspected Gonzales of messing up his bunk before inspection, informing on him to the drill sergeant because he did not do his share when on latrine duty, spreading stories about his ancestry and telling everyone that the Airman had a small penis.

His hatred for Gonzales finally came to a climax.

At the end of the sixth week, everybody was given a two-day pass to go into the nearby town. But on the following Monday morning Gonzales was nowhere in sight. He had not returned. His buddies were shocked that Gonzales had gone AWOL.

The Monday morning after _that_, Gonzales' body was found in the woods outside the town. He had been dead for a week.

Staff Sergeant Dante Maas, known to his buddies as "Tay," and, Second Lieutenant Brad Eldan—married to America's top fashion model Dominique

Fabela—were assigned to the Gonzales case. Ordinarily a problem for the civilian police, the town's sheriff was happy to deliver it into the hands of the military. The gesture being that the Air Force and the townspeople co-existed so peacefully that he would let the military deal with its own affairs. Then there could be no misunderstandings. No openings for hostility. After all, the base _was_ a big source of revenue for the town.

By the end of the following week, Sgt. Maas and Lt. Eldan had completed their investigation. They thoroughly examined the crime scene and questioned everyone in the squadron. Since not a single airman appeared to have had any hostility toward Gonzales and since a typewritten suicide note had been found on the body, the two investigators concluded that the demise of Gonzales was not murder.

Their report was given to the base commander who, in turn, sent it to Gonzales' only living relatives: an older sister and younger brother.

That being the case, the Air Force adjusted the record so that Gonzales was not listed as AWOL.

Now the Airman was the number one man in the squadron!

*   *   *

One best selling novel is PEYTON PLACE by Grace Metalious

CHAPTER I —
"The New Foreigner"

Ankara, Turkey – 1956

The enigmatic stare which came from the dark brown penetrating eyes of my first Turkish acquaintance was intimidating. I had been with the man fewer than three hours, was in a foreign country whose word for "help" was unknown to me, and had no idea regarding my location. Furthermore, I was the only American in the night club.

Smoke from Turkish cigarettes rose in the beams of tiny ceiling spotlights to create wildly bizarre designs as in a psychedelic dream. My eyes danced with the swirls of smoke until I was nearly mesmerized and I inwardly mused that my sense of diplomacy had led me to this exotic, unfamiliar establishment.

The interior of the place was quite large. Its high ceiling did nothing to muffle the sound of the feverishly-tempoed Turkish music which bounced off the walls. Across the room, past the semi-crowded dance floor, bartenders hurriedly mixed drinks for anxious waiters to transport to their waiting customers in a sea of tables.

Once again, my gaze returned to those penetrating eyes. Eyes which belonged to a young man whose mere presence reeked of authority and pronounced self-assurance. He smiled as he pushed the bill in my direction and ordered me to pay it.

The most astonishing thing was how the man deftly took from his inside jacket pocket a gun which he placed on the table. The barrel was pointed at me.

The sun was shining when I arrived in Ankara, earlier in the day. Satin white clouds of exotic shapes floated against an azure background whose vivid blue was not so terribly different from that of the Mediterranean Sea some miles away. The crisp March air was tempered by golden light and the climate immediately reminded me of New York City–my home town. The weather, at least, was one thing that was not so foreign in this foreign of all foreign lands. But it was only one small comforting aspect. In reality, I was still a bit apprehensive. I had heard so many strange and weird tales about this place. "Turks are fierce; Turks are sneaky; Turks are treacherous. Don't turn your back on a Turk."

One blessing about coming here was that Kyle Muenster, my ole buddy from Tripoli, had preceded me. A laugh tickled my funny bone as I recalled the New Year's Eve we had recently spent in Tripoli. Without too much to do–and no females available–we had spent a quiet evening just drinking and getting drunk along with a third buddy, Butch–a nondescript small dog who was so ugly he was cute.

As I disembarked from the two engine MATS (Military Air Transport Service) plane, I descended a metal stairway that I'm sure was once used by Charles Lindberg. At the bottom, was a sergeant who was waiting to greet me. A friendly enough guy, he escorted me to a Quonset hut where he checked my Orders and told me to change.

"Civilian clothes?" I echoed his words.

"It's an agreement with the Turkish government," explained the sergeant. "There's only a small contingency of American military personnel because the Turks didn't want any foreign military people at all."

"Then what the hell are we doing here?"

"We have clever men in Washington, D.C. They arranged it."

"But why?" I insisted.

"A part of Turkey borders on Russia. Therefore, it's a good spot for us to keep an eye on the Russians. Up there in Hopa, Turkey–hundreds of miles away–you can actually see Russians guarding their border."

"Sounds interesting."

The sergeant continued. "You'll learn more about it when you go to Orientation. You'll also get to meet Urdanur." He grinned suspiciously, as if he had something to hide.

"Who?"

"You'll find out in due time." He duplicated his grin. "There's a vehicle waiting to take you into town," he hastened to add.

The "limo" that the sergeant directed me to was not uncommon: an old 1945 sedan that looked as if it had been through many wars, starting with the war of 1812. It wasn't painted the usual nauseating army color because,

I assumed, it would look too much like a military vehicle. And there *was* the Turkish-American agreement to consider.

Without looking at the driver, I threw my duffel bag onto the back seat and closed the door. As I got into the front seat, I heard the driver exclaim: "Another faggot in town." I gazed upon the devilishly grinning face of my best friend in the Air Force.

"Where the fuck ya been?" Kyle asked.

"Where you left me. In Tripoli."

"No, Dummy, Ah mean today. Ya plane was supposta git here hours ago. And Ah have a big date for tonight."

"There was a delay in taking off because the crew sergeant said he hadn't enough parachutes for everyone on board. I told him not to be concerned about me 'cause I'd just as soon go down with the plane."

Kyle gave his raucous laugh and I felt immediately at home.

"What's this hot date you have?" I asked.

"Wit' Nurtan, my Turkish woman."

"How are these Turkish chicks?" I inquired.

"Hot! Really hot!" drooled Kyle. "They ain't got no hair, ya know."

"They're bald?"

"No, Dummy. No public hair."

"You mean pubic hair?"

"Yeah. That's it. Ah ain't good with them fancy words."

"Why no hair?"

"They shave it."

"How come?"

"Search me! But Ah heahr tell that Turkish men shave too. Ah guess not ta catch crabs."

That bit of information which I had never read about in any military brochure about Turkey was indeed a fascinating revelation. I fleetingly wondered if it itched; also when a male and female Turk were screwing, did they cause friction?

"Ah told ya 'bout my chick in one of my letters."

"Who are you trying to put-on?" I laughed; "You only wrote me one letter. And you hadn't been here long enough at the time."

"Ya know me, Babe. It don' take me long."

"Are you very serious about her?"

"Ya bet! She's the bes' woman Ah ever met."

Vaguely I remembered hearing a similar expression such as this from Kyle on several other occasions. Each time he seemed deeply in love and each time I made no comment.

Kyle, a very personable guy from North Carolina, was tall, muscular and good looking.   He had eyes as blue as Caribbean waters, dimples that resembled miniature canyons, golden blond hair stolen from the sun, a seemingly constant tan, and an incarcerating smile. He always appeared to be in a good mood and I seldom saw him angry. And he was definitely intense—in everything he did. He was a fun-loving guy who lived his life to the fullest. I liked him a lot.

"You look well," I said.

"Do Ah still look like what's-his-name?"

"Tab Hunter."

"Yeah. That's the guy. Everyon' reminds ya'll of a movie star."

"It's a curse," I laughed.

As we rode through Ankara, I managed to catch a quick look at my first mosque and minaret. The little I had read about Turkey was suddenly blossoming into empirical knowledge.

Something I hadn't read about the place, however, unexpectedly materialized before my eyes.

We stopped for a red light in a busy section of the city that Kyle identified as Yenishire. As Kyle began to tell me more about the spot, he quickly interrupted himself by proclaiming, "Looky there, Babe."

Instinctively, I glanced in the direction to which he had pointed. A young, mustached man—dressed in corduroy trousers and a black jacket—catapulted from what appeared to be a very sophisticated-looking restaurant that was located far back from the heavily trafficked street. About fifty feet from the place, the man slowed his pace while simultaneously surveying the area as if he expected someone to be watching him. A minute later another man—clothed in a waiter's uniform—hurried from the same restaurant; he shouted anguished words in Turkish while pointing to and pursuing the first man.

"What's happening?" I asked Kyle.

"Just watch. Ya'll will see."

When the first man reached curb side, he briefly paused to observe the traffic before charging onto the street. In the next instant, he was surrounded by four men who seemed to be ordinary citizens.

By that time, the waiter had joined the group. Anger spewed from the waiter's mouth as he heatedly explained something to the four men who were holding the first man captive. The four men listened attentively, then took the first man to the corner where they savagely threw him into a dark green sedan. Then they disappeared back into the crowd.

"That wuz the Secret Police," Kyle informed me; "They seem to come from out of nowhere when there's trouble around."

Many car horns beeped behind us to inform that the light had changed and we were holding up traffic. Kyle shifted into gear and we were off again.

"Did you notice the driver of that sedan? " I asked. "He had such penetrating eyes. They were kind of scary."

"Ah didn't look at him. –How's Tripoli?"

"The same. Remember when we got the dog drunk?"

Kyle howled. "That little mutt staggered all over the room. And Ah think he wuz even laughin'."

"I'll tell you one thing, though. The next morning he looked a helluva lot better than we did. I think he was holding-out on us and had gotten drunk before."

"It's sure good ta have ya here, Corey. Ah missed ya."

"I was a bit nervous about coming."

"No cause ta be. Ya always make friends fast. People like ya righ' off and ya find out more abou' people in half an hour than other guys do in a year."

"You being here makes me feel comfortable."

Kyle stopped the vehicle in front of a fairly large two-story house on Ataturk Boulevard–a wide road running from one end of the city to the other. This particular part of Ataturk Boulevard was a mile or three out of the center of the city and in an area that was suburban. An area with smart-looking structures, some of which served as embassies for various foreign countries.

"This here place is call' the Guest House," informed Kyle. "It's where mos' guys come, for a spell, till they can fin' a place of their owns. They'll put ya'll up or if they're booked they'll find ya'll a place. The sergeant in charge is a little strange but he's okay for a Ni...excuse me, a Negro."

He was about to use another word over which we had had several arguments. Being from the South, he was used to saying it even though he never meant anything derogatory. I never actually witnessed any signs of outright prejudice on Kyle's part so I chose not to think of him as being so.

"Ah can't see ya'll tonight," explained Kyle. "Me and Nurtan are goin' to her parents' house for supper. Her daddy misses her. But Ah'll catch ya'll tomorrow in the cafeteria at JAMMAT aroun' noon. That's about the time ya'll will get out of Orientation, with Urdanur."

He emphasized "with Urdanur."

"Who the hell is this woman?" I asked. "You're the second guy who said that in the same way."

Kyle gave me his devilish, all-knowing grin. "Ya'll will fin' out," he laughed; "Boy, will ya ever fuckin' fin' out."

Although the Guest House was a two-story structure it appeared somewhat larger because of its very high basement. It was painted a comely yellow and it looked as if it belonged in an aristocratic part of Staten Island. The overall aura of the building seemed to say "Welcome."

I was greeted at a small desk by Sergeant Drew Johnson. He was just as Kyle had described. Strange but very pleasant. I guessed him to be a man in his late thirties.

He was about my height–five feet, seven inches. His hair was short–not kinky but relaxed; he had small brown eyes that seemed to be examining one. He was exceedingly good-looking. Why wasn't he a movie star, I wondered. Light-skinned with delicate and appealing features, he resembled a Greek God. The kind of guy that other guys would take a second glance at if only to question their own looks.

"I'm afraid we're all booked up at this time," he began. His voice was as soft and mellow as the freshly-laundered satin shirt he was wearing. The way he pronounced the letter "s" was virtually melodic.

"However," he continued; "I can suggest an hotel for you. One that isn't very fancy but fairly clean and adequate."

"Fairly clean?"

"Let's face it! –What's your name?"

"Corey Brotano."

"Let's face it, Corey. You're not in the States anymore. You're in a foreign land. Being Americans we are somewhat spoiled. You have to remember that _you_ are the foreigner."

It was an interesting thought. Something that hadn't occurred to me before. I had been out of my native land since October of 1955. First I had sailed on an old troop ship which had been rejected by Chris Columbus–the U.S.S. GENERAL ROSE. We left the Statue of Liberty behind and arrived in Germany eleven days later. After a month in Germany I was transferred to Tripoli, Libya. Now some months later, I was in another strange land. But in all of that time it never once occurred to me that _I_ was the foreigner.

"We have a nice little restaurant right here in the basement," remarked the Sergeant. "Why don't you grab a bite and I'll come down and give you the name of the hotel as soon as everything is set."

The restaurant had a familiar atmosphere about it. The smell of American style cooking blended well with the pictures on the walls of famous sights back home. The room was about the size of one of my old high school classrooms and it held approximately ten square-shaped tables.

It was dimly but adequately lighted. And the set-up was cafeteria style.

After eating, I pushed my chair back from the table and lit a cigarette to accompany my cup of tea. I busied myself by surreptitiously gazing around the room. A family at one table particularly piqued my interest. First I noticed the children: a boy of about eight years and a girl of perhaps eleven–both of whom appeared to be physically small for their ages. They were very cute kids who looked surprisingly alike. There could be no doubt that they were brother and sister. Both had dirty-blond hair, fair complexions, and pug-like features, but pleasant ones. They sat up straightly in their chairs, were very quiet and seemed exceedingly well behaved.

Then it struck me why the group was fascinating. No one was talking. All the time I observed them I noticed no interplay—neither words or glances. None of them was smiling. They sat there with frowns on their faces. That's it, I amused myself; they're the Frown Family. *A family that frowns together gets wrinkles together.*

The mother was extremely attractive. While no raving beauty, she had a sexiness that was immediately apparent. Strikingly exciting. Sexy in that she was completely feminine. Her build, features, unimportant movements, and gestures were unequivocally female. Even the frown on her face did not detract from her sensuousness. I was compelled to look at her.

Apparently, I stared too long for suddenly I realized she was looking back. Behind an embarrassing red glow radiating from my face, I managed what I hoped was a polite, friendly, diplomatic smile—though I was ridden with guilt.

The smile she returned seemed cordial and I tacitly advised myself never to get caught again.

A cursory glance at the husband was all I could subsequently catch. His countenance was not appealing. A salient puffiness under both eyes made him even more unattractive. He wore an expression of someone who might be in some kind of emotional pain.

This Freudian observation was interrupted by the appearance of Sergeant Johnson. He seemed even more good-looking from my seated angle of vision.

"May I sit down?" he asked.

Now he was less formal and smiled more readily.

"The Yozgat Hotel will be your home for a few days until I can get you in here."

"Thank you. –A cup of coffee, Sergeant Johnson?"

"No, thanks. I'm off duty soon and I have some things to do before I leave. –Please don't call me Sergeant; I hate that military crap. My name is Drew. –The Air Force gives you a free month's stay in the Guest House so that you can find your own apartment. "

"Sounds like great duty, here."

"It is, albeit that our small American military community sometimes resembles Peyton Place."

"Have you read that book?"

17

"No. I'll wait for the movie."

"Speaking of movies, you do remind me of a movie star."

With a slightly incredulous smile, Drew proceeded to tell a little bit about himself. In point of fact, he had been a child actor. His credits included "Another Kind of Boy," "The Boy With Green Hair," and "Teenage Beach."

"Did you ever meet Elizabeth Taylor?" I enthusiastically asked.

He laughed at my unexpected excitement. "No, but I think it's safe to assume that she is one of your favorites."

"My favorite," I profoundly added. "But why did you give up movies for the Air Force."

"They gave me up. Not enough roles for Negroes. Maybe I'll try again after I get out of the Service. After all, the 1960's are coming. The decade should bring a lot of changes. —Tell me, Corey, what's new in the U.S.?"

"If you mean movies, in particular, James Dean died at the height of his career."

"That happened last year. We're not quite that far behind."

"How about this, then. There's a new book out called THE SEARCH FOR BRIDEY MURPHY, by Morey Bernstein. It's supposed to be the true story of a girl who says she was reincarnated and lived once before under that name. Do you think it is possible?"

"Can't say, Corey. All I really know is that _one_ life is difficult enough for me."

With that philosophical comment, Drew stood up and prepared to leave. He told me to come see him when I was ready and that he'd call for a taxi.

The Frown Family got up at the same time and followed Drew out of the cafeteria. Before they left the table, however, the mother had paused to look in my direction. Once again, that sensual smile. That fascinating mystique. I returned the gesture. This time, a bit less guilty. Would there be future encounters, I wondered.

I wondered.

Drew put me in a taxi which expediently went to the Yozgat Hotel where I checked into my room. After showering, I went down to the lobby in search of a soda machine. Before I was able to fine one, a strikingly handsome young Turk greeted me and introduced himself as Turan Karapinar—a policeman. He also presented his wife. While his English was flawless, his wife's was nonexistent. He asked me to join them.

Being diplomatic—as the Air Force had told me to be—I agreed. He ordered drinks for us and I was amazed at the swiftness with which they arrived. That alone should have told me something.

Presently, he invited me to go with them to The Gece Klub, a famous night spot in Ankara which very few Americans frequented. Anxious to assimilate into my new environment, I consented.

The enigmatic stare which came from the dark brown penetrating eyes of my first Turkish acquaintance intimidated me. I had been with the man for fewer than three hours, was in a foreign country whose word for "help" was unknown to me, and had no idea regarding my location. Furthermore, I was the only American in the night club.

The Klub was crowded, lively, and filled with excitement. An hour long floor show featured a Turkish singer, acrobats, a dancing bear, and a bevy of svelte girls who did a mediocre imitation of the Rockettes.

When the show ended, the chorus girls congregated at a table. Turan insisted I ask one of them to dance. When she refused, Turan sent for the manager and suggested that the man fire the girl. He immediately did so and the girl ran sobbing from the club.

We talked for a while longer and when the bill came, Turan ordered me to pay. I refused while explaining that I had very little money. He took the gun out of his pocket and placed it on the table with its barrel facing me.

Although my knees began to tremble I tried to act bravely.

Turan's glance traveled from the gun to my eyes. No doubt he saw fear therein. Then he retrieved the revolver, only to fondle it as if he were gently caressing a woman's face.

"Do you like my weapon, Corey?" he smiled, wryly.

"As far as guns go, it looks very nice."

"Feel it!"

I looked at him as if I hadn't understood his comment.

"Go ahead!" he prodded; "Touch it!"

Gingerly, I stretched my arm across the table and patted the firearm. It felt smooth. But very cold.

As soon as my palm made contact with the revolver, Turan clasped his hand over mine and held it very tightly. I could feel his immense strength.

Then he looked deeply into my eyes. "Come, Corey! Take a walk with me! Outside!"

Somehow I was able to get my knees to stop shaking long enough to stand up. Turan's wife–who hadn't said more that two words all night–politely smiled as I followed Turan's lead to the exit. She remained at the table.

As we walked toward the door, Turan put his right arm around my shoulder. Meanwhile, he conspicuously dangled the gun from his left hand. He didn't seem to care if anyone noticed it.

Out in the spacious parking lot, he placed the gun back in his right hand, then faced me. Bright lights from a series of poles illuminated the area, making it as radiant as daylight on a dreary day.

"I wanted you to see how good my weapon is!" announced Turan.

With that said, he aimed his gun at a car which was perhaps some twenty-five feet away. He deftly squeezed the trigger, then smiled as the windshield of that vehicle splattered into hundreds of pieces.

"Is it not a magnificent revolver?" he asked.

I nodded my head affirmatively. If this cat and mouse game were designed to frighten me, it had succeeded. While the point of it was cloudy, I could only surmise that Turan enjoyed intimidating others. That he reveled in the power it afforded him.

"Is there a lesson to be learned here?" I asked.

"Not really, my new friend. I was merely testing you to see how far your patience would go!"

"And did I pass your test?" I asked with false bravado.

He looked steadily into my eyes as he said, "Very nicely. I think perhaps we will be friends!"

Although his comments eased my tensions, the thought of seeing him again was not exactly on my list of favorite things to do.

"I still don't have enough money to pay the check," I heard myself announcing.

Turan smiled, put his arm around my shoulder and as we made our way back into the night club, he told me that this time the treat would be his.

It was at that point when I finally realized why Turan had looked so familiar. I had seen him earlier in the day when Kyle had stopped at the red light in Yenishire and we had witnessed the rapid action and appearance of the Turkish Secret Police. Turan was the one who was driving that ominous green sedan.

He was not just a policeman.

Turan was an agent in the Turkish Secret Police!

The Andrea Doria Sinks after Collision with the Stockholm;
50 are dead; 1,652 are Saved

CHAPTER 2 —
"A Letter Home"

*   *   *

Friday exited the front door of the Guest House and walked the ten feet ahead to a waist-high wall that separated the property from the city sidewalk. She leaned on the wall and gazed at the many twinkling diamonds that brightened the night sky. The moon was only half full but the faint glow that spilled onto the earth was enough to enlighten the darkness. Diagonally across the street, two Russian soldiers stood at attention as they dutifully guarded the Russian Embassy.

How strange, she thought, here we are engaged in a Cold War with Russia and on this quiet night the Russian soldiers and I can gaze at each other as if nothing were amiss. *If we can get along peacefully living across a street like this, how is it we cannot be in harmony across the world from each other?* But the night was too beautiful for politics so she pushed the thoughts out of her mind.

"what are you doing out here?" he asked.

His monotone shattered the peacefulness of her moment.

"I'm waiting for a fucking spaceship!" she snapped, in her deep bold voice.

"why must you always use profanity?"

"It makes me feel better."

"cursing is only for men."

Before immediately commenting, she looked at him with a sarcastic grin.

"Parallel lines," she retorted.

The reply totally confused him so she continued after a dramatic pause.

"In high school, they taught us that parallel lines never meet. You and I are like parallel lines. Our backgrounds might be the same but..."

"where do you get these crazy ideas from?"

"I'm very creative."

He chose to ignore her remark.

"what *are* you doing out here?"

"If you must know, I came out here to be alone for a while."

"and that's the only reason?"

His constant jealousy never ceased to amaze her. Why he wanted to stay married when he didn't seem to trust her was puzzling. Yet, she did nothing to help matters. In fact, she enjoyed doing little things to fire up the Captain's suspicions. It had become a game with her. She liked tormenting him because he was so easily ignited.

"No! Also to pick up a few Turks. I hear that they're hot lovers."

The Captain became slightly annoyed. As of late, he didn't know how to take her. Since Texas, there hadn't been any definite signs of extra-marital affairs but he couldn't be certain. The truth of the matter was that she had fooled him before.

"that young good looking airman," the Captain said.

"What about him?"

"i saw you stare at him and smile."

"Wow!"

The Captain hated her caustic expressions. On those occasions, he wanted to strike her. But he never could. Her sexiness ultimately left him defenseless. He painfully knew that he was under her control. She had been his first love and he felt that he was too old to start again with someone else; he truly loved her. She, the children, and the Army were his most prized possessions.

Her mood suddenly changed. **"Can't I have any male friends?"**

"why would you need any?"

"No reason. It's just nice to talk to younger people. It keeps me young, too."

"there are young girls you could be friends with."

"Where, for fuck's sake? –How many young girls do we find on military bases?"

The validity of her comment surprisingly sobered his mistrust. She was right, he thought. Most of the young people she would come in contact with **were** men. The few females in the military were not always accessible. Perhaps he was being a bit unfair, he ultimately reasoned.

She continued speaking. **"I thought we made a truce. I thought you promised to be less suspicious. –We're in a new place. A foreign land for us. Let's at least try to be civil to each other."**

He sighed. And, as usual, he was tired. Their discussions always made him weary. She was too powerful a foe. It was easier to have her as his ally. For peace of mind, he would have to try harder. He would make himself trust her.

"okay," he answered; "be friends with him, if you want. but if i see anything more than friendship i promise you one thing."

"And that is?"

"just like the rabbit."

*   *   *

When I arrived at the Yozgat Hotel–after my ordeal with Turan the Terrible–it was about 2300 hours. I was anything but tired so I decided to write a letter to my girl back home.

> *Dear Edith,*
>
> *This is my first day here in Turkey and I don't find it quite as strange as I had expected it to be. That is, except for their commodes. When I went into the community bathroom down the hall, I could not find a toilet. Instead, I discovered a huge porcelain square that was level with the floor. In the center of the square was a hole; on both sides of this opening were two imprints in the shape of feet. And no toilet paper in sight. Just a water faucet next to the square. Apparently, the Turks squat when they evacuate. Luckily, there was an American style bathroom across the hall.*
>
> *It's about 11:30 P.M., here, so that makes it 4:30 P.M. in New York City. To save you the arithmetic, that makes Turkey seven hours ahead of EST.*
>
> *Kyle picked me up at the airport and it was great to see him again. He took me to a place called the Guest House where an Air Force sergeant named Drew found this hotel for me. The taxi driver who drove me here was a very friendly guy who speaks halting English very loudly. He told me that whenever I need a taxi, I must be sure to call him. His name is Gobasi.*
>
> *After I showered, I went down to the hotel lobby for a soda and I wound up meeting a Turkish Police Inspector and his charming wife. They took me to an interesting night club and we had a great time.*

(How could I possibly tell her the truth about that? She would worry.)

They also taught me some Turkish words: "merhaba" which means "hello," and, "nasilsiniz" which means "how are you?"
I'll close for now. Will send you some pictures of the place as soon as I can. Be safe and well.
Love,
Corey

I addressed the envelope, turned out the light and jumped into bed. As I closed my eyes, I wondered what Kyle was doing.

*   *   *

Kyle took off his shirt, pants, briefs, and jumped into bed. He lit a cigarette then sipped some Turkish coffee, after which he shouted to someone in another room.

"Are ya comin' ta bed, Babe?"

"*Bir dakika.* One minute."

"Ya'll just boun' ta teach me Turkish."

"Please. It can not harm," replied Nurtan, exiting the bathroom. She was dressed in a very sheer negligee that revealed large inviting breasts.

"Can ya imagin' a rebel from North Carolina speakin' Turk? Ah got enough trouble speakin' English."

"Please. Person can do anything he want," gently admonished Nurtan, in a voice pleasantly appealing.

Kyle watched her with painful passion as she took off her thin garment and slid into bed beside him. When her warm body touched his, he was instantly aroused. With no foreplay, and little romance, he made love to her.

Afterwards, Nurtan got out of bed and went into the bathroom. Kyle watched every movement of her hips and nearly got aroused again. The next best thing was to get a drink. Jumping up, he found a small glass and filled it with *raki*–the national Turkish drink which is an anisette.

He sipped his *raki* and stared at Nurtan when she re-entered the room. A cherub, he thought. A pretty little cherub of Turkish ancestry.

Nurtan was full-figured and had large breasts which Kyle adored. While some American males might call her plump, Turkish men admired that type of shape. But her body was relatively unimportant because she possessed the best of human traits: kindness, sweetness, and warmth. Warmth which flowed like an endless waterfall.

Her fully-rounded cherub face held chocolate-brown piercing eyes–with the tiniest golden specks. And the petite dimples which lived in full cheeks were imbedded in a light-olive complexion. When she talked rapidly the dimples seemed to dance. Black wavy hair, parted in the middle, cascaded to the tops of her shoulders. Above all else, Nurtan had a magnetic smile.

When she got back in bed, Kyle slid on top of her once again and kissed her gently on the lips.

"Ah'll be ready again in abou' ten minutes."

Nurtan could not resist laughing. "Please, my Love, do you not get tired?"

"Nah. It's too much fun with ya. Ya'll the only girl Ah've ever been wit' who comes the same time Ah come."

"Is that only reason?"

"Nah. Ah like the way ya talk. Ya never say 'a' or 'the' and ya always say 'Please'. Why do ya always say that?"

"It is habit. I try talk more well."

She would really try, she thought, because pleasing him was her goal. He was the first man in her young life of nineteen years whom she had ever loved. There had been a few Turkish boys during secondary school days but she had never gone to bed with them. She had always wanted to save herself for the man she would one day marry. For that special lover. Just like one of the heroes in the Arabian Nights Tales she so admired. One who would swoop down on a golden flying carpet and sweep her away to an enchanted magical land. With Kyle, she believed she had found such a figure.

"May I have cigarette?"

Kyle reached for the pack, lit one, and handed it to her.

"Actually ya'll speak better English than Ah do. Didn' ya tell me ya spent a year in the U.S. when your daddy went there to take a law course?"

Nurtan nodded in the affirmative. "You know much of me. I do not know much of you."

"There's nothin' much ta tell. Ah lived in a small town and when Ah graduated, Ah joined the Air Force."

What could he tell her, he thought to himself. There were many things. But to what purpose?

He was the only child of two immigrants who came to the U.S. from Germany. They were exceedingly strict, were prone to avoid people, and were anything but warm. His father beat Kyle whenever the son broke the slightest rule, and the boy's childhood was void of friends because his mother kept him close to home. While his elementary school days were without warm memories, his early high school years were nearly abominable. His face had betrayed him with so many blemishes that his classmates called him the "Acne Factory." Unfortunately, he had had to sneakily make some of those tormentors pay for their put-downs of him.

Then, surprisingly, came a kind of miracle which changed the course of Kyle's life. During the summer before his senior year, the acne condition cleared, his body blossomed, and his good looks took center stage. Suddenly, girls succumbed to his incarcerating smile and boys began to look at him as a possible threat to their masculinities.

Kyle joined the basketball team, became one of the leading jocks in school and dated many girls. And he got good grades—only because he was one of the stars on the basketball team. His high school days which had begun in the doldrums ended in a flare of triumph. Good times which even diminished the emptiness of his home life.

In the summer after graduation, however, a girl named Emmy Lou Forester got pregnant and most people in town—including Kyle's father—assumed that Kyle was the sire. Without giving Kyle a chance to defend himself, Mr. Muenster beat his son.

It was just one too many beatings and Kyle literally struck back—knocking his father unconscious.

Kyle hastily packed a small bag and left town. He hitch-hiked through Virginia and found himself in Maryland where he met an older woman who supported him for awhile. When he _did_ get _her_ pregnant—faced with the fear of being trapped—he fled once more until he wound up in New York City with only ten dollars in his pocket.

Fleeing from another woman he had met in the Paramount Theatre, he encountered a wide guy in a blue uniform. Kyle liked the duds so he promptly joined the United States Air Force.

"Ah did run away from home," Kyle conceded.

"You just run away and leave your parents and no sad?"

"Ah had ta. Mah daddy beat me one too many times."

There was instant sadness on Nurtan's cherub face. Tears began to fill her eyes.

"Ah'm good now. Ya don' need ta be sad."

"If you leave me I be very unhappy."

"Ah'm not gonna leave ya."

Nurtan explained that her girlfriend had been dating an American airman who had promised to marry her. But when the time came to go back to the United States, the boyfriend listened to his Air Force superiors when they told him to leave the girl behind.

"Ah ain't that guy. Ah do what Ah want. When the time comes, Ah'll take ya back if..."

Silence filled the room as Kyle realized he had said too much. He knew he loved Nurtan–at least he figured he did–but he had never thought about taking her to the States with him. That is, until this moment.

"If what, please?" echoed Nurtan.

A quick response. "If ya still wanna come by then."

Silently, Nurtan got out of bed, poured some *raki* and walked to the window. On the street below a large truck shattered the quietness of the night. The throbbing sound it made seemed to match the sudden heavy beating of Nurtan's heart.

"What's a matter, Babe?"

"*Hicbir sey.*"

"Don' tell me 'nothing,'" said Kyle.

He got out of bed, went to her and put his arms around her.

"You're cryin'. –Don't cry. Ah won' leave ya behind."

"There is more thing," she said swiftly.

Whenever she became excited she spoke rapidly.

"Tell me, Babe."

"I like marry, now."

It took Kyle several terrifying moments to digest her words. When he said he would not leave her behind, it was a shallow comment. He had said it without thinking.

"Don' cry, Babe. Everythin' will be okay. We'll talk abou' it."

He left Nurtan at the window and walked into the bathroom. Turning on the water faucets to their limits, he began to wash his hands. He hoped the loud gushing sound of the water would wash away the words he had just heard. It was impossible, of course, but at that minute he needed a distraction. Needed time to think.

Deep down, he knew he was not yet ready or willing to become a husband. He was enjoying himself too much and wasn't primed to settle down and possibly have an unhappy relationship like his parents had. He suddenly felt as if he were on a sinking ship–like the Andrea Doria, or something. But he was damned if he was going to drown. He would think of a solution which would please both of them.

Presently, his mind spotted a life preserver. Whenever he was in a jam, he always found a quick way out of it. He could be very cunning when necessary.

Kyle returned to Nurtan and took her in his arms. She pressed her head on his hard chest while he gazed past her out the window.

"Okay, Babe," he said. "We'll get married. We'll have ah Turk weddin'."

Nurtan's face lit up with sheer delight.

"Please. Thank you, my love. –I will go Madam Sivas and have cards read."

"That woman gives me the creeps."

"Please, my love. Madam Sivas is wise. She is my *teyze,* my aunt. She will say when is good to marry."

"Okay, Babe. Like ya say," pacified Kyle. And to himself, he said: *we'll have a Turk wedding.*

In her home—which was also a boarding residence, and adjacent to the American Guest House—Madam Sivas awoke from a restless sleep in a state of anguish. The elderly woman sat up and reached for the bedside photograph of her husband who had departed too many years ago. Looking at his kindly face, she felt as close to him as she had ever been.

In moments such as this, when her clairvoyant powers troubled her, she would find comfort in staring at the photo. And though she was anything but a bitter person, she longed for the day when they would be together again. In a place where Allah ruled. In a place where there were no problems.

She stared at the picture for a long while. But in this instance, the solace was slow in coming. For the vision which had abruptly stirred her from slumber was too overpowering.

In the dream, Madam Sivas had seen someone being brutally murdered. The face and body of the person were blurred but the aura told the sapient woman that the victim was someone close to her.

Was it to be Nurtan, her Godchild? Nurtan's fine parents? Nurtan's best friend, Yuksel? Or one of the woman's American boarders?

Madam Sivas rose from the bed and slowly walked to the window. She looked up to the heavens at the half moon shedding faint silvery rays. And tears began to form in her knowledgeable eyes.

She had had a vision of murder. And her visions—sooner or later—always came true.

*   *   *

Rocky Marciano Retires from Boxing…..Undefeated

CHAPTER 3 –
"Nocturnal Encounters"

*   *   *

In the living room of the Guest House, Friday was reading a book. The hour was late but she had not felt like sleeping. It happened whenever she arrived in a new place; the excitement of unfamiliar surroundings stimulated her with the   hope of a fresh start, and perhaps an adventure.

She felt someone's presence in the room and looked up from her book.

"Sorry to disturb you, Mrs. Lebal. I was just checking up on things."

She noted that his pronunciation of "s" was virtually musical.

"That's quite all right, Sergeant. But please call me Friday. I'm not into that military decorum crap."

"Neither am I," he laughed. "And you call me Drew."

"It's a deal. –I thought you went home."

"I did but I forgot something. –What are you reading?"

"AUNTIE MAME by Patrick Dennis. It's a current best-seller. I picked it up in the airport just before we left the States."

Her deep voice intrigued Drew. She was a very exciting woman, he thought. Extremely sensuous.

"Where were you and your husband last stationed?" he asked.

"San Antonio, Texas."

"Did you like it?"

"I guess so. At any rate, I do have some powerful memories of the place."

Drew laughed at the wry smile that had accompanied her remark.

"It's always good to laugh. It helps alleviate life's everyday pressures."

"How right you are, Drew. How right you are."

He was about to excuse himself when Friday closed her book and asked

29

him to sit down. He did so and they engaged in general talk about the Army, the Air Force, things back home and aspects of Ankara. As they talked, Drew noticed how she toyed with a keychain. While it was not an ingenious piece of crafting, it was somewhat unusual. One part of it was a metal horseshoe which was connected to a small chain about two inches long. Attached to the other end of the chain was a metal heart whose red paint was beginning to fade.

"Who was that young man you were speaking with in the cafeteria earlier this evening?" asked Friday.

"He only just arrived today, also. His name is Corey Brotano and he's an airman second class–a corporal, in Army terms."

"What do you know about him?"

"Not much. He comes from New York City. He seems to be fascinated with movies and books.

"He's very good-looking. I like his smile. –Is he single?"

"From what I could gather, yes."

Although her last question surprised Drew, he cleverly hid his feelings. What was her big interest in Corey, he wondered.

"What's Corey's job here?"

Drew paused a moment. "His orders say that he's in cryptography, coding and decoding messages. –Where is Captain Lebal?"

"Sleeping."

Drew smiled as he rose.

"Sounds like a good idea. If you'll excuse me, I'll see you tomorrow."

Friday nodded and smiled back.

"I'll turn off the lights when I leave."

"No need," his voice filtered back; "I like to keep a light in the window."

Friday returned to her reading but the words remained on the page. Instead she thought about Corey. She hadn't meant to embarrass him earlier. She had felt his concentration flowing across the room and had only intended to catch a glimpse of him. But when she saw his beautiful face, she had become surprised.

It had been a rare, unusual moment. Seldom did she see someone whose demeanor was immediately pleasing and genuinely unique. She hoped they would become friends.

Even his name was nice.

Corey.

*   *   *

The door of my hotel room burst open with a great force.
As I looked in amazement, I could see the black silhouette of a tall man

standing at attention in the threshold. Much like the scene from a western movie where the dreaded gunfighter shows up to reek havoc on the town marshal who once put him away.

The light encircling the silhouette illuminated the room with the same dreary glow I had experienced earlier in the parking lot. Then the silhouette moved closer. As it did I could see Turan's penetrating eyes leering at me. There was a eerie smile on his face. In his right hand dangled a gun.

When he was but two feet away, Turan raised his arm, aimed the weapon at my head, and pulled the trigger. The noise was deafening; the pressure on my forehead gave me a headache.

Then I opened my eyes.

The room was in complete darkness and I lay on the floor. The musty smell of the carpet served as a catalyst to bring me back to reality. It had all been a dream and I had fallen out of bed.

Dizziness accompanied me as I got up from the floor and turned on the light. My wristwatch read 0030 hours. I had been asleep for only a half hour. But there was little time for me to wonder about the nightmare I had just experienced. My stomach felt extremely nauseous and I made it down the hall to the community bathroom with no time to spare before I vomited for nearly twenty minutes.

When I returned to my room, I felt somewhat better even though my stomach hurt when I subsequently coughed. It must be the excitement of arriving in a new place, I reasoned. Or maybe I ate something that apparently disagreed with me.

At any rate, I was glad that I had not stayed in the Guest House. It would have been excruciatingly embarrassing if I had become ill and that sensuous woman had seen me in that condition. For her, I wanted only to be at my best.

*　　　*　　　*

A half moon projected its silvery light through the cold night air but Drew didn't mind the weather as he left the Guest House and walked one long block down Ataturk Boulevard to Minyatur Sokak, the street where he had his own apartment. Because he operated the Guest House, he had been given a free and comfortable room therein on the basement level. It was a large chamber—with a private bath—at the opposite end of the building from the cafeteria. He would have been completely content with the space but he had found that people troubled him at all hours of the day or night, and he felt he deserved some privacy. So he had found a haven close-by.

In the sometimes long but mostly pleasant year he had been in Ankara,

Drew had taken this walk many times. About a ten minute journey, it was a warm-up for the work-out which he did immediately upon getting home.

To Drew, it was very important that he maintain his fine physique because someday–after this second and final stint in the Air Force–he planned to return to the movies. He was certain that Hollywood was changing and that there would definitely be more roles for Negroes in the coming years.

His short-lived film career was the only factor in his life of thirty-one years that had helped him keep at least a modicum of self-esteem. It wasn't bad enough that he had been the middle child in a poor family that lived in the Barrio of Los Angeles. Into the bargain, he had another problem.

As Drew neared his apartment, he saw his Turkish neighbor from across the street bringing out her garbage.

"*Merhaba*, Yuksel."

"*Merhaba* to you, Drew. *Nasilsiniz?*"

"*Iyiyim, tesekkur ederim.*"

"*Siz nasilsiniz?*"

"I am the good too," answered Yuksel.

Drew suppressed a chuckle. Her use of English was fairly good but she had the habit of inserting *the* in spots where it did not belong.

He had met Yuksel shortly after he arrived in Ankara and had seen her at various functions throughout the year. She was a close friend of a girl named Nurtan who worked in the PX in JAMMAT. Both girls liked Americans and did all they could to make the foreigners feel at home.

But Drew learned that Yuksel had a boyfriend named Turan who was part of the Turkish Secret Police and very influential therein. Turan was young to be so powerful in the Secret Police and while he seemed also to like Americans, Drew did not trust him. Turan had penetrating eyes which were very intimidating. Turan was also very jealous of Yuksel. Upon realizing these facts, Drew had resolved to keep his distance.

"Good night, Yuksel."

"*Iyi geceler*, Drew."

When Yuksel re-entered her first floor apartment, she was surprised to see Turan awake. He had sat in the easy chair an hour earlier and had promptly gone to sleep–his head resting on the high back part of the chair.

"Who were you talking to?" he demanded.

His cold-as-granite powerful voice made a booming sound.

"Drew. The American who own Guest House."

"He does not own it, *dolmus!* He only operates it for the Americans!

You do not know anything!   —And speak in English!   I want to practice! Someday I plan to go there!"

Even though Yuksel had been with Turan for two long years, she could not get used to his voice. Nearly everything he said sounded like a command.

"I no *domus*. I no pig," she retorted.

On occasion, Yuksel would muster an iota of courage to speak back to him. But it was always said with some trepidation and she knew it could be done only rarely for Turan had an incarcerating hold on her. In essence, she was his slave.

"Get in the bedroom!"

"No, Turan, *Efendi*. I am much the tired. I work all night in club. I want the sleep."

Like lightning, he sprang to his feet. Instantly he was upon her and she felt his hot breath against her face.

"You never tell me '*No!*'" he shouted. "Get to the bedroom!"

Yuksel obeyed his order. The experience in progress was one which had been done before, in theme. The steps or method were always slightly altered but the exercise of near-savage brutality never changed.

The apparent hatred living inside Turan was something that Yuksel could not fathom. The only good thing concerning their relationship came after the sex when he would say that he loved and needed her.

In the bedroom, Turan told Yuksel to undress.

"Slowly!" he ordered.

As she did, he sat on a chair near her bed, lit a cigarette, and took a flask out of his jacket pocket. He sipped some *raki* and blew smoke in her direction.

"What now, *Efendi*?" she asked in her naked state.

"Get on the bed!   On your stomach!   Spread your arms and legs!"

"No. Not this night."

She pleaded but knew it was in vain. Whenever Turan made up his mind there was no changing it. She wondered why she even bothered to ask for his mercy.

In the beginning, Yuksel had been completely intrigued by Turan. His olive complexion enhanced the handsomeness of his face. His perfectly sculptured nose blended with high cheekbones and his small nearly almond-shaped eyes gave him a faint Mongolian look which added an alluring mystery to his being. His thin, firm, muscular body of six feet made her feel protected when he pressed it against her own body. And he was kind to her.

"You are beautiful!" he would say.

"My nose big. Make me look the ugly," she would protest.

"No. It is not! You are beautiful! You are like a cat! Your green eyes are like cat's eyes! And you move like a cat! And your voice is sexy! You purr when you speak!"

"Say again," she would request.

And he would. And she would love it.

But that was two years ago. Now he was only kind for several minutes after he got his way.

For a person who had been shown many kindnesses from others, Turan lacked the capacity to be consistently considerate. A deep-seeded feral nature seemed to dominate his personality.

Turan sipped more *raki*, extinguished his cigarette and stood up. He walked to the night stand next to Yuksel's bed and took out two sets of handcuffs.

"No, Turan, *Efendi*. No tonight."

"*Sessiz!* Quiet!"

Slowly, deftly—like a starving man savoring a beautiful meal set before him—Turan grabbed her hands and secured them to the headboard. With this done, he proceeded to the foot of the bed and did the same with her ankles.

Then he discarded his own clothes and kept a wide leather belt in his hand.

Yuksel stared at his powerful body and his erect instrument which she had come to dread. Love was more than mere penetration and bizarre sexual acts she had always believed. But apparently not for her. Would she ever find a man who would not mistreat her?

With a wry smile, Turan raised the belt.

Yuksel closed her eyes.

After Turan left, Yuksel forced her weary body out of the bed and slowly moved into the kitchen. She poured much-needed *raki* into a tall glass and swallowed half of it in several seconds. Placing the partly-filled glass on the table, she returned to the bedroom to retrieve a notebook which resided in an old suitcase under the bed.

At the kitchen table once more, Yuksel began to write in her diary. To her, this record of daily events was equivalent to meeting with a psychiatrist—without having to spend a lot of money. The journal was a catharsis. By committing words and thoughts to a page, she was able to free herself of some pressures that she had to endure.

There were good things recorded as well. Those happenings she enjoyed jotting down. They often helped to lift her spirits when she had to face the unpleasant things that happened. And for such a young person, Yuksel had had more than her allotment of difficult situations. Especially with men.

The diary was to serve as something more than just the purging of bad feelings, she hoped. Given her past history of alienation from family, being the pawn of a pimp, and having a child taken away from her, Yuksel was constantly apprehensive about her future. If she kept a complete record of those who treated her badly–and something tragic were to happen to her–the diary could help the police.

Yuksel recorded that night's encounter with Turan then returned the journal to its home in the suitcase. As she drank more *raki* she wondered what Turan was doing with his wife at that particular moment.

*   *   *

CHAPTER 4 –
"Beyond Orientation"

"I would ask that you please do not leave yet," she said; "Stay and have more wine, Corey."

Her voice was slightly hoarse-sounding but as warm and comforting as a blazing fire in a living room hearth.

She continued. "It is good wine. Do you not think?"

Do you not think, I repeated in my head. *If I did* **think***, I wouldn't find myself in this situation.*

"Would you like more wine, then?" she asked.

I nodded in the affirmative while simultaneously struggling with "*Tessie krem.*"

"*Hayir.* No," she gently admonished. "It's *tes-ek-kur ed-e-rim.*"

Slowly following her prompting, I said it again and this time got it right.

"You may make a Turk out of me yet," I laughed.

She poured the wine, then changed the record. She had wanted me to hear an authentic version of "*Uskudara Giderken*" and not just the popular American rendition made famous by Eartha Kitt. Since it had played several times already, she put on a Nat King Cole album brought back from the States years ago.

I watched her intently. For a tall and older woman, she moved quite gracefully. In her youth one would guess she was a stunning lady. Even now she was quite attractive. Like a fading, glamorous movie star involuntarily playing grandmother roles.

How differently she looked to me now, I thought, compared to when I first met her earlier in the day.

My second day in my new home away from home.

I reported to the JAMMAT Building at 0930 hours. The Orientation wasn't scheduled until 1000 hours but I wanted to be early and check out the place.

The tan-colored stone facade of the JAMMAT Building–Joint American Military Mission for Aid to Turkey–was a huge structure of nondescript architecture. Long and rectangular, it comprised four floors. The top two were blatantly visible while the basement and sub-basement only partially discernible because they blended into the side of the hill on which the edifice was erected.

JAMMAT'S main entrance faced a courtyard the size of a football field and the area closest to the door sported a circular driveway. At the other end a wide road descended to Ataturk Boulevard–one of the main thoroughfares of the capital city.

The main floor interior had a spacious round foyer that served as a center and connected three large chambers: the PX, the auditorium, and the cafeteria. The floor above contained a myriad of offices while the basements housed communication rooms and various shops necessary to maintain the JAMMAT operation.

The Orientation meeting was held in the huge auditorium. With only about twenty-five people present, I was able to get a look at everyone there. I saw the Frown Family and my eyes met those of the sensual mother. She returned a warm smile which gave me a very unusual feeling.

Also in attendance was an Airman whose resemblance to Kyle was uncanny. The guy had Kyle's exact build and height, and golden blond hair. I overheard someone call him Ty.

The beginning of the Orientation was signaled by a tall, older woman who moved quite gracefully to a podium in the center of the stage. She warmly welcomed us to Turkey and introduced herself as Urdanur Besni, an assistant to the personnel supervisor and a liaison between Americans and Turks.

So this is the Urdanur that the airport sergeant and Kyle had both made such mysterious tacit innuendoes about; I could see no merit for their slyness.

Urdanur, a woman of Turkish ancestry, had a long, thin face with low cheekbones and slightly-protruding brown eyes. Her bright silvery gray hair was as smooth as the surface of a lake and just as shiny.

Miss Besni offered many interesting facts about Turkey: a large country in the Middle East, somewhat bigger than our Texas and located between the Black and Mediterranean Seas; the home of Mount Ararat, the resting place of Noah's Ark, as well as of Troy and the famed Trojan Horse; a country once occupied by Constantine the Great who built a new capital at Byzantium and renamed it Constantinople; and, finally, how the Ottoman Turks–the ancestors of today's Turks–captured Constantinople and changed the name to Istanbul.

The meeting concluded with a film on the complete history of Turkey and a question and answer period.

Since it was too early to meet Kyle for lunch, I decided to go outside for some air. As I was exiting the building, a tall frumpy-looking woman was entering so I stepped aside to let her pass. Instead of thanking me, she stopped, looked me up and down and made a distasteful expression. Then she proceeded on her way. She reminded me of a bitchy character I had once seen in a Warner Brothers movie.

*   *   *

"I will announce you," said the Airman clerk. "No nee*d!*" said the frumpy-looking woman.

"But the Colonel insists that I do," protested the Airman.

"Very well, if you mus*t!*" she answered, annoyed.

The Airman spoke over the intercom and received confirmation.

"You may go right in, Mrs. Myrons."

"Of course, I may, Young Man. And, incidentally, do you think i*t* is proper to wear dungarees to work?"

The Airman was stunned at her comment but she gave him no time to answer as she moved swiftly into her husband's office.

She was greeted perfunctorily by the Colonel. Unconcerned with his manner, she sat down, took out her holder and waited for him to light her cigarette. The Colonel did so and then sat opposite her with his desk purposely between them.

He was a tall, well built man who looked like an erstwhile basketball player. Obviously over six feet tall and with broad shoulders, he was a distinguished looking man with large features, dark brown hair with many traces of gray coming through, and, deeply set eyes. The most salient feature of his face was one continuous eyebrow. He often frowned and had an ominous veneer about him. But he was a fair man.

"Really, Henry," began Mrs. Myrons.

The word *Henry* reverberated in his mind. He heard it numerous times a day. She refused to call him Hank as everyone else did, and as he preferred. She insisted on using her so-called proper Vassar decorum. And all the other phony bullshit she learned in her revered alma mater.

Like her affected and presumably precise pronunciation. Her exaggeration of "d" and "t" at the ends of words incessantly irritated him. It was true that *he* probably made some people uneasy with his slight stuttering problem but he didn't do it on purpose and it wasn't pretentious.

"Now, what?" he asked, preparing to be bored or harassed.

"I don't think it is fitting for these young men to be wearing dungarees to work. And on the streets for that matter."

Here we go again, he said to himself; *another bitch-and-moan sess*ion. Today it just happened to be dungarees. Tomorrow it might be Turkish coffee. The topic really didn't matter for the bitch-and-moan sessions were inevitable.

She continued. "When I entered the building I saw a young man wearing dungarees. And when I arrived here, I saw that your clerk was also wearing them. And both had their cuffs rolled up, no less!"

"What's wrong with dungarees?"

"In my upbringing, I was taught that one dressed properly when he or she went to work."

That high-pitched nasal tone of her voice affected him with the same tingling feeling he got whenever he hit his funny bone.

"I can not do..."

"Don't tell me you can not do anything," she bellowed.

Another annoying aspect of her neurotic personality, he mused. That fucking constant interrupting. Not only to him but to everyone. It made no difference who the victim was.

"I can do nothing about t-them wearing dungarees on t-their off-duty hours but I guess I can issue an order s-saying t-that t-they m-must wear s-some kind of dress pants while working."

"Well, do that!" she exclaimed.

Hell! Was she ever frumpy-looking, he thought. At one time she had been fairly attractive. Her thin face with its beady eyes and small but manish features had made her interesting. Like a down-to-earth sports woman ready for fun and excitement. But the years had not been kind to her and that frail countenance had too many wrinkles which she nightly tried to rub out with a selection of miracle creams.

And those silly hats she always wore made her look ludicrous.

"Was t-there anything else?" he sighed.

"Yes. Don't be late for dinner tonight. We're having guests."

He was about to ask who they were when the intercom buzzed.

"Colonel," said the Airman's voice; "Captain Lebal is here."

Why had he ever married her, he wondered. Deep down he actually knew. His unfaithfulness was something he felt he couldn't tame and her stringent demeanor might have kept him under control, he had hoped. But it hadn't and the only good thing about their marriage was Sandy their teenage daughter–the thrill of his life. Mostly, his wife had been–and was–a singular source for causing heartache and trouble to himself, and to others.

"S-Send him in, please."

Captain Lebal was warmly greeted and promptly introduced to Mrs. Myrons who eyed the Captain from head to foot and tacitly approved. Once done she excused herself and made her exit. As interfering as she was, she did perceive enough never to let her husband seem weak in the eyes of an inferior officer. For, in the final analysis, her husband's power in the military was also her strength.

"I'm a fair m-man," began Col. Myrons; "but also a s-strict one. I s-support m-my officers but I also discipline t-them if t-they go beyond the proper m-military limits."

"i agree with you," said Captain Lebal. "army men must learn to follow rules and proper military decorum. it's the only way."

"Good," said the Colonel. "Your reputation has preceded you and I am very happy with what I have heard. I t-think we will get along just fine. –I read your file and was very impressed. For s-someone who was raised in an orphanage, Captain, you really m-made s-something of yourself."

"it's the army, colonel. the army did it for me."

"I also heard about your lovely wife."

"and that is, sir?"

"T-That s-she's a very interesting person. I'm looking forward to m-meeting her."

"and so you will, sir."

"You will be in charge of t-the m-motor pool and will be directly under m-my command. If t-there is anything you need or if you have any problems, come directly to m-me. I'm always here to help you."

"thank you, sir."

"Mrs. M-Myrons and I have a welcoming t-tea party once every t-two m-months for newcomers. Keep it in m-mind."

The rest of their meeting dealt with the various aspects of the motor pool and its personnel.

"T-There is one Airman," pointed out the Colonel; "who could be s-something of a problem. He looks like a devious punk. His name is T-Ty M-Manners. He's a blond-haired kid. Keep an eye on M-Manners."

*   *   *

After smoking two cigarettes and getting enough fresh air, I decided to head on into the cafeteria even if it were too early to meet Kyle.

As I entered the building, I beheld that same frumpy-looking woman whom I had seen earlier. This time she stopped and spoke to me.

"Are you working here?" she demanded, in a haughty tone.

"Not until next week, Mam."

"Well, when you do repor*t* for work, be sure you do no*t* wear dungarees. By nex*t* week, i*t* will be a definite order and you must obey i*t*."

In a flash, she was gone. Whoever the hell she was, I hoped never to run into again–or *any* of her kin.

The cafeteria was beginning to get crowded. I looked around but did not spot Kyle. A person I did see was Miss Urdanur Besni. She was sitting alone at a table in the far corner of the room. She seemed so lonely and forlorn. My heart immediately went out to her.

I got some food and made my way to Miss Besni's table. When I asked if I might join her, she smiled warmly and said that it was at my own risk.

"What is that supposed to mean?" I sat down.

"Only that some of these American airmen look upon me as a sort of joke. I am virtually an old spinster and young people like to poke fun at such things."

"Stupid young people, Miss Besni," I commented.

"Please call me Urdanur. I am not that old," she smiled.

We talked of many things among which was the time Urdanur spent in New York City when she was younger. On the subject of Manhattan we had a great deal to converse about.

As we chatted, I noticed several airmen at a not-so-distant table glance in our direction from time to time. They would do so, then talk among themselves as if in a football huddle and subsequently emit a ridiculing laugh. I decided they were fools and chose to ignore their collective grossness.

"Do you see what I mean?" commented Urdanur.

"They are very low class," I assured her; "and each one is a *futard*."

She looked perplexed so I explained.

"*Futard* is a word I made up. Please excuse my language but it means, *fucking bastard*."

Then it was our turn to laugh.

In a short span of time, Urdanur and I began to cultivate a friendly relationship. She was amusing, intelligent, and very warm. Furthermore, she was sensitive–a trait which is important to me.

Near the end of our lunch visit, Urdanur told me that she owned an apartment building close to the Guest House and that she had a basement flat which was immediately available. Her position in JAMMAT was almost like a hobby. Her real source of income was the apartment building her parents had left.

"When is your birthday?" she asked. "I sometimes judge people by those kinds of things, even if it is not very scientific."

"March twenty-fifth."

Her face took on a glow of complete bewilderment.

"Are you joking with me?" she smiled.

"Why should I kid about my birthday?"

"March twenty-fifth also happens to be my birthday. That is quite ironic."

"No wonder we took to each other so easily," I remarked.

There was more conversation about sundry things and finally Urdanur made ready to leave. Before going, she invited me for dinner at which time she would discuss the rental.

I arrived at her sixth floor penthouse apartment somewhere around 2000 hours. We had a delicious dinner during which time I told her my life story. Then she showed me the basement apartment that I immediately fell in love with. I was relieved to see that it had an American style commode.

We went back up to her place, drank wine, played music, and drank more wine. The result of all the vino culminated in sexual encounters of the torrid kind. And I enjoyed every fiery moment.

How differently she looked to me now, I thought, compared to when I first met her earlier in the day.

After putting on the Nat King Cole album, she sat opposite me, again, and said: "I would like you to know that there are no strings attached, Corey. What happened tonight was indeed very pleasant but I understand you are young and probably anxious to fall in love with someone your own age."

Her comment put me immediately at ease. I was no longer dubious about having spent this time with her. I genuinely liked this lady who only that morning had been a complete stranger at a podium.

"I would ask that we be friends. I would like that very much."

"So would I."

In the background, Nat King Cole was singing "Too Young" and I wondered if it had prompted Urdanur to say those nice things. Nevertheless, I wanted to have a relationship with her. But only a platonic one from that point on.

"Now it's your turn to tell me about yourself, " I announced. "I told you about me during dinner."

"Why would you want to know about me?" she asked, humbly.

"I like to know about my friends."

Urdanur generously smiled.

"I was born in Istanbul, in 1916. My mother was a traditional Turkish housewife and my father was a doctor. When I was fifteen, my favorite aunt got a job in New York City and we convinced my father to let me go along with her for a brief vacation. I was to return after two weeks but my stay was extended. My aunt eventually became a citizen and I became her ward. Several years later, my aunt died from a cerebral hemorrhage. A week after that was the attack on Pearl Harbor and I thought it prudent to stay safely put. I had a job and my parents sent me money. After the war, I returned to Turkey–too late to see my parents. My mother died from a sudden heart attack three weeks before I got home and my father died a week after she did from a cerebral hemorrhage. But I say it was from melancholy because he and my mother had been very close.

"It seems that everyone I have ever really loved has died on me. I must be some kind of curse. But, as it says in the sacred KORAN, 'Wherever ye be, God will bring you all back at the resurrection.' So one day I will see them again."

There was a long period of silence when Urdanur finished her story. She was temporarily lost in bittersweet memories and I was choked up with compassion. Nonetheless, she noticed the tears in my eyes and gently, appreciatively, kissed me on the cheek.

"It is getting late and you are probably tired. I am glad you came here and I am glad that I have a new friend. Grace Kelly is not the only one who has a prince; you are my little prince, Corey."

Back in my hotel room, I reviewed the afternoon part of my day. How Kyle had finally shown for lunch. How he had taken me to the PX to meet his fiancée, Nurtan. How Nurtan had introduced me to Sandy who also worked in the PX. And how I had made a date with Sandy to go see Ataturk's Tomb.

Sandy was cute and I liked her. But she was to have a few surprises for me.

*   *   *

Ty Manners left his temporary residence at the J. & V. Gilardi Hotel and hailed a taxi. Settling in the back seat, he lit a cigarette and displayed a painful expression.

I hate these fuckin Turkish cigarettes, he thought to himself; *why do so many people rave about them? They're wicked bad. I'll stick with American.*

43

"Where you want go?" asked the taxi driver.

"Where's a good place to have fun, *Mustafa*?"

"My name not *Mustafa*. My name *Kemal*."

In a low tone, Ty murmured, "You're all *Mustafa* to me."

"You want go *haman*?" said the driver.

"What's that?"

"Steam, rub down, bathhouse."

"No thanks. It's enough that I shower every three days."

"Where I take you?" the driver asked once more.

"I want some wicked pussy," announced Ty; "do you know what I mean?"

He grabbed his crotch for the driver to see.

"Sex, sex, sex."

The driver's eyes lit up in acknowledgement.

"You want go to Compound," he said.

"The Compound?" echoed Ty.

"*Evet, Efendi.*" He paused. "Compound is brothel."

"Take me there," bellowed Ty, enthusiastically. "That sounds wicked good!"

*   *   *

CHAPTER 5 —
"Tears on a Rose"

"Es-ki-ci! Es-ki-ci!" bellowed the voice.

The sound drifted down from the street above, along the side of the building, and into my partially opened bedroom window. While my apartment was below street level, it was not underground. It had a private back entrance and a little yard for me to sun in when the summer came. Right now it was only April but an unusually balmy day for this month.

"Es-ki-ci! Es-ki-ci !"

During my short time in Ankara, I had become used to that cry whenever I wasn't working the day shift. Once a week the *eskici* would come leisurely strolling up the street and sing out his song. Following close behind him would be his donkey, pulling a small cart burdened with various articles of all dimensions and qualities. For an *eskici* is someone who buys and sells old things.

One day I'll write a Broadway musical called Turkish Delight *and have a love song entitled "Eskici–The Buyer of Broken Hearts."*

Till then my employer is the Air Force.

The officer in charge of the cryptography suite proved to be helpful, friendly and patient. My fellow workers were all easy to get along with. The work hours also tolerable. We rotated on three shifts. But coding and decoding messages could be hazardous to one's freedom if he were to send out a top secret communique uncoded. He could find himself in Levinworth Prison for jeopardizing national security and/or sabotage.

I glanced across my bedroom at a photograph of Ataturk's Tomb which I had had enlarged and framed. A three week old memory, my excursion there had been a dubious pleasure.

It was my first–and last–date with Sandy, the girl whom Kyle had introduced me to in the PX. She was a pleasant person but had a strange demeanor I could not determine.

Because she had been in Ankara for a year, Sandy had acted as my guide and gave me a brief tour of this interesting city.

We visited Yenishire, the modern section of town–with its restaurants, a movie theatre and a coffee shop in which I learned that if one stirs the tiny cup of Turkish coffee, it turns into mud; Ulus, the old sector–where one traffic circle has a small concrete island that sometimes serves as the spot for public government executions; and,   finally, the magnificent Ataturk's Tomb–a splendid tribute to the man who revolutionized Turkey.

The latter is a multi-pillared structure that houses the Chief Turk's body. The rectangularly-shaped tomb sits on a man-made hill and has a series of wide steps which descend to a gargantuan plaza.

It was there that Sandy casually hit me with bombshells. Not only was she just fourteen years old, she also turned out to be the child of that frumpy-looking woman who coincidentally just happened to be the wife of Colonel Myrons–the adjutant at JAMMAT.

Then and there it was *adieu* to Sandy.

Despite those scary facts, I had decided that there could be no future for us, anyway. During the entire afternoon, I had wished that I was having the experiences not with Sandy but with that sensual woman in the Frown Family.

When I stirred my Turkish coffee to mud in the quaint cafe, I had wanted to be sharing the ensuing laughter with that woman. When I heard about the government's public executions in Ulus, I had wanted to be appalled, along with that woman. And when I strolled the acres of Ataturk's Tomb, I had wanted to be holding hands–not with Sandy but with that woman.

I could not understand my feelings, but since first seeing that woman she had haunted me. And I felt that perhaps destiny had something in store for us.

The fact that she was married to a captain in the army didn't seem to trouble me. And the truth that I had a girlfriend back home also did not affect me. Puzzling was the actuality that I had these feelings at all. For someone with such a strict upbringing in high morals–and one who was usually ridden with guilt even thinking such things–I was surprisingly blase. Perhaps that happens to one the first time he travels so far away from home.

"Es-ki-ci! Es-ki-ci!"

There he was again making his way back down my street. A signal which now said he was passing by for the final time today. Also a signal for me to get out of bed and pen that letter I owed.

Dear Edith,

Sorry I took so long to write but I've been kind of busy sightseeing. One place that I went to was Ataturk's Tomb.

Ataturk is Turkey's biggest hero. In fact, the word "Ataturk" means "Chief Turk." In 1923, he established the Republic of Turkey and became its first president. Sort of like our George Washington, I guess. Under his leadership, the country became the first Moslem state in the world to separate the powers of state and church. Ataturk believed that it was time for Turkey to turn to the Western World for its ideas, and to put aside the fez, the veil and the harem. Personally, I would have kept the harem. Why mess with something that works so well? —Within a short period of years, Turkey became a strong, modern republic with democratic ideals.

I saw Kyle and Nurtan for dinner last week and they're doing fine. Pretty soon a group of us is going out to celebrate the official announcement of their engagement. They make a great couple and I'm very happy that Kyle is ready to settle down.

I haven't seen the Frown Family in awhile. They must be hiding someplace. Will stop for now. Am enclosing some photos so you can visualize the places I tell you about.

Love,
Corey

MY apartment

Typical Shoeshine Boy

Ulus

Ataturk's
TOMB

Guest House

JANNAT

Yenishire

*   *   *

Only a driveway separated the Guest House from the dwelling of Madam Saadet Sivas–an erudite woman of Turkish blood–who operated a boarding facility catered to by American airmen. So popular was the Sivas establishment that guys never moved out until they were going back to the States.

Madam Sivas' place was preferred because the rooms were spotless, the food was the best, and the proprietress was delightful, charming, and warm. Many a lad would go to her with his problems and she would patiently listen and offer guarded but sage advice. To most of her boarders she was a surrogate mother. They all loved her. And her Sunday morning breakfast was an event. It was purported that no other pancakes in the whole world tasted as good as hers.

At age sixty-five, Madam Sivas appeared older but her welcoming countenance paled the years. Bright hazel twinkling eyes dominated her unusually small features, and brilliant white hair enhanced her demeanor. Her slim frame and remarkably short height made her immediately "adorable." One felt that he or she wanted to protect the precious woman against life's sadder ways.

Few, however, knew of her background and the long way she had come before reaching this placid stage of life.

Born in a cloistered peasant village nestled on the slope of a small mountain, Saadet grew up in an undersized hut made out of clay. Along with her five brothers and sisters, she worked in tobacco fields close to her home. When she was twelve years old, Saadet discovered that she possessed clairvoyant powers.

At age thirteen she married Kemal–a village boy one year her senior and they both escaped to Ankara on a donkey which was a wedding present. In the big city, the engineering Kemal went from blacksmith to auto mechanic. Exceedingly deft at his trade, he made a comfortable life for his wife and himself by the time he was in his twenties. They were very much in love and lived each for the other.

When Kemal died at age forty-five, Saadet thought she would not survive without him. She went into heavy mourning–via alcoholism–for several years but was eventually salvaged by the unselfish constant prodding of her friend, Aytan Ordu. They had met when Saadet first came to Ankara and they had remained fast friends throughout the years. So close were they that Aytan's daughter, Nurtan, seemed almost like Saadet's daughter.

After great contemplation, Saadet sold her husband's business and with the money she obtained opened a boarding house. It was a solace to be with young people because they were like children to her. The offspring she could

50

never have. Saadet felt that because Mohammed had given her clairvoyant powers, He had taken away her ability to produce a baby. But she was never bitter about her plight nor any other misfortune that fell upon her shoulders. She would always say, "When rain falls I have the luck to possess an umbrella." It was just one of the many sayings she delighted in couching.

When Madam Sivas opened her front door she was surprised to see the troubled look reflected on Yuksel's face.

"*Merhaba, Teyze*," said Yuksel, with a weak smile. Like Nurtan, Yuksel also addressed Madam Sivas as Aunt. "I have bring rose for you."

Roses were cherished by Madam Sivas and whenever Nurtan and Yuksel went to visit, they always brought one to prove their love and respect for the woman.

"Come into my sitting room my child. I will make tea."

Rather than conversing in their native tongue, they spoke in English. Both wanted to practice it for the Americans they knew.

With the tea poured, Yuksel began speaking through profuse tears.

"It is Turan. He is *cok fena*. Very bad. More and more the bad. He scold me and make me do bad things in the bed."

"Then you must leave him," advised Madam Sivas. Her voice was soft and soothing–like someone singing a lullaby. She generally paused within a sentence as if to emphasize something or to wonder at her own words.

"I am too the fear. He not will let me go."

"You are always welcome to come here, my Child."

"I am too the fear to see the next day. I must the know what will come on me. Please, Teyze. Read the cards on me."

Reading the Tarot cards was a talent Madam Sivas had learned when she was a young girl. An older woman from a neighboring hamlet had heard of Saadet's gift of the occult and looked upon Saadet as a kindred spirit. She would travel to Saadet's village once a week and instruct the young girl in the many ramifications of the Tarot. And according to the superstition that one must never buy his or her own cards, the woman had presented Saadet with a special deck. On one side of every card was painted a single rose.

Reading the cards was something that Madam Sivas disliked to do but when a friend would ask her, she could not refuse. One did not begrudge a cherished person something she wanted.

Madam Sivas reluctantly moved to her baroque credenza, unlocked the bottom drawer and took out a small hand-made wooden box. Upon unlocking the container, she secured her special set of cards which was wrapped in silk–another superstition among some Readers. She then joined Yuksel who knew the ritual and had already moved to a small table so that she would be seated opposite Madam.

With sincere reverence, Madam Sivas handed the cards to Yuksel and the latter shuffled them. When she returned the cards to Madam Sivas, the Reader spread out ten of them in a special pattern and began to turn each over in its proper turn.

At one point during the session, Yuksel thought that her *teyze* had hesitated so she hastened to question.

"You see bad thing?"

"There is nothing wrong," stated the Woman.

"Then I have no the fear?" summarized Yuksel.

"No my child."

When the Reading was over, the older woman returned the cards to their habitat and re-joined her young friend.

"I will try to think of some way for you to leave Turan. And you must do so."

"Thank you, *Teyze*. I not to know what to do with no you. You have take place of parents who put me out of house."

The two women then spoke of lighter things.

Before leaving, Yuksel thanked Madam Sivas again and again, and kissed her dear friend on the cheek. The old woman watched with heavy heart as Yuksel faded from her sight.

A block away from Ataturk's Circle in the Ulus section of Ankara, a young Man parked his car in front of the police building and casually made his way into the edifice. In the lobby, he was greeted warmly–if not mixed with a bit of trepidation–by the receptionist at a large desk. He walked past her and as he approached the elevators, a policeman on duty excitedly held the conveyance doors open for him. He stepped inside with an air of complete confidence and nodded to the elevator operator who closed the doors and propelled the lift to the top floor.

Alighting from the elevator, the young Man stepped into a large art-deco styled foyer which was circular in shape. In the middle of the circle was a receptionist's desk with a pretty girl seated behind it. Five feet behind her was a huge marble statue of Ataturk attired in his army uniform. The statue's arms were outstretched as if welcoming someone into his embrace.

Behind the statue was an office with a large door upon which was painted in gold leaf: Chief Inspector Jean Claude Burdur.

The Receptionist leaned forward as the young Man approached her desk.

"*Merhaba*, Turan," she whispered, with a sultry air. "I have missed you."

He walked around the desk and stood very close to her.

"Forgive me, pretty one! But I have forgotten your name although it truly does not matter because I never forget your exciting body!"

As if to prove his point, the girl rose from her chair and stood face to face with the visitor. Meanwhile, Turan could feel a rising sensation in his groin.

Savagely, he pulled the girl to his body and kissed waiting lips. Holding her tightly, he moved her backward until she pressed against the statue of Ataturk.

"I am between my two favorite Turks," she smiled, while panting.

Turan made no comment. He kissed her again and with his left hand lifted her skirt and pulled down her panties. With his right hand, he unzipped his fly and withdrew the passion apparatus waiting to be freed. With the machinery now set in motion he steadied himself by holding onto the outstretched hands of Ataturk's statue and the act suddenly became a bizarre ménage à trois.

In the midst of this pleasure, the girl asked, without too much concern, "Suppose someone comes by?"

"Let them also enjoy it!" laughed Turan. What had he to fear, he reasoned. He was one of the office's top men. *No one would dare to say anything.*

When he was spent, Turan reverted to his purpose of being there. "Is the Inspector waiting for me?"

"Yes," answered the girl, pulling herself together. "Go right in. He is alone."

Turan opened the center door and entered a large room at the end of which was his mentor, supervisor and friend–Jean Claude Burdur–a loyal Turk who was part French.

"Come in, Turan. Sit down. Have some *raki.*"

The visitor gestured to his coat pocket.

"I forgot," said Chief Inspector Burdur. "You always carry your own. –Incidentally, did you enjoy my Receptionist?"

Turan laughed but was not embarrassed. "You know me too well!"

How true that was, thought Turan. The Chief Inspector had been his friend for many years. And Turan could clearly remember the day they first met.

Although Turan had been born in Ismir, Turkey, his father had eventually sent him to live with a relative in the jewelry business in Ankara because the boy was recalcitrant. At thirteen years old, Turan became an apprentice in his uncle's trade and while he wasn't completely happy, at least he was away from a town he disliked.

At the age of sixteen, the mature-looking and personable Turan showed such great promise that his uncle made the boy a salesman. In this position, Turan eventually formed two friendships.

One relationship was with an older woman who taught him all the kinky and bizarre love processes that filled his veins with such hot intensity.

The other person Turan had made friends with was Jean Claude Burdur.

"What kind of gift would you recommend I buy for my wife?" had asked Jean Claude, a distinguished looking man at age thirty-eight.

"That depends on her much you love her!" answered Turan.

While the boy's comment had not been what Jean Claude had expected, he had found it to be very clever and extremely amusing.

"What would be your guess?"

"I would say you want to spend very little!"

The boy was brazen, self-assured and quite mature. The Customer admired those traits. He thought of himself when he was younger.

"On what do you base your answer?" Jean Claude had continued.

"On my feelings! Nothing _else_ is necessary!"

"You are quite a perceptive young man. Have you ever thought of going into police work? –If you do, here is my card. Call me."

Not too many years later, Turan got bored with the jewelry business and made that call to Jean Claude who by then had attained the rank of Chief Inspector. Burdur took the younger Man under his wing and in no time at all Turan amply proved that policing was his forte. He reveled in the power it gave him over others; he could be bold, tough, and demanding and all within the confines of the law. Soon he became the youngest inspector in the Secret Police.

Along the way, Turan married a girl of his own age, had three children and accrued great esteem–even some fear–among his colleagues. He had the city of Ankara for his personal playground and as a haven for extramarital calisthenics–even though he had a permanent mistress named Yuksel.

"Does your wife still have that cheap broach you bought her?" chuckled Turan.

Burdur echoed Turan's laugh. "Yes. She saves every little fucking thing no matter how useless it is." The man sighed in reminiscence. "It seems like only yesterday when I saw you in your uncle's jewelry shop."

"And so it does!"

"But let us get to business," said Jean Claude. "I have a special job for you."

"That is exactly what I like to hear! What is it?"

"Here in Ankara is a man named Ahmed Yalvac who works in the executive branch of the government. We suspect him of having contacts in Iran and Iraq to whom he gives information regarding everything that takes place in our offices. While all the information he is privy to is not always vital, his actions do constitute treason."

Turan smiled with delight. "And how do you want me to work this?"

"In your own inimitable way. I know you always get your man. One way or another!"

With business over, the Chief Inspector turned to lighter matters. "Do you still associate with Americans?"

"Yes! I like them!"

"What is there to like, Turan?"

The younger man laughed. "They are rich, amusing, well-educated and very entertaining! I met a new one several weeks ago! His name is Corey something! I do believe he became frightened when I exposed my gun!"

Now they both laughed.

"Do your future plans include emigrating to America?"

"I do not know yet, *Efendi!*"

"I would hate to see you leave Turkey. And I would miss you."

Turan stood up to leave. "*Tesekkur ederim*, Jean Claude! Thank you! *Allahaismarladik!*"

"*Gule, gule.*"

At the door, Turan paused and turned.

"Do not forget my standing offer, *Efendi!*"

"Thank you, my dear friend. I know and I am honored. Anytime I get tired of my wife and want to use your Yuksel, I will ask."

––––––

After Yuksel left Madam Sivas' house, the woman sat in long contemplation over the visit. Alone, and holding the beautiful rose which Yuksel had given her, the sapient lady was free to let her true emotions expel themselves. She thought back on the Tarot to the moment when she had hesitated. The sign she had seen was too hideous to fathom. And she desperately hoped that she had misread the meaning of the card. Yuksel must gain her independence from Turan, thought Madam Sivas. Before it was too late.

In the meantime she would pray. And as she did, tears swelled in her eyes and eventually crept down her cheeks.

Several of them fell upon the beautiful rose.

*   *   *

CHAPTER 6 —
"The Belly Dancer Night"

Fate is my constant guide and measurement in the enigmatic web of life. Although far from scientific it is my only way of comprehending the unexplainable. And on that Saturday evening in the Guest House destiny began a new phase of my existence. Like a spider it wove an intricate design and could do nothing else but extend it.

A radio behind the counter was playing "Too Close For Comfort" as I got my food in the cafeteria, and found the nearest table.
A few moments later I perceived someone standing over me.
"I guess you didn't need my help after all."
Peering up at Drew's now familiar face, I smiled. "What do you mean?"
"The grapevine tells me that you found a pad."
"In Miss Urdanur Besni's building."
"I know the place. And she's a great lady."
Eager for company and wanting to hear inside stories pertaining to Hollywood, I invited Drew to sit down.
"I'm having dinner with some acquaintances–a Captain and his wife–and they want you to join us."
"An officer?" I exclaimed.
"They're very nice people. And they don't bite."
Without giving me time to decide, Drew picked up my tray and moved away. Reluctantly, I obediently followed but his body blocked my view.
The radio began playing the love theme from a recent film whose name I could not recall. It was one of those hauntingly beautiful melodies which never leaves your brain. And when Drew stepped aside–when I saw my sensuous woman sitting there–the music instantly represented her and I

immediately knew that the lady and the melody would be forever entangled with my emotions.

Drew made the introductions all around and I learned that the name of the Frown Family was Lebal. The children politely greeted me then asked to be excused to go finish a game they had started.

Once seated, I had to fight diligently to overcome a sudden bit of nervousness which struck me when I was in complete awe of someone.

"How do you like Turkey so far, Corey?"

Her voice was as sensuous as she looked. The deep bold velvety tone had an amazingly calming effect on me and in no time I was pleasantly at ease.

"I'm beginning to feel at home, so to speak. Most of the people I've met to date are very friendly and warm. And my best friend Kyle Muenster is here."

"yes," offered the Captain; " i know that lad. he's in the motor pool which is under my command."

The Captain seemed to be a pleasant person despite the hard look he had about him. But his speaking voice was enough to put one to sleep.

"do you know a ty manners?" he continued.

I answered in the negative.

"well, he and your friend kyle seem to be good chums. but this manners kid is a bit of a wiseguy, i think. at the orientation he asked a few impertinent questions."

My mind flashed back to that day and I recalled the guy; he had also annoyed me.

"They may be friends," I hastened to inform; "But Kyle is a good guy."

The Captain gave me a knowing smile.

There was an unexpected lull in the conversation and I feared the Captain was offended by my coming to Kyle's defense. Drew seemed to realize the awkwardness and picked up the slack.

"Corey is from New York," he announced.

"New York is my favorite city," said Mrs. Lebal; **"After Sodom and Gomorrah, that is."**

Everyone laughed but I did so until tears rolled down my face and I started to cough.

"are you all right?" asked the Captain.

"Fine thank you, Sir. But when I cough, lately, my stomach seems to hurt."

The Captain and his wife both spoke at once and suggested that I go on sick call to check out the disorder. They agreed it could be serious.

I thanked them for their concern and then remarked how much the Captain reminded me of my father. Besides looking alike, they seemed to have the same ways. A gracious smile commanded the Captain's face and I sensed a bond developing between us. Since I could not call him "Pop," he subsequently joked, I would have to call him by his first name, Winston. But only among ourselves and not openly in public. That would be a definite breach of military procedure. The same held true for his wife; I was to call her Friday.

"That's a clever and interesting name," I commented.

"It was not my given name," she explained; **"I always hated the one my parents gave me so I legally changed it when I became an adult."**

She was not only outstanding in looks, voice, and mannerisms but also in name. Of all the unusual appellations I had ever heard, hers was the best.

The dialogue among us continued for over an hour in which time we covered Drew's air force career to date, the Captain and Friday's previous assignments, my background, things we had thus far noticed about Turkey, and Urdanur's orientation.

"Speaking of Urdanur," began Drew; "she owns an apartment building and Corey just got a pad there."

"I wish we could find a place," exclaimed Friday. **"It's nice being in the Guest House with Drew but I'm anxious to get fully unpacked."**

A bell rang in my head. "I know that Urdanur has an available apartment on the first floor. I can arrange for you to go see it, if you like?"

With agreement, they shook their heads in unison.

"Is Monday all right?"

"monday is fine," agreed Winston.

"Will you take us there?" asked Friday.

"It would be my pleasure."

"it looks like you've made two new friends," chuckled the Captain, patting me on the arm.

At that point it was time to leave. I invited Friday, Winston and Drew to join me as I was going to meet Kyle and some others at the Istanbul Palace. The Lebals appreciatively declined but Drew decided to come along.

As I stood and shook hands with the Lebals, Friday gave me a captivating smile while simultaneously squeezing my hand.

"We look forward to seeing you on Monday," she concluded.

"And, I, you."

For our trip to the Istanbul Palace, I phoned Gobasi—the taxi driver I had met by chance several days earlier. Hearing of the Roman Ruins on the outskirts of Ankara, I had decided to explore them. I had walked to Ataturk Boulevard and hailed a taxi. Gobasi's was the first cab to come along and stop.

He got out of the vehicle and while walking around the cab shouted "No" when he saw me reaching for the door. At first I was startled then realized he felt it was his duty to open the door for me. I thanked him in Turkish and smiled to myself while settling in the rear seat.

Back in the vehicle he asked our destination and seemed to understand my answer. We engaged in a tiring conversation of fractured words and pantomime since his English was poor and my knowledge of Turkish worse.

"MY NAME GO-BA-SI," he exclaimed. "I AMERICAN LIKE. THEY GOOD MAN."

Gobasi was slightly older than I and very personable. Something about his mannerism made me feel that he was a kind person whom I could trust–much unlike Turan, that frightening policeman I had met on my first night in Ankara and hoped never to see again.

When we arrived at the Roman Ruins, I gave Gobasi two *lira*. He promptly returned one of them shaking his head that I had overpaid him.

He said that he would come back for me in one hour.

Gobasi kept his word about returning and when he finally dropped me off, gave me his phone number while pantomiming that he would be my personal driver. I had tipped him generously but my feelings told me that that was not his reason. Rather, I sensed a kind of bond between us. His smile had the sincere aura of an innocent child.

While we rode in Gobasi's taxi to the Istanbul Palace, Drew made an interesting comment.

"I have the feeling that Mrs. Label likes you, Corey."

"What are you trying to tell me?"

"Nothing," he answered. "Just be careful. I don't want you to get hurt."

To Drew, I pretended not to understand what he was implying. But perhaps I was just trying to fool myself. At any rate, it seemed prudent not to pursue the topic so I tactfully changed the subject.

"Are you sure that you never met Elizabeth Taylor?" I asked.

Drew just laughed and shook his head in a gesture of hopelessness.

*   *   *

They were seated in the living room of the Guest House. She was reading the novel MARJORIE MORNINGSTAR by Herman Wouk; he was perusing the latest newspaper.

"it says here," noted Winston; "that six marine recruits were drowned during a march at parris island, south carolina."

"That's the military for you," commented Friday, sarcastically, "unfortunately those things happen. –by the way, where are the children?"

He had a habit of doing that, thought Friday. Whenever she was reading, he would always interrupt to give bits of useless information. On the other hand, she was seldom not reading.

"They're in the room and getting ready for bed. –Monday, Sandy is taking them sightseeing. It seems she has grown quite attached to them. And they to her. I think we have inadvertently found an excellent babysitter."

She returned to her book and several minutes later he interrupted again.

"what do you think of that Corey kid?"

"He seems very friendly and sincere. And your feelings are?"

"i like him also. he has a lot of respect."

Inwardly, she experienced a sigh of relief. For a fleeting moment, she thought Winston was about to start an argument and tell her that Corey could not be a part of their lives. He happily surprised her. Since their last unfriendly discussion Winston had displayed a change of attitude. He seemed much calmer and tolerant. Perhaps this transfer had been a good move. She only hoped it would last a long time.

But could things ever return to the way they were in the beginning? Doubt prevailed on that point. Yet she could still recall how she had once loved Winston. Back then. Not too long after she had changed her name.

Friday was born Filomena Sorelli. She had one sibling who died from infantile paralysis before Filomena was born and Filomena had always regretted the tragedy. She missed and longed for the sister she never knew. Being an only child was lonely.

When her parents had arrived in New York City, from Sicily, Italy, Filomena's father was anxious to become rich and thought he could do so by joining the Mafia. Instead, he was killed during a gang war. His Godfather gave a substantial amount of money to the widow, and Filomena's mother uprooted them to St. Cloud, Minnesota–far away from the dangers of New York.

At age seven, Filomena's life drastically changed. One day she was walking with her mother on a busy street in St. Cloud. When the ball she was bouncing rolled onto the road, Filomena impulsively ran after it. Her mother saw a car headed for her daughter and ran to save the child. Instead, the vehicle hit Filomena's mother and she died on the spot. Having no traceable relatives in the United States, Filomena was sent to a Lutheran orphanage where she became fast friends with a girl named Loretta. The girls found that they had much in common and Filomena suddenly had a sister.

Another turning point in Filomena's life came at the age of sixteen. She and Loretta followed the orphanage minister into the woods and by nightfall they had learned about fellatio. When the clergyman was transferred, the girls ran away and hitch-hiked to New York City in hopes of finding him.

In the reverberating metropolis, Filomena and Loretta got jobs as waitresses and lived in the YWCA until they were able to secure a cheap flat in east Greenwich Village. Filomena went to night school and soon got a job as a secretary in an insurance company on Liberty Street. Immediately, she legally changed her name to Friday because she was born on that day. She had always hated the name Filomena, especially when someone called her "Fil."

An unresolved mystery occurred after Friday had been in the Big Apple for several years. Loretta did not come home from work one night. All of the Girl's possessions—including a bank book—were still in the apartment so it was safe to reason that she hadn't run away voluntarily. Friday contacted all the authoritative offices but to no avail. She never saw Loretta again.

Saddened and alone, Friday was enticed into marriage with a seemingly sensitive guy who soon turned out to be a wife-beater. A newlywed of six months, Friday hastened to get an annulment and quickly put the bad memories behind her.

In 1941, World War II began and Friday found herself—along with all the other patriotic girls of the time—volunteering at the Stage Door Canteen.

When she met Second Lieutenant Winston Lebal there, he seemed to be a perfect mate. He was kind, older and more mature. Not very attractive but reliable. He seemed to love her a great deal and tried to show it. When she learned that he had been in an orphanage from age six months until seventeen when he joined the army, she felt that destiny had already decided her future. She had loved him as a kindred spirit.

Winston spoke again and his remark brought Friday back to the present.

"when we get settled," he said; "we must have corey over for dinner. he's the first young man i've met in a long while who seems to be mature and responsible."

"Thank you, Winston."

"for what?"

"Trying so hard to keep the peace between us. I want you to know that I really appreciate it."

For the first time in many years, she noticed that he blushed and became quietly humble. Like a little boy receiving a compliment from a parent.

Friday truly did appreciate Winston's new attitude.

But <u>why</u> did she have such a strong attraction toward Corey?

*   *   *

The Istanbul Palace fulfilled all my expectations of an exotic Middle Eastern night club. Everything I had hitherto depicted in my mind. Except, of course, for Ingrid Bergman and Humphrey Bogart.

But the **fracas** which was to occur nearly surpassed the allure of the place and the excitement of the belly dancer.

The decor was intriguing even though the place had seen better days.

After passing through a small lobby, we crossed the threshold into a huge circular room. Bordering a spacious dance floor was a sea of very low octagon-shaped tables. Instead of chairs, the customers sat on over-stuffed pillows whose coverings were somewhat faded.

Surrounding this area was a raised floor or stage containing a series of adjacent alcoves. Each one was like a small cave within which was a low table and pillows in lieu of chairs. There was also a sheer curtain which could be closed for semi-privacy.

My imagination decided that these rooms had once been reserved for sultans who used to frequent this establishment in the days when harems existed.

Gigantic light fixtures of multi-colored pieces of glass hung from the ceiling while paintings on the walls depicted tales from the Arabian Nights.

The aura of the place was augmented by a Turkish musical combo–in a strategic alcove–which feverishly played Eastern music. When the musicians rested, a jukebox–stocked with both Turkish and American songs–echoed throughout the place.

"I didn't expect to hear Elvis here," I remarked.

Drew laughed. "Why not? Turkey has everything to offer."

The maitre d' approached us.

"Good evening, *Efendi*. Where you like to sit?"

"*Merhaba*," I replied. "I was told to ask for Yuksel."

An all-encompassing smile dawned his face. "Please follow me."

The maitre d' led us to the left side of the room, up four steps to the higher level and past several caves until we reached the one which was next to the musicians. As we approached, I could hear Kyle laughing.

"Hi, Babe," he shouted upon seeing me. "How ya'll doin'? –Hi, Drew."

I had met Nurtan already but did not know Yuksel whom Kyle quickly introduced. We maneuvered ourselves onto cushions and Kyle ordered *raki* for us.

"This here is the bes' spot in the house," announced Kyle, proudly.

"Who do you know?" I smiled.

Instead of Kyle answering, Yuksel did. "He know me, Corey. I the work here. Tonight I not the work."

The purring sound of her voice was indeed quite disarming. She hadn't said anything profound but it was unbelievably sexy. I'd bet she could make the Gettysburg Address seem like a mating call.

"Are you the manager here?" I asked Yuksel.

"No," she smiled, charmingly; "only helper to manager."

Then Nurtan spoke.

"How is your apartment, please?"

"It's getting there."

"Please, if it is trouble get there, why you do not take taxi or ask me show you?"

I didn't comprehend what she was talking about until Kyle rescued me by laughing and explaining my answer to Nurtan. The more I spoke with a person whose knowledge of English was limited, the more I became away of how many idioms I lightly used.

"My English is *fena*. Bad," apologized Nurtan.

"It is good," I protested. "It is I who spoke incorrectly."

Yuksel inquired after Drew's health and then turned to me with a question.

"You live in the New York City, Corey?"

"In the suburbs."

"What suburbs is, Corey?"

Her bastardization of the English language was amusing.

"The suburbs is a quiet place where the only noise you hear is a lawn mower on Saturday and a sizzling barbecue on Sunday. –It's on the outskirts of the city."

"Oh," said Yuksel, anxiously. "It is six minutes past the nine. The show it must begin."

As if someone had heard her, the lights dimmed to blackness and the musicians began a haunting beat. Seconds later, a spotlight shone on a belly dancer who stood in the middle of the dance floor. The audience began to cheer.

My mouth dropped open in unrestrained surprise. The only exotic dancer I had ever seen in my life was Rita Hayworth in "Salome." While this girl was no doubt a very talented person, I reasoned, she was nothing like Rita.

This girl was zaftig! I wagered her weight to be close to, or over, one hundred eighty pounds.

She began the dance to a brain-sticking melody called *Tini Mini Hanim* and simultaneously clicked together tiny cymbals on her fingers. As she swirled, her waist-length hair sailed up and down in the smoked-filled air. Alluringly, her eyes peered out from above a sheer veil and each man she passed by emitted a howl of ecstasy. She moved round and round and faster and faster and built to an exciting climax in which she jumped upward and then down onto the dance floor into a split, with her arms reaching for the sky. There was one moment of deafening silence before the audience went into an uproar. I bounced to my feet and cheered so loudly that I even surprised myself.

"Need we ask what you thought of the belly dancer?" chuckled Drew.

I shook my head from side to side and rolled my eyes.

"Could there possibly be more?" I asked.

"Thirty minutes come the more," informed Yuksel.

As she spoke, I suddenly remembered the main reason we had gathered. I proposed a toast to Nurtan and Kyle on their engagement. Someone said "Speech" and though Kyle had nothing to say, Nurtan had bigger news.

"I am with baby."

Drew and I made polite noises of happy approval, Kyle seemed genuinely shocked, and Yuksel made a genuine smile as she kissed her friend Nurtan. Then they hugged each other and began to cry. Typical females, I mused to myself. Femininity was universal.

Subsequently, they excused themselves to go to the ladies room and Drew offered to walk them. Kyle and I were left alone.

"You seemed quite surprised at the news," I ventured.

"Ah sure am," he emphatically replied. "Ah likely peed my britches. Ah wonder who's the daddy."

"What's that supposed to mean?" I asked, amazed.

He became silent, as if his mind were a million miles away.

I repeated the question. This time he smiled and playfully poked me in the arm.

"Ah didn' expect a baby, but... ."

"Then why the hell didn't you use a condom?"

His reply was almost predictable. "Usin' a condom is like wearin' ah raincoat when ya go swimmin'."

Kyle gulped down his drink and I could see he was well on his way to drunkenhood.

"Why'd ya bring Drew?" he asked.

I didn't quite understand Kyle's reaction so he continued.

"Ah told ya he wuz strange. Ah heard he wuz a frien' of that there Christine Jorgensen. Never did see Drew wit' a gal."

"That doesn't mean a damn thing," I protested.

This was a side of Kyle I had never seen before and didn't want to accept.

"Drew's a nice guy," I insisted.

"Okay," conceded Kyle, smiling once again; "If ya like him then Ah like him."

The earlier conversation with Winston suddenly entered my head.

"Do you know a Ty Manners?" I asked Kyle.

"Yeah. He works wit' me in the motor pool. Ya'll will like him. He comes from Maine."

Before I could ask any more regarding Ty, the others returned and this time Drew proposed a toast to the happy couple. I closely watched Kyle's demeanor toward Drew but it was not to be a problem. Kyle acted as if he had never said a word.

Then *he* arrived and a sobering atmosphere draped our little soiree.

No introductions were necessary since everyone there already knew him. Yuksel could not know that I had met Turan, so she presented us to each other.

Turan smiled. "Now the picture is complete, Corey! Three weeks ago you met my wife! Tonight you meet my mistress!"

Automatically, I glanced at Yuksel. Her head was bent downward and her eyes studied the floor. I sensed a feeling of uneasiness. My heart went out to the Girl. How the hell did she get mixed up with him?

I noticed that Turan was wearing a similar outfit when I first saw him but in a different color combination. Like then, a pullover sweater, American dungarees, and sport jacket complimented his excellent build. *Was he still carrying his gun?*

Minutes after the waiter left from having delivered more *raki*, a young good looking Turkish Man entered our cave and greeted us with a humble and friendly politeness. His name was Nomar and he had gone to lower school with Yuksel. A few reminiscing remarks were made by both of them and then he asked Yuksel to dance. She shook her head in the affirmative and began to rise.

To my great surprise, Turan grabbed Yuksel's arm and pulled her down with such force that her knee hit the table and the glasses rattled.

"She will not dance!" bellowed Turan.

Nomar seemed unabashed and civilly argued that there was nothing wrong with his request.

"*Hayir*! No!" shouted Turan. As he did so, he made a gesture which is

Turkish slang for "Hell, No!" He tilted his head upward to the right while simultaneously making a vulgar utterance which sounded like a nasty hiss. But this did not discourage Nomar from repeating his request.

Turan sprung to his feet like a jack in the box. In the next instant, he jumped on the table–scattering glasses and ashtrays–and lunged at Nomar. Just as quickly off the table, he kneed Nomar in the groin and when Nomar doubled over in pain, Turan whipped his elbow across the Man's jaw.

As Nomar fell to the floor, moaning, three men in dark suits appeared from out of nowhere. With just one glance from those penetrating eyes of Turan, the three men hastily took Nomar somewhere out of our sight. Throughout this whole spectacle, the jukebox was playing, "Don't Be Cruel".

To my further amazement, three waiters instantly appeared and began making repairs. By the time they rapidly finished, a fourth waiter appeared with fresh drinks for everyone.

As Turan returned to his spot next to Yuksel, Drew whispered to me that those three men were part of the secret police.

"Ah have a cravin' for another drink," announced Kyle, smiling to relieve the tension. "Let's all git loaded," he laughed.

While Nurtan and Drew verbally agreed with Kyle, I overheard Turan whisper something to Yuksel.

His icy words sent chills up my spine.

CHAPTER 7 –
"A Cherished Gift"

The last thing I remembered was Winston talking to me.

Weather-wise, it was a miserable day. The rain came down in torrents and I thought perhaps we'd be in need of Noah's Ark before the day's end. But we were dry and Urdanur was showing us the vacant apartment.

"I would have you know," said Urdanur; "That the apartment was painted only last week."

"It's lovely," said Friday, looking first to Urdanur and then to me with a grateful smile.

"Do you like it, Winston?" I asked.

"very much, and it's quite convenient to jammat."

In relation to my place, the apartment was on the other side of a wide stairwell, but up one flight and street level. It was a much larger flat with a living room, dining room, two bedrooms, kitchen and bath.

"do you want the place," asked Winston.

"Definitely," answered Friday; **"if you have no objections, that is."**

"none," he answered.

"Fine," added Urdanur. "I would ask that you move in whenever you are ready."

I suggested we go down to my apartment to celebrate the occasion with a glass of champagne which I had bought in anticipation of the outcome. They all agreed and we headed for the front door.

"Incidentally," said Friday to Urdanur; **"I love that pin you are wearing."**

The pin was a representation of a butterfly whose outspread wings were gold plated and whose eyes were diamond chips.

Urdanur stopped walking, took off the pin and handed it to Friday.

"It is yours," she announced.

Friday was completely baffled and refused to take the pin, but Urdanur insisted. For Friday not to accept the gift would have been an insult. According to Turkish custom, if someone compliments the owner on a possession, the owner is obliged to give that object to the person paying the compliment.

Friday reluctantly but graciously accepted the present.

Winston laughingly said something to the effect that it was one hell of a custom. I also began to laugh and once again started coughing.

Then everything went black.

When I woke up, it was to the smiling and motherly face of an older woman. A name tag on her white uniform read Captain Agar.

"Welcome back," she said, cheerfully. "Try not to move too swiftly. You were operated on for burst appendix about two hours ago. You're in the American Hospital."

"Burst appendix?" I echoed incredulously.

Captain Agar explained that it had erupted three days earlier, that gangrene had been starting to set in, that the doctors caught the infection in time, and that everything was fine.

"Don't people die from that?"

"They certainly do," confirmed Captain Agar. "**You** were blessed. Consider it a heavenly gift."

It was early evening. I was in a large room which was the main ward. At the end of the chamber was a movie screen on which was being projected the film, "Lili." I would never forgive Leslie Caron for singing, "Hi, Lili, Hi, Low" so cheerfully when I was in excruciating pain.

"How did I get here?"

"Captain Lebal literally carried you in. The doctors operated almost immediately."

I looked down at my abdomen but could not see any stitches because of the bandages. But I sure as hell could feel the incision.

"You have two visitors," announced Captain Agar before walking away.

"I told you to go on sick call," smiled Friday.

"don't pick on the boy," defended Winston. "you can see he's in pain."

I smiled for the first time and was very thrilled and honored that they had been so concerned over me. I thanked Winston for having brought me there.

"you'll be out of the hospital by next week and then you'll get a three week sick leave to recuperate before you have to go back on duty."

That bit of news immediately lifted my spirits.

"We'll be moved into our apartment by then," said Friday; **"And we'll be able to take good care of you."**

"you rest for now," added Winston. "we'll see you tomorrow."

*   *   *

The rain dropped from the sky so forcefully that it enticed Yuksel to her kitchen window where she marveled at its intensity.

Looking into the backyard, Yuksel fixed her gaze on a small plastic birdbath which she had bought the previous summer. The raindrops filled its basin and the accumulating water spilled over the top as if the birdbath were a circular waterfall.

Close-by and hiding from the rain under the protection of a yard chair was a black cat with a thin white streak down his back. Not quite so brave now, thought Yuksel, as he was one day months ago when he tried to attack an unsuspecting pigeon.

Luckily, the bird had been a hair faster than the feline and had catapulted itself upward with wings rapidly flapping.

But the memory had stayed with Yuksel for she made an analogy between the cat's actions and those of a human. *How similar*, she had thought; *the strong often tried to pounce on the weak.* And she had written the incident in her secret diary.

The rain subsided a bit but continued to flow generously. Then came a sliver of lightning and a boom of thunder.

Yuksel walked away from the window and over to her kitchen table where she began to wrap a gift for Nurtan's forthcoming baby.

In the middle of doing so, she began to cry. The other night at the Istanbul Palace when Nurtan had first announced her pregnancy, Yuksel had had to hold back her sad feelings in deference to her friend's happiness. Alone now, her true emotions could unfurl.

At age fourteen, Yuksel was molested by a neighbor and became pregnant.

The older man denied the accusations and her parents believed him. Deciding that Yuksel was covering for an occasional boyfriend, the parents disowned and exiled her from the house.

Too ashamed to seek solace with Nurtan's family, Yuksel had nowhere to go and spent the first night sleeping under a tree in the Park of Youth, in Yenishire. Ironically, the bench she chose for a bed was adjacent to the amusement park.

When she woke up the next morning, she was greeted by an older man who referred to himself as *Amca*, uncle.

By profession Amca was a pimp. Through devious methods he persuaded Yuksel that he would take care of her. The cold, hungry, lonely, and immature girl was happy to have anyone and she eventually fell under his spell.

At first, Amca was gentle but little by little his true colors came out and Yuksel soon learned that his kindness came with payment on demand. With veritably no other options at hand, she worked for him on the condition that he would help her keep the baby after it was born.

The promise was good for two years. But one night while Yuksel was out prostituting for him, he sold the boy. Yuksel was devastated and argued and fought with the pimp but to no avail.

Having feared something like that might happen, she had had the heal of the baby's right foot tattooed with his name: Kamal. Try as she did, though, Yuksel—at age sixteen by then—could not find her son.

But she never gave up hope. She never would.

The door bell rang and brought Yuksel back from her sad memories. She dried her eyes and started for the entrance. As she did so, she tightened the cord on her robe to make sure the garment was secure. She was not alarmed that the caller might be Turan because he generally did not visit her in the afternoon.

Lightning and thunder once again announced their presence.

Yuksel opened the door to the smiling and very wet person of Kyle.

"Let me in," he laughed; "Ah'm soaked to the skin."

Yuksel was surprised to see her best friend's fiancée, and with no qualms immediately welcomed him.

"No jacket you wear, Kyle?"

"Nah. This here jersey is enouf."

"I not the understand, Kyle. Jersey is place."

The visitor laughed. "Yeah. But they also call this here kind of shirt a jersey. Ah'm takin' it off to dry."

"I hang it for you," innocently said Yuksel, accepting the shirt from the bare-chested Kyle. "What says it on back?"

"Portland, Maine. It's not mah shirt. Ah borrowed it from Ty Manners."

As Yuksel took the garment into the bathroom she called to Kyle to help himself to a cup of coffee, which he did. He stood by the window and looked out at the continuing rain. One thing he really loved to do in this weather was to have sex, he thought to himself. *There was something really hot about pumping a broad when the rain was hitting the ground.*

Yuksel entered the kitchen. "Nice you come. Nice to see you. How Nurtan is, Kyle?"

"Jus' fine."

"I see you not before, Kyle, with no shirt. You have nice physic."

Kyle laughed heartily. "Ah think ya mean physique."

While Yuksel embarrassingly apologized for her bad English, Kyle took the comment about his body as a good sign. After all, that was the true reason for this visit. Ever since he had first seen Yuksel, he had been attracted to her. Why not? *She was quite a sexy piece of ass and probably a Turkish delight.*

"Ah came here cause Ah wanna buy a present for Nurtan and Ah don' know her size."

"What you want to buy, Kyle?"

"Some nice thin lacy undies."

"Undies?"

Kyle pretended to search his mind for a word that Yuksel would understand. Then he reacted as if he had finally thought of a way to express himself. He unzipped his fly, partially pulled down his pants, and pointed to his underwear.

"Ya know. These."

Yuksel understood but began to feel a bit uneasy. Why had he not pulled his pants back up, she suddenly feared.

"Oh, shit," said Kyle, still play-acting. "Mah pants are wet too. Better take them off."

Yuksel pleaded that it would not be right for him to do so but it was already too late. He threw his pants on a chair and stood there in slightly damp briefs which were already beginning to bulge.

The hostess picked up the pants and handed them to him.

"Here. Put on, Kyle. This not the right."

For several moments neither of them spoke. She was in an unexpected panic. He was calculating his next move. The only prevailing sound was the rain which had seemed to intensify again. A blinding quivering bolt of lightning and an explosion of thunder nearly made the room vibrate.

Kyle grabbed his pants from her, threw them on the floor, and pulled her into his arms. He tried to kiss her but she kept moving her head to avoid him. She could not free herself from his powerful grasp. For the first time, she could smell alcohol on his breath.

"You drunk. That is why you act this way, Kyle. —Go drink coffee."

Her comment had no effect on his actions. He tried to kiss her again even though she began pounding on his chest while trying to keep her robe closed. Then he picked her up, carried her into the bedroom, threw her on the bed and pounced on top of her.

To her mind came the vision of the cat and the pigeon. Kyle was the feline and she the bird.

Yuksel tried to free herself but the opponent was too heavy.

"Please, no, Kyle," she pleaded. "Nurtan my best friend. You be her husband."

"It'll be our secret," he chuckled.

"Turan very jealous. He kill you."

"He'll never know."

"I can no do this," she continued.

"Don't ya'll give me that bullshit," he harshly responded, as if being cheated out of something. "Ah know all abou' ya. Nurtan told me how you wuz a whoah and how a guy accused ya of robbin' him and how you wuz sent ta the Compound."

Yuksel began to cry with complete abandon. Tears that encompassed all the pains of her nineteen years. The rape by the neighbor, her parents discarding her, the false security and degradation with Amca, the baby stolen from her, the untrue accusation of theft, time spent in the Compound, the virtual slave of Turan, and, now, Kyle treating her as an available deposit for his semen. The tears would not stop.

Kyle was completely oblivious to Yuksel's sobs of mercy. He held her arms with his one hand, tore open her robe, ripped off her panties, and lowered his briefs.

And though Yuksel cried and fought, she could not stop him from entering her.

More lightning and thunder!

Kyle moved his hips with great intensity. Through a satisfyingly wry smile, he said: "Ah'm gonna fuck ya like nobody's ever fucked ya before."

Peering in from the kitchen window was the black cat.

———————

Several blocks away, Sandy entered the JAMMAT Building and made her way to the PX. She hastily hung up her jacket in the back room and promptly reported to the front of the store where Nurtan was cleaning the top of a glass counter.

"Sorry I'm late, Nurtan, but all this rain slowed down the traffic. And my mother insisted on driving instead of putting me in a taxi."

Drops of rain fell from the ends of Sandy's hair onto the counter that Nurtan had just wiped dry.

"Forgive me again, Nurtan."

They both laughed and Nurtan once more dried the counter.

That was the nice thing about working with Nurtan, thought Sandy. She was easy to get along with and so very understanding.

"Has it been busy?" asked Sandy.

"*Hayir.* No. Please not to worry."

Sandy helped Nurtan clean the other counters and while working they spoke of various topics. Sandy mentioned that the crush she had had on Corey was definitely over. She realized he was much too old for her.

"Besides, I like somebody else better," she confided.

"Who?"

"A new boy in school."

Several customers entered the PX and the girls waited on them. When the patrons left, Nurtan went over to Sandy. In her hand was a small box.

"Please," said Nurtan; "I want show you present I bought for Kyle."

The gift was an exquisite looking wristwatch with a black face, the hours embossed in gold, a diamond chip in the center, and a gold expandable band.

"That's beautiful," gasped Sandy. "And very expensive. What is the occasion?"

"Only I love him and he such good person."

* * *

On the day before my release from the hospital, Friday came to visit as she and Winston had done every night. This time she was alone.

"Are you anxious to get out of here?"

"You bet," I laughed. "The only thing I'll miss about this place is the head nurse, Captain Agar. But she's going back to the States at the end of the month to retire."

"She's a marvelous woman. One of a kind."

Friday had put it succinctly. Captain Agar was indeed remarkable. I had met very few people in my life with the fine caliber of this lady. She was equally warm, sensitive, caring and optimistic. But her courage and fortitude were the things that amazed me. She had lost her husband in Japan, in World War II, and her only son fighting in this present Korean War. Yet never did she show a bitter or unpleasant face to the world. She bore her pain bravely—as did many other unfortunate and loyal Americans. I will never forget her.

"I brought you a present, Corey. It's John F. Kennedy's book called PROFILES IN COURAGE. Your friend Captain Agar should have been in this book."

"Another gift," I smiled, embarrassed. "You and Winston have given me so much already."

"On the contrary. You have afforded me a great deal."

Friday had a strange look in her eyes. She had stopped smiling and had become reserved. As if she were about to say something profound.

"You have revitalized me."

I did not understand the comment so she continued.

"Outside of my children, there was little else in my life that I cared about until you came along."

"But there is Winston."

"Winston and I have not been happy for years. Please forgive me for telling you this but I have the feeling we can be honest with each other."

"That's true. I am very fond of you."

"And, I, you."

A light fog permeated my brain.

What had I just said? What was I doing?

Basically, I knew.

I was falling in love with Friday but I couldn't believe it. She was an older woman. That was not a problem because I have always been attracted to mature females. But never before to a married one. And what about Winston? He had been very good to me. Hurting him was the last thing on my agenda.

Nonetheless, I had these feelings. And it seemed as if Friday also had them–unless I had dangerously misunderstood her words. *Was fate trying to play some kind of twisted game?*

"I wanted to bring you something extra special," began Friday; **"But I didn't know what. So I decided to give you this key chain. It's like a part of me. It was given to me by a good friend of mine named Loretta."**

I felt odd about accepting it but she insisted.

The gift was quite different. A thin one-inch chain connected a small metal horseshoe to an equally small metal heart whose red paint was beginning to fade. The heart had a small dent but I was thrilled and honored about receiving the present. I remembered how she had played with it when I first met her at the Guest House.

"I promise that it will bring you good luck," smiled Friday, tenderly. And I replied, "It already has."

*   *   *   *

The radio station that played only American music blared out the voice of Bobby Darin singing "Mack the Knife." The strains of the melody filled the chamber which was both a bedroom and mini-gym. A large bed with accompanying small night table and bureau had been pushed against one wall in order to leave the rest of the area free for bodybuilding equipment.

A huge barbell, dumbbells of various sizes and strengths, a tricycle-size wheel for stretching exercises, and a special type chair for doing abdominal workouts overpowered the room.

Strewn randomly throughout were numerous weightlifting magazines whose covers boasted photos of Adonises in skimpy posing straps. On one wall was a life-size poster of Steve Reeves as Hercules.

Drew did his last sit-up for the evening and paused to catch his breath from the strain of having done two hundred of them within a period of eight minutes.

With the vitality that often comes after a fruitful workout–if only for the appreciation that it's over with–he bounced off the chair and made his way into the bathroom. En route there he noted the time. He still had a full half hour before his date was to arrive.

Out of the shower, he dried, combed his hair and admired the impressive physique in the full length mirror behind the bathroom door. While the veins in his biceps, triceps and legs did not bulge as conspicuously as the magazine cover guys, he nevertheless had a fine body. The ripples on his stomach resembled a washboard. And he concluded that his anatomy was something Hollywood was going to clamor for. He could feel it in his gut.

The radio played "Mr. Wonderful" by Sammy Davis, Jr. .

Drew donned a pair of very worn dungarees, and, shirtless, fetched a bottle of wine from the refrigerator. He got two glasses and placed them on the coffee table in the living room. He filled one glass, sipped the rose colored ambrosia and lay on the couch to reminisce.

"That's it," he said, aloud. "I will change my name when I go back to Hollywood. I'll call myself Beau Eboni. No more Drew Johnson."

Who was Drew Johnson, anyhow? Just some scared kid who had had to run away from home.

When Drew began to have doubts regarding his sexual preference, he unexpectedly confirmed his feelings at the age of seventeen–one afternoon in the weight-lifting room at school.

Everyone had left except an oversized white sophomore who challenged Drew to a wrestling match. The innocent sport soon turned into nakedness and sexual agility. In the midst of the experience, a janitor appeared and threatened to report the boys to the principal.

From great shame and the fear of what might happen, Drew hurried home, packed some things in a sports bag, left a brief note for his mother and ran away to San Francisco.

Although Drew had been waiting to do another movie, he could not stick around. If a producer were to hear of the incident, Drew would not be hired. *Nobody wanted an actor who was a homosexual.*

In the Golden Gate city, it didn't take Drew long to find Castro Street where he met a thirty year old military man on a weekend pass. They formed a mutual relationship whereby the man kept Drew in an apartment. As the serviceman was stationed nearby, he had no problem getting into town. Their affair lasted for many years.

By the time the man was transferred to another location, Drew could financially take care of himself for he had finished high school and had attained a good job. Nonetheless, Drew was lonely after his friend left and so he followed in his lover's footsteps and joined the service.

The man had changed Drew's life and he had always felt indebted. He also still loved him.

But Drew wasn't a scared young guy any longer, he thought. Now he was the same age as his friend had been when they first met. And he knew a hell of a lot more about life.

The doorbell rang and Drew went to answer it. As he crossed the room the radio played "As Time Goes By" and Drew laughed out loud.

Upon opening the door, Drew greeted his guest.

"Remember this song? It was popular in 1943, when I met you in Frisco."

*   *   *

CHAPTER 8 —
"And Sorrows End"

*   *   *

The Government Ministry is located around the corner from the Police Building and directly opposite the entrance to Ataturk's Tomb. A ten story structure, it is square in shape—austere in appearance. It covers an area of three city blocks and houses a myriad of offices which pertain to national affairs.

Turan parked his car in the huge parking lot adjacent to the Ministry and made his way into the edifice. As well known there as in the Police Building, Turan was greeted by the main receptionist as he moved past her to the elevators.

On the eighth floor of the building, he made his way to the office of Corum Zile, Minister of Communications.

"How can I help you?" asked the fifty year old Zile who looked as if his obese body had been molded into his high back leather chair.

"On Chief Inspector Burdur's orders, I am investigating a certain Ahmed Yalvac! We consider him to be a traitor but we need definite evidence!"

The obese one looked up at the ceiling as he strained to recall a man by that name. Presently, he had to admit that he was unfamiliar with the person in question. He pushed his intercom button and ordered his secretary to bring Yalvac's file.

"What do you suspect Yalvac of doing?"

"Furnishing Iraq and Iran with information regarding the affairs of the Turkish Government!"

"For what purpose?"

Although Turan had only a slight hint as to Yalvac's motive, he replied self-assuredly.

"For *lira*! Money! I have been checking on him and find that he is spending a great deal! Quite beyond his salary!"

"What do you want me to do?" asked the obese Zile.

Turan spoke in his command-like manner. "I have prepared a false message which I expect Yalvac to pick up and send to Iraq and Iran! It says that the Turkish government is undergoing clandestine negotiations to allow the United States to establish secret observation posts along the Iraq/Iran borders for the purpose of spying on those countries!"

A Secretary delivered Yalvac's file. She smiled at Turan as she left the room and the latter turned his head to approvingly watch her retreat. But at that moment he was too occupied to succumb to his ever present erotic nature.

Minister of Communications Corum Zile quickly read the file and sighed.

"I see nothing here to confirm your suspicions but if Chief Inspector Burdur wants an investigation then I am in complete agreement. I will plant the message for you."

Turan stood and shook hands with Zile. "I will speak with you again!"

"Incidentally, Inspector," said the obese one, if only to prove his keen powers of observation; "my Secretary is free for lunch in one half hour. And she lives alone."

"*Tesekkur ederim, Efendi!*"

"*Gule gule.*"

*　　　*　　　*

Once again as in the hospital, a light fog permeated my brain and I could not believe what was actually happening. We were holding hands and it felt completely right. And wonderful.

Earlier in the day, Friday had rung my doorbell to announce that someone had told her of a great shopping place called the Bazaar. She shoved a mug of coffee in my hand and said we were going to "clear out the cobwebs." At first, I thought she was referring to my housekeeping techniques–or the lack thereof.

"No." she had laughed. **"Clearing cobwebs means wiping out all bad feelings from yesterday and making a clean start of today."**

The Bazaar, located in the old city of Ulus, was abuzz with activity and Eastern charm. Waist-high wooden tables of various sizes flooded an area of approximately two city blocks. Merchants attended to their customers with the traditional bargaining technique. No decent consumer would purchase an article on the first price quoted. Instead, he or she had to hassle over the cost and since the proprietor expected this, all was natural in the retail kingdom.

The market place was a cornucopia. You could buy almost anything you wanted. One half offered fresh vegetables and fruits. The other held non-food articles such as: jewelry, books, phonograph records, phonographs, radios, other appliances, household wares, furniture, and clothing. There was a special section for antiques.

A warm May sun shone upon Friday and I while we loungingly explored this paradise of paraphernalia.

I stopped by a table replete with phonograph records: 78's, 45's and long playing 33's.

"Something tells me you're going to buy a few of these."

"How could you know that?" I laughed.

"Because I feel that we think alike and since I love music, I thought you might also."

She was indeed quite perceptive.

"Do you like opera?"

"I only know one aria: 'My Donna's in Mobile'."

We both laughed like school kids.

"Who are your favorite singers?" asked Friday.

"Nat King Cole, Mario Lanza, Joni James, Doris Day and Eartha Kitt."

"So are mine," she replied.

We plowed through a stack of used 45's. I bought several oldies plus one disk without a label—just for kicks. When we paid the man, Friday thought he was pleasant so she called him a *peach.* He became insulted and chased us.

"He must be having his period," chuckled Friday, not at all troubled by his rudeness.

With each step we took, word we uttered, laugh we enjoyed, I began to feel closer to Friday. It reminded me of the thrill of my first high school love. I felt spiritually pristine—as if I had never before been so close to someone. And although I knew it was wrong, something inside propelled me down the dangerous driveway.

We passed by a counter with miscellaneous items and I spotted a box of golf balls which I decided to buy for Winston. But the purchase wasn't entirely out of guilt.

Our next stop was the book counter. There I bought a book of Japanese Haikus and a volume of Shakespeare's Sonnets. After paying for them, Friday and I escaped to a far corner of the Bazaar where a number of small white metal tables—each with its own picnic umbrella—comprised a rustic outdoor coffee shop.

"What are your plans for the future?"

I liked her asking me questions about myself.

"I want to write the great American novel or do something very meaningful like Martin Luther King. But I'll probably only be an English teacher."

"How do you feel about the Colored issue?" she asked.

"It appalls me. I can't understand why the color of someone's skin should be so important to another person. And being prejudice is not even Christian.

"There's an anecdote about a little Colored boy who lived down South and one day went into a white church. The minister chased the boy and the innocent lad asked, 'Where should I go?' The Minister told the boy to go home and ask God.

"The following week the youngster came back to the same church and the irate Minister asked the boy what God had told him. The boy replied, 'God said, Don't worry about it. I haven't been in that church in years.'"

"That's quite accurate," said Friday, with a warm smile.

Then her mood changed.

"You will do something great. I can feel it."

A boldness suddenly stimulated me.

"I'll write a novel about you."

"What could you possibly say about me?"

"How wonderful it is to be with you. How great you make me feel."

She took a deep, pensive breath.

"Most of my life I have been very lonely. I do have Winston but be doesn't fill my need for a true friend. One I can pour my heart out to and who makes me feel like the most important person in the world. Loretta did that for me. We were extremely close. I have never been that close to anyone until now. With you."

"We haven't known each other that long," I offered; "but I feel the same way."

Silence swept over the moment as we stared into each other's eyes. She unexpectedly reached across the narrow table and kissed me gently on the lips. Not a hasty kiss but one that lingered. And not a friendly kiss for it generated too much feeling.

"If I asked you to forgive me for doing that I would be lying. For I do believe I am beginning to have strong feelings for you."

Although it wasn't exactly prudent to say—and I tried not to—the words spilled from my mouth.

"Those are my exact thoughts. They have been since the first moment I saw you."

To that, she rested her hand on mine and squeezed it tenderly. I suddenly remembered why I had bought that book of Shakespeare's Sonnets. One of them perfectly fit the moment.

I bent over to fetch the book from the shopping bag and upon coming up spotted someone I didn't care to see.

"Isn't that Mrs. Myrons over there?"

"It certainly looks like her. –She's an anal orifice."

"A what?"

"An anal orifice. My euphemism for asshole."

Friday's unique sense of humor was irresistible.

"I want you to hear this sonnet. It must have been written for you. It's about a guy who's depressed about things and after meditating, he says:

> *But if the while I think on thee, dear friend,*
> *All losses are restored, and sorrows end."*

Friday said nothing. Instead, she took my hands in hers and gently stroked them. Once again, as in the hospital, a light fog permeated my brain and I could not believe what was actually happening. But it felt completely right. And wonderful.

*   *   *

When Madam Sivas opened her door, she instantly saw the turmoil in Yuksel's eyes. Neverthess, the girl held the single rose which was a symbol of respect for her *teyze*.

"Come in, my child. We will meet your problem over tea."

Minutes later, when Madam Sivas placed a small glass of tea in front of Yuksel, the young girl burst into uncontrollable tears. The Older Woman said nothing. She placed her arm around Yuksel and patiently waited.

"Oh, *Teyze*, it is Kyle. He rape me."

Although surprised, Madam Sivas deftly disguised her shock. She did not want Yuksel to feel guilty or ashamed. The poor child had already experienced too much tragedy in her young life.

Yuksel explained how it had happened.

"I need the advice from you, *Teyze*. I tell Nurtan?"

Giving counsel for Madam Sivas was generally easy. But this issue was sensitive and she needed more time to think.

"Not now, my child. If you do, Kyle will say that you are a liar. It is true that Nurtan loves you but he is to be her husband. Women want to believe their spouses."

Yuksel considered the advice and they both remained silent for several minutes; each in her own thoughts. Yuksel feeling slightly better; the Older Woman wondering if her words had been sagely.

"You are the right, *Teyze*. I say nothing now."

Madam Sivas then broached a subject she had as of late been thinking about: Yuksel's continued torment over the child who had been stolen from her.

"Why not ask Turan to find the boy for you."

The girl became visibly upset.

"I not could. Turan get mad if he know I have child. He want baby boy with me now but I say the no."

"Perhaps he will not get angry," suggested the Madam.

"I am too the fear, *Teyze*."

Madam Sivas changed the topic and tried to lift the girl's spirits with lighter conversation.

After Yuksel left, the Old Woman fetched her Tarot cards and placed them on the table. She touched the deck with the rose that Yuksel had brought because it held the girl's aura. With skillful hands, the Madam spread out ten cards and turned the first one over.

The card revealed more than the good Woman wished to see.

––––––

In the cafeteria at JAMMAT, Colonel Myrons was trying to enjoy his lunch while his wife's irritating mouth was moving at the speed of light.

"An*d* Sandy sai*d* tha*t* the teacher was unfair to her," rattled Mrs. Penelope Myrons. "I mus*t* go an*d* have a few wor*d*s with tha*t* young man. After all, Sandy is... ."

As she babbled, Colonel Hank Myrons tuned her out. Over the years he had become quite adept at turning off the volume when she incessantly chattered. Periodically he would monitor the bitch to see if she might be saying something important. If not, he went back to playing music in his head.

"Di*d* you know tha*t* tha*t* Turkish girl in the PX is pregnan*t* an*d* no*t* marrie*d*?"

Doesn't she ever fucking shut up? And who the hell invited her to have lunch with me?

"I wan*t* you to do something abou*t* tha*t* Airman Corey Brotano!"

"What about him?"

It was only the second time that Hank spoke since lunch had begun.

"I saw him and Captain Lebal's wife shopping together in the Bazaar yesterday an*d* they seeme*d* very cozy."

"S-So what?" He raised his voice in annoyance. Something he had been doing quite often, recently.

Mrs. Myrons glanced around the room to see if anyone was looking at them. She turned back to her husband and whispered, "Don't you dare raise your voice to me!"

"T-Then don't t-talk s-so s-stupid."

"It's not stupid. They looked very lovey-dovey. You can not have Airmen under you command fraternizing with wives of officers."

"Winston t-tells m-me t-that he and his wife are good friends with Brotano. It's your over-active imagination."

The Colonel pushed his plate aside and lit a cigarette.

"I thought you weren't going to smoke anymore," she nagged.

"I decided t-to s-start again," he said, curtly. And he wanted to add— because you drive me fucking crazy. Instead, he inhaled deeply and exhaled the smoke in her direction.

"You s-smoke," he retorted; "s-so what t-the hell are you moaning about?"

"It is fashionable for an educated woman such as myself to smoke with a cigarette holder. Besides, I never do it in public. Nevertheless," she resumed; "I want you to do something about that Airman!"

It was truly amazing, thought the Colonel, how just one woman could wear down a guy's resistance. Someday he'd like to use her for target practice.

In utter desperation, he gave in. Another stupid trait he had acquired over the years. But one day soon he hoped to find the impetus to successfully combat her. Right now he was too weary.

"I will keep m-my eye on t-the s-situation and if I s-see any evidence of foul play, I will s-send for Brotano and s-speak t-to him,"

Mrs. Penelope Myrons began to speak again and Hank turned off the volume for the duration. In his head, he played Ravel's "Bolero."

––––––

Writing wedding invitations in her apartment, Nurtan listened to the radio station that played American music. Although she preferred Turkish melodies, developing a taste for the foreign songs was necessary. Especially since she would be living in the States not so far in the future.

"What time is it?" asked Kyle, entering the kitchen after having just awakened from a nap.

"It 2013."

Kyle laughed at her. He seemed to be doing that a lot lately, she thought.

"Ya always give the time exactly."

"Please. It important be right," she answered, seriously.

Kyle went to the cabinet and took out the *raki*.

"Whatcha writin'?"

"Invitations."

The radio was playing "Cold, Cold Heart" by Tony Bennett.

"Ah gotta talk ta ya abou' somethin'."

Nurtan looked at Kyle's eyes and suddenly became uneasy. They seemed so distant. Instead of speaking, she remained silent.

Kyle emitted a deep sigh before beginning.

"Did ya ever think of maybe not havin' the baby?"

His words were chilling. She hoped she had misunderstood them.

"What you mean, please?"

"Forget the kid. Go ta a doctor or some place and do away wit it."

Nurtan was shocked. In her world a woman was meant to have a baby—not to destroy it. It was the only formula.

"Please! I no could, Kyle."

He waited for several minutes before trying again.

"Are ya sure? Ah don't know if Ah'm ready to get burdened with a kid. Ah'm too young."

Kyle took another gulp of *raki* and stared at his fiancée.

"Well, Babe?"

All of her life she had been looking forward to having a child. With a few selfish words he was asking her to abandon the dream.

Instead of answering, Nurtan began to sob.

Kyle's attitude changed to annoyance–a trait which Nurtan had not seen before. He took another swallow of *raki* and walked back into the bedroom. He reappeared in dungarees and Ty's jersey, and moved to the front door.

"Ah'll see ya later," he said. "Ah'm goin' drinkin' with Ty."

Nurtan was still crying as Kyle closed the door and sped down the very steep stairway. And he thought: *Ah'll talk abou' it another time. When she's not cryin'.*

Anyway, he continued to reason; *Who knows? Maybe she'll have some kind of accident.*

*　　　*　　　*

CHAPTER 9 —
"Champagne Days"

There are special days in a person's life that never fade. They live on with every passing moment of time and years later are as vibrant as if they had occurred yesterday.

The doorbell rang as I stepped out of the shower. Wrapping a towel around my waist, I went to greet the caller.

"Open up and let me in," said Friday, with a special light-hearted sound in her voice.

"I just got off the midnight shift," I announced, opening the door and walking into the kitchen. "Would you like a cup of *çay*?"

"As long as you put the *tea* in a cup and not in a glass the way the Turks do."

Friday sat at the table while I filled the kettle and placed it on the stove. Instead of sitting, I leaned against the sink to face her.

"Incidentally, I found out why that merchant in the Bazaar got so angry. The word *peach* means bastard in Turkish."

Friday laughed.

"He must have thought that I knew his mother."

Then we both laughed. We had done quite a bit of that lately. I found Friday's humor very invigorating. It was good medicine for life's low points.

"Speaking of the Bazaar, I'm headed there right now to buy an ancient Turkish floor lamp which I was too guilty to buy the other day." She paused for effect. **"Today, I don't feel so guilty."**

I poured the tea and placed it before her.

"I could use some help carrying the damn thing," continued Friday; **"that is, if you're not too tired."**

"Give me a few minutes to get dressed."

While moving down the hall, I shouted back to her.

"Where's Winston today?"

"Colonel Myrons sent him to Izmir on some business."

Switching on the phonograph in my bedroom, I played the 45 record with the indecipherable label. Two days earlier, surprise revealed the melody to be the same that was playing when I first met Friday in the Guest House. The haunting tune I had decided would always remind me of her.

I discarded my towel and opened the bureau drawer for a pair of briefs.

"Have you written words yet for this song?" asked Friday.

Startled but unabashed in my nakedness, I turned to face her. I could feel my body start to tremble slightly as I looked searchingly into Friday's eyes. My brain abruptly floated into a blinding mist and I began to move through it as in a dream. Like an out-of-body experience.

I had never before gotten so swift and firm an erection. She looked down at it then up at me and smiled. As if on cue, we walked toward each other and embraced so forcefully and closely that we seemed to fuse.

Slowly and appreciatively, I undressed Friday and gently led her to my bed. The record played over and over as it became the perfect background to our love making. I have no recollection of how long we were lost in that euphoric state but every second virtually denied description.

The climax of our love act was everything at once: the excitement of a roller coaster ride and the warm glow of a Christmas tree; the thrill of a circus and the serenity of a church. A sunrise. A sunset. Everything mysteriously blended into one.

For a long while afterwards, we lay there in contented silence. Almost too emotionally spent to talk. Presently I got out of bed, lit a cigarette, and grabbed a pad lying on my bureau.

"To answer your question from before, I did start writing words to the song. Want to hear them?"

"Of course. It's our song."

I sang the words along with the music.

> Champagne days,
> So full of golden rays,
> Where only happy music plays;
> We strolled together in the evening mist,
> And we sealed our love forever when we kissed;
> I'll remember.

"Why did you stop?"

"That's as far as I got. Can't seem to get an ending. But I promise you it <u>*will*</u> get finished. –Some day."

I sat next to Friday on the bed and we held hands.

"Poetry seems to be another thing that we have in common. I know that *you* plan to be an author or an English teacher but I got involved with literature because of a counselor I had in the orphanage. Whenever I did something wrong, the punishment was to memorize something from a classic. Consequently, I grew quite fond of certain excerpts and started learning them on my own."

"That's one way to get a kid involved with the arts," I laughed. Then my mood expectedly became solemn.

"I hope you're not feeling guilty."

"Perhaps a bit."

"Don't be. It wasn't anybody's fault. If anything, destiny is to blame."

Like me, Friday was a deciple of karma. And, I thought to myself: *fate was not only a way to rationalize the unexplainable but also a scapegoat to wash away guilt.*

"Perhaps we shouldn't do this anymore. I don't want to hurt Winston."

"He and I have been finished for years. I stay with him only because I have no place to go. And partially for the children. You and I *had* to happen. There is no way to change destiny."

Friday pulled me close to her and we kissed long and feverishly. Every fiber in my body exploded. I was aroused again and we made love once more after Friday said, **"I will always be here for you. We will always have our champagne days."**

*   *   *

Izmir–a Turkish port and trading center on the eastern coast of the Aegean Sea–lies several hundred miles southwest of both Istanbul and Ankara. Nestled on the shore of a large bay, it is sheltered by mountains. One of these is Mt. Pagos upon which rests the *Velvet Fortress (Kadifekale)*–built in the Third Century, B.C.. From its vantage point one is offered a most arresting view of the area.

In a quaint outdoor cafe along Izmir's throbbing waterfront, Winston sat with Captain Rob Rizzo–commander of the Motor Pool division of the U.S. Air Force, in Izmir.

"do you eat here everyday?" asked Winston.

"Just about. It's the best place in town to get American style food. I also like Turkish food but I prefer to vary my diet. Too much of one thing is no good. Besides, I have to keep in shape. All we Dodger fans are physically fit."

Rizzo's statement described him succinctly. At forty-three, he had maintained a good build. Complimenting his six feet height were his dirty blond hair, blue eyes and good looks.

"What would Myrons have done to me if you had found my records to be fucked-up?" laughed Rizzo.

"nothing serious," answered Winston. "myrons comes off as a prick but he really isn't. i think his wife makes him that way."

Rizzo agreed with Winston and added how he had heard many stories about the haughty, interfering Mrs. Myrons. Her nefarious reputation was well known in military cirlces.

The waiter came and cleared the table.

"*Iki kahve Amerikan, lutfen,*" ordered Rizzo.

"*Evet, efendi,*" replied the waiter.

"You **did** want American coffee?"

"definitely!" responded Winston.

Rizzo lit a Turkish cigarette and deeply inhaled the exotic aroma.

"how can you smoke those things?" asked Winston. "they smell terrible."

"It took some time but I got used to them. I always try to assimilate into a new environment."

The waiter brought the coffee.

"*Tesekkur ederim,*" said Rizzo.

"*Bir sey degil,*" was the waiter's smiling reply as he walked away.

It was a beautifully warm day in May which reminded Winston of similar afternoons he had spent in San Antonio, Texas. That was the place where he first met his luncheon companion.

Rizzo had been stationed at Kelly Air Force Base and Winston at Fort Sam Houston. Since both held the same kind of job in their respective branches, they had occasionally called upon each other's services when the part for a vehicle was needed in an emergency. They had even been occasional drinking buddies.

Winston took a deep breath and then emitted a long sigh.

"now that our military business is over i want to talk about something personal. i want to apologize and also thank you for stopping me when i was beating up that soldier in san antonio. i couldn't help myself."

Rizzo hesitated before reacting.

"I'm glad you brought it up. I had to leave that next day and didn't have time to see you. I thought of writing but decided against it. Forgive my saying this but you were totally wrong. There was nothing going on between Friday and that boy."

Winston became slightly annoyed.

"i saw them together. she had her arm around him, his head was on her shoulder, and she kissed him."

"On his cheek," corrected Rizzo.

"and how could *you* possibly know that they were not having an affair?"

"Because the boy was in the Motor Pool and under my command. He confided in me."

Winston looked surprised.

"you knew about him and friday and you didn't tell me anything."

"There **was** no affair. The boy was a fairy. A homo! That's what he confided to me."

"then why didn't you have him thrown into the brig or dishonorably discharged?"

Rizzo glanced across the road at the calm sea. Beneath its surface swam millions of fish. In a way he envied them. The only problem a fish had was trying not to get caught. A simple existence, to be sure. But humans constantly made problems for themselves. They were never satisfied to just drift along. They had to make things complicated.

"The boy was highly confused and mixed up. He didn't want to be a fairy but something deep down made him prefer men. Throwing him in the brig or getting him discharged would not have helped him. I thought if I left him alone he might eventually find himself. Besides, I believe in live and let live as long as nobody's bothering my ass."

"how do you know that friday wasn't going to bed with that boy to try to cure him?"

"Because he told me that Friday offered to drive him to Mexico where he could find a whore. Also because he respected Friday too much to use her like that."

The waiter returned and offered to refill their cups. Rizzo declined, saying that he had to return to work. Winston accepted.

"If you like, we'll talk again tomorrow before you leave," said Rizzo standing.

"thanks but i believe you've told me enough."

As Rizzo walked away, Winston bore deeply into his pysche in an attempt to re-think the incident that had taken place in San Antonio. *Had he truly over-reacted? Had Friday been telling the truth?*

All this time he may have been wrong, he mused. If so, then he was glad he had had to make this trip to Izmir. With these new revelations he would not act so impetuously and stupidly again. He would not allow himself to doubt Friday any longer. And almost as importantly, he would not have to mistrust Corey.

———-

The dinner which Nurtan had prepared for Kyle included all of his favorite foods. She had wanted it to be perfect. To please her man. Particularly after the recent discussion when she had refused to have an abortion.

During the private feast, they had laughed, talked about all the people they knew, and listened to American music. Kyle had smiled a great deal and had frowned only once when Nurtan mentioned something about the gift Yuksel had sent.

At one point over coffee and *raki*, the conversation became serious.

"Please, Kyle, I am much sorry about baby."

Kyle seemed like his old self. In fact, while Nurtan was preparing dinner for them, he had even washed the steps of the steep stairway that led from their apartment to the ground floor.

"Don' worry bout it. Ah'll figure out somethin'."

Nurtan felt at ease and content to be with him.

After dinner, Kyle wanted to have sex. Without speaking, he took Nurtan by the hand and quietly led her into the bedroom. Although she was not exactly in the mood, she obediently followed in order to maintain the pleasant atmosphere.

When they were finished making love–an act in which Kyle seemed to be more intense than ever before–he suggested they go to the Istanbul Palace and see the belly dancers. Nurtan wished not to go, but as usual gave in.

Ten minutes later, Kyle stood by the open door and called to Nurtan.

"Are ya ready yet, Babe?"

"Yes. I come."

She exited from the bedroom and when she got to him at the door, she kissed and hugged him very tightly.

"Let's go, Babe."

"Please, Kyle, you first. The stairs I not like. When you first, I feel not afraid."

He smiled and kissed her on the forehead. He moved one step down and suddenly remembered something.

"Ah forgot mah wallet. Ya go ahead."

"No, Kyle..."

"Is mah kid gonna have a scary mama?" he said, walking past her and disappearing from sight.

For Nurtan his words had validity.

"You right," she said, beginning her descent.

The next sound from Nurtan was an eerie, painful scream. When her foot touched the second step from the top, the board slid off its mounting and Nurtan fell forward. Down the steep stairwell she feared so much.

*   *   *

After Friday left, I continued to glow with happiness but came down to earth immediately when I happened to pass by Edith's photo. I also realized it was time to write her, even though my heart wasn't in it.

> *Dear Edith,*
>
> *Sorry I took so long to write but nothing much happens here so there's not a lot to say.*
>
> (That was a lie but I couldn't very well tell my girl back home that I was madly in love with someone else.)
>
> *The only thing to report is Colonel Myrons' reception which he gives periodically for incoming personnel. I accomplished nothing by going there except meeting Kyle's friend. And that was something I could have done without.*
>
> *When I first saw Ty Manners, I mistook him for Kyle. There is a very striking resemblance between the two. They have the same kind of build and the same golden blond hair with similar cuts. And they both look like Tab Hunter.*
>
> *We talked for a few minutes and he seemed to be a nice guy. I told him that he and Kyle reminded me of Carton and Darnay from Dickens' A TALE OF TWO CITIES. At the end of the story, Carton takes Darnay's place on the guillotine and the authorities don't realize it. To this, Ty commented: "If Kyle ever does somethin' wrong, I sure as hell hope I don't get blamed."*
>
> *After we chatted for awhile, Ty asked me about the Mafia. When I said I didn't know anything, he was surprised because he thought all "guineas" were in the mob. Instead of belting him—as I probably should have—I kept calm and set him straight. I also told him that I was part Italian and part American Indian. To that, he commented, "Oh, a half breed." Instead of answering the coarse jerk, I walked away. Winston was right. Manners is a trouble-maker.*
>
> *I talked to some other people for a while and then devised an excuse to leave.*
>
> *There's not much else to say so I'll close for now.*
>
> *Sincerely,*
>
> *Corey*

While signing my name, I wondered if Edith would notice the omission of the word "love".

*   *   *

Three days after Nurtan's accident in the stairwell, Kyle visited her in the hospital–as he had done everyday. But this time he was finally able to speak with her doctor.

"She has a slight concussion and some bruises, but should be fine. We have completed all the tests and she will be able to go home tomorrow."

The Doctor mysteriously hesitated.

"Is somethin' wrong?" Kyle asked.

"I am sorry to tell you that we were unable to save the fetus."

On that issue, Kyle was not concerned. In the future, she could always have another baby, he reasoned–with some other guy.

When Kyle left the hospital, the beautiful weather made him feel jubilant and free once again. A great burden had been lifted from his shoulders. He was not going to be a father, after all.

Instead of returning to work–since Ty was already covering for him–Kyle decided to pay a visit on someone.

As he expected, Yuksel refused to open the door.

"What's a matter wit' ya, Babe. Don't ya wanna know about ya best friend?"

Yuksel replied that she already knew.

"This is somethin' else," he insisted.

"Tell me."

"Ah ain't talkin' ta a fuckin' door."

Only silence answered him and he visualized Yuksel trying to decide if she should trust him.

Several minutes later, Yuksel opened the door–just a crack. To her great surprise, Kyle forcefully pushed his way into the apartment and headed for the kitchen.

"Ah need some *raki*," he boldly announced.

Yuksel ran after him.

"No you stay, Kyle," she shouted, angry and frightened.

Too horrific in her mind was the last time he had been there. She swore that it would not happen again.

As Kyle poured some *raki* into a water glass, Yuksel went to the cabinet drawer and took out a large carving knife. Rays of sunlight peering in through the window made the sharp blade sparkle. But Kyle only grinned.

"So ya wanna play, Bitch?"

"You no go, I kill you," screamed Yuksel, meaning every word of her threat.

In a calculated ruse, Kyle fell to his knees in feigned laughter. Then he threw the *raki* in her face. Instinctively, she dropped the knife and rubbed her eyes. Not letting up, Kyle tackled Yuksel and she fell to the kitchen floor.

The *raki* burned Yuksel's eyes but did not diminish her determination. She punched and kicked with the ferociousness of a wild animal.

And she continued to fight him even after he entered her.

*   *   *

CHAPTER 10 –
"Twenty Minutes"

The same coffee shop I had visited with Sandy during my first week in Ankara looked strangely different as I shared it with Friday. It seemed more colorful. Warmer. Being anyplace with Friday produced that result. Ironically, I had earlier decided this would be our last time together. My guilt was growing heavy and I was not sure about carrying the load.

It had been a quickly-paced morning. Kyle had forced me out of bed to help him find a wedding ring for Nurtan. It was getting close to that day and as the best man it was my duty to accompany the groom. To aide us both, I called upon Friday. She had had other plans for the day but willingly cancelled them.

On Turan's recommendation–which he had given to Kyle that night in the Istanbul Palace–we went to the Karapinar Jewelry Shop, the place where Turan had worked as a young boy.

Turan's uncle was a most congenial and jovial man who boasted a grey mustache. He offered Kyle a huge discount on one of the most beautiful rings I had ever seen. Surprisingly, Kyle declined and chose one much less expensive. Probably his funds were low, was my supposition, so I smiled and congratulated him on his taste.

"Let's all go get a cup of coffee," I had suggested.

"No, thanks," said Kyle. "Ah gotta get back to work. Cap'n Lebal gave me some time off. Ah don't wanna take advantage."

With that said, he drove off in a green sedan.

"How did you find this coffee shop?" asked Friday.

I told her about my date with Sandy.

"So you're the one," she smiled. "A while ago Sandy told me that she liked an airman but that he was too old for her."

It was the first time in my life that anyone had ever said that of me. I was about to ask how Friday knew Sandy but she anticipated my question.

"Sandy baby-sits for us and the kids love her. She is a very sweet girl despite that bitch of a mother. –You may be too old for Sandy, but you're just right for me."

Her comment was great but it complicated the moment. *How could I say we should end this romance?*

The waiter brought the coffee and Friday asked if they sold alcoholic drinks.

"Hayir, No, Efendi."

"Do you like to drink in the afternoon?" I asked.

"Not usually." She paused. "Maybe only this once. It might have been helpful."

"I don't understand."

"Oh, but you do. You have something to say and you can't get it out."

A radio in the back of the shop was playing a familiar tune.

Friday continued.

"I'm trying not to make you uncomfortable." She hesitated. "You think that we should stop seeing each other."

Apparently we were closer than I had suspected. She could read my mind.

"Suppose I told you that I have been thinking of divorcing Winston?"

The situation was almost amusing. I had seen this scene in so many movies and had never really taken it seriously. It was only a glimpse into lives of fictitious people on a gigantic screen. Shadows who came alive for ninety minutes and sometimes made an impact. But now it was really happening.

"That makes me feel even worse. I didn't want to break up your marriage."

"You haven't, at least not directly. I have already told you that there is nothing left between Winston and me."

"You said that you stayed with him because you had nowhere else to go. Has that changed?"

"Yes and no. Being with you has made me decide that I'm strong enough to stand on my own feet. You restored the confidence I had before getting married and becoming so complacent. And even if I were never to see you again, I still intend to leave him. I just need a little more time to figure out my strategy."

Some of my guilt gave way to rationalization which told me that as long as I had not been responsible for the rift between Friday and Winston—there was no need to end the affair. The truth was that I needed an excuse to continue. Albeit contrived.

"When we were stationed in San Antonio, an exterminator once came to our quarters to check for termites. He told me that there is a kind of termite that lives for only twenty minutes. Can you believe that? Only twenty minutes."

The expression on my face reflected confusion so Friday explained.

"If you think about humans in relation to the age of the world, our time on earth is not that much longer."

Her reasoning made perfect sense. Even at my young age I perceived that life was too short and that one had to live every moment to its fullest.

"Are we only as miniscule and seemingly unimportant as termites?" I wondered aloud.

"Who knows? Perhaps in the great scheme of things we are."

It was a disturbingly philosophical concept I chose not to ponder. At least, not at that moment.

"I don't want to lose you, Corey; and I don't want us to break up. Who knows how much of the twenty minutes we have left."

*　　　*　　　*

Ahmed Yalvac, a man of Turkish decent, beamed inwardly as he left the Government Ministry. The self-satisfying glow stemmed from the fact that he had once more fooled his colleagues. He had managed to make a xerox copy of a top secret message that he held concealed on his person. A communiqué for which he would soon receive a large sum of money.

But it was not the money alone that pleased Ahmed. Although the *lira* was great because it afforded luxuries not attainable on his meager salary, it was the fantasy that counted.

Ever since he began reading spy novels, Ahmed had dreamed of being a double agent. In the classroom many of his teachers had looked down upon him as an inferior type student. He had never received high grades but could have if so desired.

Now at the age of twenty-two, he had indeed achieved a goal. He prided himself on possessing all the traits of one particular fictitious spy: a handsome, suave male who knew the angles and had women constantly chasing him. The character had appeared in only one book but was memorable enough to become Ahmed's hero.

In some respects, such a comparison was justified. Ahmed was a tall, good-looking young man with a fine wiry physique. Many girls did desire him. But the resemblance ended there. Ahmed's intellect had been arrested when he began his *Alice in Wonderland* journey into espionage.

Morally, Ahmed felt his deeds were justifiable and merely a variation of political games that countries played. Several years ago Japan had been an enemy. In 1956, it was admitted to the United Nations. If the havoc, death, and destruction caused by the Rising Sun could be so lightly forgiven, then spying should not be that serious a crime.

The taxi which Ahmed hailed drove to Ulus along Ataturk Boulevard. It went through the public square, past the American hospital and down a long block until it stopped at the Ulus Bathhouse.

As nonchalantly as possible, Ahmed paid the fare, tipped the driver generously, and made his way into the establishment. How easy it all was, Ahmed told himself. He almost had to laugh. *For a country so proud of its secret police, they certainly were dumb.*

Several minutes after Ahmed entered the establishment, Turan followed.

The Ulus Bathhouse was perhaps the largest of its kind in the city. Both rich and poor men attended. For the latter, a bathhouse was not a luxury since most of the indigent had only a toilet and sink in their homes.

Ahmed entered the reception area, paid the fee, checked his valuables, and made his way to the locker room. There he stripped down to his underwear and donned a towel.

Anxiously, but trying to appear calm, he entered a long rectangular room with a large swimming pool in its center. On both sides of the pool was a series of eight rooms. The ones on the left side afforded the patron private bathing by an attendant–for an extra fee. The rooms on the right were for a massage. At the extreme end of the pool was the door to the steam room.

Ahmed entered one of the private cleansing rooms on the left and was warmly greeted by a familiar face. He closed the door behind himself and remained in the chamber for over five minutes.

Turan stealthily walked up to the door and listened.

For a spy, thought Turan, *Ahmed had a lot to learn*. Instead of turning on a water faucet to muffle his conversation, the would-be Informer talked clearly and enabled Turan's small tape recorder to pick up every syllable.

Turan moved away from the door in time to watch Ahmed exit and make his way down to the steam room. Seconds later, Ahmed's attendant came out, walked around the swimming pool and entered one of the massage facilities.

Turan followed the Attendant and stationed himself next to the door. He activated his taping recorder and listened to the message being transmitted over a short wave radio.

The Attendant said:

> *The Turkish Government is undergoing clandestine negotiations to allow the United States to establish secret observation posts along the Iraq, Iran borders for the purpose of spying on Iraq and Iran.*

The message was repeated.

*   *   *

The members of the bachelor party–Kyle, Ty, Drew, myself–started out together but ultimately divided.

Intim's was my favorite night spot in Ankara probably because it seemed so *intimate.* A cozy unpretentious place with plain, cream-colored stucco walls it felt comfortable. You entered into a small foyer with the hat-check room to the right. In front of you and down eight steps was a round room about the size of a lobby in a movie theatre. Indirect lighting adorned a blue ceiling dotted with sparkling electric stars.

Each table had an easily-visible number and a telephone. If you liked someone who was sitting at table number two, all you had to do was dial that digit and speak to her. And if you were shy, it could be done anonymously.

At the most distant spot in the room was a small stage on which a combo played.

It was this combo that particularly thrilled me about the place. It comprised a British singer by the name of Jane, and three men on instruments–saxophone, drums, piano. The latter was played by Jane's husband, Peter.

Jane, Peter, and I had become friends my first time in Intim's. I had asked her to sing "Love Is A Many Splendored Thing," and afterwards had invited them to my table for drinks. They had been to New York City on several occasions and loved to talk about their experiences there.

After that initial meeting, I no longer had to ask Jane to sing my song. She would do it automatically as soon as I entered.

Kyle, Ty, Drew and I sat at a table against the wall. Kyle and Ty ordered *raki,* Drew drank a watered-down beer; I had scotch and soda.

After toasting Kyle's forthcoming nuptials, I reminisced.

"Remember the New Year's Eve, in Tripoli, when we got the dog drunk?"

"Ah sure do. Ah also remember how you got crabs a week later from a local gal that some Colored guys fixed ya up with. Ever get rid of them critters?"

"With a lot of shaving. And applying alcohol which burned like hell."

Drew, Kyle and I laughed but apparently Ty was feeling neglected.

"Forget the remembering shit," he complained; "Let's tell some dirty jokes. This here's a bachelor party, ain't it?"

"Why don't you start," Kyle suggested.

"Okay, Cap'n. –A queer goes into a pool hall and asks if he can get a job cleaning the guys' balls after they shoot."

Ty turned to Drew.

"Ever work in a pool hall?"

Drew ignored him, took a sip of beer, and watched Jane singing.

My patience with Ty was waning, and I refused to laugh. Kyle seemed to find it very funny and I attributed his behavior to the *raki*. To avoid any serious trouble, I suggested that Ty phone the two girls sitting at table number six.

He followed my suggestion and just as one of the girls picked up the receiver, a large man returned to the table and took the phone out of her hand.

"*Ne istiyorsunuz, Essekogluessek?*"

Ty quickly slammed the receiver in its cradle.

"That guy's too fuckin' big for me!"

Then he turned to Kyle.

"Let's leave this joint and go to the Compound."

Kyle agreed and extended the invitation to me.

"No, thanks," I replied; "I'd like to stay here and listen to Jane sing."

"What abou' you, Drew?" taunted Ty.

"Thank you, but I'll stay with Corey."

"I hope you two will be very happy," laughed Ty.

They rose to leave. Kyle guzzled the remaining *raki* in his glass, smiled, and waved. Ty first grinned at Kyle, then looked directly at Drew. He grabbed his own crouch and pretended to play with it.

"Whenever you feel hungry, Drew, let me know."

I immediately jumped up to strike Ty, but Drew stopped me. Ty simply laughed and said, "Nasty, nasty;" pointing his finger at me as if scolding a child.

Before I could do anything else, Kyle put his arm around Ty and led him out of the place.

"Ty is a fucking piece of shit," I said.

"Don't let him bother you," consoled Drew. "He's not worth the effort."

"I wonder what that guy said to make Ty hang up so fast?"

Drew laughed. "The man has a loud voice, and I heard him say: 'What do you want, *Essekogluessek?*' Literally translated, it means son of a jackass. But in Turkish, it's equivalent to 'son of a bitch.'"

"How rude of that guy," I commented; "to insult a jackass by comparing the poor beast to Ty."

*   *   *

Urdanur sat in her penthouse apartment and read **THE KORAN**–the sacred book of the Mohammedans. She never tired of the wisdom found in its pages or the numerous passages she had underlined which seemed to fit so many aspects of life. Some bespoke lessons. Others acted as examples to be followed. Still more were merely comforting to the mind and soul.

She would read her favorites again and again.

> *O men, respect women who have borne you.*
> *O unbelievers, I will not worship that which ye worship; nor will ye worship that which I worship...Ye have your religion, and I my religion.*
> *If God should punish men according to what they deserve, he would not leave on the back of the earth so much as a beast.*

In the background, the phonograph was playing and Urdanur paused in her reading to listen to the song, *Unforgettable.* It played on the night when she had first met Corey. They had made love while the venerable Mr. Cole sang, and the encounter had indeed matched the lyrics.

That night excelled in her heart with the utmost pleasure. It was something she neither regretted nor expected to happen again. The age gap between Corey and herself was too severe. To pursue such a relationship would be unthinkable. Her pragmatic nature rebelled at such thoughts. But she and Corey could be good friends–as she felt they had already become.

There was nothing she would deny him for he had rekindled a feeling she had packed away with old souvenirs. And although the glowing memory of that night would remain salient, having his love as a friend was more precious than gold. At her age, there were very few people left in the world whom she cared about.

The telephone jolted Urdanur from her thoughts.

"Hello. Miss Besni?"

"Speaking."

"This is Mrs. Penelope Myrons. The Colonel's wife."

The sound of the caller's voice made Urdanur cringe.

"I am phoning to invite you to lunch for your birthday."

100

"My birthday's in March. This is the end of May."

"Well, it doesn't matter anyway because I owe you a lunch for helping us at the tea reception."

Having lunch with Mrs. Penelope Myrons was first on Urdanur's list of things not to do.

"Thank you, but it's not necessary."

"Oh, but I insist. My schedule is full for this week but I can make it the Thursday after next. Will that be satisfactory?"

"If you insist," answered Urdanur, sadly.

"Very well, then. I will meet you in the JAMMAT cafeteria at noon."

In deference to her colleague–Colonel Myrons, whom she greatly admired–Urdanur would try to endure the anti-Christ. And she wondered if Mrs. Myrons had three number sixes on her scalp.

Strategically located across from the prison in Ulus, the Compound is a confined penal area of several square acres. Within this perimeter is a group of tenement-style, two story high buildings that form a quadrangle. And the Compound's encompassing ten feet high concrete wall is topped with an abundance of jagged shards of glass.

In essence, the Compound is a unique site of incarceration. A woman found guilty of a crime is given a choice of serving a very long sentence in a conventional prison or a shorter one in the Compound, as a prostitute.

Any male over the prescribed age can enter the Compound through its gigantic iron gates which are guarded by Turkish soldiers. Once inside, during the hours of 1800 to midnight, a horny man can meander through the streets of the brothel and inspect the women who sit in the windows of the tenements or on the stoops in front of the dwellings–a la Amsterdam. While some of the females are reluctant to be there, others are over zealous. They call to passers-by and occasionally raise their skirts to advertise the merchandise.

As Kyle and Ty entered the Compound, they were each frisked by one of the guards. A standard procedure to assure that no visitor had a weapon to help an inmate escape.

Satisfied that the two Americans were clean, the soldier allowed them entrance.

"Ah know this one bitch with a great tongue that licks every part of mah body."

"You brought me to her last time, Cap'n," responded Ty. "Let's try somebody different."

Kyle agreed and they decided to walk up and down every street till they

found someone new to them. As they loungingly strolled along, they shared a
bottle of *raki* which they had purchased en route to the Compound.

"I guess this'll be your last time here, Cap'n."

"Says who?" grinned Kyle.

"I only figured that since you're getting hitched next week, you won't
want to play around anymore."

"Bullshit! Ah'm gettin' married. Ah ain't dying. Anyhow, Nurtan is just
another piece. Ah could probably learn to live without her."

Ty patted his buddy on the back. Kyle was his kind of guy. Up until this
time in his Air Force days, Ty had only met a bunch of wimps. Momma's boys
who were overly concerned with good and evil. But Kyle was different. Kyle
was like himself. He didn't give a fuck what anybody thought. It was his life
and nobody was going to tell *him* what to do.

"Then why the hell you gettin' chained, Cap'n?"

"Who says Ah am?"

"You calling it off?"

"Nah! Ah mean it's only a Turk ceremony. Ah ain't Turk so it don't mean
a fuckin' thing!"

They paused to take a swig of *raki*. As they did, one of the inmates
blocked their path. She was a large, zaftig woman about forty years old. Her
gigantic breasts were further enhanced by large hard nipples which nearly cut
holes in her ultra sheer nylon blouse.

"*Istiyorum*," she said, pointing to the bottle.

"I think she wants some, Cap'n."

Kyle offered the *raki*. She placed the neck of the bottle in her mouth
and proceeded to slowly move it in and out. Although the visitors spoke no
Turkish, they clearly understood her message.

Kyle retrieved the ambrosia, grabbed Ty's arm and moved away.

"Don't you like big broads?" asked Ty.

"Not this one. She reminds me of my mama."

The boys consumed more alcohol as they continued the hunt.

"Ah think you have a fuckin' hollow leg," laughed Kyle.

"I think so, Cap'n. Anyway, you sure are wicked lucky."

"How's that?"

"By Nurtan having the accident and fallin' down the stairs. At least you
ain't gotta be stuck with no baby."

Kyle's next remark caused his buddy to howl with delight.

"It weren't no accident. Ah done loosened the step so's she *would* fall!"

*　　　*　　　*

CHAPTER II –
"A Girl On The Coast"

*   *   *

Approximately four hundred kilometers from Ankara stands the beautiful seacoast city of Samsun. Viewed from on the sea, it is an impressive sight. From where the water gently kisses the shore, the city gradually and subtly slants upward on the side of a mountain which seems to be reaching for the sky.

Samsun Statistics

–**S** ights: 14th Century Pazar Mosque, 19th Century Buyuk Mosque;
–**A** mong leading products is tobacco (one sees the leaves drying on man-made racks);
–**M** ajor port of the Black Sea area and industrial center;
–**S** amsun is where Ataturk landed on May 19, 1919, to organize resistance which freed Turkey from foreign domination;
–**U** nknown to many, Samsun is one of the most conservative Moslem cities in Turkey;
–**N** ationwide, it boasts of the largest monument to Ataturk, outside of Ankara.

On a bright spring day, an article on the bottom of page one in the *Samsun Daily* read:
Pegu Gediz Arrested For Theft.

A stranger seeing this headline might dismiss it as someone else gone bad. But that person could not know the truth.

The Story Behind the Headline

Very short, slightly plump and extremely overactive, Pegu Gediz was a girl of Turkish ancestry. Her jet-black, curly cropped hair blended easily with a round pudgy face of olive complexion. Most salient were the tiny eyes, whose color resembled wheat at harvest time. She was vibrant, quick to move, a fast thinker and personable. Not very feminine-looking, she was attractive by way of a virtually irresistible smile.

In her immediate neighborhood, Pegu was best known for her strength which was reflected in her powerful build. When she had been in school, at recess she would often challenge boys at arm wrestling—and beat them. Friends called her *bebek yuz*, baby face.

Pegu lived with her father in a small rustic, four room cottage in the poorer section of Samsun.

"Do you plan to look for a job today?" Pegu asked.

They had just finished the morning repast.

"I will try, my daughter."

"And where will you look?"

"To some friends of mine."

"At the tavern?"

Unintentionally, she raised her voice and coated it with sarcasm.

The old Man did not answer. He gave a blank stare, got up from the table, then left the cottage.

Pegu departed soon after that for her job as maid in the mayor's house.

Arriving there she was greeted by the politician's chauffeur Kenan who was also her friend.

"You look unhappy, Little One."

"It is my Father. My Papa," answered Pegu.

She had a habit of speaking redundantly.

"Is he still out of work?"

"Yes, and I scolded him this morning. It was out of frustration because I do not know how to cope. —I think his feelings are hurt."

"Do not be too hard on yourself," consoled Kenan. "You are a good person. You are young and you have already sacrificed for your father."

"Not enough, I fear. And I had no choice. A few years after my mother died, my sisters married twins who were soldiers in our army, and went to

Istanbul with them when the brothers were discharged. That left only me to take care of my father. He was already badly depressed."

"Being forced to curtail your education at fifteen <u>was</u> a sacrifice," explained Kenan.

"And I was lucky to find a job with that American military family named Martucci. They taught me how to speak perfect English and wanted to take me to America when they were transferred. I miss them. And I still remember their names: Connie, Frank, Michael, Jessie, Gianna, Frank Jr., and Rose."

"And why did you not go with them?"

"You know," replied Pegu, timidly.

"Tell me again," coerced Kenan, knowing full well the answer.

Pegu lapsed into silence and stared at the ground.

"I am waiting," Kenan insisted.

"Because I could not leave my father alone. I am all he has."

"I want you to keep reminding yourself of that for it was the biggest sacrifice you have made for him. What more can you possibly do?"

Pegu kissed him on the cheek, and Kenan continued.

"It has been only a year or so since we met, but I am very fond of you." "That is also how I feel. I am fond of you," exclaimed Pegu, with much enthusiasm.

Having spoken, she waved adieu to Kenan and went into the mayor's house to start the day's work.

Shortly after 1400 hours, the cook went to the parlor where Pegu was dusting the furniture.

"Your father is in the kitchen. He wants to see you." Her tone was harsh and condescending. "You better tell him not to do this again. I am in charge when the Mayor and his wife are not here. And I do not like to be disturbed like this!"

"*Evet, Efendi.*"

Pegu had a quick temper but at certain times it was necessary to be prudent.

She made her way to the kitchen where Mr. Gediz was standing by the door with a dejected expression and his hat held tightly in his hands.

"Is something wrong, Father?"

At that point, the cook left the room and went down to the basement.

"No, my Daughter."

"Then why have you come? You know they are strict here. They do not allow me to have visitors."

"I just wanted to see you."

"Please go now. The cook is already angry with me. She is mad. I will see you later. Tonight."

Pegu returned to the parlor to resume her dusting. Several minutes later, Mr. Gediz left. When the Cook–carrying an armful of canned tomatoes–came back up from the basement, she found the kitchen empty.

After work, Pegu stopped by the market to get food for the evening meal. Upon entering the cottage, she found her father sitting at the kitchen table, with a faint smile on his face. It was the first time in a very long while that he had shown any expression even remotely resembling levity. She liked it but was leery. Something must be wrong, she quickly thought.

On the table in front of the old Man was a package wrapped in brown paper.

"What is this? What have we here?" she asked.

"It is a present for you, my Daughter."

"A present? A gift? —You found a job!" she excitedly exclaimed.

"Open the package."

She undid the wrapping to find a bright red dress made of shiny nylon.

"It is beautiful. Gorgeous. Thank you, *Baba*."

Pegu rushed to her bedroom mirror and held the dress against her body. Even though it was a most becoming garment, it was a bit too large. This posed no problem for she could easily adjust it. Her sisters had taught Pegu to sew.

As she lay the dress on the bed, she noticed the price tag. It read fifty *lira*. That was much too expensive, she reasoned. With that amount of money there were more useful things to be purchased. She would have to tactfully convince her Father to return the dress. She went back into the kitchen.

"Now tell me, *Baba*. Where did you find work?"

The faint smile disappeared from his face. "I did not."

"Then where did you get the money to buy the dress?"

"I found it."

"Where did you find it?"

"I do not remember." He poured some *raki* into his glass.

Was her father becoming senile, Pegu wondered. He found *lira* but did not know where. Something was amiss.

"Did you win the money by gambling with your allowance?"

The old Man did not answer. Instead he drank more *raki*.

"Well, did you?"

"Yes." It was said quite faintly.

Pegu started to speak but was interrupted by a knock on the door. When she answered it, there stood Kenan.

"I am sorry to disturb you, Pegu, but the Mayor wants to see you right away."

"What is the matter? Is there something wrong?"

Kenan responded confidentially.

"I am not supposed to tell you, but you are my friend. It seems that some household food money which the Mayor had given the Cook is missing from her pocketbook. When she discovered it a short time ago, she told the Mayor that you and your father had been alone in the kitchen where she kept her pocketbook. I am afraid they suspect you two of taking the money."

"*Tesekkur ederim*, Kenan. Tell the Mayor I will be right there. I am coming."

She closed the door and returned to her Father. Though she should have approached the matter more delicately, she did otherwise. There was no time to waste. The Mayor was waiting to see her. He was the most important man in the city.

"Father, I must have the truth. Were you drunk when you came to see me this afternoon?"

He nodded reluctantly–but affirmatively.

"Did you take money from the Cook's pocketbook?"

Another nod without speaking.

"Why?"

"The pocketbook was open and the money was just sitting there. It tempted me. You have been giving me *lira* and I have not given you anything. That is a shame on a father. I wanted you to have something nice."

"But you knew you would be found out."

"No. I thought the Cook would think she lost the money herself."

His childlike reasoning saddened Pegu. Her father was more out of touch with reality than she had expected. She became further distressed when he buried his face in his hands to hide the tears.

In a fleeting moment of self-pity, Pegu asked herself why he could not be like other girls' fathers–content to sit home every night and read **THE KORAN**. Just as quickly, she remembered that he could not read. He had not been as fortunate as she to have gone to school. But he had seen to it that she had been educated.

He had done many other things for which Pegu was grateful and when she thought about it, Pegu decided she could never repay him for his working hard to keep food in her belly and clothes on her back while she was growing up.

Pegu moved to her Father and gently kissed him on the top of his head.

"Don't worry, *Baba*. Everything will be okay. I will be back soon."

She grabbed her kerchief and left the cottage.

As she walked in the evening darkness, she anticipated the scene that would take place in the Mayor's house. Along with the esteemed politician, his wife, the Cook and Kenan, the police would be there. They would question her. Since she knew for sure that her father had stolen the money, she would deny it. Instead, she would say that she had taken it. Then they would escort her to jail where she would remain until it was time to appear before a judge.

There was no other solution. She had to take the blame. If her father were sent to jail, he would not last a week.

But she would never let him know of her sacrifice.

As she neared the Mayor's house, a chill enveloped her. The scene she was about to face would be frightening and difficult. She probed her mind for an encouraging thought.

One presently came.

In last week's newspaper was an article about a Woman doctor who had gone to Africa to help poor people. If that Woman could go to a strange country alone, surely Pegu could be just as brave. After all, she was a strong, healthy girl who could fight anyone or anything. *Did she not always beat the boys in arm-wrestling?*

To further confirm her decision, she thought about her Father. She could still remember how warm he had felt when she kissed him.

But Pegu could not know that she would never see him again.

*   *   *

CHAPTER 12 –
"A Private Place"

Compared to the memorable scenery in my favorite love movie of all times, our spot was only half as nice. Whereas the people in the film had a mountain top, we claimed the summit of a large hill. But it was ours.

Earlier in the day Friday had called to ask if I would accompany her in search of a wedding present for Nurtan and Kyle. Also needing to buy a gift, I agreed. No opportunity to be with Friday was ever missed. Since that afternoon when she had told me about her plans for a divorce, my guilt feelings had been slowly diminishing.

Gobasi, my favorite and faithful taxi driver picked us up at 0930 hours.

After browsing through many shops in Yenishire, we eventually found gifts we deemed appropriate.

The day was still young. I did not have to report to work until 1600 hours so one of us suggested a picnic. We bought a modest assortment of foods and Gobasi told us of a private spot–approximately ten kilometers outside of Ankara–which was perfect for an outdoor feast.

After climbing a high road, Gobasi's taxi stopped in an uninhabited area.

"YOU WALK IN TREES," he instructed.

Every time he spoke, I had to suppress a laugh. Due to his lack of English, he shouted when talking. As if the loudness would clarify his meaning.

"AT END MUCH GRASS. BELOW SMALL VILLAGE. FAR AWAY. I BACK HERE TWO HOUR."

Before leaving, however, he offered us the use of an old blanket which he kept in his trunk.

We walked through a brief wooded area and came to the clearing Gobasi had described. While the view below was not spectacular, it had a certain indefinable rural charm and we immediately claimed the area as our very own.

"Thank you, Corey."

"For what?" I smiled.

"For finding us a private place. And a hill, at that."

I could do nothing but grin.

We spread the blanket in the shade of several trees and gazed at the picturesque scenery surrounding us. It was a warm day and the fragrances of nature made me light-headed. Everything was perfect.

The impulse to make love was immediately consummated and it seemed even lovelier and more meaningful under the peaceful blue sky.

Afterwards, we loungingly ate lunch and spoke of the inconsequential things that bring two lovers spiritually close.

"Do you think those people down there are happy?" she asked.

"For their sakes, I hope so. Happiness is, after all, only relative."

"I am very happy. Now. With you."

Those were my sentiments exactly and I felt she could see it in my eyes. The worshipping way I looked at her.

"I want to know more about your past," she announced.

"It's not terribly exciting. I was born in Brooklyn and at age twelve, we moved to Staten Island. After high school, I went to college for two years and then decided to join the Air Force and see some of the world."

"And just how much of the world have you seen?"

At that I had to laugh. "A whole lot. One spot in Germany, the streets of Tripoli, and here."

"Your fascination with anything Chinese made me think you had been to the Orient."

"That stems from the Fletchers, my first neighbors and friends in Staten Island. They lived across the street in a huge three story Victorian house. They are a wonderful family whose ancestry is Chinese. Since I had only a baby brother, I was enthralled with their clan of seven kids: Paul, Diana, Maxine, Melorose, Vivian, David, and June. I spent many wonderful hours in their house.

"They taught me how to dance; I had my first champagne there one New Year's Eve; we went sleigh riding on Burry's Hill; sang and looked at the stars while on hay rides, and had many wonderful parties.

"I adored them so and wanted very much to be a part of the family. They always called their wonderful mother, 'Honey.'"

"Will you return to college when you get out of the Air Force?"

"Yes. As an English major."

"What can you do with that?"

"Teach."

"I thought you wanted to be an author."

"I also want to eat. Work with kids in the daytime and write at night. Sexy best sellers that will make us rich."

"While you're in college, I'll get a place in Manhattan. So that we can live together in scrumptuous sin!"

Friday seemed to be avoiding any serious mention of marriage, so I thought it prudent not to broach the subject, as of yet.

"That sounds great;" I abundantly smiled; "We'll have a lot of terrific times together going to movies, museums, Greenwhich Village, Broadway plays.

"I want everything for us. I want our romance to be the definitive love story of all times. I want to sing you the most tender songs ever composed. I want to quote all the amorous poems I've ever read. All the passionate lines I've heard in movies.

"Most of all, I want to collect warm, happy, beautiful memories to share with you in our later years. And to be with you in all the exotic places I have ever read about."

"That's quite a tall order and it sounds marvelous. But let's not strive for too much. Let's savor the pleasures as they come along—one by one."

*   *   *

The Motor Pool is located some two hundred feet behind the JAMMAT Building. As a haven for military cars, jeeps, and trucks it consists of six large garages attached to each other.

A small Quonset hut is close by and parallel. It is divided into two rooms: a reception area that houses a master sergeant/clerk, and a chamber which is the domain of Captain Winston Lebal.

It was 1230 hours when Winston finished writing his report regarding the Izmir trip. Although Colonel Myrons hadn't pressed him for the paper, he wanted to get it done and off his hands.

He buzzed for the Master Sergeant but got no reply. Suddenly remembering that his clerk had gone out for lunch, Winston used the intercom telephone which was connected to the garages. Kyle answered the call and upon hearing the Captain's message, promptly reported to the office.

"take this envelope up to colonel myrons' office, please. you don't have to wait for a response. come right back."

"Yes, Sur," said Kyle, turning to walk away.

"just a minute, kyle."

"Yeas?"

"tell me about corey."

"Whata ya wanna know, Sur?"

"the kind of young man he is."

"He's the best, Sur. Give ya the shirt offa his back. —Why ya ask?"

"no special reason. i was just curious. he seems like a good guy."

"He is, Sur. —Anything else?"

"no. you may go."

Winston's impromptu questioning surprised even himself. He knew Corey and liked him very much. And he had promised himself not to be jealous of the lad.

He was also aware that Friday and Corey went on many shopping trips together. Yet, they were probably innocent outings and nothing to be concerned over. The time to worry, he convinced himself, would be when—and if—he heard rumors.

Winston was startled from his thoughts by Ty bursting into the office.

"Excuse me, Cap'n. But ya gotta come quick. And bring your gun."

Winston hastened to follow as the Boy rapidly moved along. Being some years older, the Captain almost had to run to keep up.

"what's the trouble, manners?"

"There's a wolf in the last garage. He probably wandered in from the woods behind the place. He's cowering in the corner and when we go near him, he howls. Foam is also comin' out of his mouth."

As they hastened along, Winston noted how confident and smug Manners seemed. Even the Boy's gait had a certain boldness about it. Winston recalled reading a report that a military psychologist had placed in Manners' file.

Ty's father was a congressman and the boy's mother devoted her time to the husband's career. Their offspring was the youngest of six boys and by his own admission the black sheep of the family. Feeling cut off from the rest of the family, Ty had spent most of his time with his paternal grandfather. But after the old man passed on, Manners fell in with a crowd who took drugs and vandalized.

The request for a psychological examination came from a previous company commander who noted how Manners harassed and tormented a fellow airman who was timid.

When Winston arrived at the garage, he found two other Airmen standing at the entrance. A third had a huge wrench in one hand and a long broomstick in the other—trying to coax the animal out of the corner. But the wolf would not budge. Every time the stick came near him he lunged for it, then retreated to his temporary lair. His howling made the situation intense.

"How you going to get him out, Cap'n?" asked Ty.

"what have you guys tried so far?"

The Airman with the broom answered.

"We got a couple of pieces of meat from the cafeteria, placed them outside the garage and hid. The wolf came out, cased the area, snatched the meat, and ran back to his corner."

Winston calmly surveyed the scene. With the unavailability of a net, trap, cage or lasso, there seemed to be only one way to deal with the situation.

"i see no other alternative but to kill the animal," he announced.

"Can't we find another solution, Sir?" wondered a third Airman.

"what would you recommend, son?" asked Winston.

"I don't know exactly, but maybe we could all hide someplace and see if he leaves on his own."

"good idea," replied Winston. "but did you notice how he licks his left paw occasionally? i think the animal is hurt and, if he becomes disoriented, might wander up to the JAMMAT Building and possibly attack someone.

"it was a good suggestion, son, but i believe we have no choice."

"I've a mind to do it myself, Cap'n," interjected Ty. "Back home in Maine, I used to go hunting with my grandpa all the time. Whata ya say, Cap'n? Let me shoot the little son of a ho-ah."

"are you an accurate shot?" asked Winston.

Ty's reply was borrowed from his grandfather. "It's a hot day for fat folks if I miss a target."

Winston handed the weapon to Ty whose face immediately glowed with satisfaction. He raised the gun and took aim.

Deafening gunshots reverberated as he fired four times. Simultaneously, the wolf emitted a painful wail as its body fell to the floor to lie in a pool of blood.

"Two shots would have been enough, Manners," scolded one Airman.

Ty's reply: "I had to be sure he was dead. Didn't I?"

With the deed finished, Ty put the safety on the gun and returned it to his Superior.

Relieved that the problem was over, Winston became immediately repulsed by Ty's subsequent remark.

"Cap'n! Would you like the wolf's head for your wall?"

*   *   *

CHAPTER 13 —
"And Crown Thy Good"

On my first Fourth of July away from the United States, I was at a special celebration—the Turkish wedding of Kyle and Nurtan. And it proved to be a memorable occasion.

Especially since the fireworks turned out to be human!

Originally, a Turkish wedding was steeped in tradition: a contract between the families; a dowry to the bride's parents; and the permissibility of the groom taking additional wives. When the negotiations were settled, the marriage ceremony was presided over by a religious official.

In 1926, however, a civil code outlawed polygamy which was provided for in Islamic law. In its place came civil marriage and divorce, both to be registered with the civil authorities and both containing equal rights for the male and the female. Additionally, marriage of a Muslim woman to a non-Muslim man became legally permissible.

Kyle and Nurtan were married at the courthouse building in downtown Yenishire, in a civil ceremony which lasted only five minutes. Afterwards, the newlyweds, maid of honor, and best man hastily retreated to Madam Sivas' backyard for the wedding celebration.

Present at the reception were: Madam Sivas, Yuksel, Turan, Friday, Winston, Urdanur, Drew, Ty, several friends of Kyle from the motor pool, Nurtan's parents, and a few of Nurtan's girlfriends.

We popped open several bottles of champagne and when everyone had a glass in hand, I made a toast—an old Gaelic proverb which someone had taught me.

"To the Bride and Groom:

> May your days be long in the land of the living,
> And all your pain—be champagne."

With that done, the party officially got underway. Several of the female guests helped Madam Sivas bring out tantalizing and mouth-watering dishes of food—both Turkish and American—which the Old Woman had spent most of the previous day preparing. Everyone immediately began eating.

People broke up into little groups and Drew started playing the music. He had volunteered to be the disk jockey and had brought along not only his own expensive stereo set but also a great number of records, some of which were quite valuable.

The sun was beaming down amicably and a mild westerly breeze made the day a meteorological masterpiece.

Urdanur, Friday, Winston and I sat together and munched on the fine cuisine.

"Was it a nice ceremony?" asked Urdanur.

"It was short and simple."

"Civil weddings always seem so cold to me," confided Friday.

"I would agree," added Urdanur. "But the emotion can still come through if the couple is really in love."

I laughed affectionately. "Nurtan's emotions definitely came through."

"what about kyle?" asked Winston.

"I guess he liked it. But _he_ didn't cry."

"I still think that getting married by a clergyman is nicer."

Urdanur began telling us how nuptials used to be in Turkey. As she spoke, I happened to glance over at Drew where I saw Ty holding a record and saying something. A phonograph rested on a table which separated the two men.

The night of the bachelor party flashed into my mind. I excused myself and wandered closer to eavesdrop on their conversation.

"Is this a valuable record, Cap'n?" Ty was asking.

"Not especially," answered Drew. "But I did have a hard time finding this particular arrangement."

"'As Time Goes By,'" read Ty, aloud. "Is this song anything like that other one, 'As Queers Walk By'?"

"Never heard of that," answered Drew, seemingly undisturbed.

"Isn't that the queers' national anthem, Cap'n?" continued Ty.

Drew ignored Ty and resumed choosing the disks to be played.

My blood was beginning to boil.

Ty spoke again. "These new 45 rpm records are unbreakable, I've been told."

"That's my belief," responded Drew, not smiling.

"I wonder," said Ty, tauntingly.

While speaking, he bent the record so strenuously that it snapped into two pieces.

"I guess they lied to you, Cap'n," smiled Ty, triumphantly.

Drew was finally becoming angry.

"I think you need help, Manners. You should really see a shrink."

"No, Cap'n, you got it wrong. It's queers like you who need help."

Drew's arms shot across the table, grabbed Ty's shirt and pulled him close. Their faces were within inches of each other. I knew that Drew was strong enough to hurt Ty. It was also true that Drew was a sensitive guy who hated to harm anyone.

"Go ahead," grinned Ty, undaunted. "Hit me and I'll bring you up on charges. And you wouldn't dare tell anyone why you hit me 'cause you know the truth would come out about you."

Drew took a deep breath and released Ty's shirt. The latter walked away, laughing like a fool.

"You should have beat the shit out of him," I said, approaching my friend.

Drew smiled. "I guess his type does have some purpose on earth. Without them, how could the rest of us appreciate goodness?"

"You've got a point. —I wanted to interfere but waited to see what you were going to do."

"I noticed you from the corner of my eye. Thanks, Corey. You're a good friend. —I'll play 'Rock Around the Clock' for you. I hear that it's the latest fad back home. You'll like it."

From Drew, I made my way to Madam Sivas who at the moment was alone. I had heard so much about the Woman and her mystical powers. I was straining at the bit to talk with her about them.

*   *   *

Nurtan was enjoying her wedding to the fullest. The ceremony, although brief, had been very touching and Kyle seemed to be sweeter than he had ever been before. The weather was beautiful, her *teyze* had been more than generous to offer the house as she had, and all of Nurtan's friends were there, including her parents whom she loved so dearly.

"You have spoken with us long enough," said Nurtan's father. "You must now see to some of your guests."

Tears were in Nurtan's eyes as she kissed her father, blew her nose on a damp handkerchief, and walked to Corey's good friends, Urdanur, Friday and Winston.

"Corey talk much you nice people. I happy meet you now."

The guests expressed their congratulations.

"I see Corey is busy talking with Madam Sivas," said Urdanur. "He has been anxious to talk with her. He's intrigued by the occult."

"Corey's interested in almost everything," offered Friday, smilingly.

The four of them spoke for several more minutes until Nurtan graciously excused herself to find Kyle. It was time to cut the wedding cake.

————

Through his near-drunken stupor, Kyle noticed Yuksel leave the yard and walk into the house. He gulped down more *raki*, glanced around to see that no one was watching, then followed her.

He saw Yuksel entering the bathroom at the end of the hall and hastened his pace. Before she knew what was happening, he swept into the room after Yuksel and locked the door.

"Go now or I the scream," she loudly whispered.

"Cut the bullshit, Babe. Ya know if ya make any noise Turan will come. He may get mad at me but he'll probably kill ya."

Yuksel's anger did not cloud her reasoning. Turan <u>would</u> put her at fault.

"What you want?"

"Ya didn' kiss the groom," he laughed.

"You kiss *you!*" she retorted, pushing him away from her.

For a girl she was quite strong, thought Kyle–remembering how she had fought him so well when he had had his way with her.

"Ah want ya to know that jus' cause Ah'm married, Ah still wanna come by and see ya."

"You come my house again, I kill you," said Yuksel, eyes glaring with hatred.

"Ya don' mean that," he grinned, stepping closer.

As Yuksel moved away from him she simultaneously grabbed a glass lying next to Madan Sivas' toothbrush. When she smashed it against the sink, shards fell to the floor. In her hand remained its base with one large piece jutting out.

She lunged at Kyle who would have had a severe cut on his face if he hadn't been quick enough to retreat.

For several long minutes, the two stared at each other. Kyle was contemplating his next move. Yuksel's face turning red with anger.

The silence was shattered by a loud pounding on the door and Turan's slightly muffled commanding voice.

"Yuksel! Why are you taking so long?"

"I come out now," she answered, her anger partly subsiding.

"Open the door immediately!"

"*Bir dakika*. One minute. I break glass. Must clean."

Kyle's bravado lost its verve at the sound of Turan's booming voice. He swiftly moved to the bathroom window, raised the screen, and jumped into the backyard. As he closed the screen, he whispered to Yuksel.

"Ah'll see ya, again."

Yuksel let Turan into the room and cautioned him to avoid the broken glass.

"Who is in here with you?"

"No person," she retorted.

"I heard you talking to someone!"

"I talk me. I curse for break the glass."

She bent down to clean the debris but Turan stopped her.

"I will do it!" he announced to her surprise.

"I do not want you to cut yourself. Go back to the party!"

Turan's comment surprised Yuksel. It also made her happy. In a crude way, it was a sign that he cared for her. A side he seldom showed.

After his escape through the bathroom window and into a vacant part of the yard behind the house, Kyle turned the corner of the house and faced the backs of Ty and some motor pool buddies who were standing together and telling jokes. He coaxed Ty away from the group for a private talk.

"Ah want ya to know that if it wasn't for Corey, you woulda been my best man."

"Thanks, Cap'n, " beamed Ty.

Kyle continued. "Ya know that chick, Yuksel?"

"Whata 'bout her?"

"Ah heard she likes ta put-out. And she has the hots fer ya."

"Thanks, Cap'n. I'll check it out."

Nurtan approached and asked Kyle where he had been. He gave a feeble excuse as she grabbed his arm and led him to the wedding cake.

"It time cut cake," she said, kissing him on the cheek.

Corey's discussion with Madam Sivas was abruptly—but politely—terminated when he realized that Drew was playing "Love Is A Many-Splendored Thing." Dancing with Friday to that song was imperative so when he made his way to her, she seemed to be waiting.

Their graceful movements were observed by Winston and Urdanur who were engaged in conversation. But Winston's interest waned a bit when he overheard Ty—who was standing close by—talking to a buddy from the Motor Pool.

"Look at Brotano dancing with the Capn's wife."

"So what?" commented Ty's friend.

"I heard they're foolin' around together—if you know what I mean."

"That's bad talk, Man. You got no right saying that."

"It ain't me. Just look at them. —See you later. I'm gonna ask that hot looking chick Yuksel to dance."

Urdanur had also overheard the conversation and quickly hastened to contradict the absurd remark.

"That boy is a trouble-maker," she stated firmly. "You must not give credence to the malicious words of a foolish person like that."

Although Winston smiled appreciatively for her kindness, it was too late. A seed had already been planted.

———————

Filled with illusions of grandeur and shallow male pride, Ty made his way to Yuksel who was finishing the job of cutting the wedding cake for Nurtan.

"That looks good," smiled Ty.

Yuksel was immediately embarrassed.

"I am the shamed," she blushed.

"For what?"

"You catch me lick icing on fingers."

"That's the tasty way of washing your hands. —My name is Ty. I'm a friend of Nurtan."

"I Yuksel."

"It's a pretty name. —Would you like to dance?"

"Yes. But I not can. My boyfriend jealous."

Ty felt immediately challenged.

"So what," he smiled. "It's only a dance. This here is a private party and everybody are friends."

Yuksel contemplated his offer. She had been working ever since the party began. It was time to enjoy herself a little. She glanced over at Turan who was busy talking with Madam Sivas. *Surely in the presence of my teyze,* thought Yuksel, *Turan could not object.*

She timidly accepted.

As they danced, Yuksel noted that Ty was nimble on his feet as well as a good leader. When the song ended, Yuksel thanked him but he held her hand and forced her into a slow dance.

In the middle of the song, Ty pulled her close to him. Turan noticed the action and walked over to the couple.

"That is enough dancing!" commanded Turan, in unfriendly tones.

"Who the fuck are you?" demanded Ty.

"I am with Yuksel! I do not want her to dance any more!"

"Well, we are," snapped Ty. "So fuck-off!"

He visually dismissed Turan and continued dancing.

Turan's anger exploded. He grabbed Ty's arm but before he realized what was happening, Ty swung his fist and a blow caught Turan on his chin.

Like a wild animal catapulting from a cage, Turan lunged at Ty. In less than an instant, Turan's hands were around Ty's throat.

Kyle and several other guys from the motor pool separated the two pugilists. One guy held Ty in restraint; it took three to contain Turan.

"Are you fucking crazy, Cap'n?" gasped Ty, straining to breathe.

"Yes! I am fucking crazy!" returned Turan. "And I will not forget this incident! I will let you go for now because of Nurtan's wedding! But I will get you! That much I promise! I will watch you very carefully! The first thing you do wrong, I will see to it that you rot in a Turkish prison!"

Turan grabbed Yuksel by the hand and without a word to anyone they left the party. The hue of Yuksel's embarrassment nearly paled the sunlight.

To shatter the deafening aftermath silence, Drew began playing "Shake, Rattle and Roll."

*   *   *

The wedding celebration ended somewhere around 2200 hours. Shortly before then, Kyle and Nurtan called a taxi to take them to the train station. They had planned a five day honeymoon in Istanbul.

With them gone, the guests began to depart one by one. Urdanur, Drew, and I were the last to go. We stayed behind to help Madam Sivas clean up the place. Then she made tea for us and read the Tarot cards for me—at my request. My future as told by Madam Sivas seemed to be in keeping with my imagination and I was pleased that the Old Woman was kind enough to want my life to be fulfilling for me.

Finally, Drew and I escorted Urdanur home. Then I helped him carry the stereo equipment to his apartment where he invited me in for a drink.

"It seems to me that I've had enough."

"Do you want to lose that happy buzz?" teased Drew.

"When you are right, you are right!" came my astute observation.

Drew poured red wine as we sat on the couch and discussed the various events of the day. He thanked me for being ready to help him when Ty had harrassed him.

Then he confided to me that Ty's suspicions of him were true. He explained why and how he had arrived at his sexual preference. He confessed because he knew I would understand. It was a bit surprising but not that shocking.

Then I felt his hand glide up my leg and alight on my crouch.

"I appreciate your invitation, Drew, but I do prefer women."

"You really don't have to do anything but sit there.

Just close your eyes and pretend I'm a girl. I promise you I will never again bother you; I just want to get you out of my system."

When I made no reply, Drew construed that as surrender and that was exactly what I did.

I make no apologies; a person should try almost anything once.

His act of fellatio was not nearly as loathsome as expected. Truth be told, it was enjoyable. But it could not happen again.

"That was nice," I said, as if complimenting a chef on his seasoning skills. "But from now on, it would be better just to be good friends."

"You have my solemn promise," Drew smiled. "I liked you the first moment we met because you seemed genuinely kind and very sincere. And I promise to be a great friend to you. If there is anything–absolutely anything–you ever need or want, I will be there."

He paused and became even more serious.

"I know a very important person in this town and if you should ever get in any kind of trouble, I will use my influence with him to help you."

I stood up and gave Drew a hug and a kiss on the cheek.

"That's a deal. But there is one more thing you must vow to do for me. You must swear with all your being and never renege."

"I promise! What is it?"

"When you become a famous Hollywood star, introduce me... ."

Before I could utter a syllable, Drew finished my sentence: "to Elizabeth Taylor."

*　　　*　　　*

By midnight, the train carrying Kyle and Nurtan was well on its way.

The lights in the coach compartment had been lowered and Nurtan slept on Kyle's shoulder. At the opposite end of the car sat a girl with whom Kyle had been silently flirting.

He gently moved Nurtan against the back of the seat and got up to stretch. Looking in the direction of the girl, Kyle noticed her seat was empty. So he casually strolled in that direction.

The car's lavatory was immediately beyond and as Kyle approached the door, it opened widely. The girl was standing there, staring at him.

"Ah wanted to use the latrine," Kyle smiled.

"Come in," she replied. "There's room for two."

Kyle entered. He closed the door and snapped the lock.

"You're American."

The girl nodded in agreement.

"Whata ya doin' in Turkey?"

"I'm a college history teacher on vacation."

No further dialogue was needed. Within minutes, Kyle entered the girl and their erotic movements became in synch with the swift rocking of the train.

Nurtan awoke in enough time to see Kyle alight from the lavatory. But her concentration on him blocked out all else and she was delighted to see how happy he looked.

Kyle kissed Nurtan on the forehead as he resumed his seat.

"Why don't ya go back ta sleep, Babe. We still got a long ride."

"I will. First tell how you feel."

"Ah love ya, Babe," said Kyle.

She rested her head on his shoulder once again, and closed her eyes in a blissful glow.

Having spoken, his gaze met the eyes of the American girl whom he had minutes before conquered. They knowingly smiled at each other.

*   *   *

CHAPTER 14 —
"To Live With The Problem"

*   *   *

The cafeteria in the JAMMAT Building never seemed gloomier to Urdanur.

The food on her plate was becoming less and less appetizing the more that Mrs. Penelope Myrons spoke.

Finally, Urdanur put down the fork as she silently declared her lunch a disaster.

"As I was saying," blurted Mrs. Myrons, irritatingly; "In a small American community such as we are, it is not fitting for a young enlisted man to be seen in the frequent company of an officer's wife."

Urdanur quietly fought to control her temper. The *only* reason she had accepted this invitation was in deference to Colonel Myrons whom she respected. Urdanur felt that there was a certain amount of decorum that one had to exercise.

"I would ask why you are speaking with me about this, Mrs. Myrons?"

"Because I happen to know that you and Airman Brotano are good friends."

Urdanur sipped some coffee in an attempt to calm herself.

"Corey is a sweet young man and I do not understand what you are trying to say."

"I am stating," snapped Mrs. Myrons; "that he and Mrs. Lebal are having an affair."

Urdanur could feel her composure beginning to crumble.

"Do not be ridiculous! They are doing no such thing. They are simply very good friends. Corey is just as close with Captain Lebal as he is with Mrs. Lebal."

Mrs. Myrons was demonstratively dissatisfied with Urdanur's answer. She reiterated her accusation by declaring that she had **personally** seen them together several times. That they had even been holding hands.

Urdanur could feel her nerves vibrating. She had had enough of this nonsense. When she subsequently spoke, she surprised even herself.

"First of all, Mrs. Myrons, I do not believe there is anything evil in Corey and Mrs. Lebal's relationship. Secondly, if there were, it would be none of my business. I do not interfere in the lives of my friends."

The look of shock on Mrs. Myron's face was nearly as loud as her offensive voice.

"I take umbrage at the tone of your voice, Miss Besni."

Urdanur ignored the woman's ludicrous comment.

"I do not know about your Bible, Mrs. Myrons, but my Koran has some very apropos sayings. One of them is 'God loveth _not_ the speaking ill of any one in public.'"

"I am speaking the truth, Miss Besni!"

"Frankly, Mrs. Myrons, you are too myopic to know anything about truth."

The Colonel's wife proceeded to reprimand Urdanur for her uncooperative and rude behavior and concluded by threatening to have the latter fired–unless she changed her attitude and agreed to speak to Airman Brotano.

Urdanur remained silent for several long moments. Her outer appearance seemed calm but within a volcano waited to erupt.

"Well," barked Mrs. Myrons; "what do you have to say?"

Eruption!

Urdanur forcefully pushed back her chair and stood up.

She glared down at her foe with a profound vehemence.

"You can take your umbrage and stick it in one of your silly-looking hats!"

And just before walking away, Urdanur said, "To borrow a favorite American expression: 'go fuck yourself!' –Anyway, I seriously doubt if anyone else would ever want to."

––––––

When Urdanur stormed out of the JAMMAT cafeteria, she went directly to her office. She made a telephone call, then spoke to her secretary.

"Please postpone any appointments. I would have you know that I have decided to take the afternoon off. I am going to dust cobwebs."

––––––

Fewer than ten minutes after her unsuccessful luncheon date with Urdanur, the interfering Mrs. Myrons was in her husband's office. She adamantly complained about Urdanur's rude behavior, insisted that he fire her, and demanded that he do something to stop the illicit affair between Airman Brotano and Mrs. Lebal.

The Colonel reluctantly promised to look into the situation.

––––––

It was an exceedingly hot day and the electric fans inside the Police Building did not seem to be doing their jobs. As Turan got off the elevator, he removed his jacket.

The heat on this floor was even worse than it had been on the main. He was wearing a short sleeve shirt and his bulging biceps caught the attention of the Receptionist who warmly greeted him. But he was not in the mood for fringe benefits and made his way into the Supervisor's office.

Once inside, Turan found his friend seated behind the desk. While Burdur was not obese, he was a trifle overweight. And it was not difficult for Turan to ascertain that the torrid temperature was having an adverse effect on his friend.

"*Merhaba*, Turan," smiled Burdur.

"*Merhaba, Efendi.*"

"You have come just in time. If you had arrived fifteen minutes later, you would have missed me. I am going home. This heat is not good for my heart condition."

"Then I will be brief, *Efendi.*"

"Do not hurry, Turan. You know I can always spare time for you."

The young man sat down, lit a cigarette, then took a swig of *raki* from his flask.

"Regarding Ahmed Yalvac," began Turan; "I have planted one more false top secret message! I expect him to take the bait! Probably tonight! And when he does I will arrest him! I have enough evidence already, but I wanted just one more piece! As assurance!"

Burdur used a handkerchief to mop perspiration from his forehead.

"I have read your report thus far, Turan. As usual, you have done an excellent job. However, I feel very badly. Since it happens that you are so close to the case, I will not be offended if you wish to be relieved."

"No, *Efendi*! I want to finish the job myself!"

Burdur mopped his forehead again.

"Have you known from the beginning?"

"I found out shortly after the investigation began! When I first saw him,

I immediately realized who he was and that he had obviously changed his name!"

"Very well, Turan. You may do as you wish."

Turan stood up, walked to the door, and paused.

"I know you are anxious to go home, so I will not take anymore of your time! —I think the date should be as soon as possible!"

"For what?" asked Burdur, mopping his brow still another time.

With a rueful smile on his face, Turan said, "For Ahmed Yalvac's public execution!"

————

As soon as Ty exited the American Hospital, in the Ulus section of Ankara, his demeanor immediately changed. Now he could drop the act. He didn't need to pretend being ill any longer. He had attained his goal of getting the day off by deceiving the Army doctor.

Ty was also glad that the routine "sick-call" was held in the American Hospital. It was safely far away from the Motor Pool and the JAMMAT Building and conveniently located near the Bazaar, Bath House and Compound.

Ty's enjoyment of the day-off began when he entered the Marketplace. Sitting alone at one of the small tables was the girl from Kyle's wedding.

"How you doin, Yuksel?"

She looked up at him with surprise and dismay.

"I do good," she answered, cooly.

"Mind if I park it here?"

"No. —Yes! I wait somebody."

Ty ignored her wishes and slid into the chair next to her. He wore a form-fitting white T-shirt which accentuated his manly chest, rippled abs and ample biceps. He was sure his physique would entice her.

"I'll wait with you."

"No. You go! I wait boyfriend."

"Why are you so unfriendly today?"

"Why you here? It Thursday. You no the work?"

He avoided her question.

"Are you afraid of your boyfriend? Don't be. I can handle him."

Yuksel averted his leering glance. "I not afraid. I not like the you."

"We danced wicked-good together."

"You lie at wedding. You say you Nurtan friend. But you Kyle friend. *Git burda.*"

"What does that mean?"

"Go away. I alone wait friend."

Yuksel turned her head in another direction but Ty was tenacious.

"I want that you and me get close."

His words were non-existent to Yuksel's ears, yet he persisted.

"Kyle told me that you're very hot."

Yuksel's uneasy feelings suddenly came into focus. Not only did he look like Kyle, he _was_ like Kyle. The friendliness was only a pretense. Just thinking about it fired the flames of anger.

"What about going out with me sometime?" grinned Ty, moving his hand up her skirt.

It did not take much strength for Yuksel to react. Her adrenalin had been building all along.

She threw her half-finished soda in his face then dug sharp fingernails in his cheek and scratched like a ferocious feline.

After wiping his eyes, Ty instinctively placed his hand on the stinging wound and wiped away blood which he stared at in bewilderment.

"You bitch," he commented.

"You _dolmus_! Pig!" she retaliated.

He raised his hand as if to strike her but she swiftly pushed her chair back from the table and, as quickly, opened her pocketbook to take out a long nail file which she pointed in his direction.

"Touch me more," she yelled. "I put in the throat!"

Ty took a napkin off the table to stop the bleeding, but in vain for it flowed quickly and profusely. He would probably have to return to sick call.

Yuksel stood up and put the nail file back in her pocketbook. She wanted to say something but her anger blocked any words. At least in the English language. Instead, she turned and walked away.

Trailing her departure came loud, bitter utterances from Ty's mouth.

"I will get you for this, Bitch! You better watch your back 'cause someday you may wake up dead!"

As she walked from the Bazaar, one person Yuksel passed was a woman who had witnessed the entire scene between Yuksel and Ty.

The woman was Mrs. Penelope Myrons.

$*$ $*$ $*$

While I lingered over a cup of tea and a cigarette at the kitchen table, I wondered how to spend the afternoon. Friday was busy with her children at the American school. Being an excellent mother, she spent a lot of time at the place on their behaves.

Presently, the telephone rang.

"Corey," said Urdanur. "I have decided to take the afternoon off and do some painting. You once told me you wanted to try your hand at it. Do you still feel that way?"

"Yes. But I have no supplies."

"Do not worry about that," consoled Urdanur. "I have extra of everything. Shall we say in an hour? I am just leaving the office."

"I'll be ready."

Placing the receiver back in its cradle, I decided to write to Edith while waiting for Urdanur. I put an Andrews Sisters album on the phonograph and started.

> *Dear Edith,*
>
> *Please forgive me for not writing sooner but things have been pretty hectic around here. Working various shifts tends to confuse me in allotting my time properly.*
>
> *Nothing much has happened. Several weeks ago, Kyle and Nurtan got married. I think they are going to be very happy. Kyle is lucky to get Nurtan because she is an extremely sweet girl. She is very kind, gentle and tremendously naive. She never sees the bad side of things. So I'm glad that she has such a nice guy as Kyle. At least he will be able to protect her from all the rottenness the world sometimes sends our way.*
>
> *I"m enclosing a few more photos. One is the ruins of an ancient bath house that the Romans built when they traveled through this area hundreds of years ago. The other two spots are in the Park of Youth. And the last one is Ataturk's house.*
>
> *Will close for now as there is no other news. Regards to all.*
>
> *Yours truly,*
>
> *Corey*

Ataturk's House and Grounds

Actual House

Roman Ruins

The Park of Youth

The site that Urdanur chose for our painting expedition was Ataturk's House. It is located at the top of a hill where Ataturk Boulevard ends.

Urdanur supplied me with the necessary equipment for painting, and we set up our easels to capture the view of the city from Ataturk's statue. I received some minor instructions from Urdanur, then dug-in with the abandon of an over-zealous novice. After working a long while without speaking, I broke the silence.

"Do you also paint portraits?"

Urdanur smiled while negatively shaking her head.

"I would say that I prefer landscapes. Painting an actual person involves so many intricate details."

"Yeah, I agree. Such as earlobes."

"What _are_ you talking about?" laughed Urdanur.

I expounded on my earlobe observations. Different people had various kinds. Some were full and hung independent of the face. Others had varying degrees of attachment to the cheek–from partial to complete and taut.

"You never cease to amaze me," teased my companion. Then, just as quickly, her mood changed.

"Against my wishes," she began; "I had lunch today with Mrs. Myrons."

I immediately felt uneasy. Just the mention of that woman's name was enough to ruin my day. But I said nothing and let Urdanur continue.

"There is only one way to say this. Mrs. Myrons thinks that you are having an affair with Friday. She wanted me to tell you to stop it. –I told her that it was not true. I also told her something else which I have never said to another human being. But she made me very angry."

"And that was?"

"Never mind," blushed Urdanur.

When I finished laughing at my friend's charming embarrassment, I became serious to match **her** mood. I subsequently gave Urdanur a complete explanation of my relationship with Friday. How it had gone from innocence to absolute love in such a short time. And without premeditation.

"You probably always knew," I concluded.

"I probably have. But it does not matter because anything you want to do is fine with me. I will always love you as a dear friend."

Then she added. "I am afraid that Winston, also, has suspicions."

She followed the statement by telling me what Ty had said at the wedding. And that Winston had looked distressed.

We remained silent for a short time.

My next words were almost in a whisper. "Tell me what to do, Urdanur."

She hesitated while she searched for an appropriate answer.

"We both know that the decision is yours alone. You can stay away from Friday, confess to Winston, or ask for a transfer. In life, one does not solve problems; he only adjusts himself to live with them."

Although we changed the topic and spoke of lighter things, my mind was deep in thought and I decided what must be done. Now that Mrs. Myrons knew about us, the rest of the community would surely find out. To save Friday embarrassment and disgrace–and also Winston–I must not see either of them again. No matter how painful that might prove to be.

I must adjust myself to live with the problem!

CHAPTER 15 —
"Decisions"

*   *   *

On the upper floor of the JAMMAT Building, Urdanur made her way to Colonel Myrons' office.

"Go right in, Miss Besni," said the Airman clerk. "The Colonel's expecting you."

Immediately upon entering, Urdanur thought she felt tension. Usually he greeted her with a gigantic smile which always proved to be a special treat.

"Have a s-seat, Urdanur," he said politely.

The Colonel walked behind his desk. On previous occasions, he sat close to her—on the edge of his desk. With this gesture, Urdanur assumed he was being distant.

"I have s-something painful t-to discuss with you," he began, solemnly. "A personal m-matter which not only embarrasses but s-sickens m-me."

Urdanur's stamina began to wane. She had told herself that this meeting would not be easy. But she had not expected him to be quite so upset.

"Let me save you some time, Colonel. Here is my letter of resignation."

Myrons looked at her as if in a state of shock. He had thought that they got along very well together. And he was very fond of her. Very often, he wished that he had married someone as uncomplicated and as sincere as Urdanur. Then he would not have to dread going home every night.

"I don't understand," he said. "Aren't you happy here?"

"Very much so."

"T-Then why do you want t-to resign?"

Urdanur lowered her eyes.

"To save you the discomfort of having to fire me."

The Colonel got up from his big leather chair and looked out of the window behind him. He was silent for several minutes before speaking again.

"Have I done s-something t-to offend you, Urdanur?"

She was genuinely surprised. Perhaps she had misread his body language.

"Oh, no, Colonel. Not at all. I love... I mean, I like working with you very much. You have been kind, warm, and very considerate."

He turned to face her. "T-Then why do you want t-to give up your job? And why s-should I want t-to fire you?"

Urdanur took a deep breath. The words were slow in coming. In the past year that she had worked with Colonel Myrons, she had become extremely fond of him. More so than she should have been. And at various times, she did entertain sexual fantasies about the man whose stature was so impressive. She imagined him totally naked and ready to make love to her.

"Because of the conversation I had with Mrs. Myrons yesterday."

To Urdanur's astonishment, the Colonel burst into laughter which continued for many seconds. Then he walked around the desk and sat on the edge of it.

"I *did* want t-to t-talk with you regarding t-that s-situation, Urdanur.

T-That was t-the personal m-matter I was alluding t-to earlier. T-The way you handled m-my wife yesterday was t-the best t-thing you've ever done. You're t-the first person who has ever had t-the courage t-to s-stand up t-to her like t-that. I want t-to congratulate you!"

The Colonel returned to his desk chair.

"As for t-this letter, Urdanur, I can only s-say: request denied. T-That is, if you will accept m-my apology for m-my wife's behavior."

Urdanur fought to hold back tears.

"I hope not be out of line by saying this, Colonel, but I consider you a good friend. And as such there is no need for an apology."

"T-Thank you for understanding."

He cleared his throat.

"Now, what's on our agenda t-today?"

As Urdanur began discussing business, Colonel Myrons only half listened. His mind was preoccupied with the brief talk which had just taken place. Urdanur's courage in standing-up to Penelope had unexpectedly ignited something within. It suddenly made him realize that he had had enough of his wife's irritating ways. Drastic changes were going to be made. Things were most decidedly going to be different.

———————

At the Motor Pool, Ty was wiping dry one of the four sedans he had just finished washing when Kyle pulled into the garage in a small pick-up truck.

"How kum ya got this duty?" asked Kyle, smiling in a teasing way.

"Fuck you, Capin," answered Ty, half-grinning. He spit on the ground. "This is the second time this week. I think Lebal has it in for me. He probably thinks I'm plugging his wife like Brotano is."

Kyle seemed surprised. "Corey is foolin' 'round wit the Captain's wife?"

"So it's been said. But I think he's a faggot like Sergeant Johnson."

"Ah doubt it."

"Let's go to the Compound tonight," suggested Ty, changing the subject.

"Is that how ya got them scratches on ya face. From some whore in the Compound?"

"Yes," he lied. He could not admit to his buddy that Yuksel had gotten the better of him. Had made him feel inferior—albeit it only for a few minutes.

"Well, what about tonight?" Ty pursued.

"Ah'd like to but Ah gotta go to Nurtan's folks' house fer dinner. Ah can't get out of it."

"Too bad," teased Ty. "That Fatima whore was asking for you last night. I think she has the hots for you. —Where was you just now?"

"Ah had to bring some supplies to the American Hospital. Now Ah hafta bring these here papers to Captain Lebal."

Kyle began to walk away then suddenly stopped and looked back.

"Take good care of that sedan, Ty."

The latter looked puzzled.

"What's so special about this heap?"

Kyle grinned sheepishly. "It's my favorite."

"I still don't know what the fuck you're talkin' about, Cap'n." He spit on the ground again.

"Every once in a blue moon, Ah sneak it out at night and go joy riding."

"How the fuck can you do that?"

"Ah get the key off the rack on the wall in the master sergeant's office. Then Ah put it back the next morning. There are so many keys that the sergeant never even notices."

"Thanks for the info, Cap'n. It might come in handy for me some night."

As Ty dried the license plate, he read it aloud: "AF136. Maybe it's a fuckin' lucky number."

*   *   *

Once again Friday and I were at our private place. This time there was no picnic and the sky was not quite so beautiful. The sun played games with us by periodically sneaking behind dark clouds. And the texture of an unusual summer breeze hinted that rain might soon dampen the day.

We had gone there separately in case Mrs. Myrons had spies watching.

When Friday arrived, we kissed and then sat in the same spot as we had on our first visit. Silence pervaded the atmosphere for a long time as we both seemed preoccupied.

Friday was the first to speak.

"I wonder if there are any caves around here," she said, in a jovial mood.

"Why?"

"Then we could go spelunking."

"What the hell is that?"

"Spelunking is exploring caves as a hobby."

When I only faintly smiled, Friday said, **"Well, I thought it was funny."**

It was a favorite comment of hers.

If no one laughed when Friday said something that she thought was amusing, her next comment—and always with a chuckle—would be, **"Well, I thought it was funny."** She did it so charmingly and disarmingly that a person could not help but respond with at least a smile.

"You seem different today, Corey. And you were so mysterious on the phone."

The sun reappeared from behind a cloud and the brightness bolstered my courage. But not for long.

"I will not be able to see you too much anymore. I have decided to learn how to speak Turkish and I have enrolled in that school near our apartment house. So I will have to devote all my free hours to studying."

I averted her eyes.

"You're lying to me. What is the real reason? Don't be afraid to tell me. Don't try to protect me. Tell me the truth."

How did I expect Friday to believe such a tale when it didn't even seem convincing to me?

"It's Mrs. Myrons," I blurted out. "She's spreading stories about us having an affair."

Friday was atypically solemn.

"How do you know this?"

"She coerced Urdanur into having lunch with her and then she ordered Urdanur to tell me to end it."

"What did Urdanur tell her?"

"That it was not true."

"And did that convince the frumpy fuck?"

"Nothing deters an evil person from spreading gossip. —For your sake and those of Winston and the children, I feel that we should not see each other anymore. At least not here in Turkey. When you get divorced and we are both back in the States, then we can get together again."

It was a long time before Friday resumed speaking.

"Why can't we continue to meet here, secretly. The way we are doing now.

No one knows this place."

"I wouldn't be at all surprised if Mrs. Myrons followed us here someday and took photos of us making love."

Friday attempted to smile but the situation seemed too grave for her usual sense of humor.

"I'd like to think that we're not hurting anyone, but that's not really true."

"You are right. We are hurting the children. If this became public, they would be tormented by their friends in school."

Another excruciatingly long silence.

Friday continued.

" Maybe we were wrong to think we could have each other like this. But the children are important. They are so innocent. We can't make them suffer for something they haven't done."

"This is the first time in my life that I have ever been so unhappy about being right."

The sun suddenly chose to hide jump behind a cloud and the breeze increased in intensity. The weather was in synch with my mood.

"If you get back to the States before me, will you wait for me?" I asked.

"That's a question you don't even have to ponder. There is nothing else for me to do but to wait for you."

In my ever-present fascination with romance, I became convinced that the heavens were mourning for us. The rain abruptly fell. At first gently, then increasing by the second so that we had to run into the woods to take cover under some trees.

I immediately took off my wet shirt and hung it on a branch. When I turned back to face Friday, I could see the tears cascading down her cheeks. I matched hers as I took her in my arms and she rested her head on my chest.

Then we made love. For the last time, we said.

*   *   *

Ahmed Yalvac casually entered the bath house in the Ulus section of Ankara. Unbeknown to him, Turan was a safe distance behind with a squad of six men.

When Ahmed eventually entered the pool area, Turan subsequently sneaked in behind. He saw Ahmed go into the same cleansing room as the time before. But Turan also saw Ty Manners smoking a cigarette and lying comfortably on one of the marble benches which lined the pool.

Within minutes, Ahmed came out of the chamber and went into the steam room. A moment later, the Attendant also exited, walked around the pool and entered the cubical where he transmitted the false top secret message over a short wave radio.

Contrary to what Turan _knew_ were his colleagues' opinions of him, the decision to arrest Yalvac had been difficult. On the one hand, Turan was pleased to apprehend a traitor.

THE SHOWDOWN!

Turan ordered his men to action. In fewer than seven seconds, three men raced into the steam room while the other three invaded the massage chamber and confiscated the evidence therein. A minute later, the conspirators—Ahmed Yalvac and the Attendant—were presented to Turan who had stationed himself against one of the large pillars.

Curious about what was happening, Ty deserted his spot on the marble bench and assumed a position directly behind the team of men being detained. He watched and listened quietly with a perverse sense of delight.

Turan informed the collaborators that they were under arrest for treason. He ordered them to be handcuffed.

At that precise moment, Ty emitted a mocking laugh and subsequently said, "Look at the big shot Policeman."

Turan fought to contain himself.

How stupid can some people possibly be? This guy was just asking for trouble!

"You are also under arrest!" he proclaimed.

"What the fuck for?" asked Ty, indignant and unbelievingly.

"Interfering with police business!"

Ty protested loudly but to no avail. Turan ordered his men to handcuff the American.

"You can't arrest me," balked Ty. "I'm a U.S. citizen."

"Only the lowest kind!" declared Turan.

"Besides, I'm only wearing a towel. I ain't got nothin' on under this."

"You are correct," smirked Turan. "The towel is a problem."

He turned to one of his men and said, "Remove the towel! Take him out into the street naked! Let him experience how cold the walls of our jail can become! Perhaps we will get his clothes for him later, if he learns how to behave!"

As Turan followed in the wake of his men and their prisoners, Ahmed Yalvac yelled back to him.

"But, Turan. How can you do this to me?"

When Yalvac realized that Turan would not answer the question, he tried to find consolation in recalling his esteemed spy from his favorite espionage novel. Surely his hero would find a way out of this situation. So then, he would too. He would have to give it more thought.

As the entourage exited the bath house, the naked Ty found himself within speaking distance of Ahmed Yalvac.

"Tell me something, Cap'n. Why did you call this asshole cop by his first name? Do you know him?"

Yalvac answered in an embarrassed whisper.

"Yes."

"Has he given you trouble before?"

Ahmed lowered his head and stared at the ground.

"This is the first time."

"Then how do you know him?" repeated Ty.

"Turan is my brother."

In the coastal city of Samsun, the girl named Pegu sat anxiously waiting in a small room adjacent to the court chamber where her trial had taken place. Also present was the lawyer whom the State had provided because she was too poor to afford one on her own.

"I wish I could have done more for you, my Girl," said the Lawyer, sincerely.

"You did your best. You did well," Pegu responded. "The facts prove me guilty. And the Mayor is a powerful man. No one steals from him and gets away with it. Nobody."

The Lawyer sighed.

"Somehow I feel that you have not told me everything. Having talked with you all this time, I do not believe that you are a thief. —Are you sure there is not something else you want to say?"

Pegu was silent. She had confessed to taking the money out of the Cook's pocketbook and she would stick to that story. There was no way she would allow her Father to go to prison. It would surely kill him.

Thus far, she had been able to keep her Father from knowing what had happened to her. She asked Kenan to tell him that the Mayor had sent her out of town for a while.

The lawyer continued.

"Are you certain about the decision you made regarding your sentence? I have already given it to the judge but you can still change your mind."

"*Hayir.* No, *Efendi.* I will accept that. Five years in the Compound has to be better than fifteen years in prison at hard labor."

Silence abruptly reigned within the room as sounds from the world outside drifted in through the open window: vehicles blowing horns, people talking loudly, children screaming at play, and music coming from a tavern across the street.

Pegu suddenly realized she would not experience these examples of freedom for a long time.

"Are you sure you can handle the Compound?" asked the Lawyer; "You told me you are a virgin."

"I will make the men so unhappy that they will avoid me."

"*Allahaismarladik.* Go with God, my Dear."

Five minutes later, they stood in front of the Judge. His words were stark, bitter and excruciatingly cold.

"Because the jury has found you guilty, Pegu Gediz, I hereby sentence you to five years in the Samsun Compound."

*　　*　　*

CHAPTER 16 —

"Revenge"

To my partial surprise, I had been summoned to Colonel Myrons' office in
JAMMAT on a Saturday morning–for a "little talk." His Clerk had phoned to
say that 1100 hours would be a convenient time for me to see the Colonel.

One does not argue in the military. You blindly follow direct orders.
It doesn't matter if a superior officer is dense, vulgar and/or incompetent.
When said Tyrant speaks, you jump. About the only thing the military **does**
encourage its men to do is **not to think**. Along with room and board one's
thinking is done for him.

The Colonel's mere physical presence was slighty intimidating but I was
determined not to crumble. For, ultimately, I had a pretty good idea as to the
point of this meeting.

The Colonel returned my obligatory salute and offered me a seat.

"I'm s-sorry if I t-took you away from anything, S-Son. I don't usually
bother a man on his day off."

That was something I had heard about the Colonel. He was a fair man.
Stern and demanding if he had to be. But just.

"That's all right, Sir. I wasn't doing anything important, anyway."

He moved to the front of his desk and sat on the edge of it. Before
speaking, he folded his arms as if contemplating what he was about to utter.

"T-There is s-something of a delicate m-matter t-that has come to m-my
attention."

He paused as if waiting for me to say something. My rebuttal was nothing
more than a wide-eyed blank countenance.

"I was informed t-that you and Captain Lebal's wife have been s-seen holding hands in public. And t-that you have been t-together on m-many occasions."

"Well, Sir. I am good friends with Captain Lebal and his wife. Sometimes I escort Mrs. Lebal on shopping trips so that she will be safe. We are living in a foreign country, after all."

"T-That's t-true, S-Son. But I'm not s-sure you get the full gist of m-my m-meaning."

I assumed the dumbest facial expression possible.

The Colonel stood up and returned to the other side of his desk. He seated himself in a big leather chair and stared directly into my eyes.

"I'm sorry, Sir, but I really don't understand what you are saying."

"I am s-saying t-that it looks as if you are having an affair with M-Mrs. Lebal."

I became very indignant.

"That is not so, Colonel."

He was suddenly annoyed.

"Are you calling m-my wife a liar?"

He had revealed his source and I wondered if it were intentional or just a slip of the tongue. I continued my innocent act.

"Your wife?"

"S-She t-told m-me t-that s-she has s-seen you and M-Mrs. Lebal t-together on s-several occasions, and t-that t-the both of you were very amorous t-toward each other."

"We are quite fond of each other, Sir, but there is nothing immoral between us."

In my opinion, my words did not bespeak a lie. Immoral meant that someone did something wrong. What Friday and I had together was decreed by fate. It wasn't something we had planned. It occurred innocently. And inevitably.

The Colonel's annoyance disappeared as rapidly as it had come.

"If I have falsely accused you of s-something, I do apologize. However, Airman, you m-must admit t-that it does not look right for an enlisted m-man t-to be overly friendly with an officer's wife in public. T-There is a m-military law t-that forbids an enlisted m-man t-to fraternize with an officer. And especially an officer's wife."

"That's a stupid law, Sir. We are all humans and we **are** on the same team."

At first, I thought the Colonel would reprimand me for my outspoken comment. But he seemed to think better of it.

"Be t-that as it m-may, S-Son, but it is t-the s-status quo in t-the m-military.

It m-may change in t-the future. Now, t-though, we m-must abide by it. I m-must ask you not t-to s-see M-Mrs. Lebal."

I lowered my head in an attempt to convince him that his fatherly talk had hit home. Actually, I didn't want to look into his eyes for fear of exposing my true feelings and saying something that would get me into trouble. I was a free American citizen, but not to the military.

The Colonel continued.

"T-To m-make it easier for you, S-Son, I'm going t-to s-send you out of t-town for t-two weeks."

His proclamation took me off guard. That was the one thing I had not expected.

As I pondered the Colonel's order, he continued to speak. The journey would be a vacation for me. A reward for doing a good job in the cryptography room. I would be going to a town called Samsun on the Black Sea and I would travel there by private taxi.

I immediately suggested Gobasi and the Colonel consented.

Having delivered his speech, the Colonel rose.

"You will leave on M-Monday. T-The day after tomorrow."

$$*\qquad*\qquad*$$

On Saturdays and Sundays, the Motor Pool behind the JAMMAT Building was closed. It was common knowledge to most but Kyle kept it a secret from Nurtan. As far as she knew, her husband labored six days a week.

Yuksel was soundly sleeping in her apartment when the doorbell rang at 0900 hours. At first, she ignored the sound but after persistent ringing had to give in. She dragged herself out of bed, donned a robe over her naked body, and went to the front door.

"Who there?" she asked without opening the door.

"It's me."

"Who me?"

Even though she was still groggy, Yuksel recognized his voice. She could not believe he was bold enough to come there again.

"It's me. Kyle."

"Go away. I not want the see you."

"Ah have somethin' important to tell ya."

"Nothing good you say."

"But it's 'bout Nurtan. She's sick. She needs ya."

Yuksel became alarmed and instinctively reached for the lock. Just as quickly, her mind flashed back to Kyle's last visit when she had opened the door just a crack and he had forcefully pushed it open.

"Tell her call me," responded Yuksel.

"She can't get outa bed." Kyle was insistent.

"You go doctor, then."

"Ah don't know any doctors."

"Okay. I call Nurtan parents and tell them."

"No," shouted Kyle, alarmed; "Ah'll take care of it myself. If you don' care 'bout your good friend, then fuck ya."

Yuksel waited for several long minutes to determine if he had left. When she peeked out the window Kyle was walking away. Next, she went to the phone and dialed her friend's number.

"*Merhaba*," answered Nurtan.

"*Merhaba*," said Yuksel. "How you are?"

"*Iyim, tesekkur ederium.* But _you_ sound not happy. You are ill?"

Yuksel lied that everything was fine and that she had simply called to say hello. She then spoke of things in general.

When Yuksel terminated the conversation, she walked into the kitchen to make a cup of tea. She put a large pot of water on the stove. Before lighting the gas jet, she heard a noise coming from behind her.

Yuksel turned in enough time to see Kyle opening the kitchen window. Apparently, he had not gone away. He had sneaked into the backyard.

When he finally raised the window as far as it would go, he looked inside. To his great surprise, Yuksel was standing there facing him. In her right hand was a huge hammer.

Before Kyle could make a move, Yuksel slammed the hammer against his chest with all her might–with strength she never knew she possessed. Force born from the anger she harbored since having been raped. Not once. But twice.

Kyle fell to his knees in shock and pain. He grabbed his chest as if that alone would soothe the blow. As he did so, Yuksel stretched the top part of her body out of the window to reach him. She pounded him several times on top of his head until he fell to the ground unconscious.

Yuksel stood for a very long time just staring down at Kyle's motionless body. A small circle of blood lay on the ground just above his head. Contrary to Yuksel's nature, she felt a sense of relief. A perverse feeling of victory. And she experienced a catharsis. A purging of hatred flowed from her body for she had avenged herself.

After ambivalently basking in her victory for a while longer, Yuksel's feelings began to change. Kyle deserved to be dead, she rationalized. On the other hand, he was the husband of her best friend. And if he were really dead, how could she ever face Nurtan again. What proof did she have that Kyle had instigated this confrontation?

Yuksel began to quietly panic. She walked to the stove and grabbed the pot of water. She leaned out the window again and threw the water at Kyle's head.

Several seconds later, Kyle began to revive himself. He slowly opened his eyes. He shook his head a few times and sat up. He looked around at his surroundings and slowly remembered what had happened. His head ached so he touched it. When he moved his hand away it was covered with blood. Once again, he felt his head and was immediately aware of a deep cut. Then he looked up at the kitchen window. Yuksel was staring back. A slight smirk was on her face.

"Ya fuckin' bitch," he yelled. "You're gonna pay fer this."

"Go away," screamed Yuksel. "No come here no more."

"Ah'll be back, cunt; when Ah feel better."

"You come back here, I tell Nurtan."

He was on his feet now and heading unsteadily away. He held his head to stop the bleeding as he shouted back to Yuksel.

"It won't matter, Bitch, 'cause you'll be dead!"

*   *   *

I wandered around in my apartment in a feeling of uneasiness. So far, it was turning out to be a miserable weekend. Yesterday, Friday and I had painfully decided to put our relationship on hold until we met again in the States. Today the head honcho decided that I should have a paid vacation to stay away from Friday.

I made a drink, threw some records on the phonograph, and sat in the backyard. The sun seemed to be the only warm thing on this emotionally cold day.

In the middle of Tony Bennett's "Rags to Riches" the phone rang.

"I know we agreed not to see each other," began Friday; **"But a conversation over the phone can not hurt."**

The sound of her deep sexy voice was exhilarating but I knew the feeling would end too soon. In a matter of minutes I would have to hang up and never know when and if we would speak again.

When I told her about my trip to Colonel Myrons' office she became as incensed as I had been. She cursed the Colonel, Mrs. Myrons and the entire ensemble of military services–including the Commander-in-Chief.

"He's sending me to a place called Samsun. It's a city on the Black Sea.

I'm going by taxi and later will call Gobasi to make arrangements. At least I'll know somebody there."

"I will be with you in spirit," she said.

When she hung up I cried like a baby.

*   *   *

After Winston left his Quonset hut office in the Motor Pool, he decided to stop in the PX and buy some candy for his children. It was Saturday; his day off. He had inadvertently left his wallet in the desk drawer the night before and had gone back to retrieve it.

As he approached the entrance to the PX, he came face-to-face with Mrs. Myrons–who was exiting.

"Goo*d* afternoon, Captain Lebal. How nice to see you."

"my pleasure," lied Winston.

"I fin*d* this building so eerie on Saturdays. There are so few people aroun*d*."

"but it's refreshing," smiled Winston.

"Tha*t* may be."

She was momentarily silent while visualizing Winston's face–as if she were trying to reach some kind of conclusion to a cryptic thought.

"I wonder," she finally said.

Mrs. Myrons' mere presence annoyed Winston but he bore the inconvenience. Being in the army he had to practice a certain decorum. And she was his superior's wife.

"what do you wonder?" he asked, taking the bait.

The woman emitted a girlish giggle.

"Sorry. Actually, I *was* thinking alou*d*. Bu*t* now tha*t* I've given myself away, I may as well go on." She paused. "I wonder if you can spare a few minutes. There is something tha*t* you should know abou*t*."

In the Ulus prison, Ty was placed in one of the basement cells with a convicted murderer awaiting transportation to another state prison. Not only was the stench from his cellmate over-powering but the convict leered at Ty as if the latter were a delicious pastry.

Ty looked around at his new surroundings. In the left corner below a small window was a Turkish style commode. Against the right wall were bunk beds made of wood and containing mattresses filled with straw. There was one woolen blanket for each bed.

Trying to disguise a growing uneasiness, Ty sneered at his roommate then jumped onto the upper bunk in an attempt to sleep. *The sooner he dozed off, the faster the morning would come. By then, surely the Americans would notice he was missing and would come and get him.*

After a virtually sleepless night of fighting-off his cellmate's pawing, Ty welcomed the sunrise. He was given a breakfast of strong Turkish coffee and stale bread. When finished eating, he was lead across the hall to an interrogation room where he faced Turan and two guards.

The chamber was slightly larger than Ty's cell and its walls were painted a depressing brown color. There were no windows. Suspended from the ceiling was a metal lamp shade shaped like a bell. In its center was a large light bulb. The only furniture the room contained was a long wooden blood-stained table–with two leather straps on both ends.

"I want my clothes back," demanded Ty, boldly.

"In due time!" answered Turan. "First we talk!"

The police Inspector nodded to the guards. They pulled Ty over to the table and forcefully placed him on his stomach. Then they tied his hands and feet to the table straps so that his body was spread eagle. Ty tried to fight them but they were bigger and stronger.

When this was accomplished, the guards left the room.

"I want to know why you were in the bath house last night and what you have to do with the other men I arrested!"

"I was in the Compound first so I went to the bath house to get cleaned up and to have a massage. I never saw those guys before. I don't know who the fuck they are."

"They are spies plotting against the Turkish government! And they will be executed! I think you are working with them!"

The facade of Ty's courage unexpectedly began to crumble. Turan's accusation was the last thing he had expected to hear. It was one thing to ridicule a cop, but to be accused of conspiring with spies was a book of a different title.

"I swear on my grandfather that I don't know them guys," yelled Ty.

Although he pretended otherwise, Turan believed the American. But this opportunity for revenge was too satisfying to pass up.

"Then why were you standing so close to them?"

"Shit! I wuz on the bench. Only came over to see what was happenin'."

Turan was dramatically silent for several minutes then changed the subject.

"I also want to know why you wanted to dance with my girlfriend Yuksel!"

Ty's fear began to dwindle when he realized the topic was no longer espionage.

"You've got to be kidding. She's a sexy broad."

"And did you want to do anything else with her?"

One of the American's biggest flaws was never knowing when to keep his mouth closed. He had to have the last word. To antagonize. And in this circumstance, he was determined to balk at his Captor.

"Maybe," he replied.

"Did you want to fuck her?"

Ty could not resist the temptation.

"Yeah. I wanted to fuck her."

Even though Turan was angry he fought to maintain his composure. He had told himself to remain calm and simply torment the foreigner. He would teach the *dolmus* a profound lesson.

"So you want to fuck my girlfriend?"

"Yeah!" returned Ty.

"Well, let us see how much **you** will like being fucked!"

Ty's previous fear returned with a new horror attached.

Turan stood facing his prey. Slowly, he tauntingly and laughingly took off his belt and unzipped his fly. He lowered his pants and when Ty saw the policeman's soft, yet huge, penis, he began to tremble with fright.

Then Turan walked to the other end of the table, climbed upon it, and knelt between Ty's outstretched legs.

In the next instant, Ty began to literally cry. So convulsed with anxiety was he that the sweat poured off his body with abandon. The shocking horror of the situation was unfathomable. *Such a thing could not happen to him. He was too much of a man.*

What made rape seem even more believable was the fact that Turan had arrested his very own brother. If Turan could easily do that, he was capable of anything!

Turan smiled as he noted the way Ty's body was feverishly pulsating.

"What happened to your arrogance, American? Afraid you will like this and become a queer?"

Ty could stand it no longer. He began to scream, and sobbingly beg Turan not to go any further. He promised to stay away from Yuksel and never give Turan another bit of trouble. He also apologized for hitting him at the party.

After several minutes of Ty's uncontrollable rage, Turan raised his strap and began striking it against Ty's buttocks. When he was satisfied that his Captive had had enough, he jumped off the table and pulled up his pants.

His true intention had been only to teach the antagonistic American a lesson.

Within the hour, Ty was a free man.

Walking once again in the beautiful outdoors, Ty's true nature returned and it took no time for him to diminish the incident and decide that he had been the victim. With absolutely no remorse, and a renewed hatred for Turan, he was immediately his former recalcitrant self.

Someday I'm gonna get that mother-fucker, he vowed. *But first, I'm gonna get his bitch of a girlfriend.*

*   *   *

CHAPTER 17 −
"I'll Be With You in Spirit"

*   *   *

Standing in the entrance foyer of the Lebal apartment, Sandy said, "I'll bring the children home by dinner time."

"Are you sure they're not too much trouble for you?" asked Friday, sincerely.

"Not at all, Mrs. Lebal. I love being with them."

Friday thanked Sandy once more, kissed the children and returned to the kitchen. Winston was sitting at the table and drinking coffee.

"I see you finally decided to get up," she remarked, in jest.

"it's my day off. i thought i would sleep a little later."

"You missed saying goodbye to the children."

"i know. i wasn't in the mood to see them."

"Why?"

"i have something disturbing on my mind."

Friday felt a veil of tension begin to appear. The last several months everything had been pleasant between them. Both had maintained the truce. Suddenly it all seemed about to change.

"Would you care to tell me what is troubling you?" she asked, feeling uneasy.

"you and corey!"

Friday did not respond. She averted his stare by preparing a cup of coffee. Winston continued.

"at kyle's wedding, when you were dancing with corey, i overheard ty manners say that you and corey were having an affair."

She became indignant.

"And you believe vicious remarks made by a stranger? One who you, yourself, labeled a trouble-maker?"

Winston stared at her, challengingly. "not entirely." He hesitated for a moment. "i also ran into mrs. myrons the other day."

"She is a stupid woman who has no life of her own so she goes around inventing things about others."

"if mrs. myrons thinks you're having an affair then the whole community thinks so. besides, the things she told me do not sound like gossip. they are actions i do not approve of."

Employing psychology, Friday chided Winston for accepting the words of outsiders over those of his own wife. But he didn't seem to be buying her ploy and she could perceive his anger intensifying.

"i don't want you to see corey anymore. and tell him if he comes near you, he will meet with harm."

"You would hurt him all because of gossip?"

"even if the stories are not true, corey has made a fool of me. i really liked the lad and while i was trusting him he was stabbing me in the back by being free with you. "

Once again, Friday tried to convince her husband that he was wrong. She explained how much Corey respected him and that he would never intentionally hurt Winston.

"You have only the lying words of a silly woman," protested Friday.

"i have much more. i have a sinking feeling in my gut. i also have my vision and i can see how cheerful you've become. the only times that you have acted happily in the past are the ones when you have had lovers."

Friday did not immediately react. This reversal of Winston's trust was not something she had planned on. Being enthralled with Corey she had thought of little else but their meetings together.

"I am leaving you, Winston."

"then it is true. corey is your lover."

Friday raised her voice.

"It is not true! I am leaving you because I don't love you anymore. I haven't for many years but I never felt strong enough to go."

"and you're suddenly so self-reliant?"

Her instincts told her that she must protect Corey at all costs.

"Listen to me! I do not love Corey. He is only a friend! My leaving you has nothing to do with Corey. I have simply had enough and I want out."

Her proclamation deeply wounded Winston. She had said many biting things but had never mentioned leaving. Tolerable were her past indiscretions because he at least had her. And oddly enough he still loved her desperately.

But he could never let her go. Being without Friday was the same as being dead.

Winston rose from his chair and walked to his wife. For one fleeting moment Friday expected him to hit her. He had never done so but she had never spoken so adamantly.

Surprisingly, he passionately kissed her.

Friday remained leaning against the sink and her cold response to Winston's action only helped to increase his dampened spirits. He returned to the chair and lit a cigarette.

"i will not give you a divorce," he announced.

"You have nothing to say about it."

"if you try to leave me i will first kill corey, then you, and then myself!"

———————

Madam Sivas sat in her backyard at a small, circular wrought-iron table which she and her husband had purchased for the garden of their first home together. Upon moving to the current residence, she had taken the ensemble with her because it reflected memories of wonderful times. Very often, she could feel his presence. As if he were sitting opposite her like he used to when they were so very happy.

"*Merhaba, Teyze*," said Yuksel, startling Madam Sivas from her reverie.

"*Merhaba*, Yuksel."

"Do I the frighten you, *Teyze*?" She kissed her aunt and delivered the single red rose she always brought when visiting.

"That is all right my child. I was only day dreaming."

Madam Sivas could easily perceive that Yuksel's heart was heavy with burden.

"What is the trouble, My Daughter?"

"I not want the upset you, *Teyze*."

"Nonsense. You and Nurtan are my special ones. You are the daughters I was never able to have. –Tell me, child, what has made you so distraught?"

"My life. And men. I not know why men so mean. Why they touch me?"

Madam Sivas searched for a logical explanation.

"Some men are very stupid. They see a pretty girl and they want her. They think only of themselves."

"That not the right," said Yuksel, feeling vulnerable.

"No. It is not right," agreed the Old Woman. "Nevertheless, it is so."

"What other girls do?"

Years ago, thought Madam Sivas, it was much easier to give advice–even concerning love. The world did not seem to be moving as fast then as it was now. But that was no consolation to Yuksel. No answer to her problem.

"Some girls find one man and marry. So they are protected by him."

"You know I not do that. Turan not let me go. He frighten me. He say if I go, he kill me."

The Old Woman felt Yuksel's desperation. She had been agonizing over it since she first learned that her niece was involved with the lawman.

"There is something more than Turan that is troubling you," she suggested.

"How you the know, *Teyze*?"

"I just feel it." She paused. "Also a while ago you told me that Kyle raped you. Has he come back again?

The tears that flowed from Yuksel's eyes answered the Woman's question. Madam Sivas handed a handkerchief to her young friend and patiently waited until the girl was able to speak again.

Pausing to catch her breath, Yuksel explained how Kyle had raped her a second time, his friend Ty had tormented her in the Bazaar, and that Kyle had returned and she had wounded him with the hammer. Also, both Kyle and Ty had threatened to kill her.

Madam Sivas' heart grew heavy. If she lived to be one hundred and five she would not be able to understand some of Allah's ways. Yuksel was a very sweet, unassuming, and trusting child who simply wanted to mind her own business and enjoy life as best she could. How could it be that so many selfish men were attracted to her? Why had her beauty become such a curse?

"I have an idea. I think that you should go away for a while."

Yuksel looked bewildered.

"I have not much money."

"You will not need much money. You can go to my old village and stay with my family. I have been sending money to them for many years. They will take care of you."

"But what I do there?"

"Nothing. Just relax. Try to forget about your problems here. Stay as long as you want. When you feel strong enough, come back. Then I will help you to get rid of Turan. I will go to the Mayor if necessary. I will also deal with Kyle and his terrible friend."

"Thank you, *Teyze*," whispered Yuksel, with some hope in her heart.

"I will make the arrangements today," announced Madam Sivas. "You can leave Ankara this week."

* * *

The summer rain—which usually makes me feel deliciously horny—did nothing to raise my spirits as I unhappily packed for my trip to Samsun.

I had contacted Gobasi and he was more than willing to drive me to Samsun. He also planned to wait there for my return. In the early years of his life, Gobasi had lived in that coastal city. And he had some childhood friends he would be happy to see again. After his father died many years ago, Gobasi had tended to his invalid mother. But with her recent passing, he was now alone.

So everything was set. He would call for me early on Monday.

The doorbell rang and I was surprised to see Friday's smiling face.

"This is dangerous," I suggested; "Isn't Winston at home?"

"He went to the Motor Pool to check out a car. We're going to dinner at a lakeside restaurant about thirty miles out of town."

She could see the amazement on my face so she continued.

"I'm trying to appease him. He heard about us and he threatened to kill you if you come near me."

"At this point, I don't much care."

"I do," said Friday, forcefully. **"I'll do anything to keep you safe."**

"So what happens now?"

"Off hand, I don't know. But give me time. I will definitely figure out something. There is no way that I am going to stay with him. And there is no way in hell that I am going to give you up! I must go now. He'll be back any minute. Think about me while you're in Samsun. I'll be with you in spirit."

*   *   *

The Compound in Samsun was somewhat smaller than its counterpart in Ankara. It had only four blocks of tenement-styled buildings arranged to form a square. In the middle was a huge assembly area where a patron could browse or simply sit on a bench and drink *raki* before finding another girl of his liking.

But the ten feet high concrete wall was the same as the one in Ankara. The jagged shards of glass adorned the top of it as a deterrent to one who might think of escaping. And the soldiers who guarded the entrance had bullets in their weapons.

As the vehicle entered the Compound, Pegu looked back to see the outside world disappear. The soldiers closed the huge iron gates and a chill ran up her spine. But she must be brave, she told herself.

Pegu was ushered into the Warden's office where she was met with a surprise. Instead of seeing a fat ugly man, she faced a slim fairly young, fine looking man who welcomed her with a pleasing smile.

"Do not be afraid, Pegu," he said, kindly.

His gentle tone put her only slightly at ease.

"Please sit down, my dear."

Pegu sat in the leather chair opposite his desk. It was perhaps the largest desk she had ever seen.

"We do not ask for much here," began the Warden; "We require only that you do your job in servicing the patrons. You work from 1800 hours until midnight and then you are free to roam about the Compound until the next night.

"We feed you in our very adequate cafeteria and we give you five lira a day to spend in the Compound store where you can buy anything from cigarettes to new clothes.

"You must keep your room clean for inspection everyday, your clothes must be washed after each wearing, and you must get a physical from the doctor once a week to see that you have not contracted a venereal disease.

"And there is one more thing. If you should attempt to escape in any way, you will be shot on the spot!"

Pegu remained silent during the orientation but her mind was busy devising a scheme. She would lead every potential customer to believe that she had a venereal disease. Then he would go away and leave her alone. If she did that with all the patrons, she reasoned, the word would get around. She would not have to submit to sex with any man.

"Are there any questions?" asked the Warden.

"No, Sir," she replied.

"There are a few more things you should be aware of," continued the man. "You must service any man who chooses you. You can not refuse anyone. And if you do not meet your quota of men every night, you will be sent to prison to serve fifteen years at hard labor. No excuses will be tolerated!"

Pegu's spirits crashed to a new low.

The Warden then dismissed the guard who had escorted Pegu into the room. She and her Captor were alone. In that instant, Pegu began to tremble within. Horrible thoughts collided in her mind as to what might be about to transpire. And for the very first time in her young life, Pegu felt weak. Totally vulnerable.

If she physically fought the Warden's advances, she would either be beaten by his guards or sent to prison—or both. With much soul searching, she began to convince herself that there was no choice. It had been inevitable that the time would arrive. She had to make herself go into a trance and pretend to be somebody else. Strong concentration was needed but she _was_ clever enough to trick her mind.

"I am a virgin," she blurted.

Maybe he will have pity on me!

"Then Allah has answered my prayers," smiled the Warden. "We get very few of them here."

He got up from his desk and slowly moved around it until he stood behind Pegu. With delicate hands he caressed her shoulders. He could feel the tension in her small body.

"Do not be afraid, sweet one. I will be gentle with you. I consider it a part of my job to have sex with every new girl to determine how helpful she will be to my Compound."

The Warden escorted Pegu to a long couch on the side of the room. As tenderly as possible he had his way with her.

Pegu guided herself into a trance.

As a veteran of the Compound for two weeks, Pegu had ultimately succumbed to the routine and found it easier to conform than to revolt because life in a prison would be much worse. There she would also have to contend with lesbians. Resigning herself, she sat on the porch along with the other women awaiting clients.

"*Merhaba*, Pegu," came a familiar voice.

She looked down at his smiling face.

"*Merhaba*, Kenan. Please come in."

When Kenan and Pegu entered her room, she closed the window curtains. It was a sign to others that she was occupied.

"I like seeing you, Kenan. I do enjoy you coming here and giving me news but I wish you would not spend all your money on me. Do not waste your savings on me."

Kenan would give *lira* to Pegu but he would never sleep with her. She was his friend and he would not disgrace her.

"You are such a sweet girl, Pegu. You do not deserve to be here. I wish there was a way to get you out of here."

"Thank you, Kenan. I appreciate that. I am very grateful to you, but I do not want to cause any trouble." She paused. "Now, tell me how my father is doing."

Kenan became uncommonly solemn. He lowered his eyes.

"What is wrong? What has happened?" pleaded Pegu.

"Your father has gone to join Allah."

Pegu fought hard to hold back the tears.

"How?"

"He died peacefully at home. In his sleep. They think it was a heart attack."

In the ensuing silence, Kenan thought about the lie he had just told. While Pegu's father did expire, it was from a different cause. In a tavern one night, he heard a neighbor say that Pegu was in the Compound. He attacked the man, they fought, and he sustained a blow to the head when his opponent knocked him to the ground. He perished defending his daughter's honor.

Kenan saw the tears profusely flowing down Pegu's cheeks. He stood up and kissed her gently on the brow.

"He is at last with your mother and is probably very happy. –I will see that he has a proper burial."

Pegu cried for a long time after Kenan left. When she finally stopped, her sadness turned to anger. She had made the sacrifice knowing that her father was too weak to go to prison. But it had all been in vain for her father was dead and she was trapped in that horrible place.

Then Pegu made an adamant vow. Somehow, someway, she would escape. And if she had to get killed doing it, then so be it.

*   *   *

CHAPTER 18 –
"July 21, 1956"

After what seemed to be a very long weekend, Monday finally arrived. The day for my journey to Samsun. Gobasi, as usual, was on time. We drove from my apartment to the JAMMAT Building. For reasons beyond my ken, Colonel Myrons had insisted that I meet with him before departing.

When Gobasi stopped in front of the building, the Colonel was waiting outside.He smiled as I alighted from the car.

"Good m-morning, Corey," he beamed. His personal and cheery manner disarmed me.

"Good morning, Sir. Looks like it's going to be a hot day."

"M-Maybe s-so, S-Son, but at least you're getting an early s-start. It's comfortable right now." He paused. "Does your driver know the way?"

"Yes, Sir. He was born in that city."

"Fine."

The Colonel looked around the area as if he were worried about someone observing us. The vicinity was virtually void of people that early in the morning.

"I guess you're wondering why I asked you t-to come here before leaving."

I nodded in the affirmative. The Colonel continued.

"For t-three reasons, S-Son. First, I wanted t-to give you t-this m-map, in case your driver gets lost. S-Secondly, I wanted t-to m-make s-sure t-that you had s-some cash for t-the t-trip."

The look of surprise on my face made the Colonel chuckle.

"I'm really not as bad as s-some people t-think, Corey."

His sudden kindness and my unmasked bewilderment embarrassed me.

"Sorry, Sir. I didn't mean to imply anything disrespectful. I just didn't expect this extra treat. That's very nice of you."

He went on. "T-The t-third reason is t-to t-tell you t-that you will be s-staying at 548 Karasu S-Sokak. It is a house, near t-the center of t-town in which t-the enlisted m-men live. T-They know you're coming. T-There is a s-small JAMMAT Building s-several blocks away but you need report t-there only once—upon your arrival. After t-that, your t-time is your own. I have already s-spoken with t-the commander s-so t-there will be no problems for you. And t-there's no need t-to check with t-the S-Samsun Commander when you're ready t-to come back."

"Thank you again, Colonel. I appreciate it."

It was time to start. The Colonel shook my hand and I got into the front seat of the taxi.

"Let's go, Gobasi. We're off on the yellow brick road!"

"WHAT MEAN THAT?"

"Nothing," I laughed. "Just an American saying."

"*EVET, EFENDI.*"

In order to dismiss my sadness at leaving Friday, I concentrated on the journey ahead. I playfully pretended to be Huckleberry Finn traveling the Mississippi River. Gobasi was Jim and he was guiding a raft which looked mysteriously like a taxi.

I wondered if there were an adventure waiting for us in Samsun.

*   *   *

Having walked deeply into the Park of Youth, Turan easily found the designated bench on which he was to meet Chief Inspector Jean Claude Burdur.

As he approached, Turan noticed prayer beads in his friend's hand. It was a common ritual with many Turkish men. Resembling a small bracelet, the beads were strung together and each marble-sized bead was made of wood. The Inspector held them in his right hand as his fingers rapidly moved from one bead to the next.

"*Merhaba,* Turan," smiled the Inspector.

"*Merhaba, Efendi!*" replied Turan, sitting down next to Burdur.

"I guess you are wondering why I asked you to meet me here instead of in my office. I realize it is a strange request."

"You and I often do strange things, *Efendi*! And I like that about us."

"While I waited for you, Turan, I thought back about your first day on the job. You made six arrests before sundown. Do you remember?"

"Like it was yesterday!"

As regarding the site for their meeting, the Chief Inspector explained that he had been to see his doctor earlier in the day and had then decided to take the afternoon off to bask in the fine weather.

While not a very old man, Burdur was at retirement age and his visit to the physician had helped him reach a conclusion regarding his immediate future.

"What did you want to see me about, *Efendi*?"

"Several things, My Son. First, I want to congratulate you on the good job you did apprehending Ahmed Yalvac. I know it was difficult to arrest your own brother, but you had no choice."

"I am not happy about that! On the other hand, he deserved it! If he were not stopped now, his future actions might have caused innocent people to lose their lives!

Nevertheless, I do not wish to attend the public execution!"

"That is quite understandable. I will arrange a paid vacation for you. Incidentally, the execution is scheduled for August."

Inspector Burdur became pensive.

Turan drank from the flask he carried in his coat pocket, then lit a cigarette. He waited for his friend to speak but the Inspector seemed miles away.

"Was there something else, Efendi?" asked Turan, politely.

"Yes. News that I have been waiting to tell you for a long time."

With a serious look coming from his eyes, Jean Claude announced that he had definitely decided to retire, that he would recommend Turan to replace him, and that he had privileged information that Turan would assuredly get the job.

"You will be the youngest man in the history of the Service to receive such an honor. The only thing I must caution you about is your temper. You must learn to control it for the position requires great diplomacy." He paused. "Do you want the job, Turan?"

"Why are you retiring, *Efendi*? Is your health unsatisfactory?"

The Inspector gave a knowing smile. "You ask that because you see me with my prayer beads?"

"I have never seen you with them before!"

Another smile from the Inspector.

"My blood pressure is a bit too high. And as for the prayer beads, I decided maybe it was about time to use them." He repeated his question. "Do you want my job, Turan?"

"It is a fantasy come true! I will buy a book about diplomacy tomorrow and start studying! I vow not to disappoint you!"

Turan bid farewell and began to move away when his friend called after him.

"By the way, Turan, how is that drug bust on that house on Ataturk Boulevard coming along?"

"It will be finished later this afternoon!"

––––––

Ty Manners checked the time on his wristwatch with the reading on the wall clock in the JAMMAT cafeteria. It said 1445. He had been on a coffee break for the past half hour and was in no mood to get back to the Motor Pool.

Why bother to go back, he reasoned. Captain Lebal was at a meeting somewhere and was not expected to return. And the master sergeant on duty seldom checked on the men. *It's a hot day for fat folks if I get caught skipping out,* thought Ty.

He extinguished his cigarette, left the cafeteria and headed for the PX to buy more butts. At the entrance to the store, he encountered Yuksel who was exiting. He was still angry about the scratches she had imprinted on his face but couldn't resist the opportunity to taunt her.

"What are you doing here, Babe?"

Instant hatred commanded her face.

"I come see Nurtan but she not the work today."

"You want to go someplace and give me a blow job?"

She raised her hand to smack him but he blocked it in enough time.

"You stay the away from me, *Dolmuz!*"

Yuksel bolted past him and left the building.

Minutes later, Yuksel was walking down the long hill from JAMMAT to Ataturk Boulevard when she perceived a sudden aura of danger. Instinctively, she turned around and saw Ty Manners following.

She quickened her gait but had to stop at Ataturk Boulevard because of the heavy traffic. Once on the other side, it was only a matter of two short blocks to the safety of her apartment.

––––––

Parked across the street from Yuksel was a dark green sedan with four male occupants.

"When are we making the arrest?" asked one of the men under Turan's supervision.

"As soon as the suspect enters the house on the corner!"

"Is that our man getting out of the taxi?"

"Yes!" answered Turan. "Get ready to move!"

With the last word barely out of his mouth, Turan happened to glance to his right where he saw Yuksel waiting to cross Ataturk Boulevard. He also noticed that Ty Manners was not far behind her.

Turan was immediately incensed. *Were they both on their way to Yuksel's apartment for a rendezvous?* His impulse was to jump from the sedan and kill both of them on the spot.

But rational behavior prevailed because he had promised Chief Inspector Burdur to practice self-control. And at that moment, Turan's main concern was the drug bust. He would deal with Yuksel later on.

"*Efendi,*" yelled one of Turan's men; "our suspect is entering the house."

"Very well! Drive up in front of the place!"

As Yuksel waited to cross Ataturk Boulevard, she was startled to see Turan sitting in a parked car across the way. If he had seen her, she feared, he would think that Ty Manners was following at her request. But before she could do anything, Turan's sedan moved forward a bit, stopped, and Turan with his men hurriedly entered the corner house.

Yuksel crossed the street then glanced behind. Ty was approaching Ataturk Boulevard. He had gained on her and was much too close.

Yuksel swiftly walked past the corner house that Turan and his men had entered and turned left onto her street. Her apartment was finally in sight. As a nervous gesture she glanced at her watch; it read almost 1500 hours. Then she looked behind once more and saw that Ty had turned the corner.

And so Yuksel began to run.

At 1700 hours, Drew entered his apartment building which was located across the street from Yuksel's place.

While closing his door, he saw someone walking away from Yuksel's entrance. He smiled to himself and shook his head in disbelief. He had thought Yuksel's taste was better than that.

Drew then did his daily work-out. Afterwards, he showered and finished in enough time to answer his doorbell.

"Come on in," said Drew; "I've been keeping the wine cold for you."

As the male visitor entered, he handed a box to Drew.

"You didn't believe I would forget your birthday, did you?"

The host smiled. "Not you. You're among the very few people that I _can_ count on."

The visitor sat on the couch and watched Drew pour the wine. "Open your present," he affectionately ordered.

Inside the box Drew found an 18 karat gold chain attached to a pendant of the Turkish flag.

"I feel it is a nice keepsake of our days here."

"It's perfect," answered Drew. "I love it. —How long can you stay?"

"A good while."

Drew poured more wine. "You're lucky you didn't get here about two hours ago."

"Why?"

"Because you would have run into Ty Manners. I saw him leaving Yuksel's apartment around that time."

"Did you exchange words?"

"No. I only saw him from the back."

"How did you know it was him?"

"Because he's blonde, has a good build and was wearing a jersey that says 'Portland, Maine' on the back of it."

––––––

A week after July 21, 1956, Madam Sivas awoke in the middle of the night from a vision and nightmare which frightened her as never before.

The sapient Woman did not return to sleep. Instead she prayed for the remainder of the night and even with her deep faith in Allah, she knew her words were in vain. When morning came, she found herself at Nurtan's apartment.

"*Teyze*," exclaimed Nurtan. "What nice surprise. Please. Is there problem? You come so early."

Nurtan saw the redness in her aunt's eyes and immediately knew that the Woman was in emotional pain. She ushered Madam Sivas into the living room where they sat close to each other on the sofa.

"Is Kyle home?"

"No. He went work. What is trouble, *Teyze*?"

"I am worried about Yuksel. She was supposed to come see me Monday night because she was to leave from my house on Tuesday morning for a vacation in my village. But I have not seen her. I have been to her apartment everyday but no one is there."

Nurtan became painfully solemn. "Please. I too worry. Maybe she go and not say goodbye."

Madam Sivas continued to talk through her tears.

"We must find her because… ."

"Please. Why?"

"Because I had a vision."

The subsequent words spoken by Madam Sivas sent Nurtan into a trance. The room started to spin and she eventually blacked out.

"In my vision I saw a man brutally murder Yuksel. I know she is dead!"

*　　　*　　　*

CHAPTER 19 –
"Interlude"

(A TALE WITHIN A TALE)

Part One of Three Parts

The trip from Ankara to Samsun took approximately eight hours. The sun accompanied Gobasi and me every mile of the way and as the day grew older the heat became more intense. Riding in a taxi for a long period of time was not very exciting but there was the waiting reward of a no-cost vacation in a quaint city on the Black Sea.

The natural sights along the way were pretty much the same as various parts of the United States: plains, mountains, valleys and rivers.

At our journey's end, the road abruptly changed from plane to mountain terrain. We drove higher and higher and eventually reached the summit. We rounded a bend and all at once the sprawling city of Samsun lay below us like a mystical land that appeared from out of nowhere. Just like in a movie.

Stopping to take a photo of the beautiful panorama, I once again thought of Friday–making it an average of six times every hour since the trip had begun. I couldn't wait to show her this shot.

Back in the car, we descended past acres of sloping rural fields displaying countless racks of Turkish tobacco loungingly drying in the sun. Eventually we reached flat land and the city proper where Gobasi had no trouble locating my new home for the next two weeks.

"THIS 548 KARASU SOKAK," yelled Gobasi. "I COME YOU EVERY IKI, TWO, DAY. YOU NEED ME?"

Gobasi had eventually become my protector and felt responsible for my safety. Inwardly, I greatly appreciated the gesture. It said a great deal. Here was a virtual stranger being so kind and caring. And never once considering the difference in language and religion.

Gobasi wrote down the address he would be staying at and was on his way. I turned to pick up my carrying case and nearly collided with a red-haired guy.

"How ya doing?" said the stranger. "I'm Rick Brock."

"Nice to meet you. I'm Corey Brotano. And thanks for your hospitality."

"No problem," said Rick, a huge smile adorning his face. He showed me into the two story house and explained that I would have to shack up in the living room as there were no bedrooms available. I was content with any place to stay.

The next day I reported to the Commander of the Samsun JAMMAT who provided me with several pamphlets about the city. I half expected him to give me a work assignment but he told me to enjoy my leave.

After that visit, my days were spent in a leisurely existence. I got up late every morning, ate, showered, and spent the time photographing all kinds of sights–famous or otherwise.

Over coffee one morning, I asked Rick and his friends about the exciting things to do in the city. They gave me the names of several drinking holes. One guy jokingly commented if boredom set in, I could always get a tattoo.

The power of suggestion really had impact. Later that afternoon I found myself wandering past a tattoo parlor. Putting her name on my arm might not be prudent but I did anyway.

The artist tattooed "Friday" in the middle of a red heart. Directly under it, he wrote "*Masallah*" which means "wonderful and/or what wonders God hath willed"." Gobasi had used the expression during our trip. *Masallah* summed up my feelings for Friday in one word.

I missed her more than ever but the tattoo on my arm somehow made me feel a bit closer to her.

*　　　*　　　*

Gobasi sat on the small front porch of his friend's very modest house. Seventy-five feet in front of him were railroad tracks. A short distance beyond that was the Black Sea.

"You have a beautiful view," said Gobasi, kindly.

"At least when there are no freight trains parked here."

They both spoke in Turkish.

"Remember how we used to swim in this sea?"

"You used to swim with my brother," corrected Gobasi's friend. "You are forgetting that I was much older than you two."

Gobasi thought a moment.

"Sorry. You are right. You used to come and get us to go home for supper." He momentarily paused. "How long has he been gone?"

"Twelve years. I miss him a lot. He would have done very well by now. He was a smart boy."

Gobasi attempted to change the subject.

"**You** have done quite well. Being the Mayor's chauffeur is a very respectable job."

"There are better positions but I am content. I was happier when my wife was alive. Now I am resolved to work and to live peacefully. —Why is it that you never got married?"

"You know, Kenan. I could not have left my invalid mother. But now that she is gone, if I found a nice girl, I would gladly get married."

Kenan became silent. The words "nice girl" made him think about the unfortunate Pegu. Impetuously, he spoke.

"I know a very nice girl, Gobasi."

"Well, introduce me."

"Her name is Pegu. And she's in the Compound."

Gobasi laughed.

"A nice girl in the compound?"

Kenan proceeded to tell Gobasi about the events that had taken Pegu to the brothel. When he was finished, Gobasi's amusement changed to sympathy.

"I would like to meet her, Kenan."

"Out of curiosity?"

"Yes, but also because you have aroused my sympathy. I have two weeks before I go back to Ankara and there is nothing else to do."

Kenan thought a moment before speaking. *What harm could be done by introducing Gobasi to Pegu,* he wondered.

"Very well, my friend; tonight we will visit her."

The Compound in Samsun was somewhat smaller than its counterpart in Ankara. It had four blocks of tenement-styled buildings arranged to form a square. In the middle was a huge assembly area where a patron could browse or simply sit on a bench and drink *raki* before finding another girl of his liking.

But the ten feet high concrete wall was the same as in Ankara. The jagged shards of glass adorned the top as a deterrent to one who might think of escaping. And the soldiers who guarded the entrance had bullets in their weapons.

On the way to the Compound, Kenan once again told Gobasi about Pegu's unfair circumstances. Kenan raved so much about the girl's fine nature that Gobasi felt he already knew her. He also questioned the chauffeur's interest.

"I think perhaps that you love her, Kenan."

"That is true, my friend. But only as I would love my own daughter if ever I had had one."

"Are you sure?"

"If it were otherwise, Gobasi, I would not be introducing you. I would save her for myself."

In silence, the two friends passed through the gate of the Compound and into the square.

"There she is," announced Kenan.

Pegu was sitting on the porch and gave Kenan a big smile. When Gobasi saw Pegu, his eyes conspicuously widened. He had not expected her to look so innocent or so young. She looked like a mere child. *Bebek yuz*, baby face, he wanted to call her.

Pegu's presence enchanted Gobasi and he was immediately touched by something he could only recall from his school days: the irresistibly enchanting feeling when one is smitten for the first time.

Kenan made the introductions and the three of them chatted about useless things over Turkish coffee which Pegu prepared in her room. After an hour, Kenan excused himself and left Pegu and Gobasi alone.

They spoke for a long time and discovered how many things they agreed on. To Pegu, it was the first time that she felt so comfortable with anyone—except Kenan—since her troubles began. But she looked upon Gobasi with a different fondness.

Gobasi was not handsome of face, yet there was an appealing attractiveness about him. He was a big man whose strength was instantly noticeable, especially wearing a tank top undershirt. His shoulders were broad, his biceps bulged and his broad chest tapered to a narrow waist. He was very much like herself, reasoned Pegu. She, too, was strong. And he was the first male she had ever felt like identifying with.

Although Gobasi was sexually attracted to Pegu, he basically wanted to have an ethereal relationship. One that would last. For the present, then, he preferred to abstain.

Gobasi returned to see Pegu on the next night, the one after, and the one after that. He told himself that he must find a way to comfort Pegu because she was rapidly becoming someone very important to him.

*   *   *

Sitting alone in the kitchen of my temporary pad, I glanced at the tattoo on my arm and smiled. Did Friday miss me as much as I longed for her?

Thinking of her made me suddenly remember Edith back home. It was about time that I tell her the truth.

> *Dear Edith,*
>
> *I am writing from a place called Samsun. I was sent here by my Colonel to learn how the boys up here in the crypto lab operate.*
>
> *Took some photos of the place and some scenery along the way. I'm enclosing them.*
>
> *There's not too much exciting to tell you but I did have an idea about something.*
>
> *Since it's been so long that I've seen you, and because it's going to be even longer till I get home, I think it's only fair that you go out with other guys. We were both very young when I left and we didn't realize that sometimes distance and time make people change.*
>
> *You will always be my dearest friend, and if we both feel as strongly about each other when we meet again, we can decide what to do at that time. Will close for now. Let me know how you feel.*
>
> *As ever,*
> *Corey*

First view of Samsun

Tobacco drying in sun

the waterfront

View from a rowboat

Haystacks like cookies on baking tray

Sparkling river

I re-read the letter four times. At first, it sounded harsh. The next time, not so cold. Finally, I decided that my honesty was necessary. Funny how I could always rationalize my way out of a difficult situation.

As I sealed the envelope, I looked up into the smiling face of Gobasi and an older man whom I did not know.

"*MERHABA*, COREY. THIS FRIEND, KENAN."

After the ordinary amenities, I made tea for my guests and we sat in the kitchen. We were the only ones in the house at the time.

Gobasi had brought Kenan along because the latter's command of English was excellent. Gobasi's was too weak to explain the situation he had found himself in.

First Kenan told me a long story about a Turkish girl named Pegu Gediz. Then he explained that in the past five days, Gobasi had fallen in love with Pegu and had come to a profound decision.

Gobasi had decided to remain in Samsun with Pegu until her sentence in the Compound was satisfied. Then he intended to take her home to Ankara and marry her. But Gobasi would first see that I got safely back.

"Why wait for five years?" I said, my romantic nature consuming me. "Why not help her escape from the place?"

Both men looked at me in bewilderment. I could not blame them because the sum of my words was bizarre. I didn't know what made me utter such a ridiculous remark.

"Forget it," I quickly said. "It was a stupid thing to say."

"No, no, no," blurted Gobasi," through Kenan's translation; "It is a great thought!"

Then he asked if I might have any notions as to how it could be done—emphasizing that it was not a request for help. Such a venture was dangerous and he did not wish to cause me any trouble with the police. He was only seeking suggestions and he would do the rest.

I had suddenly opened Pandora's box and put my friend's foot in it. If I hadn't so lamely made that comment, Gobasi may not have even thought of such a thing. Therefore, any bad consequences would be virtually my fault.

If you're going to watch someone dance, I chastised myself, you have to pay the admission price. Throwing caution completely to the wind, I informed them that not only would I make a plan, but would also help.

Though they both sincerely tried to discourage me, I insisted. Finally, they acquiesced and I asked them to give me a few days to figure out a strategy.

Kenan subsequently told me that Gobasi would be eternally grateful to me and that he looked upon me as a brother. I returned the compliment.

That night, I went with Gobasi and Kenan to the Compound. Since I was now a part of the show, I had to meet the main attraction. Pegu was indeed everything that Gobasi claimed. The injustice which had befallen her appalled me. I could not understand why such a sweet person as Pegu should have to spend five years of her young life in such misery. To add to everything else, Pegu reminded me of Edith, the girl who I hoped would forgive me.

I reviewed the situation. I was very fond of Gobasi, his friend Kenan seemed impeccable, Pegu was a charming creature who had been severely wronged, and I felt guilty about Edith. There was nothing else I could do. Dangerous or not, I had to find a way to help them.

Before retiring for the evening, I scanned my mind of Hollywood films and found a solution thanks to Warner Brothers and their prison flicks.

The next thing I did was to draw a map of the Compound from memory, and various bits of information that Kenan had supplied.

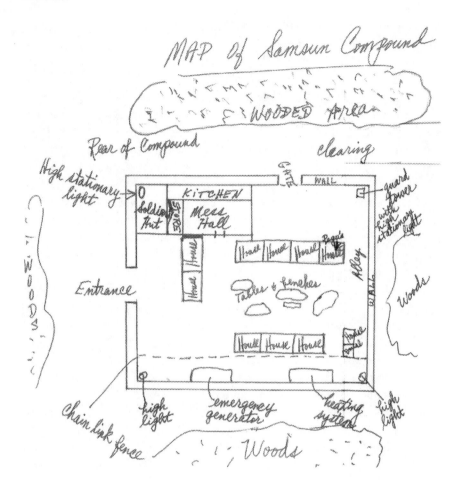

CHAPTER 19 –
Part Two of Three Parts

Two mornings later I went to see Gobasi at Kenan's house. I apologized for not going the day before because I had had previous plans to visit Lake Amasya with Rick and his friends. I explained how lovely the lake was but that the trip had been dampened by some unfortunate woman drowning. The accident had happened before we arrived but her body still lay on the beach–covered by a blanket and guarded by two soldiers–four hours later, when we left.

As I told the story, I noticed a twinkling in Kenan's eyes as if he had suddenly thought of something. But I dismissed it, attributing the observation to my overactive imagination.

Then I gave them my plan which they both seemed to think would work out nicely–even though I was a bit apprehensive.

In the days that followed, Kenan continued chauffeuring the Mayor around town while Gobasi and I busied ourselves with the preparations for the escape. We went to the local marketplace and bought American-styled dungarees and a grey sweatshirt. At various other places, we purchased a scissors, a thin hat veil, skin-tone make up, and peroxide.

All that remained to do was wait for that fateful night. I was both scared and excited and felt a rush I had never before experienced.

*　　　*　　　*

When Gobasi and Kenan finished an early supper in a restaurant not far from the Compound, Gobasi prepared to leave.

"Are you not coming to see Pegu tonight?" asked Gobasi.

"No, my Friend," answered Kenan.

"But it is the night before her escape and you will not be able to see her again, unless you visit us in Ankara."

"I would like to go with you, but something very important has come up."

"Is it anything I can help you with?"

"Thank you, my Friend, but I must do this alone."

Gobasi seemed confused but respected his friend's privacy. *If Kenan had a secret, it must be with good reason.*

––––––

In the twenty years that he had worked as chauffeur to the mayor– several different men throughout that time–Kenan had inadvertently learned many secrets that came with the job. Conversations held in the rear of the limousine, stories related in long hallways, and informal chats drifting out of doors slightly ajar.

Occasionally, a mayor even confided in Kenan because the latter had the demeanor of a sagely gentleman. In essence, Kenan was thoroughly knowledgeable concerning behind-the-scenes activities in the city. Some of the things he learned were helpful while others just useless bits of information.

Earlier in the day when he had reported to the Mayor's office to transport the Politician to a meeting, Kenan overheard his boss speaking on the phone.

"Thank you for alerting me," said the Mayor into the receiver; "I appreciate your discretion."

He had paused to listen.

"Very well, then. Since no one has identified the woman and you say she died from an overdose of drugs, keep her in the morgue tonight and cremate her tomorrow. Then destroy any paper work that might show you ever found a body. There is an election coming up and I would rather not have this incident publicized."

He paused once again.

"Yes, my Friend. You are doing a splendid job operating the morgue. Goodbye."

The Mayor's conversation–coupled with something Corey had said some days before–had merged in Kenan's brain and developed into a plan.

First, Kenan went to City Hall. The small building was guarded but Kenan knew all the soldiers there and they always allowed him unquestioned entry.

He went to the Mayor's office, found the duplicate set of keys for the City Morgue, then left.

The night Attendant at the Morgue had worked there for as long as Kenan could remember, and Kenan knew exactly when the Man left the place to go home for supper. Kenan waited for that time and quietly sneaked into the building.

He made his way to the room where the bodies were kept and began looking for the deceased woman he had heard the Mayor talking about earlier in the day. Since there were not many bodies, he had no difficulty locating her.

He wrapped the corpse in a blanket he had brought with him, then went to the desk near the door. He found the paper work which the mayor had mentioned and put the documents in his pocket. He would destroy them later.

Kenan carried the body out of the building and placed it in the trunk of the Mayor's car. It would be safe there because the limousine was always in Kenan's possession.

Finally, Kenan returned to City Hall and put back the morgue keys. With that done, he went home to drink lots of *raki*.

*   *   *

On the morning before the great escape, I awoke sweating. In my dream our plan had failed and we had all been arrested. But I knew that could not be true because Madam Sivas' Tarot cards had predicted a good future.

I was to meet Gobasi and Kenan at an outdoor café along the waterfront in case there were any last minute decisions or problems. We were also to review everything to make certain we hadn't overlooked something important.

I made my way along the seaside and among the train tracks. Here and there railroad freight cars were being loaded by oversized men with broad shoulders and sweaty torsos. The predominant cargo was tobacco. This came as no surprise because the Tekel factory in Samsun is known for producing most of Turkey's cigarette supply.

As I leisurely walked, I thought about Friday. I couldn't wait to tell her about my adventure. Then it hit me, again. Would I even get to talk with her?

Actually, I didn't know what I would find when I returned to Ankara. All I knew was that my love for her continued as strong as ever.

The outdoor cafe where I was to meet my colleagues was no elegant establishment. It was frequented by dock laborers but its food was renowned among the workmen. The view from the eatery was the beautiful Black Sea.

Gobasi and Kenan were waiting for me when I arrived. The lunch crowd was thinning out so they had easily found a table which gave us a reasonable amount of privacy. After the waiter served our lunch we got down to the main point of our conference.

As on the other occasions, Kenan acted as interpreter.

"There are two soldiers with loaded rifles at the front gate," began Gobasi.

He wished to refresh my memory.

"There are two more who roam around the square in the middle of the buildings, and one guard–under a stationary light–on a tower in the rear of the Compound."

On his frequent visits to the Compound, Gobasi had done quite a bit of reconnaissance. He would make a good spy, I chuckled to myself.

Kenan then made a strange contribution.

"There is a small iron gate in the rear wall of the Compound. It is used by workmen who bring in supplies. The guard's tower is at the far corner.

"However, I must explain that between the rear wall with the iron gate _and_ the back of the girls' tenement houses _is_ a large open area which is brightly lit. The soldier in the watch tower has a complete view of the area–as well as of the adjoining, perpendicular alley that leads to the square in front of the tenement houses."

"Then the gate is of no use to us," I asked. "Why did you even mention it?"

"No special reason. Just thinking aloud, I guess. But I do know that one afternoon an inmate tried to escape while deliveries were being made. She ran down the alley, into that clearing, and was killed on the spot by one of the soldiers."

We followed this phase of the discussion by confirming the list of supplies we had obtained, reviewing our strategy, and verifying the **MAP** that I had drawn.

Instead of leaving Samsun the next afternoon, as we had originally intended to do, we decided to leave later–under the cover of darkness.

Gobasi would park his taxi in a busy part of town approximately four blocks from the Compound. We would walk the rest of the way and nonchalantly stroll past the guards and into our waiting destiny.

Kenan spoke once again. First in Turkish then in translation for me.

"My Friends, I beg to be excused from accompanying you on this venture. Because I am the Mayor's chauffeur, I am too well known by many of the soldiers there. The same ones are usually on duty. You do understand, I trust."

At that point, Kenan stood. The Mayor had told him to return from lunch by 1400 hours and he could not be late. Before going he added that he would meet us at the top of the hill on the road out of Samsun, following our coup. He wanted to bid us farewell.

After he left, Gobasi and I went back to speaking in fractured English. We communicated as best we could but I was only half-listening. My thoughts were preoccupied with the words Kenan had spoken. I was upset over what he had said. Disappointed. I had figured Kenan for a good friend. I had thought he wanted Pegu to escape from the Compound. Suddenly, he seemed to be doing an about-face.

A sinking feeling abruptly invaded my being. Could we trust Kenan, I wondered. Did he have something up his sleeve? What was worse: would he betray us? And why did he want to meet us at the top of the hill afterwards?

CHAPTER 19 —

Part Three of Three Parts

*　　　　　*　　　　　*

When Kenan left Gobasi and Corey at the waterfront café, instead of returning to the Mayor's office, he drove to the Bazaar. He parked the limousine near one of the entrances and walked through the marketplace until he found the object of his search: a Man with a bear.

Kenan waited until the unsightly Male stopped playing his worn-out tambourine and the raunchy bear finished its dance. A small audience of bargain- hunters applauded enthusiastically and put money into the tambourine which the Man subsequently passed among them. When he faced Kenan, the Man became apprehensive.

"Have you come to give me trouble, *Efendi?*"

"No," replied Kenan. "I want to know if you wish to make twice as much money as you just collected?"

With a suspicious look on his face, the Man nodded in the affirmative. Kenan took him aside and spoke in a near whisper.

————

At the city morgue, an Attendant knocked on the Supervisor's door and was given permission to enter.

"What is it, Habib?" asked the Supervisor.

"The woman's body that you told me to cremate is not there."

The Supervisor stared at his employee in wonderment.

"Well, where is it?"

"I do not know, *Efendi*." He was becoming nervous.

"A body is missing and you do not know what has happened to it?"

"No, *Efendi*. I am sorry."

The Supervisor was momentarily silent before continuing.

"Did you check the paper work to see if anything was recorded concerning the body?"

The Attendant looked embarrassed. "No, *Efendi*, I did not."

"Then I suggest you do so," returned the Supervisor, sharply.

Habib turned to leave.

"One more thing," added the Supervisor. "I want you to make a thorough search. I do not care if you have to work all night. I demand a report on my desk by tomorrow morning!"

––––––

Intently thinking about the corpse he had stolen from the city morgue, Kenan walked from his front porch to the side of the house where he kept the Mayor's limousine.

Under the cover of darkness, he took the body out of the trunk and placed it on the ground. Unwrapping it from the blanket, he saw—in the light from the trunk—that the nameless creature was one of the Mayor's several clandestine girlfriends. That explained the Politician's blaze attitude.

Kenan dressed the body in male clothing and poured a generous amount of kerosene on it. Then he wrapped the cadaver in plastic and returned it to the trunk.

Perhaps Kenan's favorite part of working for the Mayor was that the limousine was always at his disposal. No one ever bothered the vehicle or questioned where it was parked because everyone knew whom it belonged to.

The first stop that Kenan made was the Mayor's office where he once again secured a duplicate set of keys—this time for the gate in the rear wall of the Compound. He snatched them off the hook and into his pocket. But before leaving, Kenan sat in the Mayor's chair. He had wanted to do that for twenty years but never before had the opportunity. It was not all that comfortable. *You can never fit in another man's chair,* he thought, and was on his way.

Kenan parked on a rarely used road in the woods behind the Compound. He took the dead body out of the trunk and the plastic, and carried it through the quarter-mile brush that ended at the brothel.

Before alighting from the woods with the dead body, Kenan visually perused the scene. The clearing between the Compound wall and himself was brightly lit by floodlights. In the center of the wall was the gate to which Kenan held the key. The problem was the soldier in the guard tower to the left of the gate.

Kenan concentrated on the spot. To his relief, the soldier chose that moment to light a cigarette and Kenan darted across the clearing into the shadow of the wall. He unlocked and opened the gate just wide enough to squeeze through. Once inside, he locked the gate and crept along the wall until he reached the far corner and was directly under the guard tower.

He impatiently waited. Presently, he heard tambourine sounds and laughter emanating from the square. The arrangement he had made earlier in the day with the Man who owned the bear was transpiring as planned. Hopefully, the guards on duty in that locale were being distracted from their regular rounds by watching the entertainment.

Kenan still had to go from under the guard tower and through the alley to the brothel square without being seen–and within the next few seconds. The staged diversion could not last too much longer.

He got on his knees to plead with Allah who answered him by highlighting several rocks which Kenan cleverly threw at the back wall. The soldier in the tower heard the noises and directed his attention to that area. Instinctively, Kenan sped down the alley while laboriously carrying the corpse.

Reaching the square, Kenan saw that the soldiers on duty were intrigued with the mangy bear and had their backs to him. He silently congratulated himself on everything going well–up to that point.

He found a spot against the side wall and lay the body flat on the ground to make it look as if "his friend" were sleeping. Then he sat next to it. Kenan pulled his cap further down and the visor hid most of his face. Finally, he emitted a sigh of temporary relief. Only one more thing remained for him to do.

*   *   *

I glanced at my watch and it read 1830 hours. A half hour earlier, Rick and the other guys in the house had gone their respective ways and I had said my final goodbyes to them. My carrying case was packed and the escape supplies were ready. All I had to do was wait for Gobasi and the appointed hour.

I checked out the meager supply of books in the parlor cabinet and became mesmerized by THE KAMA SUTRA, a fourth century A.D. book from India, and a guide to physical sex; it proved to be quite educational. Just as I was reading about the *Yang* accepting the *Yin,* a husky male voice jolted me. I looked up at a tall guy with jet black curly hair. While he was not handsome, he possessed a certain attractiveness some women might call sexy. His perfect posture was nearly intimidating. Outstanding of all were his cold green eyes. Like two pieces of ice which had been colored.

"What are you reading?" he asked.

"Just something to pass the time. —Are you looking for someone in particular?"

"No," he smiled. "I live here. At least some of the time. I'm Vance Leigh."

I vaguely remembered that Rick once told me there was another guy sharing the house. But I had never seen him.

I introduced myself and we shook hands.

"That's a very expensive-looking watch," remarked Vance. "You must be rich."

"Not really."

"Then maybe you were born into a family with money."

What strange initial comments to make. He certainly was not a shy guy. I attempted to end the strange conversation.

"I'll be leaving very soon."

"I know."

When he finished chuckling from the surprised look on my face, he continued speaking.

"I know all about you, Corey. As clerk to the commanding officer of this site, I'm aware of everything that goes on. I know you're on furlough, and what you've been doing these past two weeks."

This guy was certainly an unusual conversationalist, I deducted. No conventional dialogue for him. Right to the groin. I tried to appear calm but his declaration had shaken me a bit.

"You make my stay here sound mysterious," I commented.

"Don't be upset, Guy," he grinned. "I'm only teasing you."

"How is it that we've never met?" I pursued.

"Because I spend most of my off-duty hours at my chick's pad. But I did get to see you once."

When I declared no recollection of meeting him, he laughed again.

"I came home one day and spotted you talking to two Turks in the kitchen. It sounded like a heavy discussion so I just went up to my room to get some things. I didn't want to disturb you."

Although his words seemed simple and direct, something inside me created a feeling of uneasiness. I could not decipher the sensation. But it was definitely unpleasant.

"Nice talking to you, Guy," said Vance Leigh. "Maybe I'll see you in Ankara some time."

Coinciding with his departure were three blasts of a horn which signaled Gobasi's arrival.

Consequently, I had no time to dwell on the strange tete-a-tete with Vance Leigh and immediately dismissed it.

I shoved THE KAMA SUTRA into my carrying bag then left the house. This book was one piece of literature I had to show Friday; I knew she'd get a big charge out of it.

Entering the Compound turned out to be easier than I had expected— thanks to a nondescript Man and his mangy bear. They were performing in the center of the square. All the patrons of the Compound were enjoying the little show and the guards at the entrance were equally enthralled. They didn't bother to frisk us for weapons—as was their custom.

Gobasi and I circumvented the sideshow and entered Pegu's building. As we did, I noticed two Turkish men against the far wall. I could not see their faces but the sight temporarily amused me because one of them was flat on his back and, I assumed, quite drunk.

Pegu was happy to see us. She hugged and kissed her heroes and said, again, how lucky she was to have found such good, loyal, and brave friends. Her enthusiasm helped to allay some of my fears.

We immediately got to work. While Gobasi and Pegu prepared the peroxide solution, I took off my shirt and pants. Under them I was wearing a second pair of dungarees and a grey sweatshirt. I shed this sub layer of clothing and donned the ones I had entered with. By this time the peroxide solution was ready.

Gobasi cut Pegu's hair even shorter than it was in order to make it look like the popular current American flat top style.

While we waited for the solution to make Pegu into a blonde, we worked with the small piece of thin hat veil. Out of this, and a tiny bit of Pegu's hair, we made a mustache and glued it above her upper lip. The skin tone make up was used to cover up the holes in Pegu's ears which had been made by her earrings.

Finally, we washed out the peroxide. Pegu donned the grey sweatshirt and dungarees. I was delighted because she really looked like a boy. And since she was stocky, it was all the more convincing. We would have no trouble getting her past the guards, I reasoned. All was well and I became less worried.

As the three of us left Pegu's tenement, I looked to see if those two Turkish men were still against the wall. Sure enough they were. *That was some drunk they had tied on,* I laughed to myself.

Instead of immediately walking out of the Compound, we meandered to the middle of the square. By that time, the Man and the bear were gone. About a dozen patrons lounged about on benches. Our plan was to wait for a group of men to exit the Compound and to blend with them.

We sat on one of the benches and acted out our charade. Once again, I glanced at the two men against the wall. To my surprise, one of them stood erect. He tapped his companion and when he got no response, he literally picked up his friend and carried him in his arms. I assumed he was about to take his friend home. Instead, he carried his buddy into Pegu's building. I almost laughed out loud. Some people didn't know when to stop.

Five minutes later, we saw four men start for the exit. We stood up and began to follow them. At that very moment, flames shot out of the windows in the top floor of Pegu's building. As a far as I could tell they were coming from Pegu's room. We looked at each other in amazement.

All hell broke loose.

Women and men came running out of the building, the guards patrolling the square ran to see what was happening, and a fire alarm loudly sounded. Even the guards at the gate moved closer into the Compound to see the fire. And I immediately thanked God for abetting us.

As casually as possible, the three of us approached the gate. While one of the guards was preoccupied with what was transpiring, the other maintained his alertness.

He keenly stared at Gobasi and halted him by fully extending his arm and touching Gobasi's chest with his hand.

My knees swiftly turned to water and I found solace by repeating every prayer that those brown-robed Catholic grammar school Brothers had ever smacked into me—and all in the span of forty-five seconds.

The Guard spoke in Turkish which Pegu later interpreted for me.

"Where are you going?"

"Home," answered Gobasi, calmly.

"I do not believe you," continued the Guard.

"But it is the truth."

"Impossible! I remember your face. Every night for the past two weeks you have been the last horny man to leave. But now you are departing so early?"

Gobasi smiled as if taking the Guard into his confidence.

"The fire reminded me that it is my wife's birthday."

"How can that be so?" wondered the Guard.

"Because my wife is very old and when we put all the candles on her cake it looks like a big fire. And I am leaving early so as to give her a special birthday present." Gobasi grabbed his own crotch.

The Soldier guffawed and playfully smacked Gobasi on the back.
"You are my kind of man, *Efendi!* Good night."
We then walked out of the Compound and into freedom.

*   *   *

At the city morgue, Habib–the Attendant who had reported the missing dead body to his Supervisor–lit another cigarette and moaned to himself. His shirt was drenched with sweat because he had spent many hours plowing through mounds of papers.
The door to the office opened and a fellow worker entered.
"Are you still here, Habib?"
The exhausted man answered in the affirmative.
"But why are you torturing yourself, Habib?"
"Because I could lose my job."
"Do not be a fool, my Friend. Lie about it."
Habib looked puzzled so the man continued.
"You are my only brother-in-law, Habib. Would I give you bad advice? Just tell the Supervisor that you had told *me* to cremate the body–and destroy the paper work–and that you had forgotten you told me."
"You would do that for me, *Efendi* ?"
"Yes, Habib." He paused. "Now go home. My sister has been asking about you."

*   *   *

Gobasi drove his taxi at a normal speed up the ascending mountain road which led out of Samsun. It was the route by which we had entered the city. Sitting in the back of the car with Pegu I wondered if Kenan would be at the top of the hill as he had promised. Somehow I doubted it. When he begged off coming to the Compound with us I began to suspect him of being either a coward or–much worse–a traitor. But I tried to put the unpleasant thoughts out of my mind.
When we reached the rendezvous point, I saw an army truck and three Turkish soldiers forming a road block. My pulse quickened and my nerves began to vibrate but I tried to exhibit a calm appearance.
One of the soldiers greeted Gobasi as he stopped the car. He spoke in the Turkish tongue so Pegu whispered the translation in my ear.
"There has been trouble in Cypress and we are at war again with the Greeks," said the Soldier. "We must check the papers of everyone entering or

184

leaving our city. And remember;" he added with authority; "You must be off the road by the 2300 hour curfew. Our country is under martial law!"

Gobasi explained that his passengers were two Americans on their way back to Ankara. But the Soldier insisted on seeing everyone's papers.

There would be no problem for Gobasi or myself, but Pegu had no identification.

After Gobasi showed his credentials, he stretched his arm back to get mine. The Soldier looked at my passport closely then returned it to me. Gobasi turned on the ignition and began to move forward.

"No!" harshly yelled the Solider. "Must see the other one's passport also!"

The Soldier opened the door on Pegu's side of the cab and stretched his body toward her when he felt a tugging at his arm.

To my extreme delight, the person who stopped the Soldier was Kenan.

He spoke a few words to the Soldier and the latter allowed us to move on. Gobasi drove ahead about a hundred feet and stopped on the side of the road.

Kenan entered the taxi and sat in the front seat. He motioned for Pegu and I to lean forward and he spoke in whispered tones.

To make certain that our plan would go well, he had decided to give us some insurance. Kenan was the one who set the fire in Pegu's building. He had secured a dead body from the morgue, sneaked it into the brothel, arranged for the mangy bear to be a distraction, waited until we left Pegu's tenement, carried the body into her room, and ignited it. Consequently, the authorities would think Pegu had perished in the fire. Then they would have no reason to think she had escaped. And Pegu would truly be free.

How very Alfred Hitchcock, I thought.

We all thanked him at once. Kenan gave us an embarrassed smile but I could see in his eyes that he was pleased to have helped his friends. –And I cursed myself for having been so suspicious.

There were several subsequent moments of tearful farewells and then we were on our way. As Gobasi drove ahead, Pegu and I looked through the rear window to wave to Kenan who stood in the middle of the road sadly smiling back.

Within seconds, Kenan's figure blended with the darkness of the night. All that remained was the beginning of a lifelong memory–one which I would never forget. I had strengthened my friendship with Gobasi and had made two new friends. And I had helped to perpetrate an impeccable escape.

Or so I thought.

CHAPTER 20 –
"Stronger Than Before"

The sun was rising as we arrived in Ankara. The early morning bustle of the city was music to my ears. It made me feel as if I were home.

Except for an occasional relief stop, Gobasi had driven straight through since the Martial Law curfew was not enforced in the small hamlets along the way.

When I made an attempt to pay for food and gasoline, Gobasi adamantly refused.

"You are now my brother," he said–translated by Pegu. "I could never accept money from you."

Our journey back to Ankara seemed faster than the trip up to Samsun. Having Pegu as an interpreter was a big treat. We talked about many things as the miles whizzed by. One was the impending marriage of Gobasi and Pegu. To do this she would need a new name and legal identification.

Goabasi thought he could find someone who might be able to construct a set of false papers for Pegu. Then they could get married and move to Istanbul or even another country. I offered to help them get to America. In the meantime, the two lovers would play at being newlyweds.

Shortly after entering Ankara, we passed Ataturk Circle, in Ulus. There we saw a large number of soldiers infiltrating the area. When I asked Pegu what was happening, she informed me that–according to posters adorning the lamp posts–there was to be a public execution. Everyone was invited to see the termination of Ahmed Yalvac who had been convicted of treason.

Gobasi and Pegu dropped me off at my apartment and promised to keep in touch.

After making a cup of tea, I called Urdanur to inform her of my return and to catch up on the latest news. We spoke briefly as she was leaving for work. She informed me that Yuksel was missing.

Urdanur and I planned to get together soon.

Browsing through my mail, I found a letter from Edith. To my delight, she was in agreement about seeing other people and that we should remain good friends. No longer did I have to feel guilty.

But desperately on my mind was Friday, and I longed to see her.

*   *   *

A large crowd gathered at Ataturk Circle, in the Ulus section of Ankara. The people surrounded the small concrete island which housed a metal statue of Ataturk on horseback and a soldier just below him. The throng of approximately five hundred spectators had assembled for the public execution of Ahmed Yalvac.

A scaffold had been erected immediately in front of the monument. But instead of a trap door upon which the prisoner would stand was a very high chair.

Among those in attendance were Kyle and Ty. To them, the entire scene was exciting. Another story they would be able to tell their buddies back home.

Far behind them in the crowd was Mrs. Penelope Myrons waiting patiently with her expensive German-made camera to take photos of the event. A memento for her scrapbook.

To the crowd, the imminent execution had taken on a perverse aura of celebration. At strategic spots, street vendors respectively plied their wares: *shiskabob,* soda, *raki*, costume jewelry, balloons, Turkish flags. People cheerfully purchased these items as if at a festival. Few children under the age of ten could be seen but plenty of teens and other age groups were in evidence. There was also a small representation of older folks.

Scheduling the execution for 1230 hours on a Saturday attracted more curiosity seekers than would have appeared at a less propitious time. The area had been cordoned off and the usual vehicular traffic had come to a standstill at all approaches to the site.

At the foot of the scaffold stood four drummers whose roll of their instruments signaled the commencement of the ceremony. A hush echoed throughout the crowd as an army General mounted the platform and spoke into a microphone–in his native tongue.

"Today, you will witness the termination of a man who stole secrets from our government and sold them to foreign powers. His name is Ahmed Yalvac and he is a traitor to us all!"

A loud murmur from the crowd permeated the air and the General waited for it to subside before continuing.

"Fortunately, we were able to apprehend him in time and no harm was done."

The crowd let out a roar of appreciation. Once again, the General waited for silence to reign.

"We will now sing our National Anthem."

Loud cheers, whistles and applause followed the singing and the General introduced the Mayor who gave a short speech on the importance of patriotism. The assembly responded with a tumultuous ovation.

The General spoke again.

"We will now carry out the traitor's sentence."

Between the scaffold and one of the street corners feeding into the Circle, two columns of soldiers had formed a path through the mob so that four other soldiers could escort the prisoner to his destiny.

Though Ahmed Yalvac was booed and hissed at–along the way, and as he ascended the scaffold–he was almost jubilant. The novice spy who was a hero in his own psyche never stopped his mental calisthenics. In his fictionalized world, he was a secret agent from a foreign country who was in trouble but about to be rescued by a colleague, at any moment.

The General asked Ahmed if he wanted a blindfold and the latter replied: "No. I wish to see him when he comes."

Since the General did not understand Ahmed's cryptic reply, he simply chose to ignore the prisoner.

But Ahmed knew that his Rescuer was on the way. And that the latter would swoop down in a specially designed aircraft and snatch Ahmed from the face of death.

A soldier tied Ahmed's hands behind his back and guided the condemned man to the tall chair. He helped Ahmed onto the chair and the latter calmly cooperated. Then another soldier placed a noose around the prisoner's neck.

Ahmed looked out at the hundreds of eyes fixed on him. *They will be very surprised in a few minutes,* he said to himself, *when my Rescuer appears!*

A long drum roll crescendo reached its peak and abruptly ended. The ensuing silence became profoundly ominous and deafening. The brief nervous cough of an old man on the perimeter of the crowd sounded like a canon's roar. An airplane passing thousands of miles above could be faintly heard.

The confidence on Ahmed's face presently changed to shock mixed with horror as the chair he was sitting on was swiftly kicked out from under him and the weight of his body pulled him downward. An eerie gagging sound spewed out of his mouth as he gasped for air. Little by little, his lungs refused to function and his last thought before blacking out was: *Where is he?*

The drums briefly sounded once more to signal the end of the execution as the traitor's body slumped into the afterworld.

When the General was certain that Ahmed was dead, he ordered the soldiers to take the body away. While they were doing so, the General once more addressed the citizens.

"Thank you for coming, my Countrymen. And for the one or two of you who might even remotely think of being disloyal to our great nation, let Ahmed Yalvac's death serve as a lesson to deter you. Goodbye!"

In the final analysis, Ahmed Yalvac accomplished the fame he had sought. Ironically, it came in the form of death.

As people began to disperse in their respective directions, the silence crumbled and gave way to whispers which eventually reached ordinary volumes.

Mrs. Penelope Myrons put her expensive German-made camera into the purse which was color-coordinated with her silly-looking hat. She literally pushed through the peasants to get to the sedan that was waiting to take her home.

Kyle and Ty unhurriedly shuffled along with the rest of the people.

"That was wicked-good, Cap'n," said Ty, lighting a cigarette.

"Sure enough," concurred Kyle; "Ah ain't ever seen anybody lynched before."

"He wasn't lynched," disagreed Ty; "he was hung."

They bickered for several minutes with each trying to prove the other wrong.

An older man who was walking beside them in the slow moving crowd decided to settle their argument.

"It was neither, Boys."

"You speak English, Cap'n?" asked Ty.

"I am English, my Friend. I am in Turkey on business."

"Then what did they do to him?" prodded Kyle.

"It was death by strangulation."

Neither Kyle nor Ty understood so the man continued.

"With hanging, the victim's neck snaps and his death is fast and more humane. With strangulation one's wind is cut off. The latter is a much slower demise."

"Ah still don' get it," Kyle announced.

"Semantics, my dear Boy. But in the long run, the result is the same."

The man smiled and bid them farewell. When he was out of hearing range, Kyle spoke again.

"What the hell was he talkin' about? And what the fuck is semantics?"

"Don't know, Cap'n. It's probably another one of those countries in these here parts. But forget it! Today is Saturday and what's opened this afternoon?"

Kyle beamed with delight.

"The Compound! But Ah just thought of a betta name fer it."

"What's that, Cap'n?"

"The Hotel Vagina!"

*   *   *

Urdanur phoned and asked if I would put up some book shelves in her penthouse apartment. I suggested that after work would be fine and since she had a dinner appointment and would not be home, she told me where to find the key.

After attaching the last shelf to the wall, I went out on the back terrace to have a cigarette. The combination of the summer heat and my working made me hot so I took off my shirt. Yet, I kept it close by. If anyone were to visit unexpectedly, I'd have to quickly cover my tattoo.

As I gazed out at the now familiar city sprawled before me, the doorbell rang. I quickly donned my shirt.

"Don't worry, Love," said Friday; **"it's safe. Winston's out of town. —I missed you."**

"The same here. I wanted to call the minute I got home but was afraid that Winston might answer. —How did you know where to find me?"

"A little bird phoned me."

Apparently Urdanur was playing Cupid.

I ushered Friday to the back terrace where we scanned the city and pointed out all the places we had been together.

"Do you still feel the same way about me?" I suddenly blurted.

She looked at me in surprise.

"How could you doubt it even for a moment? I told you I would always love you."

"I just wanted to be sure," I said, apologetically. "I've longed for you so much and my love is even stronger than before."

Then I asked if she had come up with a plan for our future together. She explained that we had been given a reprieve. Winston had been sent out of town to a place called Diyarbakir to clear up some kind of problem. He had left about an hour earlier and was not expected to return for three weeks.

Fate was truly on our side, I thought. Three glorious weeks to be together.

"But when he returns, we can not see each other. He has become very

difficult and I'm getting a bit frightened of him. He absolutely refues to let me go."

"What are we going to do?"

Friday paused for a moment before continuing.

"Remember that tiny lump on my breast that I told you about?"

I nodded in the affirmative.

"Is it giving you trouble?"

"No. But I plan to tell Winston that. And I hope to convince one of these army doctors to send me back to the States for tests. Then, when I'm back home and settled in New York City, I'll go about getting a divorce and he won't learn of it until it's too late."

Friday, in her usual bedazzling way, then tried to lift our spirits.

"Come on, cheer up," she said. "You're the literary man. Give me one of your encouraging quotes. Or has your well of famous sayings gone dry?"

"Suddenly my mind is blank," I laughed. "But I do have something to show you."

Discarding my shirt, I turned so that she could not miss seeing the upper part of my left arm. Her eyes filled with bewilderment.

"That is about the nicest thing anyone has ever done for me. I am very touched."

She kissed me tenderly on the cheek.

"I wish the world could see your tattoo but I know that we must keep it concealed—at least until I'm free."

Tacitly drawn into a single thought, we joined hands. Then we left Urdanur's apartment and went downstairs to mine—where we could have complete privacy. I wanted to show her THE KAMA SUTRA.

And then make love.

*　　　*　　　*

Turan entered the PX in the JAMMAT Building with his usual self-assurance. Several females in the foyer favorably glanced at him and although he was aware of the attention, he chose to ignore it. He was in too much of a hurry.

Turan was spotted by Nurtan who immediately walked over to him.

"Thank you for coming," she said.

"I got your message! And my secretary said it was a big emergency! What is the problem?"

They both spoke in Turkish.

"We can not talk here," she said.

191

Nurtan led him to a far corner of the store where they could have privacy.

"Now tell me what was so urgent!" he demanded.

"I have not seen Yuksel for two weeks. And no one has seen or heard from her. I am very frightened that something bad may have happened to her and I was wondering if you saw her?"

Turan looked surprised.

"I returned only last night from a fourteen day holiday in Istanbul with my family! I have been very busy this morning! But obviously I can not help you!"

He made a gesture to move away. Nurtan stopped him.

"There is something more terrible. Yuksel was to go on a trip to Madam Sivas' old village and was to leave from my Aunt's house on the morning of July twenty-second. But she never showed up."

Turan's facial expression began to change and he seemed concerned. He knew Yuksel's deep feelings for Madam Sivas. Only something bad could stop Yuksel from keeping a promise to the Old Woman.

"Did you or Madam Sivas go to Yuksel's apartment?"

"We both did. Separately and together. Several times. But no one seems to be there."

Turan was momentarily silent.

"Did you go to the Istanbul Palace where she works?"

"Every day for the past two weeks but the manager said she has not been there."

Turan could see tears forming in Nurtan's eyes. The emotional pain showing on her face was profound.

"There is one more thing," added Nurtan, almost in a whisper. "Madam Sivas had a vision in which she saw somebody kill Yuksel."

The words startled Turan and a strange uneasiness settled in his gut. The last time he had seen Yuksel was when he was making the raid on drug peddlers. She was crossing Ataturk Boulevard and being followed by that American Ty Manners.

At that point, Turan had suspected the two of having an affair. He had called Yuksel that night but did not get an answer. And the next day, he left to go on vacation with his family.

While Turan sensed that Madam Sivas did not care for him, he nevertheless had great respect for the Old Woman. He had personally known several venerable people who claimed that while Madam Sivas gave her visions or predictions sparingly, she was extremely accurate.

By now, Nurtan's tears were profuse.

"All right," Turan said, almost tenderly; "I will see what I can find out! And I will call you later or tomorrow!"

Nurtan was too choked up to speak so she stretched upward and kissed Turan on his cheek. Her action both surprised and touched him.

Yuksel was lucky to have such a good friend as Nurtan, he thought.

Turan walked away with a firm determination to unravel the mystery of Yuksel's strange disappearance.

*   *   *

When Kyle and I entered Intim's, only a juke box was playing as my entertainer friends were off for the evening.

"Ah'm standin' in need of some *raki*," announced Kyle.

"What's this bit of news you seem so anxious to tell me?" I asked, after the waiter deposited our drinks.

"You gotta promise me ya'll keep it a secret," he said solemnly.

"Of course," I affirmed.

"Ah askt fer a transfer."

"To where? And when?"

"Any place."

"But why?"

"Ta get away from Nurtan."

"I don't understand. You married her. Didn't you plan to bring her back to the States?"

"No way, Man. Ah like her and she's allota fun but not enough to take home. Ah'm too young to be chained to a wife."

This was a side of Kyle I had never before seen. It was like being with a complete stranger.

The waiter passed by and I ordered more *raki*. This discussion was calling for heavy drinking.

"Then this marriage was just a legal shack-up?" My voice said.

Kyle was not smiling.

"She talked me inta it. She wanted it real bad so Ah wen' along with it."

My brain could not believe the message it was receiving.

"Are you going to ask her for a divorce?"

"No need. It was only a Turk wedding. Don't count afta Ah leave here."

The waiter left another round of drinks.

"What does Nurtan say about this?"

In the long pause before he answered, I perceived his response.

"Ain't told her yet."

I tried to attribute Kyle's confession to the *raki* but my mind regrettably knew it was otherwise.

"When do you plan to tell her, and how do you think she will react?"

"Ah don' know. Ah gotta do some more thinkin'."

"What did you tell Colonel Myrons when you asked for the transfer?"

"That Nurtan is buggin' me to bring her back to the States and that I don' wanna. Since they don' like us to marry foreigners anyway, he agreed wit me. Said he'd arrange a transfer as soon as possible. Probably next month."

At certain times in my life, I have wished it were possible to turn back the clock so that a particular event would not come to fruition. This was one of those times. My heart pained for Nurtan. I knew how much she loved Kyle and this unfortunate circumstance would surely be a blow. My heart was also sad because the Kyle I admired so much was suddenly a person whom I did not actually know.

I desperately searched for something to say but nothing was forthcoming.

Presently, Kyle finished his drink and stood up to leave.

"Ah gotta go now," he announced. "Nurtan is awaitin' on me. And Ah can't have her gettin' mad."

He smiled and I felt myself having to strain to return the gesture.

"Ah borrowed a sedan from the Motor Pool ta take her fer a ride. So she don' expect anythin' is wrong."

In the next instant, he was gone.

An evolution seemed to be taking place. Friday and I were being pushed apart, Yuksel had mysteriously disappeared, and Nurtan was about to have her heart broken.

I had thought of my days in Ankara to be like champagne because that wine tastes delicious, sparkles, bubbles, looks pretty, and when you drink a lot of it everything feels great. Also, it makes you happy, tickles your nose, and celebrates wonderful times.

But what was suddenly happening to my champagne days?

CHAPTER 21 –
"A Stranger In Town"

Drew handed me a beer then returned to the easy chair. Sitting on the other side of the coffee table was his tacit way of showing he intended to keep the promise of no solicitation. I respected that. And being alone with him was not threatening. Only guys who are insecure about their own sexuality are fearful in the presence of a homosexual.

Because Friday was busy, I had been wondering what to do with the evening when Drew had called to invite me over. He had just received the cast recording of a new Broadway play called BELLS ARE RINGING with Judy Holliday.

"What do you think of this music?"

"Sounds great. I'd like to see the show."

Drew abruptly changed the subject.

"Did you know that Yuksel is still missing?"

"Urdanur told me. She said that Madam Sivas is very upset."

"Well, Turan has launched an unprecedented investigation. Earlier this evening, I saw a light on in Yuksel's apartment, so I went over there hoping she had returned. Instead, I found Turan searching for clues."

"I bet Turan was his natural sweet self."

"At first, yes. But as we talked, he seemed different. Surprisingly, he said that it had taken Yuksel's disappearance to make him realize how much he loved her. And that if she were safe, he planned to treat her better. Then he asked if I had any information."

"Do you?"

"Only that I saw Ty Manners walking away from Yuksel's apartment on July 21st, and that I haven't seen any signs of occupation in her place since then."

This news came as a shock to me. Out loud I wondered if Yuksel were having an affair with Manners.

"I don't think so," replied Drew. "It's more likely that Manners was bugging her. You remember that scene at the wedding party when Manners was dancing too close to Yuksel."

The picture was indeed very clear in my mind. It was yet another example of Ty's talent for ruining things and for being a disagreeable prick.

"Does Turan connect Manners with Yuksel's absence?"

"He didn't exactly say so. But he did ask me to write a statement telling what I had seen."

Trying to raise the depressing level of the conversation, I told Drew about my visit to Colonel Myron's office earlier in the day. How Myrons had sent for me to ask about the trip and whether I had learned my lesson to stay away from Friday. The lie to Myrons that I was back to normal had made him very happy.

When I finished speaking, Drew laughed, then repeated a previous offer.

"If you ever need anything—and I mean anything—please ask for my help. I know a very influential person here."

*   *   *

At this point in his married life, Colonel Hank Myrons was running out of songs. Whenever his wife went into a filibuster, he blocked her out by humming melodies in his head.

This morning was no exception to the rule as they ate breakfast in the dining room of their spacious apartment.

In the middle of Hank's mental rendition of "Star Dust," he heard Sandy ask to be excused as some friends were waiting. She kissed both parents and was gone.

"Now that Sandy has left the apartment," began his wife; "I want to talk to you about something."

"What is it now t-that you don't like?" asked Hank, sarcastically.

Penelope ignored his tone and continued.

"I want to know where you go in the evenings."

Over the past year, Hank had discovered a slow change taking place within himself. The impetus for this feeling stemmed from several factors. First was the realization that his operation of JAMMAT was successful—giving him a new confidence. Next came the re-discovery of something he had thought he lost forever. And the best was Urdanur Besni's courage in standing-up-to his wife; some of that had mysteriously rubbed off on him.

"Well, where do you go every night?" she asked, again.

"It is not every night," he corrected. "I go out m-maybe t-two or t-three t-times a week. And it's none of your business!"

Penelope's face glowed with surprise but she did not stop babbling.

"You have never spoken to me so harshly before. What is the matter with you of late?"

"M-maybe I have come t-to m-my s-senses. I am t-tired of your reign of t-terror. Your demanding ways. Your idiosyncrasies."

She became defensive.

"Everyone has those."

"Not like Penelope M-Myrons! A car t-taking you t-to t-the public execution was not remotely necessary since we live only t-three blocks away from t-there."

"Is that all?"

"No, it is not all. Your fucking interference in everything is bizarre. Not wanting t-the m-men t-to wear dungarees t-to work, badgering Urdanur Besni, t-telling m-me stories about Corey Brotano and M-Mrs. Lebal."

"That is true," she protested. "You know that. Why else would you have sent him out of town. He practically admitted it to you."

"Perhaps s-so but it was s-still none of your damn business!"

Her voice rose with importance.

"Whatever effects military decorum in this area is my business. It reflects on me because you are my husband."

"Not for long!" he snapped.

"What are you saying?"

He stood up with such force that his chair fell backward to the floor.

"When we get back t-to t-the S-States in s-six m-months, I'm getting a divorce!"

Hank threw his napkin onto the plate of unfinished eggs and stormed out of the room, and the apartment. For the first time, Penelope sat with her mouth open and no sounds coming out.

*　　　*　　　*

There were two phone calls involving Urdanur. The first was mid-morning. The second came shortly after 1800 hours. The former was inviting; the latter was tragic.

When the initial call came I was sleeping and drowsily picked up the receiver while squinting at the alarm clock that read 1100 hours.

197

Urdanur's voice brought a smile to my face even though I was suffering from a bit of a hangover.

"Young people are entitled to get drunk and to party frequently," laughed Urdanur. "It is part of their culture. And speaking of culture, I am taking the afternoon off to do some painting. Thought you might like to join me."

Though difficult to refuse Urdanur, I had plans to see Friday later on. Since there was so little time left before Winston returned from Diyarbakir, I did not want to miss any opportunity. I graciously declined.

"Maybe you shouldn't go today," I suggested. "Yesterday's weather report predicted thunderstorms."

"The weatherman is often incorrect. The day looks too beautiful. Anyway," she exclaimed; "what could possibly happen to me? The most is that I would get a little damp."

"In that case," I chuckled; "go paint the view from my hill, for me."

"Why not?" replied Urdanur, in her jovial way.

"Call Gobasi; he'll show you where it is. And do a good job."

"I will call you later," concluded Urdanur.

*   *   *

It was easy for any onlooker to see the happiness that flowed from Nurtan's eyes as she and Kyle browsed through the Bazaar. Her gait was slow and casual but it had a spring about it. Yet Kyle was too deep in his own self to even notice.

"Ah like that thing over there," he announced, stopping at one of the stands. "Wha' is it?"

"It is saddle for camel," explained the Merchant.

"Ah see it as a good hassock."

"I buy for you," said Nurtan.

Kyle perfunctorily protested, then gave in. *What the hell*, he reasoned to himself. *If the chick wanted to spend the money, then let her.*

"Let's git somethin' to drink," he suggested, after Nurtan made the purchase.

They sat at a table under the shade of a small multi-colored umbrella—in the café area. Kyle asked for *raki* but only soft drinks were available. To ease his craving, he promised himself to drop off Nurtan at home then find an excuse to go out. He'd call Ty and they could go drinking. Maybe even to the Compound.Since Martial Law and the curfew had been lifted and Turkey was no longer fighting with Greece, the Compound would not be closing early.

Kyle remained silent after the waiter left their soft drinks but Nurtan was bursting to talk.

"You believe God?" she asked.

"Ah haven't thought much about it. –Do ya?"

"Allah very good," she continued. "He give me gift again."

As Kyle digested her simple words, a strange feeling seemed to grip him. A sense that she was about to say something he would not care to hear.

"Please. I have baby, again."

"Is thata question?" he asked.

"No," smiled Nurtan. "It is fact. I am with child again."

––––––

Upon entering Gobasi's taxi, Urdanur immediately informed him where she wanted to go.

She spoke in Turkish.

Gobasi was delighted to meet a friend of Corey and spoke at great lengths extolling the fine qualities of their mutual comrade.

"What did Corey tell you about Samsun?" inquired Gobasi.

"Only that you and he had a good time," lied Urdanur.

The rest of the journey was spent in silence.

When they arrived at the destination, Gobasi helped Urdanur out of the car. He carried her easel, a box with painting instruments, a backless folding chair, and a small portable radio. Taking the lead, Gobasi guided Urdanur from the main road, into and through a dense wooded area, to a clearing on a sloping hill.

"Do you want me to wait for you?" he asked.

"No, thank you, my Friend. But please return in two hours, if you will. And come to this spot because I can not find my way through that brush without you. It is like a maze to me."

Gobasi smiled in confirmation and was on his way.

Alone in the midst of the natural beauty of the countryside, Urdanur surveyed her surroundings with heartfelt appreciation of the splendor. This locale was just as Corey had described it. Actually, the area was even more enchanting.

Urdanur set up the equipment and began to paint.

An hour later she had accomplished a large portion of her goal. Only when she stopped to take a brief rest came the realization that the sun was fast disappearing and there was a crackling sound on the radio.

Before she had time to think, raindrops started falling on her. At first, their touch was soft and refreshing. All too soon, they became heavier and more intense. Thunder sounded frighteningly close.

Now in a panic of having her painting ruined, Urdanur hastily gathered her materials and ran into the wooded area that Gobasi had led her through. She could not find the same path which he had used but at least she would be partially sheltered from the unexpected torrent.

Glancing at her watch, she realized there was still another hour before Gobasi was to return. In the next instant, when lightning illuminated the shrubbery in which Urdanur stood, she screamed terrifyingly and a look of horror engulfed her face.

Then she fainted.

––––––

A taxi stopped in front of the Yozgat Hotel in the Ulus section of Ankara. A young man in the back seat raised his voice so as to be heard over the din of the heavy rain that was pounding the roof of the cab.

He spoke in Turkish.

"Are you certain this is the only Yozgat Hotel in town?"

"Yes, *Efendi*," answered the driver, a bit annoyed.

The young Man paid the fare and ignored the dissatisfied expression on the Driver's face regarding the meager tip. Then he grabbed his duffel bag and ran through the downpour and into the hotel lobby.

"How long will you be staying, *Efendi*?" asked the reception Clerk.

"It all depends. Probably a week."

"Are you here on business, *Efendi* ?"

"Of a sort," replied the Guest–his cold hazel eyes giving off a mysterious look.

"Where are you from, *Efendi*?" asked the Clerk, while noting that the Guest's mustache was dripping rain on the registry book.

"Waco, Texas."

The Clerk was amazed.

"Your Turkish is perfect. I was sure you were a countryman."

The Visitor smiled with self-satisfaction. *Knowing a native lingo often proved to be profitable. You could usually get things at a cheaper price.*

The young Man inquired about nearby restaurants and the Clerk made some suggestions.

The Guest thanked the Receptionist and went up to his room. He stripped off his wet garments and sat on the edge of the bed. Even his naked body was wet. He rummaged through his duffel bag, found a woman's compact and laid it on the night stand. He gingerly opened it until both halves were flat. He took some white powder from the right side and placed it on the mirror–arranging the substance into several thin parallel lines. He sniffed the substance then lay on the bed with a happy glow upon his face.

"I'll rest for now," he said aloud. "Tomorrow will be time enough for me to start my mission."

*   *   *

A short time after Friday had left my apartment to go pick up her kids at school and take them out to dinner, the heavens opened up and rain fell like a waterfall. Immediately, I thought of Urdanur and hoped she had left the hill before the downpour.

So when the telephone rang, I assumed it was she.

"Am I speaking to Corey Brotano?" asked a strong male voice.

"Yes "

"This is Turan Karapinar!"

"Is there a problem, Turan?"

"I am afraid there is! I am calling in regard to Urdanur Besni! I know from Nurtan's wedding that Miss Besni is a friend of yours!"

My heart began to race and quickly collided with an horrendous fear. *Something terrible must have happened to Urdanur. Why else would Turan call me? Don't the police always deliver tragic news?*

"Is she all right?" I virtually shouted.

"I am afraid she is..."

The phone went dead.

Complete panic engulfed me. I didn't know which way to move. Should I phone the telephone operator for the number of the police station? Should I wait for him to call me back? Was the phone permanently out of order?

Only sixty seconds passed before the phone sounded again, but it seemed like an eternity. I had the receiver off the hook the instant the ringing began.

"Turan?" I yelled.

"Yes. Sorry, we were disconnected!"

"What about Urdanur?"

"I was about to say that she is indisposed right now! She was greatly upset and we have been trying to calm her for the past two hours!"

Thank God that Urdanur is all right, was my first thought.

"A taxi driver named Gobasi found her, and then telephoned us! He suggested we contact you!"

"What happened?" I insisted.

"Miss Besni was painting when a thunderstorm occurred! She ran into a wooded area and stumbled over a dead body!"

I could imagine the state that Urdanur was in. She may have often given the outward appearance of someone who was stern and tough, but underneath it all, she was as delicate as a grasshopper.

"The body was slightly decomposed!" continued Turan, his voice taking on an almost mellow tone, one I would never have associated with him.

"Upon further investigation, we discovered that the deceased was... ." He paused.

When he resumed, his tone was heavily burdened with sorrow—the commanding sound of his voice no longer present.

"The body is that of Yuksel."

CHAPTER 22 –
"MasAllah"

As Friday and I helped Urdanur into bed we tried being cheerful in hopes of diverting her mind from what she had earlier witnessed in the woods. But she was in a near state of shock and, though appreciative, only managed a weak smile. So we quietly sat by her side.

When Urdanur finally drifted off, Friday and I quietly left the room and went on the back terrace for a while to be on hand in case our hostess suddenly awakened with fright.

"Life is so strange," I exclaimed. "One never knows what is going to happen from one moment to the next. What can be the purpose of Yuksel's death?"

"There's probably no good explanation. At least, not now. Maybe after _we_ die, the answer will be clear. But it seems that some folks suffer more than others."

"Personally, I have been extremely blessed. Yet sometimes I do not feel a part of everything. It's as if I am watching a movie on a super-large screen and people, both familiar and foreign, are acting out a story for my benefit alone. The world goes on and I'm standing outside."

"That philosophy shit gives me a headache," laughed Friday. **"I never have understood Descartes' 'I think, therefore, I am.' –Let's please change the subject."**

My mood was hard to shake.

"When is Winston coming back?"

"Perhaps by the end of the week."

"How soon after that will you be going?"

"August 30th."

The faint sound of Turkish music drifted up from a neighbor's opened window. Its exotic melody and intriguingly haunting arrangement brought another dimension to these dwindling moments together.

Friday broke a long, pensive silence.

"I would rather fly directly home but the kids are anxious to see Istanbul. Sandy filled their heads with it and I hate to disappoint them. Who knows if we'll ever come back to Turkey?

"I'm going to buy the train tickets in a few days. I'll keep them in Urdanur's care so Winston won't find them."

"When do you plan to tell him?"

"A few days before I leave. –How much longer do you have to serve here?"

"Approximately a year."

I knew the months would be very long but refrained from saying it out loud. The actual expression of a thought makes it seem even worse than it actually is.

Friday asked if I had ever finished writing the words to our song.

"No," was my reply; "but I promise to have them done by the time we meet in New York."

"And I promise you a surprise within the next few days," she smiled, warmly.

*   *   *

Turan's promise to Inspector Burdur was being upheld. He was controlling his temper so well that the results amazed even him. The news of being the next Chief Inspector had more of a profound impact than he had anticipated.

The confirmation of Yuksel's death was proving to be a test of Turan's reformed personality–especially since he now realized that he had actually loved her. And while it was obviously too late to tell her, he could at least find Yuksel's murderer and bring the *essekogluessek* to justice–in one way or another.

Turan began the investigation by calling on Madam Sivas. He wanted to give her the tragic news before she read it in the newspaper.

The good Woman did not smile when she opened the door and saw Turan standing there. Intuitively, she knew why he had come and silently ushered him into the parlor.

"There is no easy way to say this!" Turan began; "but your vision about Yuksel was right! From what we can determine, she has been dead for approximately three weeks! Her body was... ."

Madam Sivas held up her hand in a gesture for the Visitor to say no more.

204

She lowered her head as tears profusely flowed. Her heart was shattered and now filled with hatred for the man responsible.

Turan remained patiently silent.

Eventually, the Old Woman collected herself and looked into the eyes of the Inspector. Something about his countenance was different. She could not pinpoint it but Turan did not seem like his usual self. Even his voice was strangely unfamiliar.

"Is there anything you can tell that might help me find the murderer? Even the simplest thing!"

This was one situation that Madam Sivas did not intend to handle diplomatically.

"I know of three men whom Yuksel feared."

"Who are they?"

"The first is you, Inspector."

The former Turan would have flown into a rage. The new Man fought his demons.

"What do you mean, Woman?"

Madam Sivas related every story that Yuksel had ever told about Turan. All his jealous moments. His abusive sexual acts. Even the fear that he would kill her if she ever tried to leave him.

When the Old Woman finished, she expected Turan to be outraged. Instead, she was amazed to see tears in his eyes.

"Will _you_ forgive me on behalf of Yuksel? I did not know how much I loved her until I discovered she was dead."

"That is no excuse."

"You are correct, *Efendi*! But I have never known how to love somebody or how to show it! As a child I was beaten a lot and that produced an adverse effect! I swear to you, Madam Sivas; I did not kill her! Nor would I ever have! It was just my jealous tongue!"

There were several minutes of silence before Turan continued.

"Who are the other men that Yuksel feared?"

Madam Sivas told the Inspector of the two times that Kyle had raped Yuksel and how Yuksel had injured him during his last unsolicited visit. And of his actual threat to kill her.

Then she explained how Ty had harassed Yuksel in the Bazaar and she had scratched him on his face. And that he also had promised to kill her.

The Old Woman's information—coupled with Drew's statement of seeing Manners walking away from Yuksel's apartment on the established date and time of the killing—convinced Turan that Ty was the prime suspect.

As for Kyle raping Yuksel, Turan knew it would be legally difficult to verify. Without some sort of proof, he needed to find another charge before he could arrest the preying American. That was going to take a little time.

After leaving Madam Sivas' home, Turan walked to his sedan and got down on one knee. His self-control had reached the limit. Rapidly moving his fists, he pounded the car's door with great ferociousness and anger. When he finally finished, there were huge dents in the door, and his knuckles were bleeding.

A telephone call, a purchase, a bacchanalia, and an indiscretion comprised the essence of Winston's day.

In the city of Diyarbakir—located in Kurdistan, the region of Turkey inhabited by the Kurds—Winston sat in the lobby of a small hotel. Wearily, he finished writing his report to Colonel Myrons concerning the Motor Pool operations of the American contingency in that locale. He had spent the past week and a half plowing through records, checking supplies, examining equipment, and holding mini-conferences with the Commander of the site.

Satisfied that everything was in order—and that he had finished the work sooner than expected—he was ready to go back to Ankara. The only thing keeping him in Diyarbakir was transportation. The next flight out would not be till the following afternoon.

Winston signed the report and placed it in an envelope. Then he looked at his watch. Sixteen hundred hours. He'd give Friday a buzz to let her know he was coming home earlier than planned.

The hotel desk Clerk placed the call.

"Hello," said a young Girl's voice.

"hi, sweetheart, this is father."

"Hi, Daddy, when are you coming home?"

"i'll be back tomorrow. —let me talk to mother."

"She's not here, Daddy."

Winston was surprised. *Friday never left the children unattended.*

"are you sure, sweetheart?"

"Yes, Daddy. I think she's downstairs with Corey."

Winston's mind flew into a rage. Was Friday crazy? Hadn't he warned her about seeing that boy! This was the last straw. When he returned to Ankara, he would deal with both of them.

"Are you still there, Daddy?"

"yes, sweetheart. just tell your mother that i called."

After the little Girl placed the receiver in its cradle, she walked to the kitchen to get a glass of soda.

"We're going to eat supper soon so don't have any snacks now," came Friday's voice from the back porch.

"Mother," said the little Girl, very surprised. "I didn't know you were home."

The phone call left Winston seething. *They would not get away with this,* he told himself. He would see to it. He would settle this matter once and for all. At any cost.

In front of the hotel, Winston hailed a taxi which took him to the city's business district. He surveyed the myriad of shops until he found a weapons emporium. Though he already had a firearm back in Ankara, he decided to buy one that was not registered with the Army. Then, after he shot the both of them, the gun could be disposed of. And even if it were eventually found, it could not be traced to him.

Carrying the weapon in a paper bag, Winston walked out into the diminishing sun. Having made the purchase, he was a bit less tense. But still not calm enough to completely quench his anger.

With nowhere to go—and an abundance of time to fill—he strolled down a narrow cobble-stoned street and presently found a cocktail lounge.

He ordered a scotch and water and surveyed his surroundings. Almost immediately, he recognized a young American who had been in the Motor Pool the day before.

Winston walked up to the Man and started a conversation. They talked of varied topics and reciprocated in buying drinks until they were both inebriated.

"Hey, Buddy," said Winston's new acquaintance. "Let's go to the Compound. It's after 1800 hours. They're open now. Get it? The girls are open!"

Winston missed the joke but laughed nevertheless.

"i'm afraid not, Steve. i'm a married man and have never cheated on my wife. although she has done so on me."

"Me, too. I'm married but she ain't here right now. Anyways, it's okay for guys to casually explore other pastures. It ain't like we're in love. It's only just getting your rocks off."

Winston declined again.

"Look," continued Steve; "if she was unfaithful to you, then it's pay back time. You might even like it a lot."

After imbibing two more drinks, Winston decided to liberate himself.

"why the hell not?" he reasoned; "let's go."

Winston was feeling no pain as he and Steve entered the Compound. The scotch had done a good job. It had even made him forget his anger with Friday and Corey. For the first time in a long while he was in a state of euphoria. He had to get drunk more often, he smiled to himself. *It was good medicine.*

It did not take Winston very long to find an attractive woman.

When he and the prostitute were in her small room, he found himself in a new world. The woman serviced him in ways that Friday had never done. And he enjoyed every delicious minute of it.

The walk from the Compound back to his hotel helped to make Winston sober again. He still carried the paper bag with the gun in it but somehow it suddenly became less important. Maybe he would give Friday and Corey one more chance to stay away from each other.

This unexpected flight of infidelity had tempered his anger. It was the only time during their marriage that Winston had ever been unfaithful. But it was not actually his fault. If she hadn't been down in Corey's apartment when he phoned earlier in the day, he would never have gotten so drunk and slept with another woman.

At any rate, he told himself, he still had time to make the decision: to kill or not to kill.

––––––

The Young Man who had checked into the Yozgat Hotel left his room and went down to the lobby. After asking the desk Clerk a question, the Guest left the establishment and followed the Clerk's directions.

At the Bazaar, it took him fewer than twenty minutes to identify the cocaine merchant and to buy an abundance of the substance. After that, he hailed a taxi and told the driver to take him to the JAMMAT Building.

Once there, he stationed himself at a spot not far from the entrance. He leaned against the wall and surreptitiously sniffed some of his purchase. He glanced at his watch which read 1600 hours.

Then he lit a cigarette and waited for his prey.

In a matter of minutes, Corey Brotano exited the building and stopped to speak with a woman wearing a silly-looking hat.

The Young Man told himself that he would be patient for the time being.

But his tete-a-tete with Brotano would be very soon.

* * *

After decoding my last message of the day, I finished the necessary paper work and filing. It was 1600 hours on the nose.

I bid farewell to the guy who was my relief and headed down the long hallway and up several stairways to the main floor of the JAMMAT Building.

As I walked, my mind rehashed Urdanur's horrendous experience.

When she had run into the brush to escape the heavy rain, Urdanur screamed and fainted after discovering the body. Upon regaining consciousness, she found herself in the taxi of Gobasi who had come back earlier when he realized the tempest was imminent.

They decided to go to the police station where they were questioned. When Turan was summoned, Gobasi took the Inspector and a group of officers to the crime scene to retrieve the corpse. Upon their return to the police station, a forensics team examined the body and identified it as Yuksel.

That was when Turan had called me.

Besides the confirmation of Yuksel's death, the thing that prayed on my mind was that her body had been found on our hill. Did someone pick that spot on purpose or was it just a weird coincidence? Was this an omen that Friday and I might also perish soon: she ironically from breast cancer; me by Winston's gun?

We had been on a veritable honeymoon since Winston left town. Everyday we found time to make love because we knew it would be a very long while till we met in the States.

I exited the building and had the misfortune of encountering Mrs. Myrons who actually addressed me.

"Good afternoon, Airman Brotano," she said, with an expression on her face that vaguely resembled a smile.

Apparently she made it a practice to greet the people whose reputations she sullied.

"How convenient," she announced. "I wanted to talk to you."

She explained that on August 30th, there was going to be a huge dance and party to honor Victory Day which is a tribute to the memory of warriors who died in the 1922 Battle of Dumlupinar—the final struggle for Turkish independence.

"We are having the party to show our appreciation to the Turkish politicians, and absolutely everyone will be there," she exclaimed.

Impatiently, I waited for the point of the story.

It came within the next several seconds and I had to control myself from bombarding the Bitch with a tirade of curses.

Mrs. Myrons announced that all the sixteen American female teenagers of officers were attending the dance with escorts. One unfortunate girl did not have a date.

I knew the girl she spoke of. A quiet and exceedingly plain person, Vashti was awkward, without personality and bordering on homeliness.

With an audacity beyond the realm of reason, Mrs. Myrons wanted me to take Vashti to the dance. Even offered to provide a tux and transportation.

"But this conversation mus*t* be kep*t* a secre*t*," she added.

The Gossip who didn't know the meaning of the word was asking me to be discrete.

It was a case of reality being stranger than make-believe. After virtually ruining the lives of the Lebals and myself, generously marking us as immoral and lower class, and being appalled at our "inappropriate behavior," this person was asking me for a favor. Primarily because she wanted to be a heroine in the eyes of Vashti's mother.

Suddenly I was good enough to be associated with.

When I graciously declined stating prior plans, her reaction was typical.

"You shoul*d* have sai*d* tha*t* before I starte*d*," she snapped, abruptly turning and briskly walking away.

Upon returning home, I found a tiny box wrapped in shiny gold paper lying in front of my door. I quickly tore off the wrapping and opened the box to find an 18 karat gold dog tag with the word "*Masallah*" inscribed thereon. Attached to it was a most exquisite gold neck chain.

Along with the gift came a note:

> *Please wear this dog tag over your heart as a constant reminder*
> *And know that I am always with you.*
> *Love, Friday*

I have never received a lovelier present.

CHAPTER 23 –

"Never Say Goodbye"

Having poured a cup of coffee, I decided to lie on a blanket in the backyard and catch some rays. With a portable radio at my side, I listened to an American army station broadcasting from Germany.

As it played "Friendly Persuasion," a shadow hovered over me. Sitting upright, I was happy to see Friday–even though the expression on her face predicted less than joyful tidings.

"You look upset," I said; "Is something wrong?"

"Not seriously," she replied, calmly. **"But Winston is coming home today. He's probably on his way. He called earlier and said he'd be back by noon."**

As I rose, my first instinct was to enfold her. But someone might be watching.

"Time is certainly a devious demon," I uttered. "When things are going poorly, it drags. At fun times, it flies like sound."

"I don't know when we'll see each other again. Now we must be extremely cautious."

"What will we do?"

"Stay away from each other. We dare not take any chances. Perhaps I can sneak a phone call now and then but anything else is out of the question."

"Should I say goodbye now?"

"Never say goodbye," she lovingly admonished; **"it's too final. Just say, so long or I'll see you soon. –I only say goodbye to people who are not important to me."**

Without another word, she was gone.

I didn't even get a chance to thank her for the gold dog tag.

*　　　*　　　*

In separate vehicles, Winston and Turan arrived at the Motor Pool behind the JAMMAT Building at approximately the same moment.

Forty-five minutes earlier, Winston's flight from Diyarbakir had landed. Waiting for him was the Air Force sedan bearing the license plates AF 136–being driven by Ty Manners.

Of all the men to send, thought Winston, *did the sergeant have to pick Manners?*

Avoiding conversation with the Airman, Winston lapsed into thought and by the time they arrived at the Motor Pool, he had reached a decision. With a modicum of guilt for his own indiscretion in Diyarbakir, he would postpone any harsh action against Friday and Corey, for the present. To be patient a little while longer was the prudent thing to do. *Give them more rope to hang themselves.* But the next time he saw them together it would prove fatal.

When Winston got out of the sedan, he was greeted by Inspector Turan Karapinar, leaning against his own vehicle.

"Good afternoon, Captain!"

Winston returned the amenity as Turan approached.

Ty immediately began to walk away but halted at the sound of Turan's booming command.

"You are to remain Manners!" Turan ordered.

Ty stopped and faced the two men. Turan then addressed Winston.

"I am here on important police business! We suspect this American" –he pointed to Ty– "of killing Yuksel Ispir!"

Ty gasped in what appeared to be genuine shock while Winston–although taken off guard–was less amazed. Nothing bad that Ty was accused of could come as a surprise.

Manners started to protest but was ignored as Turan continued to speak.

"The head of the Secret Police–Inspector Burdur–and myself have agreed that because of the seriousness of this matter, we want to cooperate with the American government! Although it is our right to arrest Manners, we do not wish to cause any unnecessary international difficulties with our American friends!"

"i am this man's immediate supervisor," explained Winston. "i appreciate your diplomacy and I am also willing to cooperate but why do you suspect manners?"

"We have a witness who saw him outside Miss Ispir's apartment at 1700 hours! The established time of her death!"

"What witness?" shouted Ty, indignantly.

Before answering, Turan quickly reminded himself of his promise to Inspector Burdur to remain calm.

"My witness has promised to testify in court!"

While Turan spoke, Winston looked at Ty and marveled at the boy's composure under such circumstances. If he were guilty, thought Winston, he was one hell of an actor. On the other hand, the boy did have a calculating nature. He had seemed to enjoy killing the wolf.

"I was at the Compound around 1700 hours," Ty exclaimed, a smug look suddenly appearing on his face. "You can ask Fatima. I was with her."

"You were seen leaving Yuksel's apartment at that time! You were wearing a jersey with the words 'Portland, Maine' printed on the back of it!"

"That's not so," insisted Ty, the smug expression beginning to fade. "Besides, I don't even have that jersey. I loaned it to Kyle and he wears it a lot. Maybe your witness saw Kyle there. People are always mixing us up."

To that the Inspector harshly retorted.

"I, myself, saw you following Yuksel at 1500 hours when I was about to arrest a drug dealer! You were wearing a white jersey."

Ty looked worried. "It ain't the same one. I got a couple of jerseys. But I only got one that says 'Portland, Maine' on the back."

Turan lit a cigarette to quiet his nerves. He was becoming exasperated but determined to maintain his composure.

"And why were you following Yuksel?" asked Turan.

Suddenly, Ty became silent. If he told the truth, there would be trouble. He clearly remembered what had happened when Turan had arrested him. Admitting to stalking Turan's girlfriend could be fatal.

"I wasn't following her. I just happened to be walking the same way."

"And your walk took you to her apartment?"

"No," Ty continued; "I didn't go down her street."

"It appears that you were in her apartment for two hours. I saw you at 1500; my witness at 1700!"

"He's a liar!" protested Ty.

"How do you know my witness is male?"

Ty opened his mouth to speak, but Winston intervened.

"excuse me, inspector karapinar, but are you going to arrest him now?"

"Not at this time, Captain Lebal! I feel that there is enough proof but, to be perfectly fair, his alleged alibi should be checked. If it does not hold up, then I will return!"

"what will happen then?" asked Winston.

"He will stand trial in a civil Turkish court! But he will be permitted American representation! If he is found innocent, apologies will be made! If guilty, he will be imprisoned or executed!"

"thank you," said Winston. "once again, i commend you on your diplomacy. if you will excuse us now, i would like to talk with this man in my office."

Turan nodded in agreement and watched the two Americans walk away. He then turned to enter his vehicle when he noticed Kyle staring at him from a garage about a hundred feet away. Realizing that Turan had spotted him, Kyle disappeared behind one of the trucks.

A passion suddenly gripped Turan. He began to walk in Kyle's direction. Just as quickly, reason replaced anger and Turan forced himself to retreat. He would do as originally planned. He first needed to find another charge on which to arrest Kyle since there was no concrete proof of rape.

*   *   *

Pegu phoned me at home and asked if I were busy. Begging her pardon I explained that I was getting ready to report for the midnight shift and would get off at 0800 hours.

"Fine, good," she replied. "We will pick you up in front of JAMMAT at 0805 hours and take you to breakfast."

Always on time, the familiar taxi pulled up at the precise moment. Pegu jumped out of the front seat, rushed over, and gave me a huge hug and kiss on the cheek. I hadn't seen her since our return to Ankara.

In the taxi, she sat in the back with me and excitedly talked. She and Gobasi had sold his mother's house and were leaving for Istanbul on August 30th. Gobasi had a distant cousin there who could get papers for her. They planned to be married and wanted me to be best man. They even offered to pay my train fare.

How ironic it was, I thought to myself. That was the same date that Friday and her children were leaving for Istanbul. It seemed as if fate were giving us a opportunity to be together one very last time before she went back to the States.

I thanked Pegu and Gobasi for the honor and told them I wouldn't miss it for the world.

*   *   *

When Winston entered their apartment, Friday was reading on the back porch. The children saw him first and ran to find out what their father had brought them.

The little Boy immediately retreated to his room to play with the truck.

The Girl held the Turkish doll, but lingered–as if something were troubling her.

"what's the matter, sweetheart?"

"I'm sorry, Daddy."

"for what?"

"I lied to you yesterday on the phone. I told you Mommy wasn't here but she was. I didn't know she was on the back porch reading."

"did mother tell you to say this?"

The little Girl was genuinely surprised. "No. I didn't even tell her about it."

Winston thanked his daughter and sent her off to play. Delighted at the Girl's confession, Winston realized there was no longer a need to confront his wife.

Friday closed the book and looked up when Winston entered.

"Did you have a good trip?"

"fine," he answered. "what has been happening here?"

"I went to the doctor about the lump on my breast."

Winston became sincerely concerned and sat in a chair opposite her.

"what did the physician say?"

"He wants me to go back to the States to have it checked out. They are not equipped here to handle such cases."

Winston was quiet for a long while before he finally spoke again.

"when?"

With a bit of trepidation, Friday replied that the doctor suggested she leave as soon as possible, so she had started making arrangements to leave on August 30th.

"Because the children are fired up about seeing Istanbul, I thought we might spend a few days there before our trip home. If I should need an operation, I will not return to Turkey. My recuperation will be a long process."

"then i will go to istanbul with you and the children and make sure you all get safely off," said Winston. "when i get back to ankara i'll see about getting a transfer."

Inwardly, Friday was relieved. Winston had taken the news better than anticipated. She hadn't expected him to go to Istanbul with them but could bear it if necessary. As far as the transfer was concerned, she knew it would take him a while to manage that.

So far, her plan was working out nicely.

––––––

In the Ankara Compound, Fatima sat at a rickety table in her small room and counted fifty American dollars—in mixed denominations—for the third time. If there was anything more than sex that Fatima enjoyed, it was getting money. Especially American dollars. They had greater worth when traded on the black market.

During her years in the Compound, much *lire* had crossed Fatima's palms because she was one of the most popular women. Her repertoire of tricks was so varied, abundant and bizarre that Fatima would have been banned in Babylon.

And there was more of this cash to come her way, she had been told. Every month she would receive fifty American dollars. For an indefinite period.

An hour earlier, a handsome young Man had visited her. After a session in bed he had made a proposal. If anyone came to question her regarding someone named Ty Manners, she was to deny knowing him. That was all she had to do.

For that amount of money every month, Fatima knew, she would deny her own mother—the slut who had taught her the business.

––––––

Kyle entered his apartment in a cheerful mood.

"Where are ya, Hon?"

"I am in bathroom. I get clothes ready wash," answered Nurtan.

Kyle walked into the room and kissed her on the cheek.

"Why you so happy?" she asked.

"Ah've been drinkin' *raki* with some guys from the Motor Pool. Ah feel good. Let's go out and git somethin' to eat."

"But I have wash clothes."

"Do it later," he insisted.

Nurtan sighed, then acquiesced. Seeing Kyle in such a great mood made her feel that things were better between them. As of late, his attitude was not very good and she was greatly worried about their relationship.

"Okay," she said. "Later I wash."

"Hurry up now, Babe. Ah'm just gonna change and Ah'll be ready to go."

He walked into the bedroom and discarded his shirt. As he put on another, Nurtan called from the bathroom.

"I no find shirt that say Maine."

"That's 'cause it ain't here, Babe. Ah gave it back to Ty. It's his."

*   *   *

Turan telephoned me and in an uncharacteristically polite tone, requested that I meet him at Intim's for drinks around 2000 hours. Also that I come alone and keep our rendezvous a secret. There was a matter of vital importance he wished to discuss.

Upon entering Intim's, Turan immediately spotted me and walked over with a smile. We shook hands, he sat across from me, and a waiter instantly appeared to take the Inspector's order.

"Thank you for coming, Corey!"

"Your request has really aroused my curiosity?"

The pleasant look never left Turan's face.

"I wanted this meeting to be informal because it involves a grave matter, and from having observed your personality over these past months, I greatly respect you!"

The waiter delivered the bottle of *raki*, and retreated.

"As you know, Corey;" he said haltingly; "I am investigating Yuksel's death!"

His pleasant expression abruptly faded to a solemn look and his eyes appeared watery.

I offered my condolences which he silently accepted by nodding. Then he resumed.

He explained—to my sheer astonishment—that Ty Manners was the prime suspect. Drew Johnson had seen Ty walking away from Yuksel's apartment at the established time of her death. Also, a woman named Fatima—whom Ty had cited as an alibi—disclaimed ever having met him.

"If you have any knowledge of Manners' recent whereabouts or if you have observed even the simplest thing, I would appreciate knowing about it—no matter how unimportant it may seem!"

My mouth felt as dry as cotton and I guzzled down more *raki*.

"But Urdanur found Yuksel's body on that hill far out of town," I managed to get out.

Turan informed me that Yuksel had been killed somewhere else, most likely in her apartment. And that was the one aspect which puzzled him: how Manners could have moved the body to those woods without a vehicle and not being seen.

The thought instantly popped into my head.

"Perhaps I _can_ help. Kyle and Ty both work in the Motor Pool and Kyle told me that he often sneaks a sedan out after hours and his superiors never know about it. If Kyle told me, surely Ty knows it. They often go out drinking together."

Turan's face lit up. "Thank you, Corey! You have provided the missing link!"

With this said, he was now anxious to speak with the Chief Inspector and begged to be excused while concurrently summoning the waiter for the check.

When the bill came, I moved to take it but Turan snatched it first. Another surprise.

"I will pay this check!" said Turan.

"But I thought it was my turn. You said so."

"On the first night we met," began Turan; "you were a mere acquaintance! That was a long time ago! Now, Corey, I want to call you my friend!"

In the next moment, he was gone.

Too bad my musician friends were off; they could have raised my spirits.

*   *   *

The Young Man staying at the Yozgat Hotel took a taxi to the JAMMAT Building and waited for Corey Brotano to exit.

Sooner than expected, he saw Corey emerge from the building and walk past him. Keeping at a safe distance, the young Man followed Corey for several blocks until his Prey entered a six-story apartment house on a residential street.

The young Man waited for several minutes after Corey disappeared into the edifice. Then he did the same and read the tenants' directory until finding Corey's name and apartment number. At a casual pace, he walked down the flight of stairs to Corey's apartment and pressed the doorbell.

*   *   *

CHAPTER 24 –
"The Bus From Bitlis"

I had not been in the apartment more than five minutes when the entrance bell rang. Opening the door, I faced a tall muscular guy with cold green eyes.

"Hello, Corey, remember me?"

My denial did not seem to dampen his spirits so he continued.

"The only thing really different about me is my mustache."

His obvious self-confidence and tone of voice suddenly stirred my memory.

He was that annoying guy on my last night in Samsun.

I nodded my head in recognition and he reminded me that his name was Vance Leigh. Just discharged, he was passing through the area and taking a vacation before going Stateside.

"You said to visit when in town."

While I easily invited people to my place, he would not have been one of them. Our last unsolicited encounter had left me as cold as his eyes.

"Do you entertain all your guests in the hallway?" he asked, a strange smile covering his face.

Against my better judgment, I allowed him in, showed the way to the living room and automatically offered a drink. He preferred *raki*. I poured some and left the bottle on the small table between us.

"Very interesting room," he commented. "Black walls, a bar, and wicker furniture."

As in Samsun, his mannerisms were extremely antagonizing.

"How long do you plan to stay in Ankara?" I asked.

"That depends."

"On?"

219

"You." He made a very long pause. "And your friends."

If anyone else had replied in such a fashion, I would have found it amusing. But not with this guy. Under that wry grin was another face ready to unfold. I could feel myself becoming tense.

"Your answer is a bit cryptic. We can show you around the city, if that's what you mean."

He imbibed more *raki*.

"What you and your friends can show me is money."

"If you need some cash, I can probably lend you a few bucks."

"You misunderstand, Corey. No loan. I expect you to give me currency!"

He stretched out the pronunciation of the last word. And while I didn't seem to be understanding the point he was making, there was no time to decipher it because he hastily continued.

"Ten thousand dollars is not too much to pay for me keeping a secret."

"You're being very mysterious. I don't follow you."

"The secret of how you helped a girl escape from the Compound."

In an attempt to hide my surprise and anger, I rose from the chair, walked to the bar and lit a cigarette.

"I don't know what the hell you're talking about. You have a very vivid imagination."

"The girl's name is Pegu and you helped her breakout of the Samsun Compound. Let's not waste precious time, Corey. You know exactly what I mean."

As stoically as possible, I denied his accusation. But he didn't buy it.

"I came in the house once when you was talking to those two Turks. In fact, it was your idea to help her fly the coop. After that day, I kept a close eye on all of you guys."

No longer could I stomach his presence. His overbearing cockiness was getting to me. I put out the cigarette and delivered the only response that came to mind.

"The joke has gone far enough, Leigh. I'd like you to leave. Now!"

"Sorry you feel like that, Corey. I thought I was being a good guy. Never even bothered the old Man who helped you in Samsun."

The remark was ludicrous for he knew that Kenan was poor.

Raising my voice, I repeated the request for him to go.

He casually rose while stretching his arms toward the ceiling. Like a tired guest reluctant to leave.

"Since I *am* a good guy, Brotano, I'll give you and your friends four days to come up with the money."

Without realizing it, I lunged forward and swung at him with all my might and pent-up frustrations. But he was faster! Stronger! He caught my outstretched arm and twisted it until I fell to my knees in pain.

"Don't try fuckin' with me, you little Whimp," he exclaimed, the smile on his face becoming a smirk. "You're out of your fuckin' league!"

He watched me closely as I stood up and rubbed my arm. The anger within me became intense and compelled one more attack. But attempting to kick him in the groin proved to be another failure. He grabbed my leg, jerked it upward, and I fell flat on my back. Then he looked down at me and laughed.

"Tried to kick me in the balls, Brotano? Well, I've got news for you, Whimp."

His large hand grabbed my testicles and squeezed hard enough to prove his point.

"I got *you* by the balls! And if you don't come up with the money, a lot of Turks are gonna have a good time with your cute little ass in a very friendly Turkish prison."

He withdrew his grip and helped himself to another shot of *raki* before exiting the parlor. I slowly got up from the floor and went to the threshold. Watching him calmly meander down the hallway, I had another urge. But two futile attempts were enough; one more might prove very hazardous to my health.

When Leigh got to the front door, he opened it, then turned to face me. Once again that repulsive grin.

"I changed my mind, Corey. You hospitality is shitty."

He made his final dramatic pause.

"I'll give you three days to get the money. I'm staying at the Yozgat Hotel. If I'm not there when you call, leave your phone number. And if you should forget to call, don't fret; I know where you live!"

*   *   *

When Chief Inspector Burdur and Turan entered Colonel Myrons' office, he welcomed the duo with proper diplomatic amenities.

"Although I am always happy t-to s-see our T-Turkish friends, I regret t-the circumstances," began the Colonel.

Inspector Burdur acknowledged the greeting and let Turan take the reins.

"We have come to arrest Airman Manners for the murder of Yuksel Ispir!"

The Colonel had been warned of the visit by Winston.

"You have our full support, but if you will permit me, I would like t-to ask what evidence you have."

"Certainly, Colonel! I, myself, saw Manners following the deceased at 1500 hours on July 21st! Sergeant Drew Johnson witnessed Manners leaving the front of Yuksel's apartment at 1700 hours, the established time of her death! Johnson recognized him from the blond hair, his build and a jersey which said 'Portland, Maine' on the back of it! Finally, when we questioned a prostitute whom Manners claimed was his alibi, she denied ever having seen him!"

But Inspector Karapinar was not finished.

"We also have another witness who heard Manners threaten the deceased;" he paused; "your wife!"

"How does m-my wife figure into t-this?"

Turan explained how she had seen Manners and Yuksel together in the Bazaar one day and overheard him threaten to kill Yuksel.

Silence suddenly reigned as the Colonel thought about Penelope interfering again. Presently, he spoke.

"It s-seems t-to m-me all has been said. At present, M-Manners is working in t-the M-Motor Pool. I will s-send for him if you like."

Turan explained they would rather go there than wait.

"In t-that case, I'll notify Captain Lebal t-that you are on t-the way," offered Myrons.

"To be sure that the Suspect will not give resistance," said Burdur; "we have brought two extra Policemen who are waiting in the car."

The three Gentlemen rose and again shook hands. With the departing amenities fulfilled, the Turkish emissaries left and the Colonel instructed his Clerk to phone Captain Lebal. He then decided it was time for lunch. He left his office and walked down the hall.

At the top of the marble stairway which descended to the first floor, he stopped in amazement.

*   *   *

Since the encounter with Vance Leigh, I had done much thinking about how to handle the matter. The only solution seemed to be to discuss it with Gobasi and Pegu—even though I hated to make them upset.

I phoned under false pretenses and was warmly invited to their home. Instead of us meeting at my place, I asked that they call for me at JAMMAT.

As the soon-to-be best man, I wanted to buy a very special present. In my estimation that would be a camera. The PX had a small but expensive selection so I chose a Voightlander. The girl was kind enough to gift wrap it.

As I walked out of the PX, I ran into Friday who was coming from the adjoining cafeteria.

"This could not have happened better if we planned it," she laughed. **"Doing your Christmas shopping early this year?"**

Friday always had the right wisecrack. I perceived that the rest of our lives would be spent in one laugh after another.

"What are you doing here?" I asked.

"I'm on my way to visit my dear husband." The sarcasm flowed from her lips. **"But before going, I needed a caffeine stimulant."**

I hadn't spoken to her in several days and was unable to tell of my plans to leave for Istanbul on the same day she was departing. I was about to announce it when she reported that Winston was also going.

"You know it's dangerous for us to be talking like this," she suggested; **"Someone might see us. –I'll call you the next chance I get."**

She was gone as quickly as she had appeared. I tucked the prettily wrapped present under my arm and headed for the exit.

*   *   *

Colonel Myrons stood at the top of the stairway and stared down in amazement. On the bottom landing, Airman Brotano was engaged in a private conversation with Mrs. Lebal.

What the hell was happening to his airmen, thought the Colonel. In the wake of a discussion about one of them being a murderer, he finds another blatantly disobeying direct orders. Brotano would not get away with this, Myrons reasoned.

Seething, the Colonel did an about face and returned to his suite. He walked up to the Clerk's desk and practically shouted at the young Man.

"First t-thing t-tomorrow m-morning, I want t-to s-see Airman Brotano in m-my office!"

––––––

Winston cordially welcomed the police Inspectors into his office.

"colonel myrons phoned me," he announced. "i have just sent for manners. he should be here any second."

"Are you finding our country to your liking?" offered Burdur, making conversation.

"very much so," replied Winston.

223

Turan was about to add something when the phone rang.

"yes, sergeant," said Winston; "send him in."

The door opened and Ty Manners entered. Upon seeing the Men from the Turkish Secret Police, he stopped dead in his tracks.

"these gentlemen have something to say to you," began Winston.

"We are here to arrest you for the murder of Yuksel Ispir!" proclaimed Turan.

Without a betrayal of his intention, Ty abruptly turned and ran–slamming the door shut behind him. Turan was momentarily taken back but wasted little time reacting. In a flash, he also flew from the office.

Winston came out from behind his desk and halted when he noticed that Inspector Burdur was still peacefully sitting.

"You go ahead, Captain," suggested Burdur. "I will catch up. I am too old and too fat for such nonsense. Besides, very few ever get away from Turan."

Outside the Quonset hut, Ty turned to his right and ran past the series of garages which were parallel to Winston's office. Just beyond the last one was a wooded area. If he managed to get there he could probably lose Turan. Afterwards, he would contact his buddy Kyle who could help him get out of the country.

When Turan came out of the hut, his keen eyes immediately spotted the American and he sped off in the same direction. *There was no way in hell that this devious criminal was going to outsmart him.*

The two additional Policemen that Turan had brought along left their post at the side of the sedan and intuitively joined in the pursuit.

By this time, Winston and Burdur had come out of the office. Shielding their eyes from the blinding sun, they watched the contest underway.

"If we walk at a casual pace," offered Burdur; "we will get there just in time for Turan to apprehend the suspect."

Winston strained to repress a laugh for although the situation was in no way humorous, something about the portly gentleman's calm attitude made the whole event seem less bleak.

Turan was fast closing in on Ty.

Then it happened.

Quite mysteriously, a truck tire came rolling out of the opening of the furthest garage. Ty tripped over it and fell on his hands. Ignoring the painful scrapes on his palms, he righted himself and made an attempt to continue.

Turan–like an acrobat bouncing off a trampoline–leaped into the air and, in descending, his hands caught Ty's shoulders. Manners fell once again; this time on his knees. Turan was literally on top of his prey and both men struggled furiously.

Although Ty put up a good fight, the Policeman was stronger and managed to end the confrontation by handcuffing his suspect.

Turan hoisted Manners to his feet and was about to strike him but stopped at the sound of Inspector Burdur's voice.

"I see you have apprehended the criminal."

"Yes!" replied, Turan, panting. "His running days are over!"

Addressing the two other Policemen who had been close behind him, Turan said, "Take him away!"

Nearly out of breath—and with a broken spirit—Manners simultaneously yelled and cried as the two Men escorted him to the sedan which was waiting to take him to Turkish justice. He swore over and over that he was innocent.

Winston and Inspector Burdur followed the trio in silence.

Turan wiped the sweat from his brow and looked into the garage that the tire had mysteriously come from. No one was there.

*   *   *

When I came out of the JAMMAT Building, Gobasi and Pegu were patiently waiting for me. I squeezed into the front seat and we got underway.

As Gobasi drove out of the courtyard, he yielded to a sedan which was exiting an adjacent road. When it passed by, I noticed that Turan was driving. Next to him was a fat Man playing with prayer beads. In the back of the sedan sat Ty Manners between two brawny Men.

It was obvious that Ty had just been arrested. From the looks of his disheveled self, I assumed he had put up a fight. And if it were proved that he did kill Yuksel, then I hoped he would fully pay for his heinous crime.

At the house of the soon-to-be-married couple, we sat on the grass in the small backyard because the living room furniture had already been sold. In a matter of seventeen days, Gobasi, Pegu and myself would be on our way to Istanbul.

Pegu made lemonade and served some Turkish pastries which she had bought for the occasion. I watched her with great delight and affection as she placed the plate of offerings on the huge blanket upon which we sat. She was such an effervescent and enchanting person. In no way did I regret my part in her escape from the Samsun Compound.

Before getting down to the unpleasant part of my visit, I presented the wedding gift. They might want to have some photo memories of Ankara before starting their new lives elsewhere.

The expression of gratitude on their faces was unbelievably splendid. Definitely a precious moment I would never forget.

Smilingly, I began to instruct Pegu on how to use it. She proved to be a quick-study and after following my directions only once, she had mastered the photo-making gadget. It had taken *me* three times that long to learn.

Pegu took pictures of: me, alone; Gobasi, alone; Gobasi and me together; and, using the timer, the three of us.

When the enjoyment settled a bit, I broke the news of Vance Leigh's blackmail scheme.

"He must be a crazy man," exclaimed Pegu. "He must be insane. I have never even seen that much money."

Gobasi rattled off something in Turkish and when I asked Pegu to translate, she said that Gobasi forbade it. He did not want to offend my ears with such language.

"Do not worry, Corey," comforted Pegu. "Gobasi and I will make a plan. You just forget about it."

"But I want to help," I protested.

"NO TO WORRY," exclaimed Gobasi. "I TAKE CARE. WHERE BE HE?"

"He's staying at the Yozgat Hotel and he knows the three of us by sight."

"NO TO WORRY," repeated Gobasi. "I TAKE CARE."

*   *   *

Slowly moving through the pitch-black darkness on a rural highway leading to Ankara, an antiquated autobus chugged along with more faulty mechanical noises than it had passengers.

The departure point of the bus had been Bitlis, one of the chief cities of Kurdistan—an area of approximately 74,000 square miles in a mountainous region of Turkey, Iran, Iraq and Syria, and ruled by those countries. Most of the inhabitants of Kurdistan are Kurds, a rugged people of Islamic faith who are much like the Iranians in race and language.

Nearly all the passengers on the bus were sleeping save for the two young Men who sat virtually alone in the bumpy rear. A pair of seventeen year old Kurds embarking on a journey.

The Boy closer to the window lit a cigarette.

"When we get to Ankara, Cizre," he announced; "I want to buy some American cigarettes. Turkish are all right but the others much lighter."

"You should not smoke at all, Midyat," scolded his friend.

"Did you not smoke at one time?"

"True. But I read about it being bad so I stopped."

"You read too much," complained Midyat.

"And you, not at all."

"It gives me a headache."

Though Cizre and Midyat had been friends since the age of four, they were diverse in both thinking and personality.

Rather than spend wasted evenings with the other boys in the village outside of Bitlis, Cizre stayed home to read everything he could find. And encouraged by his Grandfather who had recently passed on, he diligently studied the history of the Kurdish people—especially how they had been oppressed.

Cizre's relationship with Midyat was convenient. He liked Midyat because they had been friends for such a long time and were used to each other. Also because he needed someone to back him up in case of necessity.

Midyat, on the other hand, disliked anything that bordered on intellect. Give him some *raki*, cigarettes, a girl and he was content. History was dead and he pictured himself as very much alive. But he was grateful to have Cizre as a good companion because the former explained things to him and treated him better than anyone else in the village ever had.

Midyat broke the silence.

"Does your uncle know that I am coming with you?"

"I have already said 'yes'. And you are most welcome," answered Cizre, with his customary tone of annoyance when Midyat would repeat the same question.

"Can we go to the Compound while we are in Ankara?" asked Midyat.

"Every night if you wish. As long as our funds last."

"I would also like to see the Victory Day parade. People say it is a very big event in Ankara."

"Anything you wish," said Cizre. "Now, I would like to get some sleep."

Midyat nodded affirmatively and rested his head against the window. Within minutes, he was asleep.

Cizre slouched and closed his eyes. His body was weary but the mind keenly awake.

Little did his friend know, thought Cizre, *that this particular Victory Day parade would go down in history.*

*   *   *

CHAPTER 25 —
"Revelations"

It came as no surprise to receive a message saying that Colonel Myrons wanted to speak with me immediately after I finished the midnight shift.

Upon entering his office, we saluted in the proper military fashion and he motioned for me to have a seat while his countenance remained stern.

There were several minutes of heavy silence.

"I hesitate, Airman Brotano, because I'm t-trying t-to control m-my t-temper. I explicitly ordered you t-to s-stay away from M-Mrs. Lebal. In fact, I was very considerate about it. I s-sent you on an extra leave and even provided you with additional funds. And how do you repay m-me?"

I opened my mouth to speak but he held up his hand like a cop directing traffic.

"You repay m-me by deliberately and blatantly disobeying m-my orders. I s-saw you t-talking t-to her yesterday, right here in JAMMAT."

"Sir, it was a purely accidental meeting. I haven't seen Mrs. Lebal since my return from Samsun. I didn't even know she was in the building. I went to the PX to buy a present for someone and upon coming out, unexpectedly ran into her."

The Colonel repeated himself.

"But I s-saw t-the t-two of you t-talking. I watched from t-the t-top of t-the s-stairway and you chatted for over five m-minutes."

"Having made contact I couldn't very well ignore her."

"You s-should have," he yelled. "You could have walked away but you didn't, t-thereby openly s-scorning m-my orders!"

Besides the annoying stuttering, his demeanor was getting on my nerves. As far as I was concerned he had no right to question my personal life.

Although there was an existing military law which forbade enlisted men from fraternizing with officers and their kin, I deemed the decree to be asinine.

"I'm sorry, Colonel. But I acted in the only way I knew how. Snubbing Mrs. Lebal would have been rude. I'm sure you wouldn't have liked that either."

He raised his voice even louder.

"It is not a m-matter of what I like. It's your breech of m-military decorum."

"As I said before, Colonel. The meeting was strictly innocent and you cannot prove otherwise."

The Colonel was silent once again and I complimented myself on stunning him with boldness. However, when he spoke again, the surprise was on me.

"I have done s-some checking on your work in t-the Crypto room, Airman Brotano." His voice was eerily calm. "I discovered t-that your s-supervisor s-sent you home early because you weren't feeling well, s-several weeks ago."

What could he possibly be getting at, I wondered.

"Also, it s-seems t-that you almost s-sent out a t-top s-secret m-message uncoded, but you were s-stopped in t-time."

I protested that I had been dizzy from my illness. That my mind was not functioning at its full capacity. Nonetheless, the Colonel overrode my explanation and continued to speak.

"Consequently, Airman Brotano, I have decided t-to bring charges against you for attempting t-to divulge t-top s-secret m-military information."

I bounced up from my chair yelling that such an action was a lie. The Colonel ordered me to sit again and warned that I would make matters worse if some control were not exercised.

Then he read aloud several military laws which sounded like folderal. As he spoke, I reviewed the situation in my mind. The chances for clearing myself were less than fifty-fifty. There was no proof on my part that I had not deliberately tried to sabotage a top secret message. Yet, I had gone on sick call.

Colonel Myrons finished reading the regulations, laid the book on his desk and looked me straight in the eyes with a chilling glare.

"I am instigating court-m-martial proceedings against you, Airman Brotano, for dereliction of duty. Until t-the actual hearing is s-scheduled, you are under house arrest. You are t-to go directly home and s-stay t-there until you are notified by m-me. You are not t-to leave your premises for any reason!"

He paused and a very nasty grin encompassed his face.

"At t-the t-time of your court-m-martial, we'll see if _you_ can prove otherwise."

He had zapped me with my own words!

*   *   *

Because there was no radio in the sedan bearing license plates AF 136, Airman Franklois alternately whistled and sang to himself as he drove. He had done the same thing on his route from JAMMAT to the airport where he had picked up several small packages of medicine and delivered them to the American Hospital in Ulus, on Captain Lebal's orders. Now he was on his way back to the Motor Pool.

While stopped for a traffic light in Yenishire, Franklois glanced at his watch. The Captain had given him about two hours to complete his delivery. Since he had forty-five minutes to spare, he decided to use the time to have lunch. The Washington Restaurant nearby made excellent shish kebab and it was Franklois' favorite Turkish dish—especially when washed down with some *raki*.

Thirty minutes later when Franklois emerged from the restaurant, he approached his sedan and let out a string of obscenities. The right rear tire was unmistakably flat. He stared at it for a while in disbelief. Finally he pushed himself into action with the resolve that what needed to be done should be acted upon immediately.

He undid the lug nuts on the tire, raised the car with the jack, took off the flat, and guided on the spare. Upon lowering the vehicle, Franklois let out another string of curses. The spare was also flat.

"Who the fuck drove this car last?" said Franklois, aloud—to the bewilderment of several pedestrians passing by. "When I get back to the Motor Pool, I'm gonna kick some ass!"

The Airman picked up the original flat tire and was about to place it in the trunk when he noticed something strange which was in the well where the spare had been stored.

In his office, Winston was reviewing the week's work rosters when the phone rang.

"This is Airman Franklois, Sir. I'm stuck in Yenishire with a flat tire."

Winston sighed with annoyance. Apparently, it was going to be one of those days.

"well, change it, son."

"The spare is also flat, Captain."

Winston was amazed.

"how could that happen?"

"Don't know, Sir, but it did."

"okay, Franklois. i'll send somebody. where are you exactly?"

"In front of the Washington Restaurant, in Yenishire. And whoever didn't bother to fix that flat even left his shirt in the trunk."

"shirt?" echoed Winston, confused.

"Yeah. I mean, yes, Sir. It's a jersey that says 'Portland, Maine' on the back of it."

"what vehicle are you driving, franklois?"

"AF 136."

"stay there, franklois;" ordered Winston; "i'll be right over with another spare."

When Winston replaced the receiver in its cradle, he knew what must be done. After delivering a good tire to the Airman, he needed to take the jersey to Inspector Karapinar. It was a bit of important evidence in a murder case. It could clear Manners. Or hang him.

––––––

In the lobby of the Yozgat Hotel, two Gentlemen made their way to the reception counter. The thinner of the two took out his wallet, flashed it in front of the clerk's eyes, and quickly returned it to his pocket. The Receptionist had virtually no time to get a good look at the credentials but it was of little consequence because that gesture was universal, he knew. Only policemen did such things.

The chubby Man spoke.

"Do you have a guest here by the name of Vance Leigh?"

"I will look in the registry, *Efendi*."

He moved his finger from top to bottom on several pages of the book. On the third, he located the name.

"Here it is. He checked into room 409 several days ago."

"Do you know him by sight?"

"No, but I can identify him from the hotel key."

"Is he in now?"

The employee turned to check the rack and answered in the affirmative.

"Very well," said the thin one. "We will sit and wait. Do not tell him we are here. When he comes down and gives you his key, address him by name so that we can hear."

The Receptionist nodded that he understood and went back to his duties.

Two hours later, Vance Leigh descended the stairs into the lobby. He noticed two Men resting themselves in easy chairs but thought nothing of it.

As the Clerk accepted the room key, he said, "Thank you, Mr. Leigh."

Instead of jumping up at the mention of the name, the two Gentlemen patiently waited until the American left the hotel. Then, maintaining a proper distance, they followed.

A twenty minute walk eventually led to the marketplace where they saw Vance Leigh perform some kind of transaction with a merchant who sold plants on a pushcart.

"What is he doing?" asked the chubby Man of his partner.

"I think he is buying dope," said the thinner one.

"What shall we do?"

"Nothing right now. We will continue to observe him."

With his transaction completed, Leigh walked to the corner and used the pay phone.

The two Men attentively watched him.

*   *   *

I lay in the back yard enjoying the warm sun and the pleasant music coming from the portable radio beside me. Though I had been under house arrest only since the morning, it was beginning to get on my nerves.

Ordinarily I didn't mind staying home. But when told to do something, I just instinctively revolted. Taking orders was something I abhorred.

Various thoughts which shuffled around in my brain were interrupted by the phone ringing. I jumped up and ran to answer it.

To my chagrin, the caller was Vance Leigh.

"Hello, Corey."

I made my voice frigid.

"Why are you calling?"

"To tell you that I changed my mind."

Knowing his sleazy character, I perceived he had another surprise for me. He was the type who reveled in tormenting others.

"About what?" I asked.

"My waiting to get my dough."

Several seconds of silence ensued and then he continued.

"This town is getting to me and I wanna leave. So you have until tomorrow evening to come up with the bills."

"And if I don't?"

"Then I go to the Turkish authorities and you and your friends get a long and free vacation, courtesy of the Turkish government."

*   *   *

Drew glanced at the clock. It read twenty hundred hours. Earlier in the day, his Lover had called to announce that he would drop by for a visit. Accordingly, Drew had followed his usual procedure of putting the wine in the refrigerator to cool. They both preferred the grape that way. Now he sat on the couch and listened to music while he patiently waited. Tonight's tête-à-tête was going to be special.

In the middle of a favorite song, the doorbell rang.

"It's not locked," Drew yelled, getting off the couch and heading into the kitchen.

"No physical greeting?" asked the Lover, humorously.

Drew re-entered the living room.

"I was getting the wine."

He motioned for his guest to sit on the couch and after he poured the ambrosia, he joined him. They kissed but Drew stopped it from lingering.

"Are you being distant?"

Before answering, Drew sipped some wine.

"That depends."

"Please explain."

The expression on Drew's face was serious.

"I have a favor to ask and if you don't grant it, I will be very upset."

The guest lit a cigarette and nervously laughed.

"Well, go ahead."

Drew had earlier decided he would not hesitate but jump into what he perceived could be a very delicate discussion. Depending on his lover's reaction, their bond could become stronger, or maybe lessen.

"Corey Brotano called today and told me what happened." Drew paused. "I want you to drop the charges. Forget the whole thing."

"I can't, Drew."

The Host became slightly annoyed. In their years together, he had seldom asked for anything. This was the first important request ever made. And he was determined to win.

"You have the power."

"But Brotano disobeyed orders."

Drew got off the couch and began to pace.

"Will you listen to yourself," he exclaimed. "You're being hypocritical."

The Lover was astounded. He had never seen Drew in such a state, or heard him speak so disrespectfully.

"You and I have broken the rules for years," continued Drew. "According to your premise, we should both be in jail on charges of sodomy. Why is it all right for us and not for anyone else? Actually, Corey hasn't done a damn thing wrong – except maybe to fall in love with an officer's wife."

He paused and exuded a deep sigh.

"Look at me. I am worse. I fell in love *with* an officer!"

Employing another tactic, Drew sat on the floor near his lover's feet and rested his hands on the man's knees. When he spoke this time, his voice was mellow with a pleading quality he hoped would be persuasive.

"In our relationship, I have not asked for much."

"I know," conceded his friend.

"But this is important to me. Corey is a good friend of mine. He knows about me and accepts what I am. There's not a condescending bone in his body. He doesn't deserve this treatment."

Several minutes of silence ensued before Drew made his final plea.

"Please do this for me, Hank. I love you, but not when you're Colonel Myrons."

In the kitchen of a small modest house at 325 Tokat Sokak in the Ulus section of Ankara, Cizre and Midyat chatted with their hosts.

"I remember your Grandfather well," said Cizre's Uncle. "He was a fine man and never spoke ill of anyone–except the Turks, that is."

Cizre laughed. "I know that all too well. For years he told me stories of the things the Turks have done to us Kurds."

The Uncle's wife interrupted. "It seems that you men are about to speak of war things. That is not to my liking and since I am tired, you will please forgive me if I go to sleep now. Since my daughter is now married, you may stay in her room. And you are welcome in our home for as long as you wish."

When she left the room, the Men continued their dialogue.

"Which story of your Grandfather's do you remember most?" asked the Uncle.

"The one that happened in 1925, when the Kurds were attempting to secure an independent government. There was combat in many villages. In Grandfather's town, he was one of the biggest rebels and he fought side by side with his boyhood friend. One minute they were laughing because it seemed like they were defeating the Turks. In the next instant, Grandfather's friend lay dead. It happened that fast."

"The Kurds should have won," interjected Midyat.

"We all agree with that," said the Uncle. "But the Turks were mightier in number and power and they crushed the rebellion."

"Grandfather never forgave them," continued Cizre, solemnly. "He cursed them everyday of his existence for taking the life of his dear friend. And for trying to suppress a proud people."

"Now he is at rest," consoled the Uncle. "And his problem with the Turks is over."

Cizre looked directly into the Host's eyes. "That may be so, Uncle. But he left it after him. As my legacy."

*   *   *

CHAPTER 26 —

"Strangers Who Had Once Shared"

*   *   *

Incongruous with the moods of Nurtan and Madam Sivas, the August day was as beautifully pleasant as the one which had preceded it. Incongruous because they stood on a small sloping hill in front of the grave of their dear friend Yuksel. Waiting for them on the road below was Kyle. It was his lunch hour and he had consented to drive the women to the cemetery—with Captain Lebal's permission. Yet, going up to the actual grave was something he had refused to do.

"Say prayer, please, *Teyze*," asked Nurtan, having finally stopped crying. The Old Woman bowed her head and spoke softly.

"Dear Allah, may Yuksel please lounge around in heaven in peace and happiness; please let it be that she felt no pain or fear when passing; and, please help her deserving loved ones."

After several minutes of silence, Madam Sivas suggested it was time to leave.

"Please. I like stay here alone some minute."

"Certainly, but is it too much for you?"

"No. I good, now."

"Very well," said the Woman. "I will wait for you below with Kyle. Try not to stay too long. He must return to work soon."

Feelings of tortuous confusion encompassed Nurtan. It seemed that Yuksel's death had had no effect on the scheme of things. The sun rose and

236

set and life went on as if nothing had happened. But in Nurtan's heart and soul, the world had changed so profoundly that it would never be the same again. The emptiness that Yuksel's death brought would be a burden until her own last day on earth.

When Madam Sivas reached the bottom of the hill, Kyle was waiting. He extended his hand to assist her as she moved from the slope to the flat road. Neither of them spoke as they walked to the jeep which was parked several feet away. Kyle helped the Woman into the vehicle then leaned against it and lit a cigarette. After several minutes, Madam Sivas spoke.

"Why do you not face me?"

"No reason," he replied; "Ah wuz jest lookin' at the city."

On the left side of the road, the terrain sloped downward. Above the small trees which dotted the descent, one could see Ankara in the distance.

"Where's Nurtan?" asked Kyle.

"She will come down in a moment. I am glad."

Not fully understanding the Woman's words, Kyle silently waited for her to explain.

"I was hoping to speak with you alone," continued Madam Sivas.

"Abou' what?"

"About you and Yuksel."

If Madam Sivas had had any doubt concerning the truth of Yuksel's claims, they were surely satisfied. The surprised expression on Kyle's face verified his guilt. He crushed the cigarette under his foot, then quickly lit another. Though not turning his back to the Woman, he avoided eye contact.

Madam Sivas further related that Yuksel had told her everything, including his threat on her life.

"Are ya sayin' that Ah killed her?" snapped Kyle.

The Woman slowly shook her head from side to side.

"If I thought that were true, you would not be breathing at this moment. I have many friends. They would have dealt with you by now."

"Then Ah don' know what you're talkin' abou', Woman," lied Kyle.

"I think you do," countered Madam Sivas. "If not, you would look me in the eyes and deny it."

"Ah can't look at ya cause the sun's blindin' me."

An obvious lie but the Woman ignored it.

"I also want you to know," she persisted; "that I gave this information to Turan when he came to question me about Yuksel's death."

Kyle fought to suppress his anger.

"Why'd ya do that?"

"I had no choice. Turan needed all the facts he could get."

Kyle was about to say more in his defense when Madam Sivas held up her hand to indicate that Nurtan was approaching.

"I will say no more now," whispered the Woman. "I do not want Nurtan to be hurt any further."

Kyle briskly moved forward to meet Nurtan who was drying fresh tears but managed a weak smile for her American husband.

"Please. Sorry I make you late. It is 12:23."

"No sweat," he answered, escorting her to the jeep; "Ah got plenty of time."

As they neared the vehicle, Kyle stole a quick glance at the Old Woman.

Madam Sivas returned a look that was an explicit, tacit warning even Kyle could perceive.

In a bedroom of the house at 325 Tokat Sokak, Cizre got out of bed and awakened Midyat who had been sleeping next to him.

"Why must we get up so early, Cizre?" he protested; "I am too tired."

"Get dressed," commanded Cizre, putting on his pants. "We have a lot of places to see today."

"Can I not sleep a bit longer? That woman named Fatima worked me very hard last night."

The Compound had been something of a treat after a day of exploring, thought Cizre. He had enjoyed it better than expected. And it appeared that the nightly visits would be a definite part of the schedule, at least for Midyat.

"I like that American we met in the Compound last night," exclaimed Midyat. "He is much fun and he likes *raki* the same like me."

"Do not get too friendly."

"Why?" asked Midyat, confused.

"Because he is a foreigner and many times they take advantage of the people whose country they are in."

Midyat did not fully understand his companion's logic but accepted it without question.

"Where are we going today?" he inquired; "to another education place?"

Cizre shook his head in the affirmative.

"Why did you not take that American's offer to see where he works?" continued Midyat.

"For two reasons, my Friend. First, we do not want too many people to know us. Second, because we are not interested in the Americans. It is the Turks we have come to deal with."

Before Midyat could decipher the hidden message, Cizre was out the door and on his way to breakfast.

*   *   *

Two good things about house arrest are not having to work and being able to sleep very late. But around 1030 hours, the doorbell rang so I nakedly meandered down the hall to answer it.

To my surprise, the caller was Colonel Myrons' Clerk who handed me a sealed envelope, visually surveyed me from head to toe, and smilingly departed.

Before opening the communiqué, I made a strong cup of tea. There was no burning desire to read the scheduled date of my court-martial.

But this day was to bring several revelations.

The message from Colonel Myrons was written on a sheet of paper without any official letterhead. It was simple and to the point.

> *Dear Airman Brotano,*
> *In view of certain pertinent evidence which has just come to my attention, I am rescinding my order of house-arrest, and there will be no court-martial.*
> *You are to return to work tomorrow as if nothing has happened. However, my orders for you not to communicate with Mrs. Lebal are still in effect.*
> *Yours truly,*
> *Hank Myrons, Col.*

Not understanding his strange change of heart didn't matter because it made me very much relieved. A great weight had been lifted from my shoulders.

After a quick shower, I got dressed and was just leaving when the phone rang. It was Kyle who asked that I meet him for lunch at JAMMAT.

When I got to the cafeteria, I found him seated at a table in the rear.

I watched him light a cigarette and waited patiently for the important news that he promised to tell.

"Ah got my orders," he announced, beaming from ear to ear.

Initially, I felt sorry for myself. With Kyle here in Ankara, I was comfortable. Though I had made several other excellent friends since arriving, I always looked up to Kyle as a hero.

"Ah'm leavin' on August 30th. Goin' ta Istanbul for a short leave then back ta the States."

I asked if Nurtan would also be leaving or joining him later.

"She ain't comin'. Ah haven't even told her yet."

My mind quickly flashed back to that night in Intim's when he told me about the transfer and that he was too young to be saddled with a wife. But I had attributed his cavalier attitude to the *raki*.

"Try ta understand, Corey," Kyle began, moving his face close to mine in a confidential way. "It ain't that Ah don' love Nurtan. It's just tha' Ah ain't ready ta be married. If Ah took her back wit' me, Ah'd leave her alone a lot and she wouldn't be happy. The best thing fer her is ta stay here wit' her own kind."

How does one cope with the sometimes ambiguous facets of friendship, I mused. My heart went out to Nurtan but Kyle had disappointed me. In the final analysis, judging him was perhaps unfair. I was not in *his* shoes.

"I'm also going to Istanbul that night," came my announcement; "along with Gobasi, Pegu, Friday, Winston, their kids, and now you."

"It oughta be a pretty interestin' train ride," predicted Kyle.

With that spoken, he rose and announced he had to return to work. As I watched him walk away, I wondered if we'd ever see each other again—after Turkey. And if we did, would our feelings be the same or would we be like strangers with vague recollections. Strangers who had once shared a meaningful moment in time.

*   *   *

In the Ulus prison, Ty was escorted from his cell to a small interrogation room. There he was introduced to his lawyer—Second Lieutenant Nina Debra Connie Kent.

Ty hid his disappointment of having been given a female lawyer, and for once in his life managed to be civil. With his monumental problems, he would have to settle for any help offered—no matter where it came from.

Lieutenant Kent was a pleasant woman in her early thirties. She told Ty several personal things about herself in the hope of gaining his confidence. She also brought gifts: cigarettes, candy bars and writing materials.

After the formalities, they discussed the case and Ty obediently listened as his lawyer reviewed all the evidence against him.

"Nurtan and Madam Sivas have sworn that Yuksel told them you threatened to kill her; this was also substantiated in Yuksel's diary. Mrs. Myrons reported that she overheard you threaten to kill Yuksel when you were in the Bazaar. Inspector Karapinar saw you following the victim at 1500 hours on July 21–the day of the murder. Sergeant Johnson saw you walking away from Yuksel's apartment at 1700 hours–the established time and place of death. Kyle swore that he returned your jersey to you several weeks before July 21. An anonymous report claims that you had knowledge of sneaking a vehicle out of the Motor Pool without permission so as to move the body. There were traces of Yuksel's blood in the sedan. And, the woman Fatima whom you claim to have been with in the Compound at 1700 hours, swears that she does not know you. Nor has ever seen you."

When the Lieutenant finished, Ty spoke with a pained expression.

"I swear that I did not kill her!"

"Then why did you run away when they tried to arrest you?"

"Because I was scared and thought nobody would believe me."

They continued their dialogue and the Lieutenant sincerely tried to appreciate the explanations Ty gave her. But in truth, her Client offered no kind of proof and his past record with the law was anything but pristine.

Lieutenant Kent further explained that Ty's jersey had been found and that it contained blood stains which matched Yuksel's.

To this news, Ty was stunned.

"Kyle did not return the shirt! I think he's the real murderer and is trying to frame me. It's not a crazy idea. People are always confusing us. It's like those two guys in A TALE OF TWO CITIES that Corey Brotano told me about."

Lieutenant Kent made no comment. She ended the meeting by promising to return within the week–hopefully bearing news about the date of his trial.

"Are they treating you all right?" she asked, before exiting.

"Yes," answered Ty. "But I miss my roommate. They had put me in a cell with a guy named Mohair and we got along wickedly good. After two days they took him away and now I'm alone."

When the visit was terminated, Ty was brought back to his cell. After lighting a cigarette, he took advantage of the stationary Lieutenant Kent had given him.

Dear Father,

I'm in serious trouble. Please come to Turkey... ."

———————-

The Fat Man and the Thin Man waited outside the Yozgat Hotel until Vance Leigh exited and walked to the corner. They inconspicuously moved up to him on both sides, secured him under the armpits and literally raised his body off the ground as they carried their prey into an empty adjacent alley.

Initially dumbfounded it took Leigh several minutes to realize what was happening. He then struggled but his strength was nothing compared to the combined powers of the two strangers.

The Fat Man slammed Leigh against the wall and pressed a cold steel blade against his throat. The Thin Man pressed a gun painfully on Leigh's groin.

"You plan to sell marijuana to your American friends and make a profit, do you not?" asked Fat Man.

"What the fuck you talkin' about? I ain't got no dope."

"We saw you buy it on three separate occasions."

Leigh denied the accusation but his Captors did not believe him.

"We do not like foreigners trying to cut in on our business!"

Vance Leigh's bravado and tough guy demeanor suddenly vanished. He was unmistakably frightened.

The Fat Man lightly dragged the tip of the knife along the side of Leigh's throat and the latter could feel blood dribbling downward under his shirt and onto his chest.

The action seriously convinced Leigh that this was a life or death situation and he began to heatedly plead and cajole.

"I'm planning to leave Ankara tomorrow but I'll do so right now if that's what you want . I'll even pay you to let him go!"

While only a few minutes had actually elapsed it seemed a virtual eternity to Leigh. And when his Captors tacitly shook their heads, he closed his eyes in anticipation of death and began to sob like a toddler.

"If we spare your life, do you promise to leave Ankara today? No matter where there is a flight to?"

Leigh shook his head so strenuously in agreement that he gave himself a headache.

As expeditiously as possible, the Fat Man and the Thin Man escorted Vance Leigh back into the hotel where he collected his belongings, and then directly to the airport where he boarded the commercial 2100 hours flight for Seoul, Korea.

Turan smoked a cigarette as he leaned against the green sedan which was parked in front of his office building. He took a deep drag and contemplated while he exhaled the smoke. As of late, he was doing a lot of thinking– especially regarding Yuksel's death. Surprisingly, it was slowly and profoundly changing his personality. From a harsh martinet he was becoming a kinder, more sensitive man.

Turan was interrupted from his thoughts by a tall, clean-shaven, young colleague who approached with ease.

"I did as you asked, Turan."

"And the results, Mohair?"

"Quite good. He told me a lot of incriminating things. —You owe me a promotion, Boss."

*   *   *

Seated across the table from me was the vivacious Pegu. We were in the Ulus section of town—at an outdoor café which was frequented mostly by Turks. Gobasi was not present but sent his warmest regards. He was at work.

Pegu began her tale after the waiter placed our orders on the table.

"Corey, our troubles with that man Vance Leigh are over. They are finished."

I smiled with relief which seemed to make Pegu even more happy.

"Gobasi has two friends," she continued. "One is fat and one is thin and they both look very scary. But they are very sweet men and Gobasi has known them all his life. They grew up together.

"Anyway, they followed Vance Leigh when he came out of his hotel and took him into a nearby alley. Pretending to be drug dealers they threatened to kill him for trying to horn in on their territory.

"Leigh begged for his life and promised to leave Turkey and never come back. He offered them all of the money he had if they would spare his life. Money he had accrued from stealing, blackmailing people, selling dope, and even his salary. —They accepted.

"First they took him back into the hotel to get his belongings. Then to the airport where they put him on a plane. They did not leave until the plane was in the air. Is that not great, Corey? Is that not wonderful?"

"Yes," I smiled. "That's fabulous."

"Gobasi's friends offered us Vance Leigh's money but we refused and they did not want to keep it either. So we all agreed to give it to a needy orphanage here in Ankara. Is that all right? Is that okay?"

I concurred, then inquired as to the amount.

Beaming from ear to ear, Pegu was overjoyed to announce it.

"Vance Leigh gave them ten thousand American dollars!"

CHAPTER 27 –
"By A Symphony Orchestra"

I phoned to see if Urdanur was feeling any better after the horrendous experience of finding Yuksel's body. She appreciated the gesture and asked if I would care to accompany her on a small journey that afternoon.

To my surprise and delight we traveled to her favorite mosque which was located in Ulus. En route, Urdanur gave me a brief explanation of the Moslem religion. It can never hurt to extend a little culture to someone.

"The angel Gabriel met Mohammed on the road one day and gave him the FIVE PILLARS OF ISLAM which represent the essence of the religion:

FAITH–which says, 'There is no God but Allah, and Mohammed is his prophet;'

PRAYER–five times a day;

ALMS–donations to the less fortunate;

FASTING–on the feast of Ramadan; and,

PILGRIMAGE–journey to Mecca, where Mohammed was born."

"What is Ramadan?" I inquired.

"The month in which the Koran was first revealed to Mohammed; we fast only in the daylight hours but business goes on as usual."

"You seem to be very religious," I noted, as we arrived at our destination.

"Not overly so, but I like to maintain some semblance of my faith. And reading the Koran is very satisfying."

Urdanur's mosque was about the same size as any average church. Its high dome–with a minaret on both sides–towered above us in awesome splendor.

In front of the mosque was a courtyard complete with a water fountain for the ceremonial washing before prayer. And just before entering the mosque through its high arched entrance, we left our shoes.

Inside was a large rectangular chamber with huge windows through which sunbeams lit-up walls adorned with bright arabesques and sayings from the Koran, inscribed in elegant Arabic calligraphy. There were no pews, statues or other objects as in Christian churches.

"How do people pray?" I whispered to Urdanur.

"Standing, or like that."

She pointed to a worshiper.

He was in an almost prone position with his face nearly touching the mat.

"During Friday meetings," offered Urdanur; "prayers are performed by bows and prostrations. The men stand barefoot behind the *Iman* or priest, and follow his movements. The women may participate but in a separate space."

"Do the kids go with their respective sexes?"

"Yes. But they are not required to pray until the age of puberty."

In my religion and at that stage in life, I had already said hundreds of penitent prayers for committing sins I never even understood.

"Actually," continued my friend; "the word mosque comes from the Arabic, *masjad*, which means a place of kneeling. And its structure was patterned after the courtyard of Mohammed's house at Medina where the followers first heard the Prophet preach."

Having said that, Urdanur lowered her eyes and I followed suit. Each in our own way became arrested by the solemnity of this holy place as we silently prayed for Yuksel.

Though this was not my house of worship, I felt no strangeness. Tacitly, I marveled that with the excessive religious disputes among people, it was all in vain. There was really no profound difference. We were basically the same and all we needed was kindness, love and simple respect.

When Urdanur and I exited the mosque, a compulsion to look up at one of the minarets overcame me. The loftiness of the tower was enchanting. It was late afternoon and a priest was calling the faithful to prayer.

"I've often wondered what he's chanting."

"He is saying:
> *'God is most great, I testify there is no God but Allah,*
> *I testify that Mohammed is the Messenger of Allah, Come to prayer;*
> *Come to salvation, God is most great!"*
> *There is no God but Allah'."*

We walked in silence for a long time and when the mosque was several blocks behind us, Urdanur shattered the stillness.

"When we were in there I also thanked Allah for sending you to Turkey, and to me."

"That goes both ways, my dear Friend."

"Oh," she exclaimed; "I almost forgot. I have a surprise for you."

"I love surprises. What is it?"

"On the morning of Victory Day, I am taking you to a breakfast which is given by President Mahzun. Only special people are invited to that reception."

"That's fantastic! I'd love to go. Not many Americans get a chance to meet the president of a country. But how did you get an invitation?"

"We went through school together and our families have always been friends. He is the one who convinced me to take the position of liaison to JAMMAT. I am also a Godmother to one of his children. The breakfast is being held from nine to ten-thirty."

"Afterwards, around noon," I suggested; "we can meet Drew, Kyle and Nurtan and go to the parade. That night, I'm going to Istanbul for the weekend to be the best man in Gobasi and Pegu's wedding."

Since Urdanur already knew that Friday and the children were leaving the same night, her subsequent words to me did not come as a surprise.

"Please be careful, Corey. I do not want anything bad to happen to you."

*   *   *

Hank Myrons sat alone at the huge desk in his office. In front of him lay a report by Lieutenant Kent concerning the facts, evidence, and ramifications on the Turkish government's case against Airman Tyler Manners.

The tragedy and horror of the situation saddened Hank and he lamented about the status quo of the present age.

His generation knew how to show respect and to act responsibly. Today, in these fiery fifties—with the pink shirts, mooning, Davy Crockett hats, mambo, panty raids, ducktail haircuts, and that maniac Elvis Presley—the country was headed for destruction. The fall of the Roman Empire revisited. Conditions were no longer like a Norman Rockwell painting.

From the recesses of his subconscious, the Colonel unexpectedly resurrected an idea which he had once buried. An unfulfilled dream of entering politics. Being a lawyer already was a perfect foundation for the job.

"I think I should, and I think I will," he said, aloud—not stuttering for the first time in many, many years.

He got up from his chair and walked to the mirror. Standing at attention, he studied his image. There were a few assets to be noted: a pleasant looking face, an imposing stature, and years of maturity. A clever Public Relations man would know how to utilize those features.

With an unexpected bolt of renewed energy, Hank went back to his desk and grabbed some writing materials. He had made up his mind. Furthermore, he intended to stick to this decision no matter what. If Penelope did not like the idea, then she could divorce him. It was time that he reverted to the man of his youth. The guy who knew what he wanted and rushed forward to get it.

His enthusiasm grew with intensity as he put the pen to paper and began to write his letter of resignation from the United States Army.

––––––

When Ty entered the interrogation room in the Ulus Prison, he was warmly greeted by Lieutenant Kent who presented more cigarettes and candy bars. In addition, she opened a small suitcase to show Ty a fresh change of clothing–right down to white briefs.

"What's this for?" he asked, slightly puzzled.

"The outfit I've chosen for you to wear at your trial. Captain Lebal took me to your apartment to pick it out. I hope you don't mind."

That was the least of his problems, thought Ty. He didn't care who went into his pad; there was nothing of much value in the place anyway. Getting out of this mess was all he cared about. And the quicker the better.

"When is it?" he asked.

"On Monday, August 23."

Ty's face lit up in amazement.

"That's only three days away. Are we ready?"

"As we will ever be," came her sullen reply.

The Lieutenant's demeanor alarmed Ty.

"I'm getting bad vibes," he announced.

The lawyer toyed with a pen for several minutes as she tried to determine her delivery.

"You don't seem to have much of a defense. All the evidence is stacked up against you. Honestly, I am a bit worried."

Ty's anxiety began to mount and the tension was evident in his voice.

"Well what the hell are you going to do for me?"

Another period of hesitation on the Lieutenant's part.

"The best I can suggest is to plead temporary insanity."

Ty echoed her words in high-pitched tones of incredulousness. He jumped up from his chair and aimlessly paced back and forth in agitation.

"I'm wickedly cooked! I'm finished! I'm dead!" he shouted.

Hopelessly defeated, Ty sat down at the table and covered his face as tears rolled freely down his cheeks. His voice choked with emotion.

"But I'm innocent," he moaned; "I'm fuckin' innocent."

The Lieutenant got up from her chair to move around the table. She gently cradled his head and then pressed it against her bosom. For a long time they remained as such.

To the lawyer, it was the only comfort she could offer; to Ty, a fleeting haven from the horrific world he had suddenly been launched into.

Presently, the Lieutenant returned to her seat opposite Ty and he composed himself.

"If we plead insanity," she began; "we may have a better chance of eventually getting you out of the asylum here and negotiating a transfer to one in the States. But to accomplish that from a prison would be virtually impossible. You have told me that your father is a Congressman. Perhaps he could do something."

Ty abruptly remembered the letter which he took out of his shirt pocket and handed to her.

"I decided to write to him and ask for help. Would you see that this is mailed?"

Lieutenant Kent accepted the envelope and nodded in the affirmative. Then Ty's mood changed. He pounded his fists on the table.

"I swear that I'm innocent," he repeated; "It's that miserable two-faced bastard Kyle. I'm sure he killed Yuksel. He wanted her as much as I did. She probably refused to go to bed with him, threatened to tell his wife, and he killed her."

The lawyer waited until Ty calmed down. She then verbally reflected on his theory. If what he said were true, the proof of that would be difficult to establish. To convince the police that Kyle was the murderer, she and Ty would have to produce some sort of evidence.

"Where, when and how can we accomplish that?"

"We could get a private detective."

"That's a good thought," she conceded; "But we do not have the time. Your trial is Monday."

"What about the blood stains on the jersey? If I strangled her like they say I did, why is there blood?"

While Lieutenant Kent disliked having to suppress the little encouragement Ty was trying to muster, she had to be truthful and not abet him in having false hopes.

"The girl was probably beaten before she was murdered. That would account for the blood stains on the jersey."

Ty digested the Lawyer's words for several seconds before persisting.

"Then why didn't I burn the fuckin' shirt? Why would I leave it in the trunk of the car?"

"Our opposition would no doubt say that you simply forgot it because you were in a rush to dispose of the body."

"Why didn't they fuckin' question Kyle?"

"They probably did but he must have had a good alibi. And none of the evidence points to him. —If you want, I will tell the court of your opinion. Perhaps they will give us more time to investigate your accusations."

Though Ty was slightly elated by her suggestion, it was short-lived. The subsequent words from the Lieutenant's mouth brought him crashing once again.

"There is one more complication."

Ty looked at her with utter complexity.

"What is it?" he mumbled.

"Inspector Karapinar says he has a witness who will testify that you boasted about many previous crimes that you committed and that you admitted to threatening Yuksel."

"Who the fuck can that possibly be?" moaned Ty.

His brain was becoming numb.

"Your former cell mate Mohair," she continued; "is a cop. He was a 'plant' put in with you to gain information."

Back in his cell, Ty sat for several hours in an almost catatonic state. The events of the past several weeks were becoming overpowering. Suddenly his life was falling apart. He felt like a small wooden vessel being battered about by a tumultuous sea. And the storm was slowly making him lose contact with reality. He was drifting further and further away from shore.

But there was one thing which Ty could not know.

There would be no trial.

Destiny had other plans.

*   *   *

I was sitting at my kitchen table writing an overdue letter to my understanding parents when the entrance bell rang.

Upon opening the door and seeing Friday, my spirits soared.

"Sorry that I'm breaking our agreement not to see each other, but may I come in?"

Obviously a rhetorical question, we met in a firm embrace and a penetrating kiss. Then we sat at the kitchen table.

"I can stay only a few minutes. Besides wanting to see you, touch you, be with you, I wanted to ask a favor."

"The answer is 'yes', whatever it is."

"It would give me great pleasure to have something of yours to take back with me. Any little thing will do."

The request pleased me as did everything about her. I excused myself and went to the bedroom. From a tiny box used to house a meager collection of jewelry, I took out my school ring. Suddenly perceiving Friday's presence in the room, I turned to face her and reverently placed the ring on the third finger of the left hand.

"It's merely from a two year college but I guess that doesn't matter cause it's only temporary."

Friday smiled and gently kissed me. Then she spoke again.

"Someday, we'll be totally happy. Right now, our song is being played by a piano. But someday it will be performed by a symphony orchestra."

"And we'll be sitting in the theatre box reserved for dignitaries. Everyone will be able to tell that the music is sounding just for us."

"I'm sure of that," she retorted; **"even if things do seem rather bleak right now."**

Of all the words in the English language, why did she use that one? The other time that someone had said "bleak" to me proved to be tragic.

I loved my tiny dog more than anything else in the entire world. An Italian greyhound named Snoopie. After too few years of being with me, she became ill. When I asked the vet for a prognosis, he had replied, "It looks bleak." Two days later, Snoopie died in my arms. Though it's been a long time, tears still flow and my heart breaks when I think of her.

Now Friday was using that fucking word and I could only hope it would not be another bad omen.

*   *   *

Midyat was relaxing on the bed in the guest room of his Hosts while tacitly reminiscing about the previous night in the Compound.

Shaking him from his reverie was the abrupt opening of the door as Cizre entered the room with a paper bag in his hand.

"Where have you been all afternoon?" asked Midyat.

"Shopping. —How did you pass the day?"

"I went with your Uncle on his job. Being an *eskugee* is fun. Buying and selling old things is interesting. When we go home, I will go into that business."

"There is no call for such a trade in Kurdistan. Our people have too few possessions as it is. We cannot afford to sell anything."

Midyat was perplexed.

"Why should our city be different from Ankara?"

"Because Ankara is in Turkey. Bitlis is in Kurdistan. That region should be ours. We should be an independent country! But we are not!"

The thing that Cizre could not understand was Midyat's lack of knowledge and concern regarding his own kind. He was probably the only Kurd who had to be constantly reminded that his people had been betrayed by such countries as Britain, France, Iran, Iraq, Syria, and Turkey.

Though Cizre sometimes found it a losing battle to educate his friend, he had vowed never to let up. He would make Midyat into a responsible Kurd, no matter how much energy it took. Even if it killed Midyat.

"If you hate the Turks so much," wondered Midyat, aloud; "why did you want to come here? Why do you want to know so much about them?"

"The more weaknesses that a man knows about his enemy, the greater foe he can be."

"What is in the bag?" asked Midyat.

Rather than answering, Cizre turned the sack upside down. Onto the bed fell several small clocks, lots of wires, and a large number of dynamite sticks.

Midyat studied the paraphernalia in a vain attempt to understand. Eventually, he was able to find his voice.

"I know what these are, Cizre, but why do you have them?"

Speaking calmly–and with a joyous gleam in his eye–Cizre answered.

"It is my very own independent statement. On behalf of my Grandfather and all the Kurds. Our contribution to the parade on Victory Day."

*   *   *

In Football news: College All-Americans:
Jim Brown, Syracuse; Ron Kramer, Michigan;
Alex Karras, Iowa

CHAPTER 28 –
"The Meat Delivery Truck"

My kitchen wall clock read 0945 hours. It was time to get ready.

August twenty-thrid and too nice a day to be stuck indoors. But that was exactly where I was going to be–at the Turkish court trial of Ty Manners.

Telling Turan that any Airman who worked in the Motor Pool could occasionally "borrow" a sedan without permission was the right thing to do. That information had helped Turan determine how Yuksel's body had been surreptitiously moved to the site where it was found.

Turan had promised to keep my identity confidential, but asked if I would make a public statement–should it be absolutely necessary. My answer was affirmative.

Consequently, I was requested to sit in the courtroom and act as a spectator unless Turan actually needed me as a witness. Anyway, I felt somehow involved because Yuksel had been a fond acquaintance.

I glanced at the clock again; it was 1000 hours. That gave me thirty minutes to get there. But the way Gobasi drove his taxi, we would arrive at the court house in fifteen. More than likely, he was already waiting for me in front of my building.

Gobasi was always welcome in my home. But never wanting me to feel rushed, he would patiently stay by his cab until I came out. One of my many blessings was having him and Pegu as my friends.

*   *   *

In Portland, Maine, Congressman Charles Manners entered the living room of his spacious home and found his wife Emily arranging multi-colored flowers in a cut glass vase. She glanced at her husband then re-directed her attention to the flowers.

"Your suitcase is in the foyer. How long do you think you'll be gone?"

"Maybe a week or so," he answered; "depending on the meeting with my office staff."

She finished with the flower arrangement and moved to the bar.

"Would you like a martini?"

"Not a bad idea," he concurred.

Charles Manners joined his wife. Sitting on a stool opposite her, he watched as she filled two sparkling clean glasses.

But Charles knew his wife's idiosyncrasies. This was a ceremony she practiced prior to any discussion of a serious problem which had arisen. One that he was not yet cognizant of.

Emily Manners remained behind the bar and silently sipped her martini.

"Let's have it," said Charles, finally. "What has happened to upset you?"

Seemingly from out of nowhere, she produced an unsealed envelope.

"This came for you over the teletype."

Charles read the contents then placed the communiqué on the bar; his wife continued.

"We also received a phone call from his lawyer, Lieutenant Kent."

"What do you think about this?" he asked.

With an air of indifference, she replied, "I think the paper makes a lovely coaster."

"It sounds as if Ty is in a lot of trouble."

"Is that something new?" she said, sardonically.

Her attitude came as no surprise to Charles. This was a situation they had faced many times before. Of all their six children, Ty had always been the most difficult, rebellious and uncontrollable. With five older brothers as examples, Ty should have learned the qualities of respect and responsibility. But he hadn't.

One incident that Charles could vividly remember was Ty being recalcitrant at a parade and Emily angrily hitting the boy a number of times.

"Should I go to Turkey and help him?" asked the Congressman.

His wife's answer was adamant.

"No! You have done enough in the past. If it weren't for your secret talk with that judge, Ty would be in an American prison right now instead of hiding out in the Air Force."

Charles could offer no defense. If he did go to Turkey and managed to get Ty out of the mess, it would probably be in vain. Several years down the road,

Ty would wind up in trouble again. Maybe even kill someone else. Besides, it was probably too late. The trial no doubt had started already.

"This is the first time we've heard from Ty since he enlisted over a year ago," continued Emily Manners. "If he wants to be such a loner, then let him. Sometimes, a parent has to abandon a failure."

Her words made good sense to the Congressman and he could think of no further argument to defend his wayward son. He gulped down the remainder of his martini.

"You're right," he announced, standing. "My business in D.C. is more pressing. —Where did you say you put my suitcase?"

————

Seated shoulder to shoulder in the back seat of the Air Force sedan were Colonel Myrons, Captain Lebal and Lieutenant Kent. The vehicle was en route from the JAMMAT Building to the Turkish courthouse in Yenishire.

For a long while they rode in silence. Finally, Colonel Myrons spoke.

"Lieutenant Kent, I was wondering what your t-true feelings are concerning t-the guilt or innocence of Airman M-Manners."

A large meat delivery truck whizzed by the sedan and abruptly cut in front of it. The Driver of the Air Force vehicle had to forcefully hit the brakes to avoid crashing into the truck, thereby causing his passengers to fall forward.

"Sorry, Sirs,…and Mam," said the airman Driver.

"that's quite all right," replied Winston. "it was not your fault. the driver of that truck is very reckless. i saw what happened."

As if to prove Winston's observation correct, the truck went through a red traffic light ahead of them. Then it pulled over to the sidewalk where the Driver got out and nonchalantly walked into a bar.

"a careless driver like him shouldn't be given a license," commented Winston. "he could cause a serious accident for someone. maybe even get someone killed."

With the incident over, Lieutenant Kent responded to the Colonel's question.

"My gut feeling is that Manners is probably guilty. He keeps swearing to his innocence but in our talks together, I have caught him in several lies. I don't think that he meant to kill the girl. It was probably done in a fit of passion."

"Briefly put, t-then, Lieutenant," said the Colonel; "M-Manners' chances don't look so good."

"The word that I would use, Sir, is bleak!"

*   *   *

I stood on the spacious top landing of the wide descending concrete stairway of the Courthouse Building.

Rectangularly shaped and four stories high, the edifice has a series of six huge pillars which support a mock terrace above them. When the sun is behind the building, the mock terrace offers a soothing shade. But it is also useful as protection from the rain for people entering the Courthouse through one of the three wide-door entrances.

Because the building was void of air-conditioning, I planned to wait outside until most of the principal players arrived. While smoking another cigarette in the cover of one pillar, I saw Sandy, Mrs. Myrons and a few other females enter the Courthouse.

Also ascending the steps were Colonel Myrons, Winston, Lieutenant Kent, and several guys from the Motor Pool. But conspicuously absent were Kyle, Nurtan, and Madam Sivas.

Putting out the cigarette, I was about to go into the building when Turan exited.

"Hello, Corey! Thank you for coming!"

"Yuksel was someone I admired and justice must be served."

Turan smiled, nodded in agreement, then added: "I intend to keep my promise! I will not call upon you unless it is absolutely necessary!"

"Where are you going?" I asked.

"I am late! I had to stop here first to verify something! Now I must go pick up Chief Inspector Burdur! Along with two policemen, we will go to the prison and transport Ty Manners here to the courthouse! Please excuse me!"

In the next instant, Turan moved down the wide sprawling steps and entered a waiting green sedan parked at the curb.

*   *   *

To Ty, the scene was like a repeat-performance of the day he had been arrested. He sat in the back seat of a green sedan between two tall, brawny Turks who uttered not a word and simply stared ahead as if in a trance. In the front, Turan drove the vehicle while Chief Inspector Burdur sat beside him in the passenger seat.

Having to face this court trial was proving to be more harrowing than Ty had imagined. He had had very little sleep during the night because his mind was befuddled.

The evidence against him was so overwhelming that he had finally agreed with Lieutenant Kent to plead temporary insanity.

Turan pulled away from the prison and drove the several blocks to the Ulus circle. He waited patiently for an opportunity to blend into the dense morning traffic. As he did so, his mind wandered. In just a few hours, he thought, Yuksel's murder will have been avenged. Then he would be free to pursue that other American–Kyle.

In the midst of these contemplations, Turan saw an opening in the traffic and accelerated the gas pedal. He drove around the right side of the circle and approached the spot where Ataturk Boulevard begins.

Then it happened.

Coming from the opposite direction was a meat delivery truck. It was moving too fast and was too far to the left. When Turan realized that the truck was about to hit them, he tried to swerve to the right. But it was too late. The truck plowed into the left fender of Turan's vehicle with a loud resounding noise. Both vehicles came to a crashing halt. All of the passengers in the green sedan were catapulted forward.

Turan hit his head on the steering wheel and was instantly rendered unconscious. Additionally, the left side of his body was pinned under a mass of crushed steel. The top half of Inspector Burdur's body broke through the windshield; his head, chest and abdomen lay on the hood with huge shards of glass penetrating various parts. He was mercifully unconscious as his own blood profusely engulfed him.

The three passengers in the rear had also felt the impact of the crash. The Man seated behind Turan found himself on top of the unconscious Driver. The weight of the other Guard had pushed the passenger seat forward so that his body pinned the legs of Inspector Burdur. Ty had landed between the Driver and Passenger and had hit his head on the dashboard.

The two brawny Men quickly righted themselves and alighted from the vehicle to survey the damage and assist their colleagues. Not upper-most in their minds was the prisoner who had been cradled between them.

Ty quickly shook his head from side to side and sat back in his seat. Slowly, the blurry vision began to clear itself. He looked at the two still bodies directly in front of him but did not know them. He looked at himself. The clothes were strange and he did not know whom they belonged to. Then he casually got out of the vehicle. People were buzzing all around him but he did not understand what they were saying.

So Ty aimlessly walked away from the scene and no one noticed.

The Driver of the meat delivery truck casually strolled away from the accident totally unharmed.

*   *   *

I glanced at my watch. It had been forty-five minutes since Turan had gotten into the sedan and driven away. It shouldn't take him that long to get back.

Or was I just being dense? Perhaps Turan and his party had already returned and went into the Courthouse through a back entrance. I decided to investigate.

Upon entering the huge lobby, I spied all the Americans previously seen entering the building. They were coming out of a far portal. Recognizing one of the guys from the Motor Pool, I pulled him aside.

"What's going on?"

"Weren't you inside when they announced it?"

"No. I've been waiting in front."

"Well, there isn't going to be any trial. At least, not today."

"Why?"

"One of the judges announced that Manners and the others were in a car accident. Turan Karapinar is unconscious with a broken leg, and some sprained ribs. The other guy, Inspector Burdur, is dead."

"What about Ty?"

"They don't know. He seems to have disappeared."

*   *   *

Cizre and Midyat sat on a bench in the enormous plaza of Ataturk's Tomb.

"What a waste of money and material all of this is," exclaimed Cizre.

"But it looks very nice," offered Midyat.

"Do you not understand? These people are our enemies. As a Kurd, you are not supposed to like this."

Midyat looked down at the ground.

"I am sorry. You must have patience with me, Cizre. I do not know many things. Since you are much smarter, you have to teach me."

Cizre placed a hand on his friend's shoulder.

"Forgive me, Midyat. I am not angry with you. I know you are doing your best. I have waited so long to avenge my Grandfather, and the time is so near that I can hardly believe it is about to happen."

"That is the highest flag pole I have ever seen," said Midyat. "And the biggest flag."

257

Cizre looked up at the red banner with its five-point star and crescent.

"What do the moon and star mean?" asked Midyat, innocently.

"That is a crescent," corrected Cizre. "I do not know the exact meaning because there are several versions of the flag's history but the crescent and star are symbols of Islam, and the national colors of Turkey are red and white."

"I am not very bright," confessed Midyat. "Why do you want me as your friend?"

"Because Allah has decreed it so."

Midyat looked Cizre directly in the eyes.

" I want you to know that I value your friendship. I will always do anything you want."

"Then you will help me with the bomb?"

Midyat solemnly nodded his head in the affirmative.

"It may be dangerous," added Cizre.

"I do not care because you will be at my side."

Cizre sat down next to his friend.

"We will set off the first bomb along the parade route on Ataturk Boulevard, near the American Embassy."

"There is to be more than one?"

"Yes," continued Cizre. "The second bomb was to be here. Since it is far enough away from the American Embassy, the Turks would think the whole city was under attack. But now that I am looking at it, I have doubts. I must think of another spot for our second bomb."

"Are not other Kurds going to help us?" inquired Midyat.

"Negative. We are working entirely alone. This is for my Grandfather. It is to show the Turks that some Kurdish people are a force to be reckoned with."

"But how will the Turks know this?"

"The next day, before we leave Ankara, I will telephone the newspaper and tell them. But I will not give our names."

"Good for us Kurds," chanted Midyat, excitedly.

"But bad for the Turks," added Cizre; "for the red in their flag is going to be spilt Turkish blood!"

*　　　*　　　*

CHAPTER 29 –

"All the Moments of the Day"

*   *   *

Just before closing time in the Motor Pool, Kyle was given a surprise party by a group of coworkers as it was his last day on the job prior to going Stateside. They presented him with a cigarette lighter bearing his initials.

Kyle thanked each of them as pieces of cake and shots of *raki* were handed out, and the boys began telling stories about their tour of duty in Ankara.

In the midst of one tale, a guy named Mike interrupted himself.

"Kyle, isn't that your wife over there?"

The party Boy turned to see Nurtan standing just outside the garage door. She waved to him and smiled as he excused himself and went to greet her.

"What are ya doin here, Babe?"

"Please," she replied. "Please we talk. By selves."

"Okay. We'll go on up to the JAMMAT Building."

Telling the group he would quickly return, Kyle led Nurtan past the rest of the garages, beyond Captain Lebal's office, and along the dirt road which ascended to the JAMMAT Building–approximately five hundred feet ahead of them.

"Why are ya here, Babe?" asked Kyle.

"Please. To ask what must I pack. How much take with me I can."

"What the hell are ya talkin' 'bout?"

"We go to States. No?"

"What makes ya say that?"

Nurtan opened her pocketbook and took out Kyle's transfer orders.

"I find by mistake and no understand. American girl neighbor explain to me."

Kyle quietly listened as Nurtan gently admonished him for not having told her sooner. There were so many things to do before leaving and would she have enough time?

This was the scene Kyle had planned to avoid. His intention had been to write a letter, leave it on the kitchen table, and sneak out of the apartment before Nurtan woke up on the morning of August 30. By the time Nurtan found the letter, he would be gone and she'd be unable to find him.

"Ah didn't tell ya sooner 'cause Ah can't take ya back."

Profoundly shocked, Nurtan stopped walking. Her eyes clearly asked why without having to say the words.

"Ya wouldn't like it. Ya wouldn't fit. Ya'd miss this place."

"I not understand," she said. "You are husband. Wife goes with husband."

Kyle became annoyed. *The girl must be dumb. Don't she get the message?*

"Only in Turkey. You're only mah wife here. In American law, we ain't married."

"Still not understand. What are you say?"

He took a deep breath then spit out the words.

"It's over, Babe. We're finished. Ah'm goin' back. You're stayin' here. Just like we never knew each other."

His cavalier demeanor jolted Nurtan into a near trance. The cold words spewing from Kyle's mouth seemed to be coming from someone she did not know. This man with whom she had lived for nearly a year was suddenly a stranger. She tried to digest the reality but it was choking her.

"One time I tell you of friend. Her boyfriend go back States and leave her. You say you not do that. You promise me."

"What can Ah tell ya?" blurted Kyle, now becoming defensive, "Ah was wrong. Ah spoke without' thinkin'."

Nurtan felt faint but adamantly fought it. She refused to hold onto Kyle by playing on his sympathy. And the idea of pleading was dismissed because she would not belittle herself as other girls had done. Though she loved Kyle more than anything else, and did not want to lose him, it was obvious that there was no choice.

"How you can do this, Kyle? I not understand."

"Ah'm doin' it fer you. You're better here than in the States. Ya skin's too dark. People might think ya was a ... ."

Nurtan began pounding his chest with her hands while crying hysterically.

Kyle allowed the passionate attack for a few seconds but finally stopped it by taking her in his arms.

With her head resting on his strong chest, Nurtan cried for awhile—as if trying to keep the moment from being true. But even in her desperate state, she could tell that his arms were not clutching her lovingly, only as a necessary ploy to free himself.

Presently, Nurtan composed herself and slowly backed away from him. She looked at Kyle with silent tears falling down her cheeks and sighed in defeat. Without saying a word she turned from him and laboriously began walking up the hill toward JAMMAT.

"Ah'll write ta ya," Kyle yelled after her. "Ta see how you're doin'."

Nurtan's confused mind could no longer process any words—only messages of pain and complete emptiness as she moved away from her lifelong dream of being a loving wife and wonderful mother.

She thought of the fetus within her. Perhaps it would be better if the baby never saw the light of day. Perhaps she and her unborn child should join Yuksel.

Kyle watched Nurtan until she reached the top of the hill. Then he turned and started walking back to the end garage. There was a party going on. He didn't want to miss any more of it.

———————

Madam Sivas awoke from a late afternoon nap with sweaty palms—her body trembling. An horrific vision had shaken her from slumber. In a dream she saw Nurtan fading away. The life draining from the Girl's body. The coldness of death waiting to pounce.

The time was 2000 hours. The anxiousness and stress Madam Sivas felt catapulted her into a powerhouse of determined energy. She had already lost one treasured niece. There was no way she would allow anything to happen to the other.

Madam Sivas sprung from the couch and swiftly moved to the telephone. She gave Nurtan's number to the operator and patiently waited. The phone rang once, twice, three times. Then five, seven, nine.

"Sorry, *Efendi*," said the operator. "Your party does not answer."

"Please! Please try one more time," urged the woman.

The operator reluctantly complied. Once again it happened: seven, eight, nine rings. No answer.

With great agitation, Madam Sivas slammed the receiver in its cradle and contemplated her next move.

*   *   *

Because I had the afternoon off and was looking for ways to distract my mind from Friday, a trip to visit Turan in the hospital seemed in order. Also because I wanted to go. Since our meeting in Intim's that night concerning Yuksel's misfortune, my feelings toward the handsome Turkish policeman with the penetrating eyes had changed. I began to look upon him in a different light. He was no longer a frightening figure. Instead, he was becoming something of a friend.

Turan's greeting was delivered with a broad smile.

"Corey, my Friend! How nice that you have come!"

We shook hands. I gave him a carton of American cigarettes, a box of chocolates, and sat on a chair next to his bed.

"Tomorrow I will be going home!" said Turan.

His words came as a surprise. He was even stronger than I imagined. Though a small cast covered the lower part of his left leg, and there were bandages wrapped around his ribs, he seemed as healthy as ever.

"Four days ago, when the accident occurred, they carried me in here on a stretcher! A few people thought I was close to death! A few others probably hoped so! Obviously, I looked worse than I was!"

Turan excused himself as he picked up the telephone to order tea and Turkish pastries.

"That's great news about tomorrow. Is someone coming to drive you home?"

"Yes, thank you! I have been assigned a driver! Now that I am the new Chief Inspector of the Secret Police!"

The comment made him fall silent for several minutes. I casually looked away so as not to embarrass him as tears formed in his eyes. It was apparent that Turan was upset over the untimely death of his predecessor.

"I will deeply miss my dear friend," announced Turan, with a hoarse-sounding voice. "He was closer to me than my father!"

When I offered my condolences, he nodded in acceptance and continued to speak.

"Tell me what you have been doing, Corey!"

I spoke of the upcoming events that promised to be exciting: the President's breakfast party on August 30, the parade, and the trip to Istanbul. To the latter, Turan promised to give me the phone numbers of several superb girls he had met there many years ago. To the former, he would also be in attendance as the President planned to officially install Turan in the Office of Chief Inspector of the Secret Police.

"Will you be well enough to go to the breakfast?" I asked.

Turan laughed in a kindly manner.

"I intend to return to work on Sunday! There are many things to catch up on! Thank you for being concerned but I am fine! My leg is itchy from the cast and my side hurts a bit! Other than that, I feel very fit!"

While he was speaking, the thought crossed my mind to ask how he was coping with Yuksel's death. But seeing that he had been so saddened over Inspector Burdur, I decided to avoid the topic.

Then he surprised me by stating that Ty Manners had been picked up in Yenishire the day before when he had stopped to ask a policeman for directions.

"It appears that he has amnesia!" stated Turan. "He may be faking or it may be legitimate! At any rate, he has been sent to the mental ward of the Ulus prison and is undergoing extensive examinations! And he will stay there until his memory is restored! Then we will resume his trial for Yuksel's murder!"

An orderly delivered a tray with tea and Turkish pastries and left as quietly as he had entered. We munched on the delicacies while continuing our conversation.

"But enough about everyone else, Corey! I want to know how you are really doing!"

"Fine."

" I mean your romance with Mrs. Lebal!"

He smiled at the surprised look on my face.

"That is supposed to be a secret. How do you know about it?"

"My job *is* secrets!" he laughed.

"And so it is."

"Furthermore, my new Friend, no one will learn of your affair from me! I promise you that much!"

My smile and nod of appreciation seemed to please him.

Since he was already aware of it, I told him the entire story—from the innocent beginning to the present moment and Friday's fears because Winston had threatened to shoot me if I came near her at the station or on the train itself.

"Would you really try to see her?" asked Turan.

"That might be a possiblity. I generally do succumb to temptation easily."

In the wake of these words, Turan honored me by speaking in the same way that Urdanur had. Practically the same words.

"Please be careful, Corey! I do not want anything bad to happen to you!"

By a tacit agreement, we changed the subject and Turan began asking questions about New York City as he had on the first night we met–almost a lifetime ago.

A half hour later, we shook hands and I left.

"*Allahaismarladik*, Turan."

"*Gule gule*, Corey."

*   *   *

Seated at an outdoor cafe across from the hospital, two Turkish Men were drinking coffee as they acknowledged a third who approached them.

"*Merhaba*," he said.

"*Merhaba*, Mohair," they chanted in unison.

"Get someone to replace me guarding the boss," ordered Mohair. "The Inspector wants me to follow that American walking down the street. His name is Corey Brotano."

"Immediately," answered one of the men. "But what is Brotano suspected of doing?"

"If I tell you that," replied Mohair; "you will know too much and then I will have to turn you both into frogs."

With the words proclaimed, Mohair grinningly left his open-mouthed colleagues to follow Corey.

Madam Sivas alighted from the taxi. Hurriedly reaching Nurtan's front door, she discovered it was unlocked. She went into the private vestibule, climbed the steep flight of stairs and loudly banged on the apartment door. When no answer came, her body began to tremble again. Another foreboding possessed her. She became genuinely frantic. She banged harder and harder but to no avail.

Coming from inside the flat was music. This told the Woman that Nurtan must be at home. The girl would never leave the radio playing if she were out. Nurtan was much too frugal for that.

Madam Sivas continued to pound on the door until her fists became numb. She would not give up! She descended the steps and sought out the building custodian. Together they returned to Nurtan's apartment where Madam Sivas demanded that the Man unlock the door with his passkey.

Once inside, Madam Sivas immediately went to the bedroom–where the music seemed to be coming from. Upon entering she found Nurtan lying peacefully on the bed. The girl was very still. And her eyes were closed.

Madam Sivas turned to the Custodian and screamed at him: "Call an ambulance! Call an ambulance!"

*   *   *

There was great danger in the chance we were taking but with only three days remaining before she left, the risk seemed justifiable.

Two hours earlier, Friday had slipped a note under my front door asking me to meet her at our special spot because our final farewell should be memorable.

Gobasi dropped me off first and then returned to get Friday.

It seemed forever by the time she arrived.

We kissed with a passion that had never been so intense. So strong and profound. Then we made love. It was the most ecstatic of all our times together.

Afterwards, as we lay on the grass enjoying nature and our last time with each other, guilt suddenly consumed me.

"Are we being evil?" I asked.

"Not at all. We're only acting out a script that Destiny has written." She paused and a smile adorned her face. **"Besides, everyone knows that 'evil' spelled backwards is 'live'!"**

Leave it to Friday to find humor in a sad situation. She could always be counted on to make me laugh. In the future I would have to frequently remember her quaint sayings in order to console myself when she wasn't around.

"Will you come back here and think of me?" asked Friday.

"Never. This spot has no meaning without you."

"In your favorite movie," teased Friday; **"the girl goes back to the mountain after she learns that he has died. Against all odds, she hopes to find him there."**

"That will not happen," I protested. "Fate has no misfortune planned for us."

Changing the subject, Friday announced, **"I will write as soon as I'm settled!"**

"Every day that you're not with me will be an eternity."

"And how often will you write?"

"Every week. But I will think of you all the moments of the day when my eyes are open. Maybe even when I'm asleep. They will be the sweetest dreams."

A cloud momentarily shadowed the sun and we both became silent. We knew the last instant had painfully arrived.

Rising, we joined hands then reluctantly moved toward the brush area beyond which Gobasi was waiting to take us back to the dread reality which lay ahead.

Suddenly, she stopped walking.

"Did you ever finish writing the words to our song?"

"I think you asked me that once before, and again my answer has to be 'no'. Something seems to be blocking me. Perhaps I can't finish them until it is certain that our future together is secure."

"It doesn't matter, my Love, just as long as I have you."

"And that's a given," I smiled.

One absolute last kiss and then she got into the cab which slowly drove away and became smaller and smaller as my heart grew heavy and heavier.

Perhaps it was my sadness. Perhaps it was the unexpected loneliness. Perhaps it was fate silently whispering. But suddenly I sincerely wondered if Madam Sivas' prediction for me would really bring a happy ending.

Soviet Attacks Hungary, Seizes Premier Nagy

CHAPTER 30 —
"The Day Before the Day"

The morning's mail proved to be illuminating as I received a letter from Edith in which she announced her engagement to a former classmate of ours who was studying to be a lawyer; the wedding was planned for spring of 1957.

The news came as a delightful surprise because there was still some lingering guilt on my part. So I smiled broadly while placing the note on the bureau and grabbing a small athletic bag to start packing for the weekend trip to Istanbul on the following night.

My smile lingered and widened as I listened to a news story that came over the American radio station broadcasting from Germany.

In Korea today, a former American serviceman was arrested for selling drugs and if convicted could serve up to twenty years in a Korean prison. All of us here wish you luck, Vance Leigh.

*   *   *

Madam Sivas sat in an easy chair in her parlor and gazed at her Godchild who was peacefully sleeping on the couch. Seeing Nurtan now was a relief compared to that day in the girl's apartment.

After Madam Sivas had ordered the custodian to send for an ambulance, she discovered an empty bottle of sleeping pills on the table next to Nurtan's bed, and hastily threw it into her pocketbook.

By the time the medics arrived, Madam Sivas and the Custodian had managed to stir Nurtan out of the extreme drowsiness by employing a series of methods which included pouring coffee down the Girl's throat, and assisting her in walking.

When the Intern from the ambulance had asked what happened, Madam

Sivas nonchalantly replied that she had given Nurtan the wrong medicine. Without her glasses, she thought the bottle contained aspirin. The Intern accepted the explanation without question but took Nurtan to the hospital for follow-up treatment and examination.

Madam Sivas was suddenly very grateful for her clairvoyant powers. If it had not been for the sometimes questionable gift, she would not be calmly sitting there–watching her niece peacefully sleeping.

But one side of Madam's mind had shifted to another subject. And her emotions fanned the embers. Though uncharacteristic, she was harboring hatred. No matter what it took, she would not let Kyle get away with hurting her nieces. She would make him pay for his dastard deeds!

––––––

Indulging in a lazy afternoon, Drew lounged on the sofa in his apartment and listened to some of the latest phonograph records which had arrived from the States. When the doorbell rang, he answered it to find Hank Myrons.

After a quick kiss, the Colonel made his way to the parlor.

Rather than sit on the sofa next to Drew, he situated himself in an easy chair while Drew left the room and quickly returned with wine.

"What can be so important that you visit me on a Sunday?"

"A crucial decision I have m-made."

"And that is?"

"I'm resigning from t-the Army, going back t-to t-the S-States, and entering t-the political arena."

"You never mentioned such aspirations in the past."

"T-There are s-some t-things you don't know about m-me."

"Please continue."

"I had a long t-talk with m-my wife. I t-told her t-that divorce was a certainty unless s-she s-straightened out and s-started doing what I wanted. S-She realized I was s-serious and s-so s-she agreed." He paused. "Also, s-she likes t-the idea of being a S-Senator's wife s-someday."

Drew was silent for a while before giving his observations on the matter.

"Repeat performance," he announced.

"What is t-that s-supposed t-to m-mean?" asked Hank.

"Only that we've been through this before. We met in Frisco, I fell hard, and then you left. Now, years later–after I had gotten over it–you come back into my life and do the same thing."

Hank lowered his eyes.

"I'm s-sorry if I hurt you. I never m-meant t-to. It's just t-that m-my life is all fucked-up t-the way it is and if I don't do s-something drastic, I m-might have a nervous breakdown."

Drew began to console himself. *Probably Hank's decision was all for the best.* After his own tour of duty was up, Drew intended to go back to Hollywood and resume a career. That being the case, there would be no room in his life for the Colonel, anyway. Especially if Hank never intended to divorce his wife. In the final analysis, this split-up was inevitable. What did it really matter if it happened now or later?

"When is this going to be effective?" asked Drew.

"M-My last day in t-the Army will probably be s-somewhere around late October or early November."

Drew sighed.

"I want you to know that there are no hard feelings. I wish you well."

Though he said the words bravely, his heart was aching. Throughout the years, Hank had always meant so much to him. More than just a lover, the Man was a friend, hero and mentor. To give him up was a painful deed. But there was no stopping the sorrows that life brought one's way, and you had to face them courageously in order to survive while maintaining your sanity.

"By the time you decide to run for president, I'll be a famous actor and you can call upon me to endorse your campaign."

"T-That's a deal," smiled Hank.

———————

In the mental ward of the Ulus Prison, Ty sat on a chair next to an opened window. Across from him and in close proximity was a psychiatrist who jotted several comments in a notebook on his clipboard.

Sunday, August 29, 1956.   Second session.

Patient does not respond to his name. I repeated a list of names belonging to people he knows. Not the slightest bit of recognition was shown by the patient. Today, I will repeat the names.

"Can you at least remember your name?" asked the Doctor.

"No," replied Ty, solemnly. "You told me it's Ty Manners. But that doesn't mean anything to me."

"Do you know where you are?"

"A hospital, I guess."

"In what country?"

"The United States, of course."

Considered to be most astute in this relatively new field of psychiatry, the Doctor used the technique of not coercing his patient to recall things, just sort of nudging him.

"Are not any of these names familiar?" asked the Doctor, after reading them to Ty.

"Maybe the last one, sir."

"Corey?"

"Yes."

"Do you know him, Ty?"

"I don't think so."

It was not a substantial breakthrough, thought the Doctor, but at least a beginning.

"Then why do you say it sounds familiar?"

"I don't know. It just gives me a strange feeling. I don't like the name."

———————

Turan sat in the huge leather chair in his new office and began to attack a stack of reports waiting for him in the desk tray. The first was by Mohair Tercan, a brand new agent who reminded Turan of himself. A younger man with whom he was forming a relationship exactly like the one he had had with Jean Claude Burdur; except that Turan was the mentor.

> *To date, there is nothing suspicious to relate about Corey Brotano. When subject left the hospital, he shopped in the Bazaar and bought several phonograph records. He then went directly home and had no visitors for the rest of the evening.*
>
> *The next day, the subject had a rendezvous with a woman in the vicinity of that wooded area where Yuksel Ispir's body was found. Their meeting was of a sexual nature and they left immediately afterwards.*
>
> *Since that time, the subject has done nothing else but go directly from his apartment to the JAMMAT Building, work his hours, and return to his apartment.*
>
> *As far as I can ascertain, the subject has spoken to no one other than his fellow workers. And he has had no contact with Kyle Muenster.*
>
> *I will continue the surveillance.*
>
> *Agent Mohair Tercan*

Turan tossed the paper aside, and spoke out loud.

"You can rest assured, Corey. We have our eyes on you."

The Inspector's next focal point was Kyle Muenster and he reached for the phone.

"This is Inspector Karapinar! Have several men pick-up the American named Kyle Muenster! You can find him by contacting personnel at the JAMMAT Building! Keep him confined overnight and I will personally question him tomorrow!"

"But that is Victory Day," protested a voice at the other end.

"Crime does not take a vacation! Now do as you were told!"

————

After the incident with Nurtan at the Motor Pool, Kyle had to return to the apartment and get his belongings without having another confrontation with her.

He telephoned the apartment and receiving no answer, felt that the coast was clear. On his arrival there, he saw Nurtan being carried out on a stretcher. Next to her was that old Woman, Sivas, and together they entered an ambulance. So Kyle hid himself across the street until they left.

Upon approaching his building, Kyle met the Custodian who voluntarily told him what had happened. He thanked the man, got his belongings, and left for some fun at the Compound.

Until train time on August 30th, he'd stay in a cheap hotel. Going to Corey's was a bad idea because the Guy had changed!

*   *   *

With the packing for Istanbul finished, I found plenty of time on my hands. The thought of going to Intim's crossed my mind but since I had to get up early in the morning for the President's breakfast, the idea was quickly dropped.

From out of nowhere, an urge hit me. Why not start that novel I had been thinking about for so long? Why wait until my return from Istanbul?

Fired with a renewed energy, I got a stack of paper, several pens, and sat down at the kitchen table.

I stared around the room for inspiration and marveled that there was plenty of fodder from the souvenirs lying about:

   —a napkin from the Gece Klub: my first night in town when
      Turan frightened the hell out of me;
   —a monogrammed glass from the Istanbul Palace: my first belly
      dancer, and Kyle and Nurtan's engagement party where I met
      the unfortunate Yuksel;
   —PROFILES IN COURAGE : a book presented by Friday and
      Winston, and the start our relationship;

—a rhinestone tie pin: gift for being best man at Kyle and Nurtan's wedding, and the brawl between Turan and Ty Manners;

—Tarot cards: given to me by the clairvoyant Madam Sivas;

—a weight-lifting magazine: a symbol of Drew, along with my realization that alternative lifestyles are not abnormal or bad, just different;

—a miniature copper replica of a Turkish barbeque: purchased in Samsun, and a remembrance of the adventure of Gobasi, Kenan, and I rescuing Pegu from the Compound;

—an autographed picture: of Jane and Peter, the entertainers at Intim's;

—a copy of THE KORAN: with love from my dear Urdanur to help guide me through life; and,

—a metal heart/horseshoe key chain, plus a dog tag representing Friday's love.

These were all good sources for refreshing my memories.

Why not be like Ernest Hemingway, I decided. He wrote stories based on his experiences in foreign countries.

And so I wrote:

> Chapter 1 - "The New Foreigner"
> Ankara, Turkey – 1956
>
> The sun was shining when I arrived in Ankara earlier in the day. Satin white clouds of exotic shapes floated against an azure background whose vivid blue was not so terribly different from that of the Mediterranean Sea some miles away. The crisp March air was tempered by golden light and ....

I paused to add the title of the book: *CHAMPAGNE DAYS*.

*   *   *

Friday was reading on the back porch when Winston entered and interrupted her.

"what is the book?"

"SAYONARA by James A. Michener. Very appropriate, don't you think?"

Winston looked puzzled so Friday explained.

"It means 'goodbye.' And that's just what we're doing."

"only for the time being," he replied.

Friday closed the book and laid it on the table beside her.

"Perhaps it will be permanently."

"what is that supposed to mean?"

Friday shrugged her shoulders.

"Who knows? If I need an operation, I might not come out of it alive."

"don't talk so stupidly," said Winston, annoyed. "you're going to be fine."

"Well, it has been known to happen."

"not to you. you're too... ." He halted to search for the right word.

"Too ornery? Is that what you want to say?"

"don't put words in my mouth. don't imagine things."

"Why not? You always do."

The last thing Winston wanted was to argue with her—especially with the illusion of what could happen to her. And no matter what had come between them during the years, he was still in love with her.

"have you finished packing?"

"Yes. Most of the clothes we need. You can send the rest as soon as the kids and I get settled."

"do you have enough money?"

She shook her head in the affirmative.

Friday had decided that when she and the children arrived in New York City, they would get a hotel room until an apartment could be found. Probably in Greenwich Village; it was one of her favorite spots in the Big Apple.

"well don't forget to send me a telegram as soon as you arrive. so i know that you're safe."

"Will do," she replied. **"If you have nothing else to say right now, I'd like to finish reading. I'm almost at the end and I promised to give the book to Urdanur. She's been waiting for it."**

Winston nodded then left the room. He went into the bedroom and from a secret hiding place took out the gun anonymously purchased in Diyarbakir. He checked to see that it was loaded.

This was the firearm he would take with him to Istanbul. And in case that back-stabbing Corey tried to come anywhere near Friday, the Lad would be greeted with a big and fatal surprise—just like the rabbit!

*   *   *

CHAPTER 31 –
"Victory Day – Morning"

August 30, 1956, was to be a day of entertaining highs, unexpected lows, and frightening chaos. A day whose climax would find me unwillingly bewildered.

It began with Urdanur and I attending the President's breakfast.

We arrived at the huge Civic Hall Building at 0845 hours and followed the line of other chosen ones through tall brass doors, over a marble-floored lobby and into a titanic assembly hall. Soldiers were posted everywhere and a person was admitted only by showing the lavishly designed invitation with embossed gold leaf print on it.

We attacked the amply stocked buffet then found our assigned spot. It was very close to the main table and I was able to get a good look at President Mahzun and the other dignitaries, including Turan.

Two of the men at our table happened to be former classmates of Urdanur. One of them turned out to be a "snitch" for he exposed Urdanur as a prolific joke teller when they were in secondary school. That was a cue for us to encourage her to tell one. She was a bit reluctant but finally consented.

"There was a great atomic explosion and everyone on the face of the earth perished. Somewhere in North Africa, from a pile of refuse emerged a little monkey. He traveled far and wide until he finally met a female monkey–the ONLY other living creature on earth. They joined forces and traveled together. Soon they came to an orchard of apple trees. The female monkey picked an apple, took a bite, and offered it to her male companion. He suspiciously looked at her and said, 'Oh, no! Let's not start that again!'"

Everyone laughed heartily then retreated into private conversations while eating.

Approximately thirty minutes later, the President gave a brief speech followed by the official installation of the new Chief Inspector: Turan Karapinar. My friend looked especially handsome in his bone color suit and I felt privileged to know someone in such a high governmental position.

As Turan and the President left the banquet hall they waved to us: Turan to me, and the President to Urdanur.

With the return smile fading from her face, Urdanur looked at me.

"I do not want to ruin the happiness of this day for you," she began; "but there is something I must tell you. Late last evening Winston called and asked me to speak to you."

"Is he off his rocker?"

"Maybe so because he requested that I warn you not to go near Friday at any time today, neither at the apartment nor at the train station. Not even for a friendly goodbye."

"Does he know that I'm leaving on the same train?"

"If he does, no mention was made of it."

"What did he say exactly?"

"If you so much as approach her, he is prepared to kill you—regardless of the consequences. He would willingly do that rather than see Friday leave him for you."

Silence reigned for a short while as I tried to digest the message. On more than one occasion, Friday had told me of his feral nature. She feared that Winston was on the brink of a nervous breakdown, or worse. She had further stressed that he was definitely capable of violence. She had once seen him almost fatally beat an Airman.

Urdanur continued.

"For your sake, Corey—and mine, because you mean so much to me— swear that you will not go near Friday tonight."

Reverently, I nodded my head in a promise so as not to worry my dear friend. But the harsh words of Winston's message kept reverberating in my brain: *"kill you!"* And was I capable of staying away from Friday?

*   *   *

When Turan and President Mahzun left the Civic Hall, Turan escorted the esteemed politician to his waiting limousine. Before entering the vehicle, the President hardily shook Turan's hand.

"I think you will make a very good Chief Inspector, my Son. I know that Jean Claude Burdur thought so."

"Thank you, *Efendi;* I am quite honored. I will see you later at the parade."

As the President got in his car and it drove away, Turan reached in his pocket for a walkie-talkie similar to the ones he had distributed to many of his agents. It was one of his first innovations since assuming the Office.

The radios would prove to be very useful in avoiding crimes and apprehending perpetrators.

Turan spoke into the radio.

"Mohair, come in!"

The reply was instantenous.

"Yes, *Efendi.*"

"How are things going?"

"Fine. Corey and that lady are still at the Breakfast."

"That lady's name is Urdanur Besni," corrected Turan. "And she is a good friend of President Mahzun!"

"Sorry, *Efendi.* Next time I will know her."

"You are doing a good job, Mohair! Stay with Corey all day; it is imperative that you not let him out of your sight!"

––––––

Most of the patients in the mental ward of the Ulus Prison were not concerned about the holiday festivities stirring outside their walls. But one of them was mildly interested as he sat by the open window and looked down at the portion of Ataturk Boulevard where the members of the parade were excitedly readying their floats.

"What is happening down there, Ty?" asked the Doctor.

"You called me that name again. Is it mine?"

"Well, you did respond; you knew who I was talking to."

"I'm the only one fucking sitting here," retorted Ty.

The doctor conceded a grin. *The patient had amnesia; he was not dumb.*

"Tell me what is happening down there."

Ty sighed with annoyance. He did not know who he was or why he was in the hospital, only that this fuckin' doctor was starting to piss him off. *Everyday he bugs me about names and places and things*, whined Ty to himself.

On the other hand, the answers he gave the Doctor surprisingly seemed to bring him closer to the past.

"They're having a parade," Ty reluctantly answered.

"Do you like parades?"

"I guess they're okay."

"What kind of feeling do you get from watching a parade?"

"Like I've been in many of them, and in the front. Maybe even on a float."

The doctor knew that Ty's father was a Congressman.

"Were you ever in a parade with your father?"

"Maybe," offered Ty.

While he answered in only one word, something in Ty's memory came back. He was twelve years old and standing next to several other boys. He must have done something wrong because when he got off the float some woman began smacking him until his nose bled and someone forced her to stop. Could that have been his mother?

"Please think, Ty. I am trying to help you."

"I don't know anything else about any fuckin' parade." He feigned a deep sigh. "Besides, I'm getting sleepy. I wanna lay down."

"Very well, Ty. You may get some rest. We will talk again later."

— — — — — —

In the house of his uncle, Cizre was sleeping soundly and the hour was 0800 hours. Midyat anxiously shook him awake while promising that he had something important to show.

When Cizre's eyes were fully opened, he watched Midyat pour out the contents of a paper bag and successfully assemble a bomb.

"That is good," exclaimed Cizre. "I am proud of you."

Midyat gracefully accepted the compliment and blushed.

"You are going to do very well today," continued Cizre. "And please remember your promise. If anything should happen to me—such as getting killed or arrested—you will set off the second bomb the way we planned."

Cizre looked directly into Midyat's eyes and waited for an answer.

"Do not talk like that, Cizre. I would be lost without you."

"You would do very well without me. You are capable of much more than you think. And if you are truly my friend, then you will honor my wishes!"

He paused.

"Please promise me!"

"So be it," said Midyat, reluctantly; "I promise you."

— — — — — — — — —

While the sun shone brightly at 1100 hours, a taxi stopped on one of the level roads in the mountainside graveyard on the outskirts of Ankara. A young Man conspicuously high on liquor emerged from the cab and ordered the Driver to wait.

The young Man looked at the slope above him and decided he had come to the correct part of the cemetery. As he recalled, her grave was close to the top.

Other mourners were also paying their respects, but not in his immediate area.

Grinning and softly humming, he meandered up the incline and eventually found the right spot.

He sat directly on the grave, guzzled down some *raki* from the bottle he had been carrying, lit a cigarette, and spoke out loud.

"Ah told ya that ya wasn't gonna get away wit' it, Bitch! Now Ah reckon that ya believe me. No female fucks with Kyle Muenster and gets away wit' it."

He gulped more *raki,* silently grinned down at the grave, and recalled the day it happened.

*

*

*

*

July 21, 1956

Kyle looked over at Nurtan who was peacefully sleeping beside him. He firmly shook her. She moaned but remained in deep slumber. Very good, he thought; the sleeping pills he had put in her tea had done the trick. She would not wake up until the next morning.

He got out of bed, donned dungarees–with Ty's jersey–and left the apartment. This was the day for his revenge to take place. He was so full of hatred for Yuksel striking him with the hammer that he could stand it no longer.

Having reported to sick call earlier, he had been instructed to spend the remainder of the day resting in bed. He knew that Nurtan would definitely insist on staying home to care for him. His Turkish wife was a perfect alibi. She would easily swear that he had been with her the entire day.

Kyle walked to Yuksel's apartment, sneaked into her backyard and peered through her kitchen window. He could not see Yuksel but heard her talking on the telephone. He covered his head with a stocking then quietly raised the kitchen window which opened very easily.

Yuksel was too preoccupied with her conversation to sense that anyone was entering the apartment, so Kyle successfully crept in and stood against the wall near the bedroom doorway. There he patiently waited.

Yuksel finally finished her call and walked into the kitchen. As she stepped over the threshold, a foreboding struck her because the window was open. But she had little time to wonder for Kyle made his move. He grabbed her by the arms and pushed her against the wall.

She let out a scream and Kyle forcefully smacked her across the face. Blood spewed from her mouth and drops of it landed on the jersey that he was wearing.

But the blow did not stop Yuksel. She hesitated for several seconds, then instinctively sprung back with fear-fueled adrenalin. She kicked Kyle in the groin, and, when he doubled over in pain, tore the covering off his face.

She stared at Kyle with disbelief and unrivaled hatred.

"Now I go tell Nurtan," Yuksel shouted. "Now, I telephone my friend!"

She swiftly moved back into the bedroom and headed for the phone which was on the nightstand–on the far side of her bed.

Still in pain, Kyle straightened himself and pursued his prey. He lunged for Yuksel who by then had the phone in her hand. He pulled the receiver away from her, yanked the cord out of the wall, and threw her on the bed. Then he pounced on her and she moaned from the force of his weight.

In the next instant, Kyle's strong hands were around her throat. When she tried to fight back with renewed vigor, his hands automatically tightened until her head slumped backward and her body collapsed.

Kyle stood looking at her for several minutes. Then he bent down and put his ear to her chest. She was definitely not breathing, he concluded. He hadn't meant to kill her. But he had. And she was dead. And that was that!

Out of habit, he glanced at the small alarm clock on the bedstand. It read 1700 hours.

Kyle easily composed himself and calmly walked out of the apartment, being sure to close the door. He casually strolled to the end of the street and turned right onto Ataturk Boulevard–humming as he proceeded along the way.

By the time Kyle arrived home, his mind had rationalized the crime he committed. There was no remorse in his soul, only the unyielding concern for self-preservation.

He immediately changed his shirt and stuffed Ty's blood stained jersey in the back pocket of his dungarees. He would later decide what to do with it.

Kyle involuntarily recalled how he had gotten the shirt in the first place. While he and Ty were on an errand for Captain Lebal, Ty had asked to stop so he could pick up his laundry. Since there was a bar next door, they had had a quick beer and when Kyle spilled some of the nectar on his shirt and couldn't go back to work smelling like a brewery, Ty willingly loaned Kyle the Maine jersey–a dubious birthday present from his mother.

Nurtan was still sound asleep so Kyle poured some *raki* and began to calculate.

There was absolutely no way he would confess to the crime. He valued his life too much to see it ruined by spending the rest of it in a Turkish prison. Or worse for that matter. They'd probably hang him.

An idea casually came to him. He would hide the body someplace and maybe the cops would not find it until he was out of the stinkin' country.

The telephone rang and Kyle rushed there before it woke Nurtan. The caller was Ty Manners who wanted to know why Kyle hadn't come to work that day, and if he wanted to go to the Compound later. When Kyle refused Ty's repeated invitation, the latter got angry, said "Fuck you–Buddy," and hung up.

Annoyed at Ty's attitude, Kyle casually thought: I ought to pin this rap on Manners. He laughed and gulped down more *raki*. Suddenly, he stopped smiling. If the Turks thought an American had had anything to do with Yuksel's death, they would find the killer at any cost. That being the case, Kyle could be considered a suspect, especially since Madam Sivas had told Turan about the rape.

What had popped into his head as an amusing idea quickly became a plan. A way out for him. Why _not_ blame Ty? He'd probably be a suspect, anyway.

Realistically, the idea seemed to have everything going for it. He began to examine the facts. Ty and Turan had had a fight over Yuksel at the wedding party and Turan knew that Ty wanted her. Also, Ty had once bragged to Kyle that he had threatened to kill Yuksel. More than likely, Yuksel also told that old woman Madam Sivas about the threat.

Finally, he had been wearing Ty's jersey. The blood stains on the shirt would be evidence against Ty. And if any neighbors had seen Kyle leaving the apartment, they would have thought he was Ty because of their similar physical features–and the jersey!

He liked Ty well enough but if framing the guy kept him out of prison, so be it. In this world, every man had to look out for himself. If not, he was just plain stupid.

Yet, he _would_ give Ty a fair shake, he subsequently conceded. He'd hide Yuksel's body. There was always the chance that it would not be found at all. In that case, Ty would have no worries.

When darkness fell, Kyle sneaked out again and went to the Motor Pool. He borrowed sedan AF 136, drove to Yuksel's place and parked in front of her apartment with the sedan's trunk directly parallel to the front door.

He opened the trunk lid and kept it that way as he entered Yuksel's apartment. The door was still unlocked, just the way he had left it. He had brought along a flashlight so he wouldn't have to turn on the lights and attract attention.

He found the stocking that Yuksel had earlier pulled off his head and stuffed it into his pocket. Later, he would burn it.

The next thing to deal with was Yuksel's body. The sight temporarily startled Kyle because her eyes were open but, undauntingly, he closed them and proceeded with his business.

Pretending this was just a weird game, he picked up Yuksel's cold body and hastily walked through the living room, out the front door and to the waiting car. Kyle put the lifeless body in the trunk. He closed the lid and then closed Yuksel's front door.

Getting in the sedan, he calmly drove away and headed for a little known spot that Corey had once told him about. He found the place without much trouble. The darkness was smothery black but the flashlight cut sharply through it.

Kyle opened the trunk, picked up the body, and carried it into a dense bit of shrubbery. The cops might not find the corpse for months–if at all.

He then headed back to Ankara.

Kyle congratulated himself on everything going so well until one of the sedan's tires went flat as he reached the city. He hastily changed the tire and threw it back in the trunk. As an after thought, he took Ty's blood-stained jersey out of his back pocket and put it in the well next to the defective tire.

If Ty were to be accused of the crime–and the police found the jersey–the shirt could be used as evidence against him. As far as Kyle was concerned, he was in the clear. All he really needed was for his transfer to come through.

Weeks later, when the body _was_ found, Ty immediately seemed to be the prime suspect. Through the grapevine, Kyle quickly learned that there was much evidence to incriminate Ty. As assurance, Kyle fanned the flames. In the hope that Corey would pass on the information to his cop buddy, Kyle told him how easy it was to sneak a car out of the Motor Pool.

Then Kyle visited Fatima in the Compound and promised to pay her fifty American dollars every month for the rest of her life if she denied being with Ty on July 21st.

It had all been so easy. And Kyle was proud of himself for being so clever.

*
*
*
*

Kyle lit another cigarette, sipped more *raki* then spoke out loud to the grave.

"Ya shudn't have tried ta put me down, Yuksel. Ya shudda just let me have mah way. Ya would ov' bin alive right now. Ya wuz just as thick-headed as that asshole Gonzales back in basic trainin' at Sampson Base in New York. Ah followed him inta the woods where he went to take a piss. But 'fore he had a chance ta, Ah hit him on the back of his head and he passed out.

"Then Ah put the gun in his hand and squeezed the trigger. They all thought it was suicide 'cause ov' the note that Ah typed and forged."

Kyle threw the empty bottle on the grave and descended the hill to the waiting taxi. It was just a matter of hours now, he told himself. He'd go look for Corey to see what was happening. Then he'd find his new friend Midyat at the parade. After that, to the Compound—for a last ride on Fatima—and to the train station.

"In no time at all," he yelled; "it's *Allahismarladik*, Turkey!"

*   *   *

CHAPTER 32 –
"Victory Day – Afternoon"

After leaving the President's party, Urdanur and I met Drew at the Guest House. The first floor of the building has a small balcony on which Drew placed chairs so we could have an unobstructed view of the parade.

A high school band passing in review was holding my attention when Drew nudged me.

"There's Madam Sivas. Seems like she's coming over here."

Looking in the direction he indicated, I saw the venerable Woman crossing her driveway and heading our way. There was a vague smile on her face but it seemed only perfunctory. She greeted us cordially then asked to speak with me.

I climbed over the railing, jumped off the low balcony and followed Madam Sivas' lead as she moved closer to the waist-high wall which separated the lawn from the public sidewalk.

On the other side of the wall a crowd of people had lined Ataturk Boulevard. Happy little groups of spectators waving tiny Turkish flags, sipping soft drinks, talking, laughing, and generally indulging in the merry mood of Victory Day.

"I am very sorry to disturb you, Corey."

"It's always a pleasure to see you, Madam Sivas."

The weak smile she had been sporting faded into an expression of solemnness.

"I must know where Kyle is."

"I honestly have no idea. He phoned yesterday to say that he might meet me here to watch the parade. But I haven't heard from him since."

"Do you know what time he is leaving Ankara? And how?"

"He is leaving tonight. On the 1800 hours train for Istanbul. He will fly back to the U.S. from there."

"Thank you, Corey for being so honest. You _are_ a good boy."

With that said, she nodded a sad-faced farewell and crossed over the driveway back to her house.

It was ironic, I pondered. Before my coming to Turkey, several individuals had made derogatory comments about the people and country. Where these informants had gotten the bogus data is a mystery. But too many people have a perverse way of spreading rumors about a place. Even a spot they have never visited. They will easily pass on the gossip as fact rather than arrive at their own opinions empirically.

I would like to tell those informants that it was two Americans who did some horrific things to two trusting and innocent Turkish girls.

"Are you all right, Corey?" inquired Drew.

"Sure."

"What the hell did she say? You look so depressed."

"Nothing. I was just suddenly being philosophical."

"Good for you, Plato," he joked; "but you're missing the parade."

*   *   *

When Madam Sivas entered her house, she went directly to the telephone and dialed Turan's office number.

"Sorry, *Efendi*," sounded the pleasant voice of a young male Agent; "Inspector Karapinar is not here. However, he plans to check-in with us later for any important messages."

"It is imperative that he gets this information. Please relate to him that Madam Sivas called to say Kyle is leaving on the 1800 hours train for Istanbul, tonight. From there, he will fly out of the country."

"I will tell him as soon as he contacts us, *Efendi*."

With that done, Madam Sivas made iced tea and brought it upstairs where Nurtan was half-heartedly watching the parade from the window. One look at the girl made the old Woman dissatisfied with having left only a message for Turan. It was possible that he would not receive it in time to apprehend Kyle.

She could not permit the American to get away with raping one niece and heartlessly abandoning the other. He had to pay for his abuses. And if Turan were unable to stop Kyle, she would have to do it herself.

Madam Sivas knew that she was not physically strong enough to be an impediment in Kyle's path. But she _was_ familiar with the gun which her late husband had once taught her to use for protection. The firearm would definitely make her a worthy opponent.

The old Woman gave the tea to Nurtan then walked to her bedroom closet. The weapon was exactly where her husband had left it. Though a bit dusty and soiled, it was still loaded.

She picked up the gun and began to clean its surface with her apron. The piece was not very large, but seemed heavy and cold in her hands. Just the feel of it sent a chill through Madam Sivas' body.

Then the picture came back to her of Yuksel being raped by Kyle, not once, but twice. And Nurtan's description of how coldly Kyle had left her standing in the shadow of the JAMMAT Building with her heart breaking. Also how he was the direct cause of Nurtan's attempted suicide.

Madam Sivas heard Nurtan call to her from the other room to come watch the parade. The old Woman put the weapon back in its hiding place. Temporarily!

——————

Delighting in the effects of the *raki* he had thus far consumed, Kyle made his way up Ataturk Boulevard toward the Guest House. The task was difficult as the sidewalks overflowed with holiday revelers.

As Kyle neared the Guest House, he halted in his tracks. On the lawn between the house and the wall, he spied Corey talking to Madam Sivas. In Kyle's intoxicated state, he had forgotten that the old Woman's boarding house was just next door to the American hostel.

Kyle zeroed-in at the expression on the face of the old Woman. It appeared to be anything but pleasant. Suddenly, he remembered the day he had driven her and Nurtan to the cemetery. She had informed him that Yuksel told her about the rape, and that she had given the information to Turan.

Surely the old Woman was angry because he had dumped Nurtan. Maybe she was planning to get revenge. What other reason would she have for talking to Corey?

Not wishing to take any unnecessary chances so close to his getaway from Turkey, Kyle made an abrupt turn and proceeded to walk in the direction from which he had come.

——————

Cizre and Midyat stood by the curb directly in front of the American Embassy Building. They had chosen the spot for its strategic location. The street adjacent to the Embassy led to a wooded area where they could find refuge in case they were discovered and had to make a quick escape.

Snuggled between Cizre's feet was a simple cardboard box which possessed deadly powers that when unleashed would avenge his Grandfather.

Having read about the parade's highlights in the newspaper on the day before, Cizre had decided which float he intended to annihilate. His idea was that the explosion would reduce the float to a useless pile of debris and kill or injure many others in the immediate area.

While Cizre and Midyat patiently waited, they made themselves blend in with the other spectators by cheering when the crowd did and appearing to be captivated by the various attractions and bands which marched by.

Though Cizre was uncharacteristically elated, he harbored slight apprehension regarding Midyat's capabilities.

He had explained the possibilities many times: the bomb would explode and do its job; they might escape without being caught; either or both of them would die; or, one of them would be apprehended and the other go unnoticed.

If the latter case were to prevail, the undetected Partner was to walk away calmly so that he could set off the other device–later on in the day. Cizre had stated this over and over again. He could only hope that Midyat would ultimately comply.

"Quickly," ordered Midyat, "Turn your back to the parade!"

"Why are we doing so?"

"Because my American friend Kyle, from the Compound, is just across the street. He wanted to meet so we could watch the parade together. But I refused because he might spoil our plans."

"That was very wise of you, Midyat."

Several minutes later, Midyat surveyed the area then announced that the coast was clear. And Cizre's confidence in Midyat was encouraged.

Loud cheering could unexpectedly be heard a few blocks away so Cizre peered down the street and realized the ovation was for the float which was to be his target. Anxiously he sat down on the curb, readying himself for the pleasurable task ahead.

––––––

On the float making its way toward the two Kurds was a host of prominent people. In addition to the country's President and the new Chief of the Secret Police were the city's mayor, several college professors, and a few foreign representatives of various countries.

The delegate representing the United States was Colonel Hank Myrons. Next to him was his wife who was wearing a silly looking hat. Their faces boasted huge smiles as they waved at the throngs on the sidewalks.

While enjoying the unwarranted attention of the spectators, Penelope

Myrons was in one of her many unexplainable moods. She had greeted the morning with an idea on her mind which she would not shake.

"I suppose your lady friend is somewhere in this crowd and watching us," she said, while maintaining a false smile.

"What lady friend?" Hank reacted.

"The one you have been secretly seeing since we've been in Ankara."

"You're crazy," he replied. "I haven't been s-seeing anyone."

"I know there is someone," she persisted.

"T-This is not t-the t-time or place t-to t-talk about it."

"I want to discuss it now."

Hank fought hard to maintain a cheerful demeanor.

"S-Shut the hell up," he ordered, through clenched teeth and a smile on his face. "If you don't, I'll knock you right off t-this fucking float and into t-the middle of next month!"

Cizre saw his target approaching. He quickly glanced behind to ascertain that Midyat was in position. Satisfied, he took a book of matches out of his pocket and switched from a sitting to a kneeling attitude. At the right moment, he would open the lid, light the fuse, close the lid again and catapult the box under the float. Midyat was to act as a shield and camouflage the actions.

Unaware to the young Kurds, two Secret Policemen were scrutinizing the immediate area for any untoward occurrences. One of them noticed Cizre on his knees and would have thought nothing of it save for one thing.

"What is that young Man doing with matches in his hand if he does not have a cigarette in his mouth?" he asked his Associate.

"I do not know. Are you suspicious of something?"

"Perhaps. My feelings tell me that he may be about to cause trouble. What is that box he is playing with?"

"Let us investigate!"

The Secret Policemen moved closer to Cizre. In doing so, they pushed Midyat aside—not realizing he was an accomplice. At that same moment, the front of the float came parallel to them and Cizre opened the lid of the box.

"What are you doing?" asked the Policeman.

"None of your concern," snapped Cizre. "Go away!"

"We are Policemen. Cease your actions and stand up."

Though startled by the Man's words, Cizre showed no fear. He had traveled too far and had spent too much time on this project to give it up so easily. Nothing was going to stop him from avenging his Grandfather.

"Your mother is a whore!" lashed out Cizre.

Then he lit the fuse.

With lightning agility and speed, one of the Policemen knocked Cizre to the ground and extinguished the tiny flame; the other handcuffed him. The entire feat was done so quickly, deftly, and nonchalantly that very few people noticed the incident.

Midyat watched in horror. He was about to open his mouth to interfere when Cizre's eyes sent him a tacit message: *It is now up to you to set off the other bomb.*

And so Midyat stood there dumbfoundedly as the Secret Policemen took his friend away–into the dense crowd and out of his sight. Perhaps, forever.

Now Midyat must return to the Uncle's house, make an excuse for Cizre's absence, secure the makings for the other bomb and find his way to the next site in their plan.

———

By the time the parade was over, Nurtan had fallen asleep on the couch in Madam Sivas' private quarters. The good Woman had been staring at her for some time and the more she did, the greater her anger grew for Kyle–especially when she considered the fetus within Nurtan.

Madam could sit still no longer. She had to do something. And fast. Ordinarily she would be in the process of preparing the evening meal for her boarders but this being Victory Day all her charges had unanimously made other plans.

Madam Sivas phoned Turan's office again and asked if Inspector Karapinar had gotten the message.

"I do not know, *Efendi*. I came on duty only a few minutes ago. –What was the message about?"

The Woman repeated her earlier words and there was a long silence as the Clerk searched through some papers.

"I am very sorry, *Efendi*. I can not find anything. But I copied it as you were speaking and I will certainly tell him for you. He has a portable radio for communication in the field but his office messages are retrieved over the line phone. –Is there anything else I may help you with?"

Madam placed the receiver harshly in its cradle and stood there trying to decide her next move. There was no doubt, she told herself. Kyle must not leave Ankara until he paid in some way. With Turan not immediately available, she would have to take matters into her own hands.

Madam Sivas went to the bedroom closet and secured the weapon. She put it in her pocketbook, telephoned for a taxi, then left the building to wait for the cab by the curbside.

She knew that there were easily two hours before Kyle's train was to depart but she wanted to reach the terminal in plenty of time to find him.

After confronting Kyle, she would give him the opportunity of coming peacefully to the police station. If he refused, she would command him at gun point.

And if he refused a second time, she would definitely shoot him!

Arrayed in a white tuxedo and looking more handsome than necessary, Turan entered one of the interrogation rooms in the basement of the Ulus prison. Because of the holiday, he was expected at the cocktail party which preceded the President's ball. But this detour was a matter of national security.

Agent Hunhar was in charge of the questioning taking place and greeted his Supervisor with much respect.

"I see you have received my message, *Efendi*."

Turan silently nodded his head in acknowledgment and fixed his eyes on a young Man clad only in a pair of briefs. The Prisoner was seated on a stool directly under a glaring, naked light bulb which radiated intense heat. Sweat covered his entire body while several welts were visible on his back and a modicum of blood trickled from his mouth. But he seemed fearless in the presence of the two brawny guards who stood directly behind him.

"Whom do we have here?" asked Turan.

"His name is Cizre Siirt. He was apprehended during the parade as he attempted to ignite a homemade bomb. He is a Kurd from Bitlis who came here, he says, to get even with us Turks for his Grandfather."

"Is he working with a group?" asked Turan.

"No. But he boasts that a friend is going to set off a second bomb and refuses to disclose the location. We have tried beating him but he seems to enjoy it. I was about to use the electric treatment when you came in."

"Let us give him one more chance! Ask him again, Agent Hunhar!"

The Agent complied with his Supervisor's suggestion but Cizre stood his ground.

"I will tell you swine nothing," he yelled. "You will know where the bomb is after it explodes."

"Suit yourself," said Turan, calmly. Then turning to Hunhar, he ordered, "Lay the prisoner on the table–on his back!"

It took Agent Hunhar and his two Assistants several combative minutes to contain Cizre, for the latter waved his arms and kicked wildly to resist them. But the policemen were ultimately stronger. They threw him onto the hard surface, raised his arms above his head and secured his wrists. Then they tied his outstretched ankles at the other end.

One policeman tore off Cizre's underwear while the other went to a far corner of the room only to return with a small black box which had several knobs atop of it and a power cord that plugged into the wall socket. Extending from the box was a coated wire whose tip was exposed to show the copper fibers underneath. One of the policemen pressed a thin metal cup against Cizre's testicles.

The defiance on Cizre's face began to fade as Turan explained what was about to happen.

"Every time you refuse to answer a question, we give you a jolt of electricity! The exposed copper wire hits the metal which becomes excruciatingly hot, as it vigorously vibrates! It is a small dose but quite effective! And you never know exactly when we are going to do so! I have seen men much bigger than you cry like babies and beg us to stop! But perhaps you will enjoy having your testicles toasted!"

At that moment, the door opened and a Clerk entered. He gave a folded piece of paper to Turan.

"Your office just forwarded this, Inspector Karapinar. They were unable to reach you earlier."

The note told of Madam Sivas' earlier call regarding Kyle leaving Ankara. Turan glanced at his watch. He could alert some of his men in the terminal but none of them knew Kyle by sight. That being the case, it was best if he went there himself. By hurrying, he might make it in time.

Acting on a sudden impulse, Turan addressed Agent Hunhar.

"We will not have to use the electric treatment on this prisoner, after all! It seems that we are too late! His friend has already set off the bomb and it has done a lot of damage!"

When Cizre heard the words, he became elated. His face glowed with delight, not only for the damage the bomb caused but also that Midyat had come through. He was ecstatic that his Grandfather had finally been avenged.

Never before could Cizre remember being so happy. And not realizing the pinnacle of his joy, he called out in thoughtless fervor.

"I knew the train terminal was a good spot!"

Turan chuckled aloud in spite of himself. His gut-feeling had paid off. Though he was never adverse to using physical torture, he had learned from his predecessor that sometimes much more can be gained by mental trickery.

Turan then exposed the ruse.

"It was all a lie! The message told me nothing regarding your case! And though we have not caught your accomplice, we now know where the bomb is and we will be able to defuse it!"

"My Grandfather was right," screamed Cizre. "All you Turks are donkeys!"

Turan had started for the door, but stopped. Turning to Agent Hunar, he said, "Give the prisoner a jolt or two for his foul mouth!"

The Inspector then left–with Cizre's screams following him down the hallway.

Turan had no time to waste. It was imperative that he alert the authorities at the terminal regarding the bomb. And that he get there in time to stop Kyle from leaving.

After the parade, Kyle went to the Compound for one last fling. He did not find his Kurdish friend Midyat but Fatima was easy to locate, and they went directly up to her room.

"You look for best Gypsy girl, no?" she asked.

"Fur shur, Baby," said Kyle, guzzling some *raki*.

"We Gypsy girls hot. We do best for our man. But never to lie to Gypsy girl. Never to cheat on Gypsy. She put curse on you, bad! It stay forever!"

Kyle paid for the session and also the monthly fifty dollars he had promised Fatima when she had agreed to deny having seen Ty Manners on July 21st.

But the dark side of Kyle was bigger than the sum of his parts. Without Fatima realizing it, he noticed where she hid the money.

When sex was over and Fatima turned her back to light a cigarette, Kyle struck her unconscious with the *raki* bottle. Stealing her money, he left with more cash than coming in with.

A short time later, when Fatima came to, she found one of the soldiers and after searching the vicinity discovered that Kyle had left the Compound.

She sat down on a bench in front of her building and spoke out loud.

"I say you no make fool Gypsy woman, stupid American scum! Now I put curse on you. It stay forever. Only I make curse go away."

Fatima closed her eyes, bowed her head and in a combination of several languages proclaimed a profound chant and curse on Kyle.

"I say your pocketbook be empty always. Your body have much pain. You be ugly. And alone!   Forever!!!!!!!!!!!!"

*   *   *

CHAPTER 33 —
"Victory Day — Evening"

*   *   *

When Turan exited the rear entrance of the Ulus Prison, his Driver was waiting with the sedan's motor running. The Man was one of the newest and youngest agents in the Service and very eager to please.

"Where are we going, *Efendi*?" he asked.

"To the train terminal as fast as possible. We must find, and stop, a terrorist before he sets off a bomb."

The Driver drove around past the front of the building and at the end of the block turned onto Ataturk Boulevard which would eventually lead them to Yasamak Sokak, the road going directly to the railroad station.

Turan spoke into his walkie-talkie and heard someone say "Yes" as the battery unexpectedly went dead.

"*Essekogluessek*," yelled Turan, beating his radio against the dashboard.

"What is wrong, *Efendi*?"

"This contraption is useless and it is the only way we have to warn the terminal."

"Take mine, Sir."

Turan felt a twinge of encouragement which was short lived since the Driver's radio was also dead.

"I will drive faster, *Efendi*. But maybe we should be looking for a public telephone on the way there."

On Ataturk Boulevard, the sedan traveled at nearly breakneck speed until it reached Yenishire. In that area, huge crowds were slowly making their way across the road in the direction of Ataturk's Tomb, where the fireworks were scheduled to take place.

The vehicle came to a complete stop and Turan let out a string of curses his young Colleague had never before heard.

"We are only five or six blocks away from Yasamak Sokak," the Driver tried to console.

"There are several cars ahead of us and swarms of people. We are just as close to the moon as we are to Yasamak!"

"Look, *Efendi*," shouted the Driver. "There is a telephone and no one is using it."

Turan jumped from the sedan and started for the phone booth. He stopped midway and returned to the car.

"Do you have any change?"

The Driver gave his boss a handful of *lire* and Turan resumed his journey.

Upon getting to the booth, he discovered that someone had cut the wire and the telephone was dead!

––––––

Madam Sivas stood in front of the Ankara Train Terminal at the far end of the right side. Her vantage point enabled her to see all of the twenty-four parallel entrance doors as well as any vehicle dropping off passengers in front of these portals.

When choosing the location, she had noticed a soldier in the area. It was not unusual to see military men guarding various establishments and neighborhoods throughout the city.

Madam glanced at her watch and noted there was plenty of time before Kyle's train was to leave for Istanbul. Though her planning was good, what she had not taken into consideration was fatigue.

She had been upset the entire day and that often made her feel tired. And she had been standing there for half an hour. But she knew that determination would sustain her.

Luckily, Kyle was taking the earlier train and while there were many people in the area it was only a quarter of the amount that would be traveling on the later train–the one departing after the spectacular fireworks display that the majority of the people would be attending.

Twenty minutes passed.

A taxi dropped off two people and as it was pulling away, a sedan with license plates AF 136 cut in front of it–nearly causing a collision. The taxi driver paused long enough to curse out the sedan driver but the latter simply laughed at him.

––––––

"That was cool, Mike," encouraged Kyle. "Ah like tha way ya drive."

"So do I," grinned Mike.

Earlier, when Kyle had left the Compound, he stopped at Intim's where his Motor Pool buddies were sure to be hanging out. After a couple of drinks, Kyle had convinced Mike to go to the Pool and secure a sedan to drive him to the train station. He wanted to be chauffeured there in style—courtesy of the Air Force.

Mike was willing so they hitchhiked to their work place and helped themselves to a vehicle. It turned out to be the one with license plates AF 136, and Kyle thought it was a cool ending to his time in Ankara—to be taken to the terminal in the very car in which he had transported Yuksel's body! If only he could have told someone.

"Thanks fer the ride, Mike," said Kyle, emerging from AF 136. "Ah'll send ya a postcard from the States so ya can remember what it looks like."

"Go seduce a moose," laughed Mike, driving away.

––––––

Madam Sivas had noticed the confrontation between the taxi and sedan Drivers and her eyes lingered long enough to spot Kyle getting out of the car.

She called to him but he was some distance away. If her voice reached him, he was not responding.

––––––

Kyle clearly heard Madam Sivas yelling but pretended otherwise. She was probably there to try and stop him from leaving Nurtan. *Well, she was definitely barking up the wrong tree.* Nothin' was going to keep him from getting out of Turkey.

Ignoring her, he ran into the terminal and high-tailed it to the closest men's room where he would remain until the coast was clear.

––––––

Madam Sivas called to the Soldier who by that time was closer to her. "Stop that young man!"

The Soldier turned around but not in enough time to see Kyle. Unsure of what the venerable Lady wanted, the Soldier then went over to her.

But being overzealous to apprehend Kyle, Madam Sivas rushed ahead. In her fervor she twisted her ankle and would have fallen to the ground if not for the Soldier catching her. Instead of worrying about her injury she ordered the Soldier again to go catch Kyle.

"*Anlamiyorum, Efendi,*" said the Soldier, cooperatively.

"Of course, you do not understand," said Madam Sivas, chastising herself. "I said it in English."

She was so used to speaking the American tongue that it was beginning to come naturally. After she repeated the request in Turkish, the Soldier left her leaning against one of the columns while he ran inside the terminal to look for the alleged blond haired man.

Two teenage girls who had witnessed Madam Sivas' struggle went to offer their help and insisted that she should go to the hospital–a belief which they conveyed to the secret Policeman who came on the scene after exiting the terminal.

"The Soldier said you are in trouble, *Efendi.*"

Madam Sivas excitedly explained that Inspector Karapinar wanted Kyle apprehended because he had raped a Turkish girl and was trying to leave the country unpunished.

The pathos with which she spoke convinced the Policeman that Madam Sivas was on an admirable mission. So he spoke on the radio and attempted to contact his boss–several times, but in vain.

"Forgive me, *Efendi,* but I can not seem to reach him. Perhaps there is something wrong with his radio."

"But it is very important that you stop the American I spoke of. Turan plans to arrest him!"

The fact that the old Woman referred to Inspector Karapinar by his first name told the Policeman that she must be a personal friend, and should be treated as such.

"I will be happy to go find this man you speak of, but first you must do me a favor. Inspector Karapinar would insist on you going to the hospital and having that ankle attended to. And if I did not entreat you to do that, he would probably fire me for not being concerned about one of his friends. –You would not want me to lose my job, would you?"

"I am fine, young Man; I do not need to see a doctor."

"These two Girls and the Soldier who sent me out here both seem to think you are injured."

"I am not. I can walk very well. I want to go into the terminal and stop him!"

"I will find him for you," assured the Policeman.

She ignored him and started to walk, then almost fell again.

The secret Policeman caught her by the arm and she unwillingly leaned against him. She hated to admit it but there was more damage than she thought. Her ankle was beginning to throb with pain.

"As I said before, you do not want me to be fired." He paused. "Or do you?"

Madam Sivas laughed in spite of herself. He was a very clever young Man and quite handsome. Perhaps she should get his name and introduce him to Nurtan.

"Very well," she conceded. "Please find Kyle and detain him for Turan. He is American with broad shoulders, blond hair and almost six feet tall. He is wearing a white polo shirt and dungarees."

"You can be sure that we will catch him, *Efendi*."

The secret Policeman then raised his arm and motioned. Within seconds a green sedan pulled up to the curb with two other Men inside. Madam Sivas was helped into the car and the Driver was instructed to first take her to the hospital, and afterwards see that she arrived home safely.

Madam Sivas was disappointed but her foot did hurt badly and Nurtan must be wondering what had happened to her.

*   *   *

I found the Ankara Train Terminal to be most impressive. Planted ten feet back from the curb, the building had a series of tall and wide parallel windows—making the façade look like a row of intermittent concrete and glass columns. At the base of each tall window was a glass door trimmed in brass. And along the entire length of the front of the building was a tan-colored canvas marquee.

Getting out of the taxi, I could see an older Woman being helped into a green sedan by two Men—at the opposite end from where I was standing. For a second, the Woman looked like Madam Sivas but that was ridiculous, I promptly told myself. She ran a boarding house and would be home preparing the evening meal.

I passed through one of the terminal doors into a mammoth chamber which seemed to have no boundaries. It was my first time there and I gasped at the size of the place. My eyes panned from one side to the other, trying to discover points of necessity—such as the ticket booth and a snack area that provided seating.

Always wanting to be someplace on time, I had the habit of getting to an appointment much earlier than need be. Luckily there was a snack area near by. After getting some goodies, I found a convenient table from which to observe passengers coming and going. People watching is always fun.

*　　　*　　　*

As the cab pulled up in front of the terminal, Friday was vividly recalling the last time she had traveled by taxi: to the farewell rendezvous with Corey on their hill.

But this was not Gobasi's vehicle and she was not meeting Corey. She was leaving Ankara, Turkey, and would never come back again. Things were rapidly changing and she was suddenly too weary to wonder what the future had in store.

The taxi Driver placed their luggage on the sidewalk, received payment, and drove away.

"do you have the tickets?" asked Winston.

"The answer is still yes," laughed Friday; **"As the other three times you asked."**

"what car are we in?"

"Car # 143. I hope it's the Orient Express. I once saw a movie and the train looked so elegant. There was so much intrigue. A spy was being pursued by the authorities and they were running through all the cars."

"well, if you're lucky," joked Winston; "maybe you'll see somebody get shot."

Then the little Girl spoke.

"I am so happy that you're coming to Istanbul with us, Daddy. I have a big list of things to see that Sandy told us about."

"Me, too, Daddy," said the Boy. "I'm going to miss you when we go away."

Friday could see that Winston was deeply touched. The fact that he was a good father had always pleased her. It was the other facets of his personality with which she found fault.

They walked through the entrance doors into the titanic terminal.

"i see a small snack shop over there," announced Winston; "would you like to get a bite to eat?"

"Not right now," answered Friday. **"It's still pretty early. Let's get settled on the train, first. They probably have other refreshment stands available."**

*　　　*　　　*

297

While sipping a coke, I saw the Lebal Family enter the terminal at a comfortable distance away from me. Nostalgically, I remembered my first look at them when they were eating in the Guest House.

It was practically yesterday but the many months in between seemed like a lifetime. In truth, it was an era that I would never forget. A period in which I felt mysterious changes taking place within me.

Trying to prevent the Lebals from seeing me, I lowered my head and searched for something in my carrying case.

In there was a bag of fruit which Urdanur had given me for the train ride. Along with that she had supplied a list of famous sights that I HAD to see while in Istanbul–such as: the famous Blue Mosque, the Sunken Palace, and the Grand Bazaar which was a shopper's paradise. Also in my possession were phone numbers of girls–supplied by Turan. In all likelihood, I would not contact them anyway. Friday was the only woman in my thoughts.

She was always on my mind and our separation unexpectedly became startlingly real. Though we had discussed it, I did not quite believe it would happen. Fate suddenly became fickle and was leading us in the wrong direction. And I thought of lines from a 45 record that Friday and I had bought in the Bazaar.

> *No one can change what is destiny;*
> *Can't rearrange what was meant to be;*
> *...*
> *We had to meet that was destiny;*
> *What had to be simply had to be... .*

I forced my mind to think of other things.

As huge as the waiting room was, it was figuratively small enough for me to feel that I was being watched. A sensation which had occurred all too often as of late. Turning quickly, I spotted a man wearing a dark green tie and a gray suit. When he perceived that I had seen him, he looked in another direction.

My immediate instinct was to go over and ask why he was tailing me. But at that second, the public address system blurted out an announcement–first in Turkish, then in English: "The Istanbul Express is now boarding on Track 13."

So, instead, I made my way toward the ticket window. En route there, I was intercepted by Pegu.

"Hi, Corey," she smiled, hugging me. "We have your ticket. We bought your ticket already."

"Let me pay you for it."

"No, no," she said, looking almost insulted. "You are our guest. It is our pleasure."

With no wish to offend, I accepted the friendly gesture.

"Gobasi is waiting for us at the entrance to Track # 13," announced Pegu. "He is watching our suitcases."

As we walked along, I pointed out the Man whom it seemed was following me. Pegu glanced at him and promised to be observant. But she didn't appear to be alarmed so I decided to ignore it. Anyway, Gobasi was probably impatiently waiting.

*   *   *

Lying on a previously soiled blanket on a lumpy old mattress in his cell at the Ulus Prison, Cizre had positioned himself in a fetal position. Against his genitals he held a small ice bag which one sympathetic guard had had pity enough to give him. But the scalding from the electric jolts was continuing to pain and Cizre intermittently moaned and cursed Turan.

Yet, the physical discomfort was not the only torture he was experiencing. Almost worse was the fact that he had been manipulated by Turan into exposing the location of the next target area.

And there was an additional problem he had to contend with.

His cell mate was a man perhaps a few years older than he who had been incarcerated for the previous five years. He was constantly randy and delighted in harassing any current cell partner into having sex.

Cizre being in the top bunk was his only defense–albeit virtually nothing. Every half hour, the Man would paw Cizre and the latter would have to push him away.

In summation of his current situation, Cizre decided that Allah was punishing him for having failed. For not having avenged his Grandfather as he had sworn to do. The only consolation he would permit himself was to pray that Midyat would be able to set off the bomb in the train station.

And he prayed hard that Turan would not get there in time to stop it!

Another highlight of Ankara that Midyat had found so interesting was the *dolmus*, an inexpensive taxi shared by strangers. The *dolmus* traveled only on main thoroughfares. It would run from the north of a given road to the south, and back again. When the cab was not full, it would stop to pick up any passenger who hailed it. There was nothing like that where Midyat came from and he admitted to himself that he preferred city life over rural.

299

The *dolmus,* which means "pig," made its final stop at the Ankara Train Terminal. Midyat nervously jumped out of the cab and headed for the building.

"*Efendi,*" yelled one of the other passengers. "You are forgetting your suitcase."

Midyat looked surprised. Then realizing the error, he took the valise from the man without thanking him. He placed it firmly between his feet as he lit a cigarette. His hands trembled and while exhaling the smoke, he chastised himself for being so stupid. How could he possibly forget the bomb when it was the very reason for his going there?

An hour earlier, he had been in the home of Cizre's family but could not tell them what had happened to their nephew. Would not confess that he was taking a bomb out of their home with the intent of exploding it in a crowded railroad station. They were older people and might not understand. Fortunately he was able to sneak out without them noticing.

But what HAD happened to Cizre? Midyat wondered. Did the police throw him into prison already? Had they beat and tortured him? Were they aware that Cizre had an accomplice? Was he, himself, being watched by the Secret Police at that very moment?

The onerous questions and thoughts burdened Midyat's brain so he pushed them aside. Though he was completely by himself–and missed the comforting support of his lifelong friend–he would have to somehow find the strength to move ahead. He would have to carry out Cizre's wishes.

All alone, he stood on the threshold of a huge task. The time had come to prove to the world–and himself–that he was a responsible man who could be depended upon. He took several more drags on the cigarette, then moved ahead with determination.

Upon entering the colossal structure, Midyat was amazed to see so few people in evidence. The success of the bomb depended on the presence of many Turks. Now, he had to decide where to place his weapon. He would have to find a spot in which lots of passengers had assembled.

As if to solve his problem, the public address system sounded: "The Istanbul Express is now boarding on Track 13."

That was it, he concluded. Allah had given him direction. He would plant the bomb on an actual platform–right near a train so that the explosion would cause a lot of damage.

With a renewed yet slightly apprehensive confidence, he made his way to Track 13.

As he walked along, he could feel it gently bouncing: the Bomb.

*　　　*　　　*

CHAPTER 34 –

"And The Minutes March On"

Gobasi was patiently waiting for Pegu and me at the entrance to Track # 13. Upon seeing us, he jumped up from the suitcases and hugged me like a long lost brother. Then he suggested we walk to our car which was # 143.

As we moved down the platform, I noted that our train was on the right side. To the left was a number of similar parallel platforms. The empty trains parked there were being made ready for passengers who would arrive after the fireworks. But it was our conveyance that intrigued me.

Ever true to my flare for histrionics, I had hoped that the transport would be the famed Orient Express. Though it wasn't, it did bear a slight resemblance since it had private compartments with doors opening outward–as the trains I had seen in so many Warner Brothers movies set in foreign countries. That alone was enough to add excitement to the journey.

Within minutes, we reached a spot in front of car # 143.

While the platform was about the same width as any I had seen in other train stations, there was something a bit unusual on this one because a refreshment stand had been erected. When I mentioned it to Gobasi, he explained that the booth was only temporary. Erected solely for the holiday. Tumultuous crowds were expected for the later trains and the snack bars within the terminal waiting room would not accommodate everyone.

So the management had provided additional booths to make its travelers happy. Each stand was equipped with its own adequate gas tank–with several spares on hand–used to keep the food heated.

Another special treat not usually happening was music blaring out of gigantic speakers strategically placed for the optimal amplification. Ordinarily used only for pertinent announcements, on this occasion they were in keeping with the holiday spirit.

Invigorating Turkish marches and other toe-tapping melodies filled the air–creating an aura of excitement and happiness. There was also a flavor of charm as Eartha Kitt's enchanting voice captured the area with her popular hit song, "Uska Dara." Apparently the terminal authorities wanted to make this Victory Day most memorable.

After placing our luggage in one of the train compartments Gobasi asked if anyone wanted to eat.

"Yes," said Pegu, smiling enthusiastically; "we are all hungry."

In keeping with tradition, the three of us had shish kebab–small pieces of roasted beef with tomatoes, green peppers and onions on a skewer.

As we sat snacking, I noticed Kyle coming our way and waved to him. He acknowledged with a smile while joining us. I introduced him to Pegu and Gobasi and asked why he hadn't joined me for the parade.

"Ah tried but Ah couldn't get through the crowds so Ah partied with some guys from the Motor Pool."

"Madam Sivas asked me if I knew when you were leaving."

"What did ya tell her?"

"At 1800 hours by train."

Kyle became enraged.

"Why the fuck did ya tell her?"

He had never before spoken to me in that tone of voice or manner. And while it angered me, I decided to condone the rudeness for the time being.

"You didn't tell me that it was a secret."

"Ya shudda minded ya own business."

From the corner of my eye I could see Gobasi getting ready to defend me. But he was being politely tacit at the moment.

"It isn't a problem, Kyle, unless you have something to hide."

"Ah ain't. It's that Madam Sivas. She's an asshole and she keeps messin' wit Nurtan's business."

Refusing to dampen the pleasant atmosphere of the day I suggested we both change the subject. Kyle agreed then went to the refreshment stand.

*   *   *

"what platform is the train at?" asked Winston.

"They just announced it," answered Friday. **"It's Track # 13. I can see it from here. It's toward your right."**

A few minutes later, the family passed through the gate and Winston once again asked after the car number.

"Did all of us stopping at the restrooms make you forget?" laughed Friday, trying to keep things light. **"It's # 143."**

"it sounds like a lucky number," suggested Winston.

Friday smirked. **"I've given up on luck. And destiny has betrayed me."**

"you're still thinking about corey, aren't you?"

"At this moment, my feelings have nothing to do with Corey. I'm just tired of this place and I can't wait to get back to the States."

They reached car # 143. Entering an unoccupied compartment, they put their suitcases on the rack above the seats. The children said they were tired so Friday suggested they lie down and try to sleep. Within minutes, they were in slumber land.

"i thought you were coming back here after your physical?" asked Winston.

"Let's go outside and talk so the kids can sleep."

They debarked and stood several feet away from the compartment door. Friday perceived that the conversation was going to be difficult and did not want the children to hear any of it.

"I can't come back," continued Friday; **"The doctors have to observe me for several months. I thought we had settled that already."**

Winston did nothing to camouflage his disappointment. He walked a few steps away from Friday, lit a cigarette, then returned. He was not smiling.

"what am I supposed to do without you here?"

"Ask for a transfer back to the States."

Friday knew her answer was a lie. A way to keep Winston bridled. Having no intention of ever being with him again as a wife, she would deal with his reactions at the divorce table. For the present there was an entire week to spend with him in Istanbul before taking off for the States. She was tired of arguing and wanted the remaining time to be as calm as possible.

Winston randomly glanced around their immediate area and noticed Corey sitting on a bench some feet away from them.

"what is he doing here?" demanded Winston, becoming irate; "has he really got the audacity to see you off?"

"Don't be ridiculous," answered Friday, annoyed at her husband's tirade. **"He is going to Istanbul for the weekend to be the best man at the wedding of his taxi driver friend. —I assume that's them he's talking with."**

"and just how the hell do you know all that?"

Winston's face became red with anger.

"There you go again jumping to conclusions before you have any of

the facts. Just like the time last year in San Antonio–when you mercilessly beat up that enlisted man.

"I know all of this because Urdanur told me earlier today when I called her to say goodbye. She wanted me to tell you about Corey's trip so that you wouldn't misinterpret his presence. She forgot to mention it the other night when you phoned her."

Friday knew why Winston had spoken to Urdanur that evening but chose to ignore his foolishness. It had made her angry as hell but since things were going fairly well at that stage, there was no point upsetting the apple cart.

The flush from Winston's face paled as he digested what Friday told him. He presently remembered Kyle mentioning one day in the Motor Pool that Corey had made good friends with a Turkish taxi driver and that Corey always called the same guy whenever he needed a ride. So perhaps it was the truth, conceded Winston.

"well he better not come over here. if he does, i promise you that i will kill him!"

Was there no end to this man's jealousy and foolishness? contemplated Friday. *Did he always have to be so damn macho? Constantly the big military man?* She was tired of it and delighted to be getting away from him.

"Okay, Winston. If he comes over here you have my permission to shoot him," teased Friday.

"don't make fun of me!   i'm dead serious!"

With a deep sigh, she replied, **"I know you are."** She paused. **"Heaven also knows that you are!"**

––––––

"Could you please go faster," calmly requested Turan, even though inwardly filled with a passion.

The green sedan was finally flying down Yasamak Sokak toward the Ankara Train Terminal.

"I am going as fast as I can, *Efendi*. You do not want me to run down any pedestrians, do you?"

"Yes," replied Turan; "But only the small ones. Those under four feet!"

The shock on the Driver's face greatly amused Turan. That was another concept that former Inspector Burdur had often pointed out. One should always try to have a sense of humor.

Not many minutes before, Turan certainly had had to practice that philosophy when they were forced to stop in Yenishire because of the traffic tie-up. Finding a public telephone unusable, he had located a new Recruit who refused to give up his walkie-talkie, and to believe that Turan was the Chief of the Secret Police.

"Under different circumstances, I would compliment you on your sense of security, but these moments being wasted are indeed very precious!" exclaimed Turan, to the new Recruit.

Several older people who were passing by recognized Turan from his photos in the newspaper and stopped to congratulate him on becoming the new Chief. Only after that—and Turan producing his identification card—did the new Recruit acquiesce and hand over his radio.

"I have been very busy studying for my Policeman's Examination to even look at a newspaper, *Efendi*. I am dreadfully sorry, Sir."

"Help me get through this traffic!" ordered Turan.

"Right away, *Efendi*."

The new Recruit worked so swiftly and diligently in dispersing the vehicles and crowd that his results looked suspiciously like the parting of the Red Sea.

Back in the sedan, Turan had used the confiscated radio to successfully contact the bomb squad.

Then he tried to reach Mohair who had been assigned to follow Corey and was probably in the terminal. But when Mohair did not answer, Turan assumed that his radio was also dead. The first thing on Monday morning, vowed Turan, the walkie-talkie company was going to be severely chastised, and maybe even sued. Perhaps the damn battery company, as well.

Dauntlessly, he sent out an open call.

"This is Inspector Karapinar. I need to speak with an agent on duty in or near the train station."

Four voices simultaneously responded but the only name Turan was able to decipher was Mustafa. *That was all that Turkey needed,* laughed Turan to himself; *another Mustafa—the first name of the country's biggest hero. Probably half of the boys in his homeland were named Mustafa.*

"I will speak to you, Mustafa."

"*Evet, Efendi.* Go ahead."

"Find the Supervisor of the train terminal and tell him that there is a bomb ready to explode. I do not know where exactly or at what precise time. Tell him to calmly evacuate the terminal without causing a panic. I am on my way there, and have already contacted the bomb squad."

"Yes, *Efendi*.

———

Mustafa signed off and quickly made his way into the terminal. He asked a random employee for the Supervisor's office and the man directed him to a door marked 'Employees Only' which was at a distant corner of the huge waiting room.

Mustafa found the door. It was unlocked so he opened it and stepped into the junction of three long corridors: one to his left, one straight ahead, and one to the right. Added to his frustration was the fact that the hallways were dimly lit. He stood there for several seconds, then finally made a decision.

He went to the right–moving slowly along and squinting to read the name on every door. There were at least ten portals: the electric shop, lost and found, baggage, and so on. His first choice of corridors was a failure–as was his second. And he was becoming increasingly nervous. *The Chief of Police, himself, has entrusted me with this important job,* he thought. *I can not fail him.*

The corridor to his left turned out to be the one he needed. At the end of the hallway was a door marked "Supervisor." He knocked loudly but there was no answer. He tried several more times without success and remembered passing the men's room, so he went in and called for the Supervisor. But still in vain.

Mustafa was beginning to get upset. He went back into the overpowering waiting room where he found the Information Booth and asked for the location of the public address system. Perhaps he could have the Supervisor paged.

That destination–at another far end of the terminal–was a small square room with large windows and perched some fifty feet high above anything else in the place. It was accessible only by climbing an iron ladder–acutely perpendicular to the concrete floor.

The next move was a challenge for Mustafa. He wanted to carry out the assignment with perfection. Wanted to look good in the eyes of his boss. But his deadly fear of heights consumed him. He could not climb a mere three rung ladder that one uses in the house.

Nonetheless, he had to get the job done. It could involve the saving of many lives. Mustafa walked to the ladder and took several deep breaths before starting. He ascended the first rung and froze. His head was dizzy and his palms were sweaty.

I can not stop, he told himself. *I must keep trying.*

Mustafa moved up several more rungs. On many occasions people had told him never to look down but he could not resist the temptation. Although only ten feet above the ground, he began to panic. It suddenly seemed that the whole room was moving and going faster with every spin.

Mustafa paused before chancing the next rung. He was semi-frozen in his present perch but was desperate to complete the mission. As he climbed to the next plateau, his foot slipped. His palms were so wet with perspiration that while attempting to grab the next rung his hands slipped and he found himself floating in air.

His body hit the ground, rendering him unconscious.

*   *   *

As Kyle left my vision and headed for food, the Lebals once again came into view. They all boarded one of the compartments of car # 143. Five minutes later, only Friday and Winston stepped out and lingered within a small distance from the train. Judging from their facial expressions, Friday and Winston seemed to be engaged in a heavy conversation but I was too far away to hear what they were saying. I could only wonder what nonsense the troubled Man was burdening on his wife.

Kyle soon returned and sat on the far side of Gobasi. They began conversing about something but I tuned them out upon noticing the same man who had been following me. He was casually leaning against the far pillar which had been decorated with red crepe paper for the holiday. I asked Pegu about him and she concurred that he was the same guy we had seen not minutes ago in the waiting room.

"I should go over and question him."

"No, no," disagreed Pegu. "Wait to see if he follows us on the train. If he does, we will all go speak to him."

Her idea made sense so I went back to eating my shish kebab and stealing glances at Friday.

"Are you all right?" asked Pegu. "You look a little tired."

"I didn't get too much sleep because I was anxious about this trip. Also, I woke up in the middle of the night from a bad dream and couldn't get back to sleep."

"Tell me about it?"

"I was on a plane and it was so dark that you couldn't see a thing out the window. Then we ran into a storm with thunder and lightning."

"Was the plane bobbing up and down like a ship?" asked Pegu.

I had to stifle a laugh because she had asked the question so seriously.

"Yes, it was. But the awful thing was that there was no flight attendant to help us. We went on like that for a long while and finally the Captain came out of the cockpit. And the Captain was Winston who came to my seat and shot me."

"Not to worry," said Pegu, most profoundly. "I will protect you. I will save you."

CHAPTER 35 –
"The Terrorists"

*   *   *

In the dimly-lit and musty humid prison cell which he shared with a randy convict, Cizre lay on his bunk. Because the pain from the electric shock treatment still lingered, Cizre continued to hold an ice bag against his genitals even though the ice had already turned to water.

"What time do you think it is?" asked Cizre.

The cell Mate rose from the bottom bunk and walked to the door. By pressing his face against the bars and holding his head at the proper angle, he could see the clock on the wall in the guards' area at the end of the hallway.

"It is 1800 hours."

Cizre repeated the hour in his mind. It should be just about the right time for Midyat to be setting off the bomb. Even though that Inspector had tricked him into telling where the next hit was to be, all was not lost. Midyat could still accomplish the mission. The terminal was very large and it would take the authorities hours to find the exact location.

"What are you thinking so hard about?" asked the cell Mate.

Cizre raised himself and sat on the side of the bunk–his legs dangling.

"Nothing, really," he replied.

But it was a lie. He could not tell the Convict anything about the bomb for fear the man might be a plant put there by the Turks to sneakily gain information. In truth he was worried about Midyat failing to detonate the bomb. It did not matter if Midyat died while doing so just as long as the revenge was satisfied.

The cell Mate climbed up to Cizre's bunk and sat beside him.

"What can I do to help you from your depression, my new Friend?"

How can you help me? Cizre thought; *you can help by killing me.*

At various low points in his life, Cizre had entertained the concept of suicide. But he had never really meant it. It was only a temporary foolish thought.

Suddenly, the idea of terminating his life sounded justifiable. One of two things waited in his future. The Turks were either going to keep him in their filthy prison for the rest of his life or they were going to execute him in a public area. Cizre strongly suspected that the death penalty would be their choice.

That being the case, Cizre hoped to outsmart the Turks. Before they could get a chance to execute him, he would commit suicide. The only problem with that plan was how to do it. He could not hang himself, there was no weapon readily available, and starvation was too obvious.

But Allah suddenly smiled at him and sent the solution.

"There *is* something you can do for me," said Cizre.

"What is that?"

"When I am asleep, I want you to kill me."

At first the cell Mate laughed. Presently he stopped when he realized that Cizre was serious. So he succumbed to the solemnness.

"I have killed many men for nothing more than their worldly possessions. Murder to me is neither sinful nor troublesome. But I had a reason for doing so. I have no purpose to kill you."

"Your reason can be that I am asking you to. You would be doing me a great service."

"And what do I get from this?"

"You are already imprisoned for killing over ten people. What more can they do to you?"

"Nothing. But I am not concerned with them. I still want to know how you will reward me."

Cizre was silent for several minutes as he tried to find an incentive for the Convict to kill him. The few possessions he had when arrested were taken from him. Chances were he would never get back his Grandfather's watch. In the final analysis, there was only one thing he could barter with. Reluctantly, he spoke.

"I have found your 'purpose'."

"And what is that?"

Cizre was having difficulty saying the words. But it was foolish, he chastised himself. If he were going to be dead shortly, what difference could it make? And as long as it was only one time, how bad could it be? He would think of pleasant things while it was happening.

"What have you wanted to do since I was thrown into this cell?"

A broad smile lit up the Convict's face.

"You keep pushing me away but I want to fuck you. You have a nice ass."

"If I let you do that, will you promise to smother me to death after I have fallen asleep?"

"Are you serious?"

"I am deadly serious."

"'Deadly serious,'" repeated the cell Mate, laughingly; "that's a good choice of words. What the hell," he continued; "No sweat off my balls. If I get rid of you maybe I will be lucky with the next guy. Maybe he will be willing to do it all the time." He paused, then laughed again. "All right, my Friend, it is a deal."

Though trembling at the prospect of what was about to happen, Cizre lay back on his bunk. It could not be that much worse than the electric shock treatment that the Turks had given him. And that had been for naught. At least he was going to get something out of this. In a short while, he would be at peace. And the thought of never having to be angry or troubled again–about anything–was the reward that death gave. Its *only* reward.

The Convict dropped his shorts and moved on top of Cizre.

"I have changed my mind!"

"But we made a deal."

"I have changed my mind about you killing me when I am asleep. I want you to kill me after you have finished abusing me."

"Are you sure?"

"Yes! I want to be awake when death comes. I want to clearly embrace the grim reaper as he reaches for me because it will be the last experience in life that I will ever feel."

Without any more words spoken, the cell Mate took his pleasure.

Within the hour, Cizre's wish was granted.

AND THE WORLD WAS ALL THE BETTER FOR HAVING ONE LESS TERRORIST IN IT!

––––––

As Madam Sivas entered her foyer and closed the door, she heard Nurtan call to her.

"Please. Where you have been, *Teyze*? I worry you."

"I am coming up," answered the old Woman, as she painfully battled each step.

"Why you limp, *Teyze*?"

"I fell while coming out of a store, foolish old lady that I am."

"Why you go store?"

"To buy ice cream for us."

"Where is ice cream?"

"It melted on the way so I threw it in a garbage receptacle."

"I no understand."

"When I fell, a nice Policeman came to help and after assuming that Turan was my friend, the Policeman insisted on me going to the hospital to have my ankle treated."

At least that part was true, Madam Sivas thought, without feeling guilty. If she had told Nurtan the whole story about her plight to stop Kyle from going, Nurtan would have become more morose than she already was. *Sometimes things left unsaid are better for everyone.*

"You sit," insisted Nurtan. "I go make tea for you."

She escorted her *Teyze* to a chair and hurriedly went to the kitchen to prepare the brew.

Perhaps it was a good omen that she sprained her ankle, reflected Madam. Her injury seemed to have brought Nurtan unexpectedly alive and out of the doldrums. *Helping others is often considered good therapy.*

For the first time since sitting down, Madam Sivas realized that the radio was playing and filling the room with pleasant Turkish music. Songs from the past that carried with them memories of the great times in her life.

How strange and frightening to get old and realize that there are not as many years ahead of you as you have already lived.

As she relaxed in the easy chair, Madam Sivas' varied emotions during the day suddenly accumulated and put her in a pensive, almost philosophical mood–making her remember a poem she had recently read.

Days of My Youth

Days of my youth still live in my heart,
This much I know, they'll never depart;
Fondly they stay and strikingly bold,
As years go on, these memories are gold;
And if my life had a second chance,
I guess I would do the same dance;
For fate did decree,
I was meant to be me;
I can weather the storm;
The days of my youth will keep me warm.

Nurtan shattered Madam's reverie by entering the room with a big smile on her face, and then pouring tea.

For the first time in a number of days, Madam Sivas felt that everything was going to be fine with Nurtan and that she would surely rise above the unhappy ending with Kyle. She knew that her niece would bounce back as wholesome as ever–especially since *she* would be there to help the Girl.

"How you ankle now?" asked Nurtan, with a smile of concern.

Already the Girl was showing signs of improvement.

"Much better, my Dear. But I have to tell you something. The Policeman who helped me is very handsome. He... ."

*   *   *

I glanced at a clock dramatically hanging down from the high ceiling of the terminal. It was secured to the end of an exaggeratedly-thick chain and the clock was so large that I felt like a Lilliputian gazing at Gulliver's watch. It hovered over the platform as a reminder that trains departed promptly.

The time read 1740 and I realized that within a matter of minutes we would be on the train and rapidly moving away from Ankara–and all the wonderful times spent there. Though I was returning after the weekend, things would definitely be different without Friday around.

I turned to Pegu and mentioned that more people were gathering on the platform than when we first arrived there. Gobasi and Kyle agreed and suggested that perhaps we should start boarding.

A stranger walked by us while carrying a suitcase. After he had gotten a short distance past our spot, Kyle called to him.

"Midyat, where ya goin'?"

Without slowing his hurried pace, the young Man turned and gave Kyle a surprised look–as if he had been caught doing something forbidden. Kyle took a step toward him and halted when the stranger said, "No. Go away, Kyle!"

He continued on his way as Kyle turned and addressed me.

"That's mah Kurd friend I met in the Compound. Somethin' must be wrong. Ah better go see."

By that time, Kyle's friend was approaching a group of people converged at the front of the refreshment stand. It was an interesting assemblage, I noted. There was an old man of perhaps seventy who braced himself on a cane and tried to flirt with a younger woman; an elderly lady who eyed the old man without his knowledge; three teenaged boys vying for the affections of two adolescent girls; a family of four with a young father, a mother dressed in pre-Ataturk garb, and two children: a boy and girl probably aged ten and eight respectively; and, a harrowed attendant behind the stand who seemed to wish he were anyplace else.

Kyle's friend passed by the waiting patrons and moved to the wooden wall

312

behind the refreshment stand. I saw him stoop down and open the suitcase he had been carrying. Then I saw him strike a match and direct it into the valise. I assumed that he was looking for something and needed extra light to find it. But then he did something strange. He closed the lid of the case without retrieving the match, and looked as if he were about to run away.

Next, I saw Kyle approaching this young Man he had called Midyat. When Midyat saw Kyle, he ran to him, shoved him backwards to the ground, then did an about-face. At that moment, Midyat noticed that all the people at the refreshment stand were looking because of the fracas between Kyle and him.

The little Girl with her parents waved at Midyat.

"*Merhaba, Efendi,*" she smiled.

To everyone's amazement, Midyat shouted, "I just set off a bomb. All of you get out of here."

Apparently the little Girl had reached a sensitive nerve within the puzzling young Man.

Yelling and screaming, the would-be customers ran in all directions away from the refreshment stand. One teenage boy had the presence of mind to help the older gentleman with the cane.

I sat there watching in a state of shock. It was impossible for me to believe that what was taking place was actually happening. Pegu's mouth was wide open and Gobasi readied himself to protect us.

Midyat began to run but he slipped on something and fell flat on his stomach, right next to the suitcase.

Kyle picked himself up. He seemed annoyed and baffled as he began to walk back toward us.

Then it happened.

When Kyle was perhaps twenty feet from the refreshment stand, there came a thunderous sound as the suitcase exploded. Clouds of dark smoke and hills of fire filled the area and carried with them the smell of Midyat's burning flesh. Within an instant, a second and third deafening noise blasted the air as the spare propane tanks in the refreshment stand erupted. In their wake came more smoke, accompanied by jetting flames which transformed the stand into a miniature bonfire.

A large coffee urn, made airborne by the force of the explosion, flew from the refreshment stand and caught Kyle in the base of his spine—sending him face forward to the ground.

At first the smoke was dense but slowly and eventually it drifted upward, leaving thin, less harmful vapors that reached us. The burning red crepe paper on the nearby pillar glided to the ground in blackened weird surrealistic shapes.

In areas immediately adjacent to the point of impact, people fell to the ground for protection as fiery splinters of wood from the refreshment stand became tiny rockets shooting out in all directions.

Simultaneously, the twang of breaking glass mostly from the windows of car No. 143–as well as from the train on the opposite track–resounded in frightening reverberations.

Small segments of various kinds catapulted in diverse paths.

As if being thrown by an invisible force, splinters of wood, shards of glass, and particles of food ricocheted off various obstacles–and each other–to eventually settle on the concrete platform. The festive area suddenly resembled a skirmish on a battlefield.

Also adding to the bleak atmosphere were horrified screams which eventually subsided to moans and shocked cries for help from those too close to the point of impact.

In contrast to–and sinfully out of place–the festive music relentlessly kept piercing the air–incongruous with the tragic scene enveloping us.

As if mesmerized, I sat on the ground near the bench and watched in horror. Gobasi had pushed Pegu and me to the pavement on the initial explosion. And though we were close to the scene, we were luckily far enough away that only small, non-threatening fragments of debris landed near us. And the least of our problems was the soot that painted our faces.

"How unbelievable!" blurted Pegu, verbalizing my own thoughts. "How awful! We must go to help!"

She made a motion to move but was stopped by Gobasi who said something to her in Turkish.

"If this was a terrorist attack," she replied; "I hope they burn in hell. The government should kill the family of any terrorist. If a terrorist murders another man's loved ones through his barbaric acts then his own family should also die. If a terrorist knew that a government would definitely do that, then the terrorist would have second thoughts about being so ruthless."

Having spoken, she buried her face on Gobasi's chest and cried for a while.

At one point when the thick smoke was rising, it seemed to me that the Man whom I thought was following me, had made an attempt to approach us. Yet as he got closer he unexpectedly turned and went back to his spot near the pillar. But it could have been my imagination.

Acclimating myself to what had happened, I began to evaluate the situation. I could see that Gobasi and Pegu were safe. Then I looked over at Friday. Winston was backing away from her. He had obviously been pressed against her as a shield of protection. But then he had turned and began walking toward the destruction area–leaving Friday standing alone by the train door.

How could he do such a thing, I wondered. *It was very stupid. If something else were to happen, Friday would be vulnerable.*

I had to go to her.

Forgetting the possible consequences, I started toward Friday. As I got closer, Winston apparently changed his mind. He turned around and began walking toward his wife. Friday observed my gesture, and held up her hand in a sign which meant "Stop." But I ignored it. Then Winston saw me moving in Friday's direction.

He stopped in his tracks as his face took on the strangest menacing grin I had ever seen. At the same time, his hand disappeared into his pocket.

When his hand reappeared, it was brandishing a gun.

CHAPTER 36 –

"The End of the Evening"

Winston toyed with me as if I were an innocent rabbit soon to be slaughtered. To say I was frightened would be an understatement. Never before had anyone pointed a gun at me.

My thoughts flashed back to things that Friday had told me about him. How he had physically beaten a young soldier interested in her, how he was an expert marksman, how he occasionally enjoyed going hunting, and how he could easily, suddenly, go off the deep end.

These reminiscences did nothing to ease my fear. I could feel my knees becoming weak and hoped that my slight trembling did not show. It was imperative for me to look unafraid even though I could hardly breathe.

With an air of great confidence, Winston took aim while his wry grin turned into sadistic, smirking laughter.

"i warned you to stay away, corey. but apparently you're too stupid to understand."

Although most of the other people in the vicinity were preoccupied with the aftermath of the explosion, a small group of perhaps ten individuals were close enough to become curious. Chances were they probably did not understand English but seeing a man pointing a gun at another did not need interpretation.

To my surprise, they instinctively formed an uneven perimeter around us but at a safe distance for themselves. Perhaps they thought Winston was one of the terrorists and that I was his next victim.

"Winston!" yelled Friday, taking a few steps towards him. **"Don't be foolish! Think about what you're doing."**

"i have never thought clearer," he answered.

"Then think about the army. Your career which you have worked at for so long."

"it doesn't matter to me. nothing means anything if i don't have you."

"But......." She took another step toward him.

"stay where you are, friday. don't come any closer."

She continued to protest. To protect me.

"Then think about our children. How will they feel to know their father has killed someone and is spending the rest of his life in Leavenworth?"

"i'm tired of thinking and i'm tired of you falling for younger men."

He said it so pathetically that I almost felt sorry for him.

From the corner of my eye, I noticed that the children were standing in the doorway of the train compartment. Their faces were filled with awe and bewilderment as they witnessed the scene.

With panic, Friday rushed toward Winston. He violently pushed her aside and the crowd of on-lookers let out a collective gasp as they took several steps backwards.

Winston checked his aim once more.

Then he calmly squeezed the trigger.

In the next instant, I heard a thunderous sound. Simultaneously, someone forcefully pulled me sideways by my left arm while the upper part of my right arm started throbbing with excruciating pain—and blood trickled downward to my fingertips.

Concurrent with the first shot, a second one shattered the air. I looked in the sound's direction and realized it came from the Man who had been tailing me.

Fortunately, Pegu had been close behind me. When she saw Winston fire, she swiftly yanked me out of the way. If not for her fast action, Winston's bullet would have caught me directly in the chest. And I immediately thanked God for watching over me.

Pegu quickly explained what had happened.

"Gobasi was carefully making his way behind Winston in an attempt to restrain him," she exclaimed. "But when I saw that Gobasi would not get there in time, I pulled you away."

"I owe you my life," I said, sighing.

Pegu blushed as I kissed her on the cheek.

Gobasi then joined us and we went back to the bench. Now my trembling was boundless. Gobasi lit a cigarette for me while Pegu affixed a tourniquet to my arm.

"We must take you to a hospital immediately," announced Pegu, upset. "We must go right now."

"In a few minutes," I pleaded. "Give me time for my knees to stop shaking."

"Okay. All right," she replied, "But only two minutes!"

"Where is Friday?" I asked. "Is she safe?"

"Yes," answered Pegu. "She is in her compartment."

I could see Friday inside the train. She had one arm around each of the children while–I surmised–she was trying to explain why their father had shot a friend of the family.

Pegu and Gobasi stopped me from going to her.

"Later," argued Pegu; "You can see her on the train."

"What is Winston doing?" I asked.

"CAN NOT TELL. POLICE WITH HIM," answered Gobasi.

At that point, a reverberating siren blasted from the public address system and the intensity of the din added to the existing chaos of people moaning, sobbing, yelling and moving about in various directions.

Though Midyat's surprise warning about the bomb had managed to save many at the refreshment stand, there were others who did not fare as well–particularly the Attendant working there.

And besides claiming the lives of other innocent people as well, Midyat's bomb had done a large amount of property destruction. I could not fathom why anyone would do such a dastardly deed.

From out of nowhere appeared a group of soldiers under the command of a tall officer with a handlebar mustache. By his order, the men quickly dispersed themselves like tiny ants scurrying in all directions. Some cordoned off the vicinity of the explosion while others carried out people who were seriously injured.

One very young Soldier was sent to the refreshment stand area for a reason I could not determine. Upon getting a close-hand view of the devastation, he fell to his knees and sobbed. The Commander looked at the Soldier with disdain, shook his head in disbelief, then resumed giving orders to the other men.

I was then distracted by Pegu's words.

"We must take you to the hospital now," she commanded. "Now!"

"But the train," I protested.

"We will get the next one," argued Pegu. And Gobasi concurred.

Though it was obvious that my wound needed attention, I did not want to leave without first seeing Friday. To learn where she would be staying in Istanbul.

The next event was unnerving and final.

The clapping sound of train doors rapidly and consecutively closing echoed along the length of the conveyance. Without warning or announcement the transport began to move. At first slowly. Then a little faster.

My eyes frantically searched for Friday because her car was now several feet past its original spot. By chance I saw her as she stretched the upper part of her body out of the train door window and shouted to me. But her voice could not be heard over the din of the siren.

Breaking away from my protectors, I ran after the departing train while clutching my arm. But the train had gained great momentum. Faster and faster Friday was being taken away from me.

The last thing I thought she shouted was, **"I love you!"** Perhaps it was only my imagination but the expression on her face seemed to confirm it.

In desperation, I unintentionally fell to my knees and quietly sobbed—just like I had seen in a movie once. But this was real life and no shadow on a screen. The emotional pain was powerful and I couldn't find that part of my body that it was possessing. Couldn't apply an ointment to soothe it.

With the trains gone, the immediate area took on a new buzz of bedlam as soldiers hustled everybody off the platform, through the gigantic waiting room and into the street while bomb squad members raced past us in the opposite direction.

Several first aid stations were set up in front of the terminal. Also on the scene were volunteers who handed out coffee, pastries and compassion.

Additionally, fire engines, bomb squad vehicles, army trucks, ambulances, newspaper cars, and radio broadcast vans all combined to create a new portrait of congestion.

At the rear of one ambulance, a friendly Intern tended to my wound and gave me some happy pain pills. He also gave the three of us moist towels to wipe the soot off our faces. The bullet had only brushed my right arm but even if it had been lodged there, I was still pleased that it missed my heart. Grateful to God, Allah, Pegu and someone else: I was soon to find out.

Approximately an hour later, things began to return to some sort of normalcy, and an announcement informed us that the terminal was once more safe to enter. Most of the firemen and bomb squad personnel had left, as well as the emergency medical stations and the comforting souls who served doughnuts and coffee.

I was about to suggest we find out about the next train when I spotted Turan exiting the terminal, and waved him over.

"Corey, I am happy to see that you and your friends are safe!"

To my great amazement, he hugged me but made no mention of my injury. I thought it odd that he did not notice.

He continued speaking.

"Unfortunately, I arrived too late to stop the bomb! My agent, Mustafa, _did_ try, but got injured when he fell off a ladder! That is no consolation to the victims, of course, and I feel very badly that I could not have done more!"

There was no attempt made on my part to introduce Pegu and Gobasi since one of them was a fugitive from justice, albeit unfair.

"It was a harrowing experience," I exclaimed; "especially when I saw the young Man set off the bomb."

I purposely avoided the "we" pronoun so that Turan would ignore Pegu and Gobasi.

"You actually witnessed it?" asked Turan, astonished.

"It happened fast and seemed so unreal."

"One of my other agents was in the vicinity but was preoccupied with something else to have noticed much!   —Tell me exactly what occurred, please! I have been questioning people for the past hour but no one has seen anything!"

I related the entire incident as it had unfolded. In addition to the bomb incident, Turan seemed especially interested in Kyle's role, so I offered the little known to me.

"Kyle met Midyat in the Compound a short time ago and said they got along well."

"That is not surprising!" exclaimed Turan. "Was Kyle working with Midyat?"

"I seriously doubt that. —Do you know where Kyle is?"

"They took him to the hospital! He is very badly injured! His back is seriously damaged and he has burns on sixty percent of his body! But Midyat _is_ dead!"

When I expressed concern about Kyle, Turan revealed that Kyle had raped Yuksel not once but twice. Yuksel had confided the wretched experiences to Madam Sivas—as well as writing about them in her diary.

Although the news saddened me, it was less shocking after remembering how Kyle had been so vicious with me earlier in the evening.

The unfavorable comments about Kyle were difficult to accept since I had always looked up to him as a hero. But in the final analysis, did I really know him that well? Our conversations had been mostly about parties and fun stuff. I never would have guessed that he had such a dark side.

Suddenly, the memory of us getting the little dog drunk on New Year's Eve, in Tripoli, was no longer amusing.

"Would you be kind enough to make a statement about what happened here after you return from Istanbul?" asked Turan.

"I'll be happy to help in any way that I can."

The announcement that the terminal was now safe to enter was repeated.

I excused myself from Turan and began to walk toward the station when I stopped and faced him. Pegu and Gobasi kept moving ahead.

"I forgot to tell you that there was a Man following me. He also fired a shot."

Turan gave me a warm smile.

"I know."

Why should that have come as a surprise to me, I playfully admonished myself; I *was* talking to the head of the Secret Police.

Turan continued.

"His name is Mohair! Days ago I assigned him to guard you very closely in case Winston tried to harm you! In fact, he stayed so close to you that when his walkie-talkie went dead he would not leave to get new batteries for fear of losing sight of you! And when the bomb exploded, he ran over to you but retreated because he saw you were safe!"

No wonder Turan hadn't asked about my injury. He already knew what had happened.

"Thank you, my Friend. And also please thank Mohair, for me."

I resumed walking to the terminal when I suddenly stopped, again.

"Would you happen to know where Winston is?"

"I did not wish to spoil your little vacation but I guess you have the right to know! –When Winston fired at you, Mohair shot at Winston to protect you!"

"What are you saying?"

"That Mohair saved your life!"

"Is Winston wounded?" I asked, innocently.

"No! Mohair's bullet went astray!"

"Then what exactly are you telling me?"

"That Winston is dead!"

CHAPTER 37 –
"Winding Down"

October 1956

I will always remember Victory Day.

Pegu, Gobasi and I caught the late train to Istanbul and arrived there early in the morning. We rented hotel rooms and rested. My repose was curtailed as I tried to locate Friday and the children.

Having explored all the places that Americans generally stay at, and gaining nothing for my pains, I finally gave up.

After the wedding and small reception on Sunday, I had to return to Ankara since only a weekend pass had been granted.

Though the Newlyweds had accumulated some money from the sale of Gobasi's house, the amount wasn't enough to get them out of the country. Their plan was to obtain "legal" papers for Pegu, and work to save up sufficient funds to enter the U.S., which I promised to help them accomplish.

Bidding them goodbye, I pledged to keep in touch.

Arriving back in my apartment on Sunday night, I had hoped to find a telegram from Friday. But none was there.

Why did so many things in life have to change? Why couldn't everything stay *Radio City Music Hall?*

The Showplace of the Nation is consistently the same; it never changes. And its uniquely beautiful splendor and ambiance suggest that nothing bad could ever happen there—making you feel safe under an indefinable aura.

After many slow-moving weeks, a turning point occurred.

One night—with the help of *raki* and *our* song repeatedly playing on the phonograph–I seriously considered committing suicide. But as usual, the Almighty was watching out for me. He brought to mind my family and friends back home, and that stopped me.

God has always graciously looked upon me: as if shining down a Spotlight From Heaven.

November 1956

*   *   *

In the coffee shop at the Ankara Airport, Hank Myrons spoke to his companion.

"T-Thank you for accompanying m-me here. I could have gotten a ride from s-someone in t-the M-Motor Pool but I _am_ glad you insisted."

"Maybe they would not have obliged you," joked Drew. "As of three days ago, you are a civilian. That's why you're flying home commercially and not on MATS. –Have you heard from your wife?"

"Yes," grimaced the Colonel; "S-She got home s-safely. Unfortunately!"

Drew laughed, Hank frowned, they sipped coffee and silence temporarily reigned.

"In what part of the country will you run for office?"

"In m-my home s-state of New York," replied the Colonel.

"I wish you all the best of luck. And I am going to miss you."

Hank stared down at the countertop as if searching for a response.

"Flight 127 is now boarding at Gate 5," announced a voice over the public address system.

Without speaking, the men slowly rose and began walking toward the area. When they reached the queue of other passengers going on the flight, they stopped and faced each other.

"Let's make this quick," suggested Drew, with tears already forming in his eyes. "One fast hug and a rapid goodbye."

Hank made no reply as he embraced his former lover. Then they both turned in opposite directions and reluctantly went their respective ways.

En route to the exit, Drew noticed a magazine stand and could not resist stopping. He spied an exercise periodical and as he browsed through it, he heard someone speak behind him.

"Are you featured in that magazine, my handsome Friend?"

Drew turned and beheld a sexy looking olive-skinned young Man wearing an Arab headdress with a European suit.

"Thank you for the compliment, _Efendi,_ but I'm afraid that's a negative."

Drew went on to say that he was being discharged in one week's time and was returning to the U.S. to meet with a former movie producer who had promised to put him in a forthcoming film.

The Arab–only slightly older than Drew and with impeccable English–explained that he was traveling from his homeland of Morocco to his other residence in Paris. While he had many other profitable business interests, he also produced "art films," a.k.a., pornography.

"Why not take a short vacation in Paris before returning to California?" coaxed the Arab, smiling sensually. "For one day's work, I can pay you three hundred American dollars. Tax free.

"It is a rising new industry, my Friend. Just imagine how much money you can make in a week's time. You could return home in style. Nowadays, an Oldsmobile car costs no more than $2,900."

"It sounds good, but I would need to think about it."

"Do not ponder too long, my handsome American. Just do it. I believe we might also become very close friends. –Here is my card."

As the Arab walked away, he looked back at Drew and smiled.

Drew stood motionless and stared at the card as if in a minor state of shock. Three hundred dollars multiplied by five days is fifteen hundred dollars. In two weeks' time, he _could_ buy an Oldsmobile.

And he thought, *just imagine what I can make for three weeks' work!*

*   *   *

February 1957 - Ankara

The gun shot wound in my arm had healed and my state-of-the-art depression slowly began to decrease. But it would still be a long time before my heart could mend–especially since Friday still hadn't contacted me.

To block out the pain as best as possible, I lost myself in a variety of ways. There were: lessons in the Turkish language at the Turkish-American Association; going to see the latest flicks from the U.S. in the JAMMAT auditorium; writing my book; painting with Urdanur; and even taking a short furlough to Athens where I stood among the ruins of the Acropolis and wished that Friday were with me.

But throughout all that time, I never once dated anyone. Turan introduced me to several girls but none of them could compare to Friday.

Even my friend Dylan, another airman who works at the military portion of the airport, wants to introduce me to his sister–someday. She is a WAF and is currently stationed in Lebanon. Her name is Giana and he says she's a knock-out.

But I have absolutely no interest in love, or sex. It will take a very extra special wonderful female to stroke my heartstrings and make them sing.

In delightful contrast to Mrs. Penelope Myrons, the wife of the new Adjutant was magnanimous and charming. She and her husband rented an apartment in my building and at Christmas time offered an "open house" to the other residents.

Urdanur and I attended and the highlights for me were cucumber "finger" sandwiches and a punch called London fog—which our hostess claimed to have originated.

Definitely destined for the Alcohol Hall of Fame, the punch contained equal amounts of brewed coffee, chocolate and vanilla ice cream, rum, and whipped cream. After several glasses of that tantalizing ambrosia, a person was really in a fog—London or otherwise.

If not for Urdanur's compassion, I may never have survived. She did everything she could think of to keep up my spirits. One evening she truly surprised me by saying that I was being mentioned in her Will. The thought deeply touched me. It also saddened me because I didn't want Urdanur to ever die. I didn't want anybody to ever die! To me, *change* and *endings* are profoundly upsetting.

As pleasant as it would have been, I did not see Madam Sivas and Nurtan that often. Nurtan had met a doctor at the hospital when she went to have an examination regarding the fetus that Kyle had left her with.

She and the Doctor were instantly attracted to each other and after dating for several months he proposed marriage, and willingly accepted the child as his own.

Born prematurely, the baby was a beautiful healthy girl who had Nurtan's magnificent brown eyes, and whom she named Yuksel.

Several months before the birth, Madam Sivas had spoken to Turan and he had launched a thorough search to find the Boy who had been stolen from Yuksel. Happily, Turan located five year old Kemal, and Nurtan and her husband lovingly adopted the Boy.

I had occasion to meet the little Guy and thought he was the spitting image of Yuksel. I had to hold back the tears while looking at him.

Madam Sivas spent all of her free time looking after Nurtan, the new baby, little Kemal, and Nurtan's husband. And all of the above adored having her around.

For their sakes, I felt it best to stay away. Although they were too polite to ever say it, my presence could only bring back bitter memories because I had been Kyle's close friend.

Ty Manners was existing in prison. He had regained his memory and was found guilty of Yuksel's murder. The trial went smoothly and I *did* have to testify against him. He received a life sentence.

Several days after the bomb explosion on Victory Day, Kyle was shipped to a special burn unit in Germany. It took me awhile to subsequently locate him in a veterans' hospital somewhere in North Carolina, his home state. And after writing several letters to which no replies were forthcoming, I was relieved when a Nurse there kindly informed me of his situation—stating that he wished to communicate with no one! I was sorry for him, to an extent, but could not condone—or forget—what he had done to Nurtan and Yuksel.

My gratitude also went to Turan for helping to lift my spirits. It was quite ironic that the man who had scared the hell out of me on my first night in Turkey had become one of my best friends. But it was delightful irony.

Once a week, we'd go out to dinner, and afterwards drinking. But the best part of our meetings was having long, philosophical conversations. Inadvertently, I learned a lot about life from him.

March 1957 – Knightdale

*   *   *

The Veteran's Hospital in Knightdale, North Carolina, easily stood out as one of the worst such establishments in the entire country. The personnel of the hospital were perfunctorily helpful. They did their jobs but not necessarily with aplomb or compassion.

Kyle shared space with two older men who, like himself, were paralyzed. The room had no air-conditioning—only several noisy inadequate electric fans, and the walls were painted a depressing dark green. Outside the window, a huge tree blocked sunlight from trying to sneak into the room.

The bed sheets were changed once a week and Kyle was bathed every other day. To use the latrine, he had to be picked up by an Attendant, wheeled to the bathroom, literally put on the toilet, and afterwards taken back. It was either that or use the bed pan which the Attendant was slow in removing.

"How are you today, Airman Muenster?" asked a Nurse, about fifty years in age.

"Fine, Chubby. Don't ya see how Ah'm trainin' for the fuckin' Olympics?"

"My patience is just about at an end with you, Airman. Every time anyone tries to show you some kindness, you become belligerent and nasty. Of all the patients in this place, you are the most ill-mannered and uncooperative."

"Yeah? Well you try layin' in this fuckin' bed all day. Ah can't even feel my feet. The whole left side of mah body is a gigantic burn scar and the side of mah face is like a horror movie. Ah can see people look at me and turn away in disgust. Ah have splittin' headaches in the day and bad dreams at night."

The Nurse ignored him and continued.

"We received this letter from the Air Force saying that you will soon be discharged. You can be released to your family and receive special compensation from the government since your injury was service-related. But if you do not have anyone to care for you, then the government will keep you here until you... ."

The Nurse abruptly stopped speaking.

"Until Ah die?"

She lowered her eyes and softly answered.

"Yes. I guess that is what I mean."

Then quickly retrieving her composure, she asked, "Do you have a family?"

Kyle answered in the negative. While he hadn't contacted them since he had joined the service, he was sure that they did not want anything to do with him. They were too old and impatient to care for him, anyway. Also, he neither cared nor knew if they were both still living.

"Very well," exclaimed the Nurse, trying to conjure up a bit of sympathy; "I guess we will be your family. –Good night, Airman Muenster."

An hour later, when the Nurse was on her break she re-read Kyle's file over a cup of coffee and a cigarette.

In a confidential portion, it said that the Air Force had had difficulty in initially getting Kyle out of Turkey because he had been accused of raping a Turkish girl. But when the charges could not be conclusively proved, they decided to let him go.

The Nurse closed the file and thought: *if Kyle Muenster did rape that girl, he was certainly paying for his crime now.*

May 1957 – Ankara

In his cell at the Ulus Prison, Ty Manners lay on his bunk while reading a letter. On the cot across from him lounged a fellow American inmate known only as Pothead.

"That must be a helluva letter, Ty. You're grinnin' from ear to ear."

"It's from my old Man, the Senator."

"I thought you two didn't get along."

"We don't. Much.   But after I got a life sentence in this fuckin' dump, he felt wickedly sorry and began to help me."

"So what's he writin' about?"

"He's tryin' to get me transferred to a prison in the States. He thinks he might be able to do it. But he said not to get my hopes up 'cause it might take a long time."

"How could he possibly spring you?"

"By appealing my case since the evidence in my trial was circumstantial. And to prove that I was framed."

Pothead let out a sarcastic laugh.

"It's true, I tell you. I *am* innocent!" insisted Ty. "I was set up by a jealous Turk cop, a faggot, a do-gooder, and a so-called buddy who I'm sure is the real murderer."

"If you ever did get out, what would you do?"

A fiercely savage light filled Ty's eyes.

"*When* I get out, I'll track down Turan, Kyle, Drew and Corey, and make them pay!   One by one, I will tear out their hearts!"

*   *   *

THE MUSIC MAN opens on Broadway
Starring Robert Preston, Barbara Cook, David Burns

CHAPTER 38 –
"Unexpected Moments"

September 1957 – Ankara

My last day in Turkey.

A *year* had passed and still no letter from Friday.

After all the personal things we had said, the ecstatic times we shared, the wonderful plans and promises we had made, and the love that surpassed all others, this was not the outcome I had anticipated.

Apparently, for Friday and me there were no more champagne days.

Be that as it may, I resolved not to try and find her upon returning to the States. Hell! I wouldn't even know where to begin.

If the truth must be confessed, Friday and I were inadvertent murderers. The sweet affair–which I had honestly believed was inevitable–actually caused Winston's death. Our actions clearly lead him to behave in the violent manner that he had.

I could blame it all on Friday because she insisted that their marriage was over, and because she was years older, but that would be unfair. I was just as responsible.

The severance from Friday, then, was punishment I well deserved.

On the positive side, my complete surrender to Friday had not been in vain. I had come to Ankara as a boy and, because of her love, was leaving as a Young Man who would forever cherish a great moment in his life. Never to forget the wonderful things she taught him, and the confidence and trust in himself that she had instilled.

I seriously doubted if there could ever be another one as fulfilling as Friday.

Time to go!

Kyle and Drew were already gone so that made two fewer people to part with. I said *Allah ismarladik* to Nurtan and Madam Sivas with much sorrow. They both gave me a book about Turkey, as a keepsake.

As for Urdanur and Turan's desire to escort me to the airport, I had to decline–knowing full well it would be too painful. That proved to be the correct decision because bidding them adieu, separately, the day before was horrendously tearful. And I did cry myself to sleep.

The only friend remaining was Dylan whose job description included all phases of managing the U.S. military section of the airport. It was he who had wangled me a plane ride to Greece. He was a good buddy.

"Your plane landed about an hour ago from Beirut," said Dylan. "Our ground crew is doing some maintenance and it will be ready to take off again in about forty-five minutes. I took care of all the paper work for you."

"Thanks a lot. I owe you one."

Dylan continued speaking.

"In case you forgot, the plane goes directly to Germany where you'll take another flight to McGuire Air Force Base in New Jersey, the good old U.S. of A. You *will* send a postcard to remind me what the States look like, won't you, Pal?"

"I'll put some air in a bottle and mail it to you as a present," I joked.

"Speaking of presents," smiled Dylan, suspiciously; "I have a great one for you. Take a seat on the bench in front of the Quonset hut and try to look even more handsome."

I protested that he had already done enough but, ignoring me, he quickly vanished into the Quonset hut.

No sooner had I sat on the bench when Dylan re-appeared escorting a young lady who almost took my breath away.

"Corey, I'd like you to meet Giana Martucci, my kid sister. She is also going back to the States."

As he introduced us, Dylan's eyes gleamed with pride.

"I hold *you* completely responsible for Giana. Be sure she gets to the States, safely."

"That's not a task," I retorted; "it's a pure honor. –Didn't you say you had some paper work to do?"

Before leaving us alone, Dylan whispered in my ear.

"I caught that wide smile on your face when I introduced you. Hate to say 'I told you so' but ain't she foxy? I could have arranged this meeting for you much sooner. And you could have even seen Beirut, into the bargain."

I smacked him on his ass as he moved away. Turning to Giana, I asked if she cared to sit on the bench.

Giana was the prettiest girl I had seen in the past year. She had a thin face, olive complexion, eyes so blue they looked almost turquoise, and a smile so encompassing that I had to talk slowly for fear of tripping over my own words.

Yet it wasn't her outward beauty alone that wholly captivated me. There was something intrinsically enchanting that she exuded. And I immediately wanted to bond with her.

"If you'd rather be inside talking to your brother before you go, I fully understand."

"Thank you, but we spent all morning together," she replied, smilingly. "I arrived on a very early flight from Beirut. Besides, I am curious about you. Dylan greatly admires you and I want to tell him whether or not you deserve his adoration."

Her teasing instantly put me at ease.

"Do you like being a WAF? Or should I correctly ask if you enjoy your life in the Women's Air Force?"

"Either way you say it, I like the traveling aspect but hate having to take orders."

The girl sounded as if she were quoting me.

"How did you find Beirut?" I continued.

"Actually, I didn't. But luckily the pilot knew what it looked like."

It took me several seconds to get the joke and then we both laughed. It was such a great feeling. It was the first time I had *genuinely* smiled in nearly twelve months.

"Beirut is a swinging city," she added. "It is the Paris of the Middle East. I had a great time there. I hope it never changes. —How do *you* like the Air Force?"

"I agree one hundred percent with what you said. As a matter of fact, it felt like I was listening to *myself* talking."

It was hard to realize that I was actually enjoying the presence of a girl without being haunted by the *ghost of champagne days-past*.

For the next half hour we both spoke profusely. All kinds of topics. All kinds of anecdotes. All kinds of likes and dislikes. Not one lull interrupted our dialogue. The instant she would finish saying something, I would commence. And, ironically, we both seemed to have corresponding opinions. It was uncanny. As I had wished earlier, we *were* bonding with each other.

Then Giana said something which totally blew my mind. As her words spilled out, I could not believe it.

"You have perfect ear lobes."

"What?" I almost bellowed, in grinning bewilderment.

"Didn't you ever notice anyone's ear lobes? They're different on different people. Some lobes are taut and tight and look like they are growing out of the person's cheek. Some are semi-attached. But the best are the ones that hang freely. And that's what you have. You could easily wear an earring."

"An earring?" came my incredulous comment.

"Sure. I bet that someday men will wear earrings. After all, we're approaching the end of a decade and who knows what's waiting for us in the Sixties?"

Regarding ear lobes, I had said those very same words to Urdanur one day when we were painting, and she had warmly laughed. Wonder what she will say when I write her about this. She'll probably exclaim that I have definitely met my other half.

In these *unexpected moments*, a weight was slowly dissolving from my shoulders—as if my heart were delightfully coming alive once more. I felt someone tugging at my heartstrings which were beginning to play again, starting as a murmur but definitely building to a complete and beautiful melody.

The forty-five minutes remaining before the plane's departure time flew by like the few seconds it takes to sigh. Suddenly, Dylan was standing in front of us.

"The plane is ready to go, Kids."

We stood up and grabbed our carry on bags. The crew had already loaded our other luggage. I hugged Dylan goodbye then took several steps back to give him a bit of privacy with his sister.

Some minutes later, Dylan said, "Please take her Corey, before she I and flood the area with tears."

Giana reluctantly turned from her brother and I offered comfort by cuddling her against my shoulder. She was about two inches below my height, and that's something I like in a girl.

As we walked the hundred feet or so of tarmac to the waiting military aircraft, I handed Giana a handkerchief and she slowly began to control herself.

"Did anybody ever mention that you look like Elizabeth Taylor?"

"No, but feel free to say it as often as you like," she smiled, beginning to feel less sad. "However, I do like horseback riding which she did so well in *National Velvet*."

332

Giana was also an avid movie fan. I had apparently found my counterpart.

"I've never ridden a horse."

"Then I will have to teach you."

"Are you saying that there's a future for us?"

She was playfully coy.

"If you give me a resume and some references, I'll certainly take it into consideration," she teased. Slight pause. "Did anyone ever remark that *you* resemble Farley Granger?"

"No; But someone told me that I look like Lassie."

"Who would say such a thing?" Giana giggled.

"My mother! She said I was one of Lassie's puppies. Yet, she also claimed to have gotten me out of one of those little windows in the Horn and Hardart Automat Cafeteria. So I don't know which story is the truth."

"Stop fishing for a compliment," she teased, poking me in the ribs with her elbow.

As we boarded the plane, I marveled at the many similarities Giana and I had, both in ideas and the expression of them. Perhaps there *was* another chance at romance for me.

We sat side by side in bucket seats and waved greetings to the pilot, co-pilot and navigator who were but a mere twenty feet away. And as the plane took off, we resumed our marathon conversation.

"The first thing I'm going to do when we land in Jersey," began Giana; "is to find a diner and order a hot dog, a hamburger, pizza, waffles with ice cream, a chocolate milk shake, and a Charlotte Russe."

"That's my favorite food group," I laughed. "You can order them for me, too."

Being intrigued with each other, we were both feeling slightly less sad about leaving.

"I don't mean to be too personal," murmured Giana, seeming a bit serious; "but I will, any way. –Dylan told how you've been suffering the past year with a broken heart. I can't imagine any girl walking-out on you. She deserves a good swift kick in the ass for doing so. You're as good and sweet as my brother."

Her comments warmly boosted my morale and I thought: although you never completely forget your first true love–if you are lucky enough to have a second opportunity–you have the right to embrace it.

"Thank you. But I don't want to be your *brother*."

"Since that job is already filled, maybe I can find another position for you."

She smiled broadly then changed the topic.

While Giana's voice was pleasantly sounding, I sneaked a glance out the

Rob Russo

window and noted that the plane had risen above velvet white clouds. Then I saw the sun appear above them with its warm, soothing glow which bathed me in calmness.

The bright light spilled into the cabin like a comforter–sweeping over us and transforming dark areas into golden rays. I took Giana's hand in mine and without even realizing it, kissed her gently on the cheek.

She seemed to accept the gesture as if I had done that many times, and she just as naturally returned it. We had known each other for such a short time, yet it seemed longer. Love is an enigma: it can be long in cultivation or happen almost instantly.

Ironically, and with a re-born feeling, my mind unexpectedly finished the words to the song which had belonged to Friday and me.

> Though your love did not last
> I won't live in the past
> For I hope to once more gaze
> On Champagne Days

EPILOGUE

September 1958 – Cheyenne, Wyoming

*   *   *

Airman Keith Karlan–brown eyes, black hair, an intriguing smile and dimples in his stocky cheeks–drove the jeep up to the curbside of the modest Cheyenne Train Station in time to see a small crowd of people exiting the terminal.

Scanning the varied faces, he quickly spotted his buddy, Jim Phaning—brown eyes, tall, natural sun tan, muscular, and quite pleasing to look at.

"How've you been, Jim?" asked Keith, smiling and jovial.

Jim threw his duffle bag in the back seat and vigorously shook his friend's hand.

"Missing you, Man. We haven't seen each other since Kelly Air Force Base in San Antonio. And I'm anxious to know about the latest loves of your life. Heaven knows that your carousing back in high school was worthy of the Kinsey Report. If I'm not mistaken, didn't Kinsey interview you for the book?"

"You're exaggerating," laughed Kevin.

"I'm realistic," smiled Jim. "You used to date a number of girls at the same time. There were Jean Gilardi, the artist; Patty Creta, the librarian; and, Janice Zarba, the nurse. Unlike you, I only romanced my right hand."

Keith grinned coyly as he maneuvered the vehicle into the flow of light traffic headed for the main thoroughfare of the city.

"Well, I'm changed now, good Buddy. I am officially and in all ways a one-gal man. We'll stop at the town's only hamburger joint and then I'll lay it on you."

Ten minutes later, they had finished lunch and were lounging over coffee.

"Did you know that Francis E. Warren Air Force Base–your home for the next year–was General Custer's supply base?" offered Keith.

"Really? And where was Asshole Custer stationed when he slaughtered the women and children in the Indian village of Black Kettle, while the Indian men were away hunting? But don't get me started on that Fuck! – I want to hear the scoop about you."

Keith's mood changed to reverent seriousness as he looked deeply into his friend's eyes.

"I'm dating an older woman."

"That can be fun, I guess."

"Jim, I tell you truly; I have never met anyone as wonderful as her and I know she is the only woman for me."

"Are you all that certain?"

"I swear on my life!"

"Maybe you're just lonely and confused 'cause you're away from home."

"My mind is as clear as cellophane. What's more, I plan to marry her. After she gets divorced, that is."

Jim tried to avoid a surprised look on his face but not in time.

"I know what you're thinking," Keith hastened to add. "But she and her husband have no love for each other so I'm not doing anything morally wrong."

Not wishing to appear judgmental, Jim smiled at his friend.

"How did you two meet?"

"She was shopping for a birthday present for her husband in the PX and asked my opinion. As gratitude for my advice she offered to buy me lunch."

"That sounds harmless enough."

"It was," continued Keith. "But then Fate stepped in. We kept bumping into each other, not only on Base but even in town. One thing led to another and here I am madly in love."

"How much older *is* she?"

"About twelve years."

Jim was pensively silent as Keith kept talking.

"But the years don't matter none. I feel as if we're the same age. I mean we like all the same things: movies, books, poetry, music."

"I didn't know you could be so seriously romantic," teased Jim.

"You think I'm being foolish? Don't you?"

"Not at all," answered Jim, convincingly. "I'm very happy for you. It sounds like you hit the mother-load. Perhaps you've been blessed by a beggar."

"What the devil does that mean?"

"Well, a beggar's blessing is a great honor because he is putting your welfare above his own–even though he has nothing for himself. Such a blessing yields great results. And what kinder wishes could you get from anyone?"

"I never heard that saying before," exclaimed Keith, approvingly. "I like it. Where does it come from?"

"It's a fifteenth century proverb," laughed Jim; "which I made up five minutes ago. —Actually, it really happened to me. I once gave a beggar some money and he said, 'God bless you.' As I walked away I thought how ironic it was that he was blessing me when he had veritably nothing."

Keith playfully hit his friend's arm.

"Be that as it may," Jim went on; "you should realize that life does not come with a book of instructions. Each person has to learn for himself through trial and error by making calculated decisions. And one should not always worry about the other guy's opinion."

Keith looked at his friend with much admiration.

"You were always pretty intelligent in high school. And I'll be damned if you still ain't!"

Jim blushed. "On a lighter note, is this woman of yours as crazy as you are?"

"Like we were twins," Keith grinned. "We're always doing cute things for each other. We like to go shopping together in yard sales and other bargain places. We bought a 45 record that is an instrumental and she told me to write words for it. Now we call it *our* song.

"What we also do is to laugh a lot because she's very funny. I nearly pissed my pants when she told a local minister one day that her favorite cities in the Bible were Sodom and Gomorrah.

"She jokes a great deal but she's really smart. Has done a lot of traveling. She's even been to Turkey. Her former husband was stationed there. She has two kids and they're really great. Strange and introverted but very polite.

"Something else we like to do is buy little presents for one another. In fact, right now she's having a key chain specially made for me. It's a tiny metal heart that is linked to a horseshoe. She used to have one just like it but somehow lost it."

"You know something, Pal?" interrupted Jim; "with all the things you've been saying, you never even told me her name."

Keith smiled happily.

"Her name is Friday."

*   *   *

SPECIAL FEATURES

Military Time – How to Decipher It

The expression of time in the American Military as well as in many foreign countries is based on 24 hours–each hour being unique and self-explanatory.

There is no A.M. or P.M.

Examples:

0800	(8 AM) Said: eight hundred hours
1200	(Noon) Twelve hundred hours
1300	(1 PM) Thirteen hundred hours
1645	(4:45 PM) Sixteen hundred forty-five
2000	(8 PM) Twenty hundred hours
2300	(11 PM) Twenty three hundred hours

Trick: If you are not sure of any hour after 1200, simply subtract 12 from the number. E.g.- 1600 minus 12 equals 4 (4 PM)

Glossary Of Turkish Words
(In Alphabetical Order)

Allah ismarladik................goodbye (said by person departing; the person staying says, "gule, gule")

bay...gentleman; Mr.

bayan...lady; Mrs., miss

bir dakika...one minute; wait a minute

bir sey degil...you are welcome

burada...here

cok...much; many; very

cok guzel..very good

cok iyiyim..very well

dolmuz...pig; swine

efendi or efendim.....................sir or madam; a term of respect

evet..yes

fena..bad

gule gule..........................goodbye (said by person staying; the person leaving says, "Allah ismarladik")

guzel...good

hayir...no

hic birsey..nothing

iyi...good

Koran........................the sacred book of the Mohammedans

Lira..Turkish money

lutfen...please

masAllah..............what wonders God hath willed; God keep it so; wonderful (often said in rejoicing and/orpatting a child on the head)

muezzin...priest

merhaba...hello

nasilsiniz?...how are you?

sessiz..quiet

siz nasilsiniz?...and how are you?

sokak...street

tesekkur ederim...thank you

teyze...aunt

MAP OF LOCALES

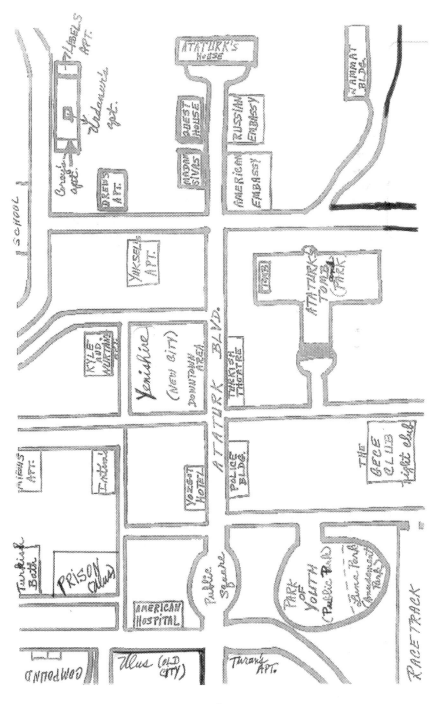

"Uncorking the Bottle"
Rob Russo
(A Behind-the-Scenes Essay)

BASICS

CHAMPAGNE DAYS is loosely based on my stay in Ankara, Turkey, while serving there in the Air Force from approximately January of 1954 to July of 1955. However, the novel is set in 1956 because I preferred that year's events. At that time, the Turkish government did not want a foreign military blatantly present, so we were not permitted to wear uniforms. Also, we lived in private apartments scattered throughout the city and received extra pay for food, rent and utilities.

Almost all of the characters in the book are *visually* based on friends and acquaintances so that I could have a mental picture while writing. *But that is where the similarity ends!* My characters do not–in any way–depict the personalities and lives of those real people. My characters' thoughts and actions are *pure fiction!*

COMMANDER'S WIFE

The gossipy Mrs. Myrons, though fictitious, was inspired by a woman I never actually met. She was the Base Commander's wife while I was stationed at Wheelus Air Force Base (for three months) in intriguing Tripoli, Libya, before going to Turkey. (Since Omar Kadafi and I are the same age, I may have brushed elbows with him while in town.) After the commander's wife commented (in the Base newspaper, I believe) that she did not consider dungarees to be appropriate attire, an order was given forbidding us to wear them.

TURKISH COP

On my second night in Ankara, I met a Turkish couple in my hotel lobby who invited me for drinks at a night club. He was a policeman and showed me his gun during the taxi ride to the place. No one had seen me leave with them.

We communicated mostly through pantomime and when the check arrived, he pushed it in front of me; (he had bought me a drink at the hotel). So I paid it. Several days later, I learned that the night club had been off limits to American servicemen.

Although I never saw that policeman again, he was a good starting point for Turan.

Though friends of mine had told me various stories about the secret

342

police, I don't remember actually seeing it in action for myself. My reference to it in the novel is subjective and fictional for dramatic purposes.

TURKISH GIRLS

Nurtan was visually based on an extremely sweet girl whom Kyle had lived with in Ankara. But there was no animosity between them when he left.

Yuksel was a girl who worked in JAMMAT and we dated on several occasions.

THE MOVIE STAR

Drew was inspired by a Caucasian fellow airman who claimed to have been a child actor and to have acted in a popular film in the late forties. Although he was extremely handsome and could easily have continued his career after the Air Force, I kept looking for him on the silver screen in subsequent years but never saw him. To my knowledge he was *not gay*.

MADAM SIVAS

The image of Madam Sivas came from a Russian woman (living in Turkey) who operated a hostel next to the Guest House. (She made the best pancakes I have ever tasted–to date.)

I lived there for a short time and one night my stomach was upset. She would have given me a laxative but she was fresh out. That following morning (mostly from Friday's prodding) I went on sick call and discovered that my appendix had burst three days earlier. Someone said that if I had taken the laxative, it would have killed me.

Also while in Turkey I contracted a beef tape worm which took me over two years to get rid of. When it was finally flushed out, it was an inch wide and two feet long.

URDANUR

For Urdanur, I recalled the faces of two women. The first, I had the honor and pleasure of meeting while stationed in San Antonio, Texas.

She had some relatives in a small town in Mexico called Rosita, and I once accompanied her to see them. While there, I met a high school senior who invited me to her prom the following week. It was exciting to attend a prom in a foreign country. But it was not so very different than in the U.S.

The other woman was an American who preferred living in Turkey and periodically returned to the U.S. just to renew her citizenship. She tipped me off that her basement apartment was available because she had finally landed the penthouse pad.

KYLE

Kyle was my then best friend. He had blond air, a captivating smile and thick Southern accent; Kyle was one of the nicest guys I have met.

After my discharge, I inadvertently lost contact with Kyle. Over the years I had always wanted to find him but did not know how. In 1991, I bought a book which told how to locate somebody. A year after all of the book's suggestions were exhausted, I was ready to abandon the search when on October 28, 1993, the phone rang and the caller was Kyle.

I never fully understood how it happened. I *think:* a very considerate nurse in a V.A. hospital where Kyle had been re-admitted, had saved my letter for him which had arrived after his initial stay there.

Kyle and I spoke for half an hour and planned to meet that summer.

In January of 1994, Kyle's sister phoned to tell me that he had passed away. His death greatly saddened me but at least God had put us in contact one final time.

Kyle was so full of fun and was willing to try almost anything. He was a great guy who had a zest for life that was contagious. On the phone, he had told me that he had been married three times and had a total of 10 kids.

FRIDAY AND WINSTON

Upon meeting them, I immediately decided they would be my family away from home. They lived on the floor above me and were quite concerned about my health after the appendix operation.

Friday made me laugh a lot, encouraged me to follow my dreams, and bolstered my self-esteem. We became fondly close. (*Nothing sexual ever happened between us.*) Winston acted like a surrogate father.

However, we lived in a small community of Americans and soon gossip arose about Friday and me, and I had to stop seeing the Labels.

A short time later, Friday decided to return Stateside for a divorce. The Commander sent me to Samsun for two weeks because he feared I would see Friday off at the station, and Winston did not want that.

When I returned, Friday was gone. Many months later, though, Winston and I did speak on one occasion.

AMERICAN TEENAGE GIRLS

There were at least ten wonderful American teenage girls whose fathers were stationed in Ankara. I had dated many of them at various times but after the so-called scandal of Friday and me, most parents didn't want their daughters going out with me.

However, one father was willing to let me take his uncomely daughter to "the big dance" because she was the *only girl* without a date.

Everything is relative and people have conveniently selective memories.

CAPTAIN AGAR

The Army nurse at the American hospital when I had the appendix op is not fictitious. I used her real name to specially honor her.

Captain Agar was one of the most courageous women I had met in my nineteen years (and I still believe so). Her husband had died serving in World War II, and her son had recently been killed in the Korean War. Yet, she was never bitter and always loving to everyone. I instantly loved and greatly cherished her. I would really be thrilled to see her again.

In this world where there are so many dissatisfied and difficult people (and man's inhumanity to man still senselessly and sorrowfully exists) it is so marvelous to know that persons like Captain Agar can, and do, exist.

DUSTING COBWEBS

After Turkey I was stationed in San Antonio, Texas. There I had the great fortune to go out with a very pretty girl named Karen who had a wonderful mother named India.

The first time I spent the weekend in the room above their garage, I was gently shaken awake the next morning to see India shoving a mug of coffee in my hand, and saying: "Get dressed. I'll wait for you downstairs. We're gonna dust cobwebs!"

Five minutes later, India, Karen and I were speeding down a Texas highway in their Cadillac convertible with the wind blowing out the cobwebs in our heads. Funny how a simple thing like that can be so monumental in one's life.

India and Karen Murray are constantly in my heart and on my mind. Unfortunately, we lost contact with each other. The last letter was from Albuquerque, New Mexico. I have been trying to find them but in vain.

MORE BASICS

Many hours of research were done concerning specific aspects of Turkey, such as places, language, customs, and history. For example, Victory Day *is* a national holiday.

Additionally, the quotes at the beginning of each chapter are fact. Plus, all photos were taken by me and are of authentic spots.

Regarding the amount of pages in the book, I actually wrote three times that much by the time my pleasurable task was completed. There were longer descriptions of people and places but I feel that today's readers want a book to move fast. So when I re-read my manuscript for the seventh or eighth time (actually lost count) if any part seemed to slow down the flow, it was trimmed.

PLACES
JAMMAT, the Guest House and Ataturk's Tomb were real places in 1955, and as I described them. Most of the Turkish sights I mention are also true except for "my" version of the police building, and certain streets. I never even saw the train terminal, and don't know if the government building where Ahmed did his spying existed.

Speaking of Ahmed, there actually was a public execution held in the Ulus circle one day. Though I chose not to attend, friends who did go said that the man was seated on a chair, had a rope tied around his neck, and had the chair pushed out from under him.

INTIM'S
Intim's (actual name/dubious spelling) was a small night club which I frequented a great deal. The entertainers were a married British couple with whom I became very friendly. Every time I entered the place, Jane would automatically sing "My Foolish Heart."

Every Sunday afternoon, there would be a "jazz session" at Intim's.

PUBIC HAIR
The shaved pubic hair is true. The Turks whom I encountered did follow that practice. My first hand knowledge of this is not open to discussion.

Recently, I met a Turkish salesman and asked if the tradition were still followed. He answered affirmatively.

I'm guessing it may have initially started for purposes of cleanliness.

While in Turkey, I could not miss going to a Turkish Bath. When I told the taxi driver to take me to one, he asked, surprisingly, "Do you not have a bath room in your house?" Probably a large number of poor people did not have such a luxury.

THE COMPOUND
My description of the Compound is mostly accurate. I recall going there and being told that it was operated by the government, but anything more than that, I have to say is my invention for the novel's enhancement.

I recall the guards at the entrance holding rifles. I vaguely remember a festive atmosphere about the Compound and many of the women being aggressively friendly.

Conditions would be so much better in the U.S. if prostitution were legalized in every state. There would be much less crime and fewer problems with venereal diseases. Why can't the U.S. be like Amsterdam?

Write your Congressmen!

IN CLOSING

My tours of duty in Ankara and San Antonio are among the most memorable and wonderful times of my life. And although I seriously doubt if I ever WILL grow up, the experiences in these places definitely affected changes. Made me a much wealthier person for having met so many great people and for having had such unique and cherished memories. Those times really were champagne days.

And even at this very minute, I most seriously and sincerely am grateful for *still* being blessed with Champagne Days!!

ACKNOWLEDGEMENTS

I wish to express my sincere appreciation to my niece, Danielle Fabela, who did such a fine job in transferring my work from the printed page to computer disk so that the novel could be published.

And to my cousin, Jean Gilardi, for her constant encouragement and warm support which helped me get over several rough times in the accomplishment of this pleasurable task.

Several other people are thanked for reading the work and offering opinions: Rose Paterno, Patricia Amodea, Anna Martinese, Frank and Lois Garbarini, Patty Creta, Janice Zarba, Connie Martucci, Wanda Rapp, Ann Coppotelli, Ruth Lampo, Tim Coatney, Jeff Ferrante, Jean Amodea, Ivy Maas, Fred Maas.

Fond appreciation to my brother, Ron Amodea, for his excellent work on the interior photographs.

Finally, Thanks to the iUniverse member who re-designed the front cover.